Edward Deering Mansfield

A Popular and Authentic Life of Ulysses S. Grant

Vol. 2

Edward Deering Mansfield

A Popular and Authentic Life of Ulysses S. Grant
Vol. 2

ISBN/EAN: 9783337416645

Printed in Europe, USA, Canada, Australia, Japan

Cover: Foto ©Raphael Reischuk / pixelio.de

More available books at **www.hansebooks.com**

A

POPULAR AND AUTHENTIC

LIFE

OF

ULYSSES S. GRANT.

BY

EDWARD D. MANSFIELD.

CINCINNATI:

R. W. CARROLL & CO., PUBLISHERS,

117 WEST FOURTH-STREET.

1868.

TO THE

People of the United States

I Dedicate this Volume,

WHICH RECORDS THE SERVICES OF A MAN WHO IS ONE OF THEMSELVES,

PATRIOTIC IN PURPOSE;

OBEDIENT TO LAW; FAITHFUL TO THE GOVERNMENT;

INDUSTRIOUS IN PEACE, AND SUCCESSFUL

IN WAR.

EDW. D. MANSFIELD.

Morrow, O., May 13, 1868.

CONTENTS.

CHAPTER I.

CHAPTER II.

CHAPTER III.

CHAPTER IV.

DONELSON.

CHAPTER V.

SHILOH.

CHAPTER VI.

CHAPTER VII.

VICKSBURG.

CHAPTER VIII.

VICKSBURG.

CHAPTER IX.

THE PREPARATION.

CHAPTER X.

CHATTANOOGA.

CHAPTER XI.

PREPARATION.

CHAPTER XII.

THE WILDERNESS.

CHAPTER XIII.

ON TO RICHMOND.

CHAPTER XIV.

CLOSE OF THE WAR.

CHAPTER XV.

GRANT IN PEACE.

CHAPTER XVI.

GRANT IN POLITICS.

INTRODUCTION.

NATIONS grow great by their conflicts. Trials are necessary to their success, movement to their growth, and the opposition of forces to direct them into those regular and harmonious orbits by which they are henceforth to move grandly on in their predestined course. The American nation is no exception to this law. We have just finished the third grand conflict of our nation. The first was the WAR OF INDEPENDENCE, in which a few small colonies struggled for a separate existence, and won it by blood and suffering. The next was the SECOND WAR OF INDEPENDENCE—the War of 1812–15—for such it was. Not till the Peace of 1815 was our flag respected, our commerce safe upon the ocean, and our frontier protected from the Indians. The third was the WAR FOR UNITY. We call it the War of the Rebellion; but the one prominent idea on every flag and in every heart was the American Union. It was the greatest of the conflicts, because as no trial of the individual is so great as that carried on in his own soul, so no conflict of a nation is so great and terrible as that in which its social forces are arrayed against one another, giving a shock to the whole political system, and threatening its final dissolution. Such was our War for Unity, such its mighty conflict, and such the danger encountered. The triumph of unity is the triumph of the American nation in the last great struggle necessary to harmonize its social forces, and make this country the dominant power upon earth.

In any picture which can be possibly made of this great conflict, two figures will ever be prominent on the scene. Turn that picture as you may, like it or dislike it, think what you will of it, LINCOLN and GRANT will ever be looking straight at you. One was a statesman, who, calm, quiet, simple, guided as if by the very hand of Providence the civil forces through untried dangers and unheard-of calamities to a safe deliverance. The other was a soldier, as plain and simple, leading the embattled armies of the Republic through multiplied trials, through flowing blood, through defeats and victories, through gloom and glory, to the achievement of a last and a glorious success. LINCOLN is gone, his work done, his glory complete. History preserves his name among the few nobly great. But GRANT remains to complete the drama of the great conflict. Something is yet to be done. The last scenes of the last act have not passed away. Grant is still on the stage, and in these last scenes he is the principal figure.

Grant belongs wholly to this generation. He came on the stage after both the wars of independence. He is, in some degree, a type of these times, and has only now become historical. For this reason, as well

as on account of the momentous events now occurring, I propose to tell simply, briefly, but accurately,
the story of Grant's active life, but especially of that
martial life in which he has embodied the true genius
and character of the American soldier. It is not
necessary that we should go through multiplied details, enter upon military criticisms or political dis-
cussions ; nor is it necessary that we should try to
make Grant any thing more than he is. I shall endeavor simply to give the plain story of what he is
and what he has done. This is enough. In doing
it I shall be obliged, even if I were not glad, to
bring out upon the canvas that noblest character in
this historical drama, the AMERICAN VOLUNTEER, and
to show not a little of what the AMERICAN WOMAN
has done as she went forth a ministering angel to the
sick, the wounded, and the dying. It is all part of
the same story. It all concenters round the commander of the American army. Then the story will
lead us as we follow Grant in the GRAND MARCH
FROM CAIRO TO RICHMOND—for such it was—by
Belmont's repulse to Donelson's glorious victory ; by
the bayous of the Mississippi and the marshes of
the Yazoo to Grand Gulf; by the Big Black to the
battles and surrender of Vicksburg—to the bloody
Chickamauga and Missionary Ridge—to the Rapidan
and the battles of the Wilderness—to Spottsylvania
and the Chickahominy ; by the bloody field of Cold
Harbor; by the James—to the storm of Petersburg,
and the surrender at Appomattox Court-House. Such
a march as this—such a series of vivid scenes, of
bloody battle-fields, of extraordinary events—in the

same space of time—has never been recorded in modern history. The march of Grant from Cairo to Richmond is without a parallel. To picture it forth, not in the visions of fancy, but in the soberest and truest colors of history, will require all the abilities of the most accomplished historian. I propose only to tell the story of that drama in such simple language and in such outline sketches as will give the reader a clear idea of what was done without being confused by terms and details not generally understood. I write for the common reader an account of great events, which is true, reliable, accurate, and to which he may refer for much of the history of these times. Fortunately for the truth of history in our day, the press records every thing. Every fact, every man, every plan, every movement, every opinion and event of our last great conflict are embodied by the press and perpetuated for the use of the historian. With such materials we may be dull, but we must be true. I shall avail myself of all these materials; and however brief I may be, or however inadequate the life of any one man is to represent the acts and movements of a great people, yet, so far as I take the scenes of that movement, and so far as I represent them, I shall make the picture true and faithful. My part is humble, and the story but one chapter in history, but it shall be just and accurate.

EWD. D. MANSFIELD.

Cincinnati, 1868.

LIFE

OF

GENERAL GRANT.

CHAPTER I.

ANCESTRY—PARENTAGE—BIRTH—SCHOOL-BOY DAYS—OCCUPA-
TION—HORSEMANSHIP—AT WEST POINT—DESCRIPTION BY
A COMRADE.

THE life of an eminent public man is a page in
his country's history.   God has so made us, that
no man lives only to himself.   We are interwoven one
with another.   We are particles in a great whole—
units in immense numbers; but not particles without
cohesion, nor units without magnitude.   Do what we
will, whether small or great, we do make part of the
public body; we have an influence, whether we choose
or not, and can not get rid of it.   But, if one of us
comes to be a leader; to be commander of an army;
to be chief magistrate of the Republic; to be eminent
in science, or, to be illustrious in letters—that makes
us, not a small, but a large particle in the body-politic;
not of slight, but of immense influence in directing
events, in forming opinions, and in shaping the course

of affairs. Such is the position of General ULYSSES S. GRANT. It matters not whether we think his fame and success are the sole result of unprecedented merit or not—it is enough that he has them; it is enough that Divine Providence, which overrules all human events, has permitted him to acquire such fame and success, and that he thus occupies a large space in public affairs, and is looked up to by multitudes as one of the principal leaders in one of the most powerful nations of the earth. This calls our attention to him, and leads us to trace out, as far as we can, his manner of life and his public career.

ULYSSES S. GRANT was, as the name implies, of Scotch extraction. The first ancestor we hear of as native to this country was Noah Grant, born in Windsor, Hartford county, Connecticut.[1] He was a captain in the King's service, and killed at White Plains, 1756. Noah Grant, son of Captain Grant, was also born in Connecticut. He was a lieutenant at the battle of Lexington, and served through the whole Revolutionary war. It seems that after the war was ended, this Noah Grant, in 1789, emigrated from Connecticut to Western Pennsylvania; and we find that Jesse R. Grant, the father of Ulysses, was born in Westmoreland county, in January, 1794.[2] This Noah Grant was a man of education and property, but, we are informed by his son, died poor. In 1799 he took his family from Westmoreland into that part of Ohio now Columbiana county. Ohio was then part of the North-Western Territory, and it was four

[1] Jesse Grant's Letters to the New York Ledger.
[2] Idem.

years before it was constituted a State. The Grants
have, therefore, as we shall see hereafter, been identified with Ohio during the whole period of its growth
and history. In 1804 the family moved to Portage
county, on the Western Reserve. In 1810 Jesse R.
Grant was apprenticed to learn the tanning business,
at Maysville, Kentucky. After serving his appren-
ticeship faithfully, he set up business for himself in
Ravenna, Portage county ; but, suffering severely from
fever and ague—always incident to a new country—
he removed in 1820 to Point Pleasant, on the Ohio
River, in Clermont county, and twenty-five miles above
Cincinnati. Here, in 1821, Jesse R. Grant married
Hannah Simpson, and began housekeeping. Here we
may inquire, what kind of a woman is the mother of
General Grant? It is said that men derive their best
qualities—certainly a large part of their character—
from their mothers. Human history presents few
eminent men whose mothers have not been remarkable for some good or bad qualities. Of Mrs. Hannah
Grant it is not proper to say, nor do we know, more
than her husband has said of her ; but this is clear
and direct. Mr. J. R. Grant says of her :[1] "At the
time of our marriage, Mrs. Grant was an unpretending country girl ; handsome, but not vain. She had
previously joined the Methodist Church ; and I can
truthfully say that it has never had a more devoted
and consistent member. Her steadiness, firmness, and
strength of character have been the stay of the family
through life."

The lineage of Grant is thus traced up to ancestors,

[1] New York Ledger, March 7, 1868.

whose descendant, we may reasonably infer from our knowledge of human nature, might be such a man as he is. Of Scotch extraction, of New England character, of Western enterprise, of moderate education, of thrifty habits—for they all seem to have prospered—Grant's ancestors were a sort of people likely to have careful, prudent, industrious, and, with moderate luck, successful descendants. When to this we add the Christian character of his mother, I know not whether Grant could have been born under better auspices in this republican country, where men are valued more for what they are, than for the nobility of their birth, or the splendor of their fortune. Born under such auspices, he was not likely to be a man of genius; but was almost certain to be a man of common-sense, of patriotic purpose, and of prudent conduct.

It was in Ohio, then, that Grant was born; in a simple, frame house, on the banks of that beautiful river, whose waters roll through the richest land on earth, and whose valley is now filled with free, energetic, and intelligent people; and whose youth are brought up in the love of republican institutions. Here universal freedom began; for here the Ordinance of 1787 had proclaimed that no slavery should endure; and that Ordinance is flowing over other States and other lands, like the widening circles in the water, till it shall fill the earth with the rejoicings of emancipated nations. Here was the cradle of Grant. Here he looked out upon a new world, which his New England ancestors, who lived amid the conflicts of the Revolution, had not dreamed of. They little knew what the war of Independence had done, and they lived not to see the mighty growth of empire in the Western valleys. But here their descendant grew up with it, and became a leader in other and greater conflicts.

ULYSSES S. GRANT was born on the 27th of April, 1822, and his boyhood was passed at Point Pleasant and at Georgetown, Brown county, to which his father removed.

At Georgetown, and at a very early age, was exhibited that remarkable love of horses which he seems to have retained. Most boys are fond of horses, but Grant not only loved them, but had a talent for them. His father tells some stories of him, some of which are quite striking. At seven and a half years of age he first began to manage a horse alone, and then in a very daring manner. While his father was gone for the day, Master Ulysses hitched up a colt which had never been harnessed, managed to get him tackled in a sled, and employed him all day drawing brush, till he had collected a large pile. Many stories are told about his horsemanship, all of which prove that he was a ready and bold horseman while quite young. Beginning at five years of age, he preferred standing to sitting on the horses, and at nine was so accomplished an equestrian that he rode his horse at full speed, standing on one foot and balancing himself with the reins. He broke his own horses, had the knack of teaching any horse to pace, and while a small boy became a regular team-driver. As might be expected, he was fond of circuses, and on one occasion seems to have beat the ring-master, the horse and a monkey, who had entered into a conspiracy to have him thrown. He was the boy who volunteered to ride pony round the ring; the ring-master cracked his whip, the horse tried to throw him, the monkey jumped up behind, and finally on his shoulders, but all in vain. The conspirators had to give it up. Indeed, had they known that this boy delighted in riding with the bridle in his mouth, standing on one foot, down a rough hill, they would not have made so useless an attempt. At this period of his life his father does not represent him as, in other respects, very different from other boys, nor is his love of horsemanship remarkable, except in one thing, which has continued to characterize him : this is perfect self-possession and unmoved nerve. Looking forward to the possibilities of such a boy, we find him already possessed of some qualities very necessary to a great soldier—good horsemanship, physical courage, and self-possession. There are men of great genius in the world, and of great eminence and command, who have neither one of these qualities, and yet who have as much merit in their several walks as any of the great soldiers.

In describing him in his boyhood his father, who is the best witness, portrays him as being very much what we should suppose the germ of such a man would be. He says:

"He never seemed inclined to put himself forward at all, and was modest, retiring, and reticent, as he is now; but he never appeared to have any distrust of himself, or any misgiving about his ability to do any thing which could be expected of a boy of his size and age. Self-possession was always one of his leading characteristics." In addition to this his father

says he was industrious, but detested the tannery!
He would rather do any thing else under the sun than
work in the tannery. So great was his dislike to
that occupation that when told to go into the tan-
yard he went to the village instead, got a job to do,
and hired another boy to take his place. Perhaps for
this a philosopher might give a natural reason—Grant
was the friend of horses, and horses dislike tan-yards,
and so Grant sympathized with his friends! Perhaps,
another would say, this was an instinctive feeling that
he was to rise above merely mechanical work, and
certainly the business of a tan-yard requires no great
activity of mind, and promised little to lead forth the
spirit, or satisfy ambition. It is common to try to
popularize a man by giving him a nickname derived
from an early and laborious employment, such as the
"wagon-boy," and the "tan-boy;" but this does wrong
both to the fathers and the sons. These occupations
are honest and honorable, but they are certainly not
very intellectual, or leading to any very noble results.
Mr. Corwin would not have been a "wagon-boy," or
General Grant a "tan-boy," if he could have helped
it. The avoidance of the tan-yard in a boy who was
otherwise industrious, was really, although it might
be unknown to himself, a latent ambition to be
something else. But, after all, Grant's boyhood was
nothing wonderful, and the only points about it, as
described by his father, worthy of our special notice
are those I have mentioned—horsemanship, physical
courage, self-possession, and avoidance of the tannery. A story is told of a phrenologist who came
along and pronounced his head no common affair,

and said it would not be strange to see him President of the United States! But as every phrenologist I ever heard of does the same thing for every head he examines, and especially if it be a boy's, this can not be deemed very remarkable. In fact, Grant's boyhood passed away without any wonderful occurrence, without any precocious genius, and without any great performance, except that of rivaling the circus-rider in horsemanship. Two characteristics, however, came out, which indicated the coming man. The first is, that he had the qualities I have mentioned; the second is, that he had no vices. His mother watched him with great care, and his father says that he never had the habit of swearing, either as boy or man,' and that he was not addicted to any pleasure, except horsemanship and playing marbles. At twelve years of age, then, we find Ulysses Grant a very respectable boy, with some qualities which are necessary to make a good soldier, and none which would retard his success if fortune should be favorable.

I come now to his education. This sometimes counteracts the natural bent and talent of youth; sometimes falls in with them, so as to give them greater force and elasticity. In Grant's case, his early life seems to have favored and strengthened his natural character; his bent was evidently for the exterior world, and for the management of exterior forces; and his education being mainly military, and his studies of the physical sciences, they prepared him for the art of war, the control of men, and the perception of what is necessary for the development of physical

---

' Mr. Grant's Letters to the New York Ledger.

resources. But little account is left of what his primary education was. What the moral and religious part of it was, we know from what has been said of his mother. A Christian mother rarely fails to impress her religious ideas upon her children, and such a mother is no more the fountain of life than she is of sentiments and principles. An old gentleman, named Barney, had the honor of being his first teacher, when Ulysses was only four years old. He was fond of school, and particularly of mathematics. The first book he read was the Life of Washington—I wonder whether it was Weems's! Long before Grant's time, Weems's Life of Washington was the wonder and delight of boys. As a literary performance it was quite inferior; but it presented Washington as a wonderful being, shielded from the rifle-balls of Indians by the hand of Providence, and reared by the same Divine Providence to be a Heaven-directed and Heaven-shielded leader of the people. When I was a boy, I talked with veteran soldiers of the Revolution, who had the same ideas, and actually believed Washington was a Heaven-sent and Heaven-guided man. Was that belief false? Is it not true that great leaders are sent into the world, as Moses was, to lead nations through trials and through difficulties to some predestined result? However that may be, Grant read the Life of Washington, and it may be the example there set before him will in some measure influence his future life.

We do not know how much he acquired between four years of age, when he first went to school, and sixteen, when he must have been fitted for West Point;

but there was time enough to attain all the rudiments of common knowledge, and he must have done it, in order to have arrived at subsequent results.

When Grant had got along toward sixteen years of age, his father was short of hands, and told him that he would have to go into the tannery and work, when he again manifested his dislike to tanning; of which his father says: "He came along and went to work, remarking, however: 'Father, this tanning is not the kind of work I like. I 'll work at it though, if you wish me to, till I am one-and-twenty; but you may depend upon it, I 'll never work a day at it after that.' I said to him: 'No, I do not want you to work at it now, if you do not like it, and do not mean to stick to it. I want you to be at work at whatever you like and intend to follow. Now, what do you think you would like?' He replied that he would like to be a farmer; a down-the-river trader; or get an education."

His father had no farm, and would not let him go down the river; so he said: "How would you like West Point?" He replied, "First-rate." Thomas Morris was then Senator from Ohio, living in Clermont county, and Mr. Grant applied to him, asking him whether there was any vacancy. It happened there was a vacancy in that district, in the control of the late Thomas L. Hamer, at that time representing the district in Congress. Application was made to him, and he had young Grant appointed a cadet, on the last day of his Congressional service. It happened that Hamer and Grant were both subsequently in the Mexican war, and Hamer being taken sick, Grant had the melancholy satisfaction of attending him in the last hours of his life.

We are now to follow the young Grant to West Point, one of the few classic scenes in our country, not made classic by any studies pertaining to ancient learning, but by events, and scenes, and preparations memorable in our country's history. Here the Hudson River, mainly a tide-water arm of the sea, seems to the spectator to have broken through a rocky range of mountains. From Newburg Bay, where the river spreads out into almost a lake, to Stony Point, where it again spreads into another bay, a distance of nearly twenty miles, the river seems to be hemmed in by frowning, rocky barriers of precipitous hills. In the midst of these, jutting out from the Western side, on a grassy plain, commanding the view both up and down, stands West Point. Every crag above is memorable ; for all around the soldiers of the Revolution camped in the woods, lit their watch-fires, and built their beacons on the mountain summits. On the Bay of Newburg, above, is " Washington's Head-Quarters;" and just below us on the water side is " Washington's Valley;" and high on the eastern side is " Beacon Hill;" and there are bold " Bull's-Head," and " Crow-Nest," and " Butter Hill," and " Sugar-Loaf," rising up on every side, and looking down upon those glassy waters, as if to " sentinel enchanted land." Above the plain of West Point, and commanding it, is "Old Fort Put," gray and overgrown, in ruins. Its massy walls yet remain, while the cedar and the wild rose grow in its crevices. Below it, on various points, and mostly hid by the cedars, are the remains of thirteen different forts and batteries erected in the Revolution. On the sides of the plain are monuments to the glorious dead who were specially associated with West Point. Among these was Kosciusko, the Polish hero, who was at one time employed as an engineer here, and of whom Campbell wrote—

> "Hope, for a season, bade the world farewell,
> And Freedom shrieked—as Kosciusko fell."

Here, too, are the monuments of the heroic Wood and the gallant Dade, among the noblest *élèves* of the Academy. On the green turf, under the elms, you may look upon many a cannon, taken from the enemies of the country by land and sea. There are pieces taken at the surrender of Burgoyne; from the French frigate L'Insurgent; at M'Donough's victory on Lake Champlain; at Vera Cruz and Cerro Gordo; from Chapultepec, Cherubusco, and the Gates of Mexico. Far above them, waving in the Northern breeze, and gleaming in the sun, is the starry flag of our country:

> "Flag of the free heart's hope and home,
> By angel hands to valor given;
> Thy stars have lit the welkin dome,
> And all thy hues were born in heaven.
> Forever float that standard sheet!
> Where breathes the foe but falls before us,
> With Freedom's soil beneath our feet,
> And Freedom's banner streaming o'er us?"

It was in such a scene the poet wrote this inspiring stanza, and such must be the feeling of every youth and every patriot, as he looks from the plain of West Point at that beautiful flag, so surrounded by all the glowing memories of his country and her glory.

Here, in some bright day of July, 1839, stood the young Grant, ready to join the Academy, and for the first time to look upon scenes, and to dwell amid associations, so different from any thing to which he was accustomed. He was then seventeen years of age, a time very suitable to enter upon a military education. His early education must have been good, for he found no difficulty in passing the examination, which often proves a stumbling-block, even to young men of good abilities. On his entering West Point, he had a little experience in what I believe is called "hazing," but which is in fact a very silly practice of plaguing the young cadets by tricks and impositions. Some one assumed the uniform and authority of a police officer, and entering his room at bed-time, ordered him to get certain lessons, and perform certain things, which would have taken him all night ; to which he replied, " All right," turned over and went to sleep. This was simply another example of self-possession, for want of which many youth suffer a great deal.

Grant's career at West Point was simply that of any one of its two thousand graduates. The system of the Military Academy is uniform, divided into a routine of duties and performances, which are repeated from day to day, and year to year, with little variation. This routine embraces substantially but three great branches: the exterior military exercises, which are sufficient in time and extent to give that strength and development of body, which civil institutions endeavor to supply by gymnastics, but with much inferior results ; next mathematics, which embraces mechanical philosophy, astronomy, and the applied sciences; lastly, the military art, which includes drawing, French, and engineering. To these are added natural and ethical philosophy. The whole is enforced by an unyielding discipline, far more rigid than, and superior in its results to, any thing adopted in colleges. The effect of this system is that no one *can* graduate at West Point who has not an amount of instruction, of disciplined habits, and of bodily vigor, which fits him for any office in an army. It is almost the same system by which Napoleon was educated in the Polytechnique School. It is, at this time, probably the best school of military instruction in the world. A graduate may not have genius; he may possibly want that moral principle necessary to a high character, or be deficient in that vital energy necessary to great success; but he *must* have the knowledge and the discipline required to fill the highest military offices. If, after that, he fails, it will not be for want of any thing which a military institution can give. This advantage every one who graduates has; and, although out of two thousand, two hundred graduates, some have undoubtedly failed in the after struggles of life, yet the number is comparatively small; and probably the catalogue of no institution of learning exhibits so large a proportion of successful men.[1]

In the great body of graduates from the Military Academy, Grant held an average standing; he was a fair type of the whole. In a class, which originally numbered near a hundred, thirty-nine only were

[1] See Cullum's Biographical Register.

graduated, and of these Grant was the twenty-first. Looking only to those who graduated, Grant stood below the middle ; but looking to the whole class, he stood much above that. Class-standing, whether at the Military Academy or in colleges, is an evidence of persevering and industrious scholarship; but not necessarily of the best minds. One of the most brilliant men, in intellectual capacity, I ever knew, in either civil or military service, was General Ormsby M'Knight Mitchel, and he stood fifteenth in a class of twenty-four. There were men in his class graduated above him, who, although worthy and successful, were never equal to him.

Of Grant's personal conduct among the cadets little is known, except a reminiscence of Professor Coppée, who was contemporary with him at the Academy.[1] He says :

"The honor of being his comrade for two years at the Academy enables me to speak more intelligently, perhaps, than those of the 'new school,' who have invented the most absurd stories to illustrate his cadet life. I remember him as a plain, straightforward, common-sense youth ; quiet, rather of the old head on young shoulders' order ; shunning notoriety ; quite contented, while others were grumbling ; taking to his military duties in a very business-like manner ; not a prominent man in the corps, but respected by all, and very popular with his friends. His sobriquet of *'Uncle Sam'* was given to him there, where every good fellow has a nickname, from these very qualities ; indeed he was a very uncle-like sort of a youth.

[1] See "Grant and his Campaigns," by Coppée, page 22.

He was then and always an excellent horseman, and his picture rises before me, as I write, in the old torn coat, obsolescent leather gig-top, loose riding pantaloons, with spurs buckled over them, going with his clanking saber to the drill hall. He exhibited but little enthusiasm in any thing; his best standing was in the mathematical branches, and their application to tactics and military engineering."

If we suppose the boy described by Mr. Grant, and the cadet described by Professor Coppée, to be grown up into a man of experience, and become General Grant, we shall find no difference whatever in the character, but only a growth, and a fullness, and an eminence, into which the natural germ, the boy, born in Ohio, bred in simple habits, and directed by worthy parents, has steadily and successfully been developed. Plain, quiet, retired, industrious, and well disposed ; such was Grant on the Ohio and on the Hudson, and thence we shall follow him to his active military career.

CHAPTER II.

GRADUATES AT WEST POINT—IN THE FOURTH REGIMENT—
ITS HISTORY—GOES TO MEXICO—IS IN THE BATTLES OF
PALO ALTO, MONTEREY, CERRO GORDO, CHERUBUSCO—IS
TWICE PROMOTED—RESIGNS—BECOMES FARMER, BROKER,
AND LEATHER-DEALER.

UNDER the severe and salutary system of West Point Grant graduated, July 1, 1843, and was appointed brevet Second Lieutenant of the Fourth Infantry. A "brevet" was originally, and is yet, an honorary distinction for distinguished services. In the case of cadets, however, it is a designation simply of the rank they are to hold, and the regiments to which they are assigned, when there are any vacancies. This designation is made according to class rank, and beginning with the engineer corps, which is esteemed the best, because the officers have no line-duty to perform, and are substantially in civil life, except in war, when they are a part of the staff of the army, and employed in topographical and engineering duties.

Grant was breveted to the Fourth Infantry, and that regiment has a history unequaled by any. A regiment, like a country, survives after the individuals have perished. I remember, when a boy, near Cincinnati, to have seen the Fourth Regiment on its march

from the victory of Tippecanoe to the army of Hull;
that army, composed partly of regulars and partly of
volunteers, marched by my father's house, on a bright
day in June, full of hope and anticipations of victory.
Never were expectations so disappointed. The army
returned as prisoners of war, having been needlessly
and disgracefully surrendered by Hull. It was the
only disgrace the Fourth Regiment ever suffered; it
fought through the War of 1812–15 with Great Brit-
ain; it took part in all the bloody battles of Mexico;
it fought at Palo Alto and Resaca de la Palma; it
was in the storm of Monterey, at the siege of Vera
Cruz, at Cerro Gordo, at Cherubusco, and Molino del
Rey; at the storm of Chapultepec, and the surrender
of Mexico. When the great Rebellion took place it
pursued the same career, and from battle to battle
carried its blood-stained flag. Hung up at West
Point are the trophies of its history and its glory.

Into this regiment Ulysses S. Grant was promoted,
and for ten years he took part in its fortunes. He
was in garrison duty for two years, till the Texas occupation took place; then his regiment made part of the
army of General Taylor, when he took his position at
Aranzas Bay. With the politics of the war which
ensued a sub-lieutenant of the army could have nothing to do, and probably cared as little; but it is curious
to observe that, although the diplomatic correspondence of Messrs. Buchanan and Donelson proved that
war was inevitable, yet the Government had taken no
measures to increase the strength of the army! The
Fourth Regiment numbered 511 men, and that was
above the average; the full strength of a regiment is

more than 1,000 men. The strength of the regiments had never been so small since 1808; but this was a matter which young Grant probably neither knew nor cared for. This want of precaution must, however, have increased the losses and difficulties of the subsequent campaigns.

On the 8th of March, 1846, the advanced column of General Taylor's army commenced its march for Corpus Christi, and on the 18th the whole was concentrated near the banks of the Arroga Colorado, thirty miles from Matamoras, but subsequently returned to Point Isabel.[1] To this army, we have seen, Grant belonged. On the 8th of May was fought the battle of Palo Alto, and on the 9th that of Resaca de la Palma, both of which were decisive victories. We need not follow the details of marches and engagements in which the army of Taylor took part, and in which young Grant participated as a subaltern, and then unknown officer. It is sufficient to say, that on the 23d of September following, Monterey was stormed, in which the Fourth Regiment participated, and that in March following it was found with the army of General Scott, in front of Vera Cruz.

After fighting the bloody battle of Cerro Gordo, and advancing to Puebla, it was there concentrated, drilled, and organized for the march on Mexico. The Fourth Regiment, to which Grant belonged, made part of the First Brigade (under Colonel Garland) in the First Division, under the command of General Worth. In the battles of the Valley of Mexico, this Division was engaged in the hardest conflicts. On

[1] See Mansfield's "Mexican War."

the 9th of August this Division commenced its march to Mexico. The main road was found to be impassable, in consequence of the impregnable fortifications of El Peñon. In consequence of this, Scott reversed the order of march by leaving the main roads to Mexico and *turning* Lake Chalco to the south.[1] Worth's Division, which had been in the rear, now became the advance, and on the 15th of August proceeded steadily to the fortified position of San Antonio. The march round the lake to San Augustine was twenty-seven miles, by a route deemed by the Mexicans impracticable, and on the 18th all the corps were in position. Then followed, on the 19th, the great battles of Contreras and Cherubusco. After these was a pause, in which war was interrupted by some fruitless negotiations. On the 7th of September Scott ordered a corps, composed mainly of Worth's Division, of which the Fourth Regiment was part, to attack and carry Molino del Rey, (or King's Mill,) which was part of the defenses of Chapultepec. On the morning of the 8th Worth moved to the storm of the fortified Mill. It was obstinately defended, and the American loss was relatively greater than in any battle of the Mexican War. I mention this more particularly because for his gallant conduct in this action Grant received his first promotion. He stands on the Register of the Military Academy: "Breveted First Lieutenant, September 8, 1847, for gallant and meritorious conduct in the battle of MOLINO DEL REY."

On the 12th of September the army stormed the

---

[1] Mansfield's "Mexican War."

hill and castle of Chapultepec. Here again Grant won promotion, and he is again recorded on the Register as "breveted Captain, September 13th, for gallant conduct at CHAPULTEPEC." On the 14th he entered the city of Mexico. In the engagements attending the capture of the city he distinguished himself by one of those gallant little actions which show the spirit and character of the true soldier. It is thus mentioned in the official report of Major Francis Lee, commanding the Fourth Infantry in that battle:

"At the first barrier the enemy was in strong force, which rendered it necessary to advance with caution. This was done, and when the head of the battalion was within short musket-range of the barrier, Lieutenant Grant, Fourth Infantry, and Captain Brooks, Second Artillery, with a few men of their respective regiments, by a handsome movement to the left, turned the right flank of the enemy, and the barrier was carried." And he mentions Lieutenant Grant as "among the most distinguished for their zeal and activity."

The battle over, Grant was one of that army now standing in the city of the Montezumas, and constituting part of a scene which, in romance and interest, is equaled by few in the drama of history. The 14th of September was a memorable day. Grant belonged, as I have said, to the Division of Worth. About daylight Scott gave command to Worth and Quitman to advance and occupy the city. The corps of Quitman rushed forward, and soon the colors of its regiments were planted on the far-famed palace of Mexico. Worth's Division had been delayed at the Alameda, that the men who had entered the Belen gate the night before might be first in the grand plaza. At 7, A. M., on the 14th of September, 1847, the flag of the American Union was hoisted on the walls of the national palace in the city of Mexico. Soon after this event, at 9, A. M., a "tremendous hurrah broke from the corner of the plaza, and in a few minutes were seen the towering plumes and commanding form of our gallant old hero, GENERAL SCOTT, escorted by the Second Dragoons. The heart-felt welcome that came from our little band was such as Montezuma's halls had never heard."[1]

Here we must stop to observe a fact, which is most singular in American history, and strikingly illustrating the infirmities of human nature and the uncertainty of human conduct. Gathered round Scott on that memorable day were young men who were the flower of the American army, who rejoiced in a common flag, a common country, and common victories, but who, in a few years after, were fighting against one another as mortal foes. Some who were there no longer followed that flag, no longer loved that country, no longer rejoiced in a common inheritance! In fact, the army of Scott in the conquest of Mexico was the great school in which the leading soldiers in the War of the Rebellion, whether for or against the Union, were taught the art of war, inured to its vicissitudes, and skilled in the handling of armies. On Scott's staff, most honored and most distinguished, were LEE and BEAUREGARD; and in the

---

[1] Mansfield's "Mexican War."

line of the army there stood GRANT, and LYON, and McCLELLAN, and HANCOCK, and BUELL, and STEELE, and a host of others, who fought gloriously under their country's flag.[1] From the plaza of Mexico they separated, never again to meet in a common army and a common cause. Over some of them, like LYON, the grave has long closed, and

> " The brave have sunk to rest,
> By all their country's wishes blest !"

The Fourth Regiment, to which Grant belonged, had thirty-seven men killed in battle ; thirty-one died of wounds, and one hundred and twenty-three died of disease. Out of five hundred and eleven men and officers who marched to Mexico, one hundred and ninety-one perished in the war. This fact is alone enough to show the active part it took in those campaigns.

The military events, which closed on the 18th of September with the capture of the city of Mexico, closed also, with the exception of some incidental and minor engagements, the war with Mexico. To all practical intents, Mexico was conquered. From Santa Fe in the north to Tampico in the south ; from the Rio Grande to the shores of the Pacific ; from the hights of the Sierra Madre to those of the Sierra Nevada, the troops and navy of the United States held every position which, either in a military or commercial view, was valuable or accessible to the channels of business and population. Henceforward,

---

[1] See Cullum's " Biographical Register " of West Point, an interesting and valuable work.

the chief movement of our troops was the advance of
reinforcements, which, had they been earlier, had been
useful, but were now too late to aid the victorious
army or share in the glory of its achievements.[1]

The army remained but a short time in Mexico.
While there occurred an incident which again showed
Grant's superior horsemanship. Professor Coppée, who
was also in Scott's army in Mexico, says:

"During our residence at the capital I heard a
'horse-story' about Grant, which has not appeared in
the books, but which is at least true. He was an
admirable horseman, and had a very spirited horse.
A Mexican gentleman, with whom he was upon
friendly terms, asked the loan of his horse. Grant
said afterward: 'I was afraid he could not ride him,
and yet I knew, if I said a word to that effect, the
suspicious Spanish nature would think I did not wish
to lend him.' The result was, the Mexican mounted
him, was thrown before he had gone two blocks, and
killed on the spot." Professor Coppée justly says:
"It must not be supposed that these services during
the Mexican War are now dressed up to assimilate
with his after career. He was really distinguished in
that war above most of those of his own rank."[2]

Thus we see this young man was making his way
ahead, yet so unknown and unregarded are the subaltern officers of infantry, that the staff officers of that
army did not even remember him. Scott thought he
recollected such a name in Mexico, and Lee, (who
was one of the most distinguished on Scott's staff,)
thought he had seen him. He certainly did see him

<hr>

[1] Mansfield's "Mexican War."   [2] "Grant and His Campaigns."

afterward on an occasion more memorable in history than any thing which took place in Mexico.

But we must now follow Grant to more peaceful scenes. His career in war was for the present ended. The conquest of Mexico was complete. Negotiations soon took place, and peace was restored. Upon the close of the war the Fourth Infantry was sent to New York, then to the northern frontier, at Detroit and at Sackett's Harbor.

Sometime prior to the Mexican War Grant had been stationed at Jefferson Barracks, St. Louis, and there visited in the family of Mr. Frederick Dent, whose son (now General Dent) had been his classmate at West Point. Here he became engaged to Miss Julia S. Dent, but the occurrences of the Mexican War prevented their marriage. Grant was hurried off to Mexico, and took, as we have seen, his first lessons in war. In August, 1848, however, they were married. Here commenced a series of vicissitudes, in place and circumstances, to which army officers are always liable. They can count upon no settled home, and often, when they get comfortably fixed, and have made friends and associations, from which it is hard to part, they are suddenly broken up, and hurried to a distant region of the country. This was particularly the case with Grant. The officers and troops were distributed in the country, as they had formerly been. He was made Quarter-master of the Fourth Infantry, and was successively stationed at Sackett's Harbor, New York; Detroit, Michigan; Fort Columbus, New York; Benicia, California; Fort Vancouver, Oregon; and Fort Humboldt, Colorado. The mere naming of these places shows how widely and frequently the officers of our army are scattered. It was probably for this reason that Grant left the army. He was made full Captain of the Fourth Infantry in August, 1853, but in July, 1854, resigned.

The civil history of Grant makes a period of seven years, and is not filled with any remarkable events, except those of a purely domestic nature. He seems to have been like many men, who get out of their element, and do not very well know how to get in again. Few army officers who undertake to retire, after years of active service, find themselves completely at home in civil life, till years have partially obliterated their former experience. In spite of the restless character of Americans, we all like, after some years of fixed habits, from which we have wandered away, to return to the routine of our old ways. The ways of the army are always a routine. It may be sent over the globe and scattered in many parts, but the habits, or daily ways of the army, are fixed. Grant had been separated from his family, and was likely to be. For this reason he resigned, without, it seems, having a very definite idea of what he was going to do. Having when a boy a detestation of the tannery, he told his father he would like to be a farmer, or go down the river. The last his father would not allow, and sent him to West Point. Now his old notion of being a farmer seemed to have returned; and, accordingly, we find him at St. Louis. At this period of his life his father says: "His wish to become a farmer was now realized. Mr. Dent, his father-in-law, gave his wife a farm about nine miles from St. Louis, in Missouri, and I stocked it. Grant farmed it for about four years, at the end of which he was not so well off pecuniarily as when he began. To be sure, he had made some improvements on the place; he had built a new house—in part with his own hands—of hewn logs, for himself to live in. During all this time he worked like a slave; no man ever worked harder. He used to market wood. He kept men to chop it in the woods, and he hauled it to St. Louis. He had two teams; he drove one himself, and his little son drove the other. Grant was a thorough farmer, and an excellent plowman—though he never plowed a great deal."

It is said, that a lady of St. Louis met General Grant at Washington, after the close of the war, when he stood amid admiring circles, and said: "General, I think I saw you at St. Louis." "Yes, madam, I used to bring you wood; that was the happiest part of my life, when I was laboring hard for the support of my family." He was probably right, for no rest is so sweet as that which follows a day's labor in the honest pursuit of daily bread; and the rewards of such a life are greater than those which attend the successful soldier. Cincinnatus at his plow is more envied than Cæsar at the Capitol.

This four years of hard work was of inestimable service to Grant. It gave him knowledge of a class of objects, and of the management of affairs in civil life, which it is necessary for a general to know, though he may not have them to do himself. The office of commander of an army, to be well filled and well performed, is something like what Cicero describes that of an orator to be. It requires some knowledge of almost every subject. The course which Grant was led into seemed as if he really were in preparation for the office of commander. Four years a farmer, he had got no richer; in fact, I suppose, did not see clearly how to make the ends of the year meet. So he stepped out of farming, moved to St. Louis, and went into the real estate business with a man named Boggs. It is probable that this kind of business, which requires some of the tricks of trade, suited him less than any other. At any rate, he saw the profits were not enough for two, and he told his partner: "You may take the whole of this, and I will look up something else to do." He next got a place in the Custom-house, which he held for about two months, when the collector who appointed him died, and he left. It is said that he undertook two or three other occupations. However that may be, he pursued none long. At length his father found an employment for him, with which he was at least more familiar, if not better fitted. His father describes it thus:

"I owned a leather store at Galena, Illinois, which was conducted by my two other sons. Grant went to Galena and joined them in that. He took right hold of the business with his accustomed industry, and was a very good salesman. He had a faculty to entertain people in conversation, although he talked but little himself. But he never would take any pains to extend his acquaintance in Galena; and after he joined the army, and had begun to be distinguished, citizens of the town would stop in front of our store, within six feet of the windows, and look in to see which of the Grants it was that was absent, and had suddenly become famous."

I can imagine that Grant must have thought to himself that Fortune was obstinately thwarting all his wishes, when she brought him to smell, if not take part in, the business of a tannery. Grant was out of his element, and although his last occupation was more familiar, it was scarcely more congenial. Here, however, he lived contented; his wants were supplied, and his ambition was certainly confined within moderate limits. When the War of the Rebellion was over, some one was speaking to Grant about what he might aspire to; what offices he might obtain; what desires he might satisfy; to which he quietly remarked, that he only "wanted to be Mayor of Galena for one year, that he might get the street paved from his house to the river." He must have been a very quiet, retired man there; for when he afterward became so greatly distinguished, the people of Galena tried to recollect who he was; few remembered him; and he was even unknown to the member of Congress from his district, Mr. Washburn. One of the papers of Galena has recently undertaken to tell how little known and how really obscure he was. If true, it only shows that he took no part in public affairs, made no noise, and was unobtrusive upon other men's business. This was his natural character, and from it nothing could be argued for or against his fitness for any particular line of public business. A man living on the sides of Vesuvius, before its last eruption, could truly say, that he never heard of its eruption; that it was always quiet;

and that it manifested no signs of great power or extraordinary brilliancy. But the time was near when it did manifest great force, and when the world was filled with the rumor of its vast commotion. Men can not do extraordinary things without an extraordinary occasion. In common times, and with no convulsions of society, the river of life flows evenly on. No great falls, no long rapids, interrupt the even tenor of its ways. It is God who furnishes opportunities for men, and furnishes them with the qualities necessary to the great occasion. Grant would not have been commander of the army, nor that army been able to accomplish mighty purposes, if it had not been for that Divine Providence, which furnished the occasion, the ability, and the means. On this part of Grant's life, between the war of Mexico and the War of the Rebellion, Professor Coppée justly remarks:[1]

"That he tried many shifts, does not betoken a feeble or volatile nature, but simply the invention which is born of necessity. As a small farmer near St. Louis, and a dealer in wood, he made a precarious living; as a money-collector, he did no more, having neither the nature to bully, nor the meanness to wheedle the debtors. He is said, also, to have played the auctioneer; but in this branch, unless he made longer speeches than he has done since, he could achieve no success. At Galena, a place which had a growing trade with Wisconsin, Iowa, and Minnesota, the industry, good sense, and honesty of Grant did at length achieve a certain and honorable success, and had not the Rebellion broken out, he would have had

[1] "Grant and his Campaigns."

a local reputation in the firm of Grant & Son, as an admirable judge of leather, perhaps Mayor of Galena, with a thoroughly well-mended side-walk, visited always with pleasure by his old army friends traveling westward, but never heard of by the public. His greatest success had been achieved in the army; his Mexican experience gave glimpses of a future in that line; he needed only opportunity, and he was to have it abundantly." Here, then, begins a new epoch for him, as well as for the nation. The even tenor of his life was to be broken by a sudden plunge into the stormy elements of revolution, amidst the angry passions of men, into the conflicts of war, and to be borne upon the waves of a mighty nation thrown into convulsions by the terrors of the tempest. The forest was filled with the winds, the vales resounded with the drum, and the war-clouds rested on the hills. Then Grant returned to his element, then he renewed his armor, and soon began that career which, commencing in the office of Governor Yates at Springfield, flowed through all the campaigns of the war, and terminated only in the surrender of Lee at Appomattox Court-House.

CHAPTER III.

GRAND UPRISING—THE CONFEDERATE CONGRESS LAUGHS—
THE PEOPLE ANSWER—LINCOLN'S PROCLAMATION—GRANT
AT GALENA—VOLUNTEERS—APPOINTED COLONEL OF THE
TWENTY-FIRST ILLINOIS—COMMANDS AT CAIRO—ATTACKS
BELMONT—GRAND RECONNOISSANCE—STRATEGIC LINE OF
REBEL DEFENSE — FORT HENRY — ITS CAPTURE AND RE-
SULTS.

FORT SUMPTER was fired upon. It was the
match to the magazine already prepared for ex-
plosion. In a bright morning in April, the telegraph
announced to the nation, from Passamaquoddy to
the Rio Grande, and from the Lakes to the Ocean—
Fort Sumpter is fired upon! Although every intelligent man saw the coming storm ; although the
heavens were black with clouds, and the air already
filled with the roar of the coming tempest, yet most
men had a desire, if not an expectation, that in some
way the storm would pass over. As we had often
seen in a sultry day of summer, the clouds gather
suddenly up, and then pass away with a brisk wind,
so we thought this threatened tempest might disap-
pear without harm. Patriotic men could not conceive
the idea of Americans deliberately firing on the flag
of their country. It was an idea utterly foreign to
their natures. So, when Fort Sumpter was actually

fired upon by the batteries on Sullivan's Island, it was even more startling than would have been the loudest thunder from the most cloudless sky. It was startling, but there was no terror. It was the strengthening, not the relaxing of the nerves. In one moment every patriotic heart was braced up; every idea was concentrated on the country; every energy put forth for its salvation. Men saw the danger, but its greatness did not appall them. The whole loyal people sprung to action, as if excited by the touch of electricity. Their souls were fired; and never did any country exhibit such a scene as did republican America on the 15th of April, 1861. Multitudes met in all the great cities, and pledged their lives and fortunes to the Government. Private estates were offered; banks opened their vaults, and before the President's Proclamation could be issued, volunteers were already assembling for the field. The Marseillaise was not sung; but the churches were opened, and the most fervent of prayers offered up to the Divine Ruler of the Universe, that the God who had strengthened the fathers in building up, would now strengthen the children to preserve the Republic from ruin. No such scenes of assembled millions; of profound emotion; of determined resolution; of universal action, had ever been exhibited in National history. It could not have existed before; for never before had republican institutions given such perfect elasticity and freedom of movement; and never before had the telegraph furnished the means of such instantaneous information. It seemed as if the National nerves had been struck at the same moment from one end of the continent to the other, and vibrated together with a common emotion. A few days before, the country seemed, to a common observer, as quiet as a lake on a summer day. Heavy clouds were indeed gathering, but no wind ruffled the waters, and no sudden alarm startled the bystanders. Then the storm came. Then the nation.rushed to arms; the drum beat on every hillside; the streets were filled with companies of volunteers; the green fields were occupied with camps; and the National flag was raised on every house and in every highway. A nation of peaceful citizens was transformed into a vast army of volunteer soldiers. The events of that day may be accurately set down in history; but no history can ever paint the scene for posterity, as it was exhibited to the eye-witnesses who were actors in it. Though we had

> " Tully's voice and Virgil's lay,
> And Livy's pictured page ——"

we should fail to represent that grand uprising of a nation, in the magnitude of its passion and the strength of its faith.

The popular emotion had scarcely been expressed, when LINCOLN, President of the United States, issued his Proclamation, dated April 15, 1861. In that, after stating that the laws of the United States were opposed and "obstructed in the States of South Carolina, Georgia, Alabama, Florida, Mississippi, Louisiana, and Texas, by combinations too powerful to be suppressed by the ordinary course of judicial proceedings," he called forth "the militia of the several States of the Union, to the aggregate number of seventy-five thousand, in order to suppress said combination," and for that purpose, he said: "I appeal to all loyal citizens to favor, facilitate, and aid this effort to maintain the honor, the integrity, and the existence of our National Union, and the perpetuity of our National Government, and to redress wrongs already long enough endured."

At this time the "Confederate Congress," as it was called, was sitting at Montgomery, and when Mr. Lincoln's Proclamation was read, received it with a laugh of derision! Seventy-five thousand men to put down the Southern Confederacy! But Mr. Lincoln was right. The object of that Proclamation was to test the spirit of the country. It announced war. It startled the people, and if the popular heart really responded to the call of the Government, not only seventy thousand, but seven hundred thousand, would rush to arms; and so it was. Before July was gone half a million of men had volunteered for the field, and the country was resounding with martial music and the tramp of troops. Thus the acts of the nation responded to the emotions of its heart. No indifference of feeling, no love of ease, no corruptions of avarice, no sluggishness of action, which had so often arrested the energies of other nations, for one moment stopped the career of our Republic. The demoniac laugh of the Confederate Congress at Montgomery was answered with the loud shout of loyal millions, and before long its triumphant boasts were buried in the graves of traitors, and the surrender of its defeated armies. Long did treason hold out, and bravely did it fight, but in vain.   The patriotic masses of the nation were hurled against it, with all the energy of a noble and exalted patriotism.   Sad was this scene of internal convulsion, but gloriously did the Republic triumph, and undeniably did it prove to the world that the Government of the people was the strongest of all governments.   How inestimable to the peoples of the earth that demonstration is, it will be for after history to record and illustrate.

Lincoln's Proclamation of the 15th of April found Grant, as we have seen, in a leather store at Galena. He was comparatively prosperous, but a soldier, bred as he was, could not remain inactive when millions were marching to the field, and the public heart was throbbing with emotion.   He was not naturally enthusiastic, but he was brave, patriotic, and well acquainted with his duty.   So he wrote to his father asking, as he had been educated by the Government, whether he had not better go into the army?[1]   But these were fast times; a week was equal in events to a year in peace, and before his father could answer, in six days after the fall of Fort Sumpter, he was drilling a company.   He declined the captaincy of the company, but marched with it to Springfield, the capital of Illinois.   There he was introduced to Governor Yates by Mr. Washburn, the representative of the Galena district.   A day or two afterward the Governor sent for him, and asked:

"Do you understand how many men it takes to make a company? And how many to make a regiment? And what officers each must have?"

<hr>

[1] J. R. Grant's Letters in New York Ledger.

"O, yes," replied Grant, "I understand all about such matters; I was educated at West Point, and served eleven years in the regular army."

"Well, then," said the Governor, "I want you to take a chair, here in my office, as Adjutant-General of the State."

After several weeks passed by the Governor asked a young man, who had been with Grant in the mercantile house, "What sort of a man is this Grant? He says he wants to go into the army, and several regiments have offered to elect him Colonel, but he says 'No.'" His friend replied, that Grant had only served in the regular army, where officers are never elected; that he had served eleven years in the army, and that, if the Governor wanted to give him a place, he should send Grant a commission without consulting him. The Governor did so, and appointed him Colonel of the 21st Illinois Infantry, while he was on a short visit to his father.

On taking command of this regiment his first object was to drill the men perfectly, and use them to military habits. They were organized at Mattoon, but he removed them to Caseyville, where he superintended their drill. Not long after, Quincy was supposed to be in danger, and he marched the regiment, for want of railroad transportation, to that place, one hundred and twenty miles. Here he was ordered to defend the Hannibal Railroad, and moved to St. Joseph, the western terminus, in the "District of Northern Missouri," under the command of General John Pope. Here, meeting with other regiments, although the youngest Colonel, he was selected as Brigadier-

General, and in July, 1861, made his head-quarters at Mexico, Missouri. Thence he made various marches to different points—to Pilot Knob, Ironton, and Jefferson City, defending the river from threatened attacks from Colonel Jefferson Thompson. In August he received his commission, dated May 17th, as Brigadier-General of Volunteers. It was the seventeenth of thirty-four original appointments.

At this time he was ordered to proceed to Cairo and take command of the "District of South-East Missouri," which included both banks of the Mississippi River, from Cape Girardeau to New Madrid, and on the Ohio the whole of Western Kentucky. Any military man, and almost any intelligent person, will see, by a mere examination of the map, that in all the country west of the Alleghany Mountains, likely to be in any event the scene of war, CAIRO was the most important point. Geographically and strategically, it is the key of the Mississippi Valley. Below was the Lower Mississippi to the gulf; above was the Upper Mississippi, including St. Louis; west was the Missouri, and east the Ohio. A garrison holding Cairo can cut off communication between three great arms of internal navigation, and then, if sufficiently strong, be able to strike the rear of any military force sent through the interior. If Cairo were held by the enemy, where would be our steamboat transportation of supplies, which proved of such inestimable service during the war? What was the actual condition of Kentucky and Missouri at that time? South-Eastern Missouri, opposite and below, was held by the rebels then, and for a long time afterward. Kentucky then professed a sort of armed neutrality; but half her young men had entered the rebel army, and from what we know now, it is evident that three-fourths of her people were on the rebel side. If we suppose a strong force from Missouri and Kentucky to have moved on Cairo, in the summer of 1861, it would have been taken, and the loss to the Government would have been incalculable. It seemed to me, then, very singular that the rebel leaders did not make the attempt, and equally strange that the Government delayed so long in making it strong and defensible. On the rebel side, it may be said that the war found the Confederates in the West without a complete organization, and without efficient leaders. The attempted "neutrality" of Kentucky, (which was at best only a flimsy disguise,) lost them several months of time, which, if actively and skillfully employed, would have struck heavy blows to the Union cause on the Mississippi. At length, however, the Government perceived the necessity of a rallying point and defense at Cairo. It was, in fact, what engineers call a *point d'appui.*

The appointment of Grant to the command of Cairo settled the difficulty, and from Cairo Grant commences a new career. He had got back to his element, and now he lacks neither energy nor purpose. He immediately entered Cairo, with two brigades, and took a calm view of the situation. Two things were quite obvious: one, that Kentucky "neutrality" would not prevent the rebel forces from occupying that State; the other, that the mouths, and as far as possible the navigation, of the Cumberland and

Tennessee Rivers, were essential to the Union army. If the reader will look upon a map, he will see that the Cumberland and the Tennessee Rivers enter the Ohio not more than ten or twelve miles apart, (not very far from Cairo,) and that they both traverse Kentucky and Tennessee. For some distance in the interior of Kentucky they run in a general parallel direction. Besides this, the Cumberland is navigable to Nashville, the capital of Tennessee. Below Cairo, on the Mississippi, some twenty miles down, are bluffs, capable of being fortified at and near Columbus. If the rebels could have done it, they would have seized Cairo, Paducah, and the mouth of the Cumberland, and have made the Ohio River the line of defense. No doubt this was their original plan; but, fortunately for the Government, and most unfortunately for them, they were too late. Kentucky neutrality, and the want of military ability, had delayed them too long. They now sought to retrieve their error by marching a large force through Kentucky, seizing Bowling Green and Hickman, and establishing themselves at Columbus, in that State, under the command of General Leonidas Polk. Grant watched their movements from Cairo, and saw their object. Fremont was then in command of the district to which Cairo was attached, and Grant telegraphed him that the enemy had invaded Kentucky, and that "he was nearly ready for Paducah, should not a telegram prevent the movement." No telegram came, and Grant left Cairo on the evening of the 5th of September, and occupied Paducah on the 6th. In the same manner he occupied Smithland, at the mouth of the Cumberland, and thus closed two gates to the enemy and opened them for himself. It was not an hour too soon, for the enemy had already approached within a short distance of Paducah, and their friends had prepared them comfortable meals to welcome their arrival.

Having done this, Grant next planned an expedition against Columbus, not with the view of making any serious impression on that place, which was heavily garrisoned by the army under General Leonidas Polk, in a commanding position, but to prevent the sending of reënforcements to Thompson and Price in Missouri, and to reconnoiter the general position of the enemy. To further this plan he sent out General C. F. Smith from Paducah, to make a demonstration toward Columbus. Prior to this, Polk had actually landed a body of troops at the little village of Belmont, on low ground opposite Columbus, and under the guns of that place. These troops had, however, moved out and made an advanced encampment. Beyond a doubt Polk was preparing to reënforce Thompson and Price. At the same time a portion of the rebel troops had their knapsacks on, preparing to reënforce Bowling Green. In fact Columbus was a commanding, fortified camp on the Mississippi, which, as appears from the concurrent testimony of Polk's General Orders, and the contemporaneous accounts, was then held by a large army, with a view to reënforcing Missouri or Southern Kentucky. It was a *point d'appui* on the rebel side, as Cairo was on ours. This Grant knew, and now prepared an expedition for the purpose of checking that scheme. The force selected was composed of:

> Twenty-Second Illinois, Colonel Dougherty.
> Twenty-Seventh Illinois, Colonel Buford.
> Thirtieth Illinois, Colonel Fouke.
> Thirty-First Illinois, Colonel Logan.
> Seventh Iowa, Colonel Lamon.
> Taylor's Chicago Artillery.
> Dollen's and Delano's Cavalry.

The whole force numbered two thousand, eight hundred and fifty men of all arms,[1] to make, as Grant said in his report, a reconnoissance toward Columbus, with the objects I have stated. The expedition left Cairo on the evening of the 6th inst., and stopped about nine miles below Cairo, on the Kentucky shore. About daylight of the 7th (November) it proceeded down the river to a point just out of range of the rebel guns, and debarked on the Missouri shore. Thence it was marched about a mile toward Belmont, drawn up in line of battle, and a sharp, quick action took place, which terminated in driving the enemy from their camp, over the bank, into their transports. Their tents, blankets, and cannon fell into our hands. The former were burnt, and two pieces of the latter taken off by our men. These belonged to Beltzhoover's Battery, of which Polk in his report said they saved four, which was true, but they lost two. Belmont could not possibly be held under the fire of Columbus, opposite: so Grant immediately retreated. In the mean time the enemy rallied, and were reënforced by at least ten regiments. Grant says the enemy attempted to surround our forces;

[1] Grant's Official Report, November 12, 1861.

but, not in the least discouraged, they charged and again defeated them. At length our troops reached the transports and returned to Cairo. The losses of this action were: *killed*, eighty-four; *wounded*, one hundred and fifty; and *missing* one hundred and fifty; making less than four hundred. What loss the enemy met with we only know from an account[1] giving the official report of four regiments at sixty-five killed, one hundred and eighty-seven wounded, and one hundred and eight missing; showing in these regiments alone three hundred and sixty-four. The account admits that if the loss in other regiments engaged were 'in proportion, the total loss must have reached one thousand. The rebel accounts substantially agree with that of Grant, except in the number of our forces, which Bishop Polk, in his dispatch of November 7th, modestly put at seven thousand, five hundred! In this action all the officers behaved well, and in that respect Belmont is much more creditable to us than were some others of much greater magnitude. Grant had a horse shot under him, McClernand three, and every colonel of a regiment was reported to have behaved gallantly. In fact, one idea of this engagement was to show that our men could and would fight. This it was absolutely necessary to do, not so much for military results as moral effects. Among the many delusions which gave rise to the war was the singular notion that the Northern men would not fight, and that there was a certain and available superiority in the chivalry of the South. Exactly what that meant it would be difficult to tell;

[1] Letter in the Memphis Appeal, dated November 10, 1861.

but this idea had the effect of a superstitious feeling, for a time encouraging Southern men to hope for success from causes entirely without the ordinary laws of military science. This idea it was necessary to destroy, and in the course of the six months, from the 1st of November, 1861, to May, 1862, it was most effectually done, and the South awakened from its delusions to find a hard and bloody war covering its homes and its fields with death and desolation. Grant in his Order, dated Cairo, November 8th, gave formal testimony to the fact that volunteers fresh from their shops and fields had behaved with the gallantry of veterans: "The General commanding this Military District returns thanks to the troops under his command at the battle of Belmont on yesterday. It has been his fortune to have been in all the battles fought in Mexico by Generals Scott and Taylor, save Buena Vista, and he never saw one more hotly contested, or where the troops behaved more gallantly."

Belmont has been sharply criticised by those who look rather to the glory of a battle-field than to the *objects* of a battle. All military movements are made, if made by generals of any capacity, with a view to gaining some end. If that end *is* gained, it is of no moment who held the battle-field. In this instance, the enemy held the field, and no other result was possible. But Grant gained all the objects he proposed to himself, and the expedition paralyzed several offensive expeditions contemplated by Polk, and gave the first real check to the heretofore triumphant progress of the enemy. It did more. It was the initial step in those vigorous, offensive operations which opened the Cumberland and the Tennessee Rivers, and broke through the entire defensive line of the enemy from Missouri to Virginia.

We return now to the steps in what we may call the preparation for the great campaign of 1862. On the 12th of November, 1861, General H. W. Halleck, of the regular army, was sent to take command of the "Department of Missouri." He divided his command into districts, of which the District of Cairo was the most important. This comprehended Southern Illinois; Kentucky, west of the Cumberland; and Missouri, south of Cape Girardeau. In this district, Grant was retained, as commander, and immediately began to organize an army for new movements. At that time, military information, as to the number and position of forces, was, as far as possible, kept from the press and the public; so that, in December and January, little was known of the immense preparations made at Cairo; and when at length that army was hurled against the rebels on the Cumberland and the Tennessee, the country was as much surprised as it was rejoiced. In the mean while, it became necessary to get full information of the enemy's positions and strength. For this purpose, an expeditionary force under General Grant was prepared for a grand reconnoissance. General Buell was at this time operating in Kentucky, and advancing upon Bowling Green, the central point of the enemy's line of defense.[1] One object of the expedition was to

---

[1] Halleck's order to General Grant, dated January 6, 1862, (which he was not to communicate even to his staff,) gives the real object of this demonstration, which was to prevent reënforcements to Buckner, and

prevent Polk from detaching reënforcements from Columbus and the intermediate country, to aid in the defense of Bowling Green. The main expedition was under the command of General McClernand, and consisted of five thousand, two hundred men, composed of the following regiments:

Tenth Regiment Illinois Volunteers.
Eighteenth Regiment Illinois Volunteers.
Twenty-Fifth Regiment Illinois Volunteers.
Twenty-Ninth Regiment Illinois Volunteers.
Thirtieth Regiment Illinois Volunteers.
Thirty-First Regiment Illinois Volunteers.
Forty-Eighth Regiment Illinois Volunteers.
Schwartz and Draper's Batteries of Light Artillery.
Dickey's Cavalry, five companies.

On the 10th of January, 1862, this force set out, by way of Fort Jefferson, for Columbus, the gun-boats Essex and St. Louis accompanying by the river. This reconnoissance was made over icy and miry roads, in a most inclement season, the infantry having marched seventy-five miles, and the cavalry one hundred and forty; returning to Cairo on the 21st of January. The expedition was in the highest degree satisfactory, having advanced to within a mile and a half of Columbus; discovered several new roads, and diverted the enemy's attention from important measures which they had planned. . The gun-boats met some of the enemy's boats, which they had attempted to fit out for offense, but soon drove them back under the guns of Columbus. At the same time, General Smith moved from Smithland, and

divert the enemy's attention. Grant, however, using it for something more, got valuable information, on which the attack on Fort Henry was based, as appears in the pages of the text following.

General Payne from Cairo, by Bird's Point. Grant himself moved with the column under Payne, and the official report of the expedition was made by General McClernand.

Unmilitary people look upon such proceedings and wonder what they are for. They expect a battle; a town stormed, or something decisive; but they might just as well ask the use of a drill. In one sense, these great reconnoitering expeditions are a drill, to teach the marches and movements of war. In another, they are absolutely necessary, to *feel* the enemy; to discover how much country he occupies and defends, and whether any new positions have been taken and fortified. This reconnoissance was one of the movements which preceded the coming campaign.

To form an idea of the successive events of the war in the West, and the part General Grant had in them, it is absolutely necessary to take a glance at the *preparation;* the material which it required time and skill to get and fit out. We have seen how the army was gradually gathering at Cairo, and along the Ohio; how it advanced in reconnoissance, and tried its hand in battle and in skirmishes; but there was another branch of service which, in the West, was of vast importance, and grew up to great magnitude. This was the River Navy; the flotillas of armed boats, which were to force and keep the navigation of the Mississippi, and to guard that of the Ohio. This was one of the first ideas in the plans of General Scott. The Mississippi, Missouri, and the Ohio were the grand arteries of the interior, and there were scarcely a hundred miles of either of them which were not continually attacked, or threatened, by rebel batteries. Even on the Ohio, the south side was, in many places, filled with rebels, who took all possible means to obstruct navigation, because, in that way, they could prevent the transportation of men and means necessary to the armies below. Such was the condition of affairs in the latter part of 1861. But the Government had anticipated this, by building or altering boats for a river flotilla. At Cincinnati, Mound City, and St. Louis, a class of vessels called "Gun-boats" were built. At first they were built with heavy timbers, and lined partially with iron. Subsequently, they were thoroughly iron-clad. In January, 1862, several of these gun-boats had been got ready, and Commodore Foote, one of the most skillful and gallant officers of the navy, was appointed to take command of them. Thus, by land and water, was rapidly gathering together that grand armament, which first burst through Kentucky, then Tennessee, then Mississippi, and culminated its triumphs in the surrender of Vicksburg.

At this time we must look at the rebel line of defense, and our line of attack, in order to comprehend properly precisely what was the meaning and results of subsequent military movements. The Confederate commander regarded our Government (and justly) as making a war of invasion and subjugation. Nothing short of that could restore the unity of the country, for the Confederate States had seceded— declared their independence, and their determination to remain independent. There was no alternative, then, but conquest or separation. The war was a war of conquest, and it could be nothing else. The first object, then, of Mr. Davis and the Confederate Generals must be to seize and fortify a line which they could defend. In the East they intended this to be the line of the Baltimore and Ohio Railroad to the Ohio. This, however, our Government understood. General Mansfield, returning from Texas before the war, wrote me: "We shall have war, and *the first thing to be done is to seize the line of the Baltimore and Ohio Railroad.*" This was done substantially before the rebel troops could reach it in sufficient numbers; and it was held permanently (though sometimes cut by invading parties) by McClellan's successful campaign in Western Virginia. On the Ohio, as I have said, they meant to take the line of the Ohio; but they were not in time, and Grant's occupation of Cairo, and his seizure of Paducah and Smithland, made it impossible. The consequence of these proceedings was, that the rebels took an interior line of defense, which, although not equal to the one they desired, was yet one of great natural advantage. The head of it in the East was Manassas, thence turning west into the Valley of Virginia, and following that to Knoxville, and thence across the head-waters of the Cumberland to Bowling Green, Fort Henry, and Columbus on the Mississippi. The first and the last were strong positions. Bowling Green, Kentucky, might have been regarded as an advanced post—a *tete-de-pont*—to Nashville, if it had not been essential to the defense of Columbus. If the reader will take a map and examine it, he will see that this was naturally a very strong defensive line ; in fact, by far the strongest between the Ohio River and the Atlantic or the Gulf. *In ten months of the early part of the war that line was never penetrated* till the events occurred which I am about to relate. Let us now turn to the position of our forces.

Our object, as an attacking, invading force, was to break that line, which involved the loss of the whole of it, and the substantial conquest of the whole country between that and the next one taken, if another was possible. The brief campaign of McClellan in Western Virginia was only a prelude to clear away the advance parties, which the enemy were projecting from their line in the Valley of Virginia, with a view to gain the Ohio River. That was effectually done in the summer of 1861. The next thing was an attack on their line to break it. This was made on their strongest position at Manassas, and failed. It was, in fact, a mistaken movement. Any successful assault on the compact line of the Confederates must come from the West, where the Mississippi River could be forced by our superior naval armament, and from which the whole rebel line, extensive and powerful as it was, could be *turned and forced back upon itself*—a strategy which the Government was obliged to adopt after ten months of unsuccessful effort and desultory attacks. We shall now see the first steps in that grand strategy which ended with the fall of Richmond. I do not suppose that this whole scheme was adopted at once, or that either the Government or the generals saw at this time what were the strategical tendency of their proceedings; but we can see it now; and we can see in it another illustration of a law of nature and of Providence which history shows to be true, not only of the material elements of creation, but of the movements of men and nations. *Forces*, however irregular at first, have a constant tendency to assume a uniformity, and several forces to combine in a common resultant. Physical forces and social forces all move on this principle. Hence, we see the moral and physical forces of the Government, in spite of errors, blunders, and inconsistencies, gradually uniting on certain definite lines, and, by the laws of Providence, tending to a certain and inevitable result.

On the 25th of January the expedition under McClernand had returned. The volunteer regiments of Illinois, Iowa, and Wisconsin had been rapidly forming and preparing, so that on the 1st of February, 1862, there had been gathered a large army at Cairo, Paducah, Fort Jefferson, and other points of the Mississippi. Large camps of volunteers were formed in Ohio and Indiana, preparing for the same objects. The gun-boats had been hurried to completion, so that some of them could be used. In one word, the preparations of a great armament had been made. Halleck and Grant were plainly intent on something. What it was the newspaper reporters for once failed to find out. They told of preparations along the border, of rumors filling the air, of forces ready to be pushed forward, but where the bolt was to be hurled they knew not. It was commonly thought that an attack was to be made on Columbus, but that, if successful, would be another Manassas in the West. It would indeed open a certain distance down the Mississippi, but would leave the interior line untouched. The state of uncertainty was, however, soon to be ended.

Near the boundary line of Kentucky and Tennessee, about sixty miles east of Columbus, and about the same distance, on the common roads, from the Ohio River at Smithland, is Dover, on the Tennessee River. At this place, to which the general direction of the Cumberland and Tennessee from the Ohio is nearly parallel, these rivers approach to within twelve miles of each other. To stop the navigation of those streams by the Union boats, and thus to prevent the approaches to Nashville by water, and to Alabama by Tuscumbia and Florence, was to the rebel defenses a matter of supreme importance. This position was, perhaps, the most essential in their line of defense. Accordingly, as soon as they could, and long before it was known to our authorities, the rebels commenced building the fortification near Dover, now known as Forts Henry and Donelson. They were planned for very extensive and powerful fortifications, which, luckily for us, the rebels never were able to complete. The real object of the forces designated by the President in his Order[1] as the "Army and Flotilla at Cairo," was these fortifications. In his return from the late reconnoissance, General C. F.

---

[1] In a most singular Order, dated January 27, 1862, the President ordered a general movement of land and naval forces on the 22d of February.

Smith, who it will be remembered took one column from Smithland, in obedience to Grant's orders, struck the Tennessee River about twenty miles below Fort Henry.[1] "There he met Commander Phelps, of the Navy, with a gun-boat, patrolling the river. After a brief conference with that energetic officer, General Smith decided to get upon the gun-boat and run up for a look at Fort Henry. The boat steamed up sufficiently near to draw the enemy's fire and obtain a just idea of the armament of the work. Smith returned at once, and reported to General Grant his conviction that, with three or four of 'the turtle iron-clads,' and a strong coöperating land force, Fort Henry might be easily captured, if the attack should be made within a short time." *Time* was here of the utmost importance, for the enemy had planned, and were rapidly constructing, an imposing fortress. Grant immediately forwarded the report to Halleck; but Halleck was a slow officer. Four or five days elapsed without a reply, when, on the 28th of January, Grant and Foote both sent dispatches to Halleck, asking permission to storm Fort Henry, and hold it for ulterior operations. On the 29th Grant wrote an urgent letter, and on the 30th, in the afternoon, a dispatch was received from Halleck, directing him to make preparations to take and hold Fort Henry. To do General Halleck justice, we should remember that he had been making a great concentration of troops, and undoubtedly intended an important expedition.

[1] Coppée's "Grant and His Campaigns" is the authority for this statement.

Let us now see what Fort Henry was, and how taken. The best account of the fort, and the attack, is given by the correspondent of the "Cincinnati Gazette," in a letter, dated February 7, 1862. His account of the fort is thus minutely given:

"The fort is of the class known as a full bastioned earthwork, standing directly upon the bank of the river, and incloses about two acres. It mounts seventeen heavy guns, including one ten-inch Columbiad, throwing a round shot of one hundred and twenty-eight pounds weight; one breech-loading rifled gun, carrying a sixty-pound elongated shot; twelve thirty-two-pounders; one twenty-four-pounder rifled, and two twelve-pounder siege-guns. Nearly all the guns are pivoted, and capable of being turned in any desired direction. The fort is surrounded by a deep moat, and, when fully garrisoned, would be almost impregnable against any force which could be brought against it from the land side. Evidently its designers did not anticipate so formidable an attack from the river, and, certainly, nothing less well defended than our iron-clad gun-boats could have attacked it with any hope of success."

The forces brought against it consisted of twenty regiments of infantry, one regiment of cavalry,[1] four

[1] The division under General McClernand was composed of the Eighth, Eighteenth, Twenty-Seventh, Twenty-Ninth, Thirtieth, and Thirty-First Illinois Regiments of Infantry, making one brigade; the Eleventh, Twentieth, Forty-Fifth, and Forty-Eighth, making the Second Brigade, with the Fourth Cavalry. The Second Division, General C. F. Smith, was composed of the Seventh, Ninth, Twelfth, Twenty-Eighth, and Forty-First Illinois Regiments; the Eleventh Indiana; the Seventh and Twelfth Iowa; and the Eighth and Thirteenth Missouri, with artillery and cavalry.

independent companies of cavalry, and four batteries of artillery, and others not named, attached to Smith's Division; the whole formed into two divisions, under the command of Generals McClernand and C. F. Smith. The naval force consisted of six gun-boats, which had recently been built, and were now to try the force of their batteries. They were the Essex, Commander Porter; the Carondelet, Commander Walke; the Cincinnati, Commander Stembel; the St. Louis, Lieutenant-Commanding Paulding; the Conestoga, Lieutenant-Commanding Phelps; the Tylor, Lieutenant-Commanding Gwyn; and the Lexington, Lieutenant-Commanding Shirk.

The land forces were under the command of Grant, and the naval, of Foote. On the 5th of February, the whole expedition had arrived below Fort Henry, and Grant issued his order to commence the attack next morning, and make the investment at 11, A. M.[1] It was agreed that the army should land, cut off the communication, and the navy attack the batteries in front. In fact, the army did land, and encamped for the night on the ridges near the fort; but the navy got to work early in the morning, and actually captured the fort alone. The intermediate proceedings are thus described by the correspondent of the " Cincinnati Gazette:"[2]

" That night our troops, with the exception of General Smith's Brigade, which had crossed to the west side of the river, encamped on a ridge of hills parallel with the river, and about half a mile from it.

---

[1] Grant's Report to Halleck, of February 6.
[2] Rebellion Record, Vol. IV, page 70.

Their camp-fires, scattered all along the sides of the ridge among the trees, for more than a mile, presented that night one of the most beautiful sights I have ever witnessed, and, no doubt, being observed by the enemy, gave the impression that our force was much larger than was really the case. Probably this might have had something to do in causing their precipitate flight afterward.

"During the night, a tremendous storm arose, accompanied with thunder and lightning, thoroughly soaking the soft clay soil, and rendering locomotion, especially in the low grounds, almost impossible.

"The writer moved with the troops, who started at 11, A. M., according to the order, and were struggling along through mud, caused by the rain of the night before. In the mean time the gun-boats commenced shelling. For some three hours we thus struggled along, when suddenly the roar of a heavy gun came booming over the hills, and another, and another, told us that the gun-boats had commenced the attack. For an instant the entire column seemed to halt to listen, then springing forward, we pushed on with redoubled vigor. But mile after mile of slippery hills and muddy swamps were passed over, and still the fort seemed no nearer. We could plainly hear the roar of the guns, and the whistle of the huge shells through the air, but the high hills and dense woods completely obstructed the view.

"Suddenly the firing ceased. We listened for it to recommence, but all was still. We looked in each other's faces, and wonderingly asked: 'What does it mean? Is it possible that our gun-boats have been beaten back?' for that the rebels should abandon this immense fortification, on which the labor of thousands had been expended for months, after barely an hour's defense, and before our land troops had even come in sight of them, seemed too improbable to believe. Cautiously we pressed forward, but erelong one of our advance scouts came galloping back, announcing that the rebels had abandoned the fort, and seemed to be forming in line of battle on the hills adjoining. With a cheer our boys pressed forward. Soon came another messenger, shouting that the enemy had abandoned their intrenchments completely, and were now in full retreat through the woods."

The battle of the gun-boats against the fort lasted but an hour and a quarter, in which time all the cannon in the fort were knocked to pieces; its garrison had literally run away, escaping early in the morning on the road to Dover, leaving Tilghman, the commander, with one company of artillerists, and the sick. It was not till the fort was made utterly untenable that Tilghman hoisted the white flag and surrendered. The surrender was made to Commodore Foote and the Navy. Foote immediately turned the fort and prisoners over to General Grant. The official dispatch to Halleck gives this brief account of the matter:

"The gun-boats started up at the same hour to commence the attack, and engaged the enemy at not over six hundred yards. In little over one hour all the batteries were silenced, and the fort surrendered at discretion to Flag-officer Foote, giving us all their guns, camp and garrison equipage, etc. The prisoners taken are General Tilghman and staff, Captain Taylor and company, and the sick. The garrison,

I think, must have commenced their retreat last night, or at an early hour this morning.

"Had I not felt it an imperative necessity to attack Fort Henry to-day, I should have made the investment complete, and delayed till to-morrow, so as to secure the garrison. I do not now believe, however, the result would have been any more satisfactory.

"The gun-boats have proven themselves well able to resist a severe cannonading. All the iron-clad boats received more or less shots—the flag-ship some twenty-eight—without any serious damage to any, except the Essex. This vessel received one shot in her boiler that disabled her, killing and wounding some thirty-two men, Captain Porter among the wounded.

"I remain your obedient servant,
"U. S. GRANT, *Brigadier-General.*"

The Confederate forces, which really had made the garrison of Fort Henry, but escaped, amounted to five thousand men.[1] These took the road to Dover, and subsequently made part of the garrison of Fort Donelson.

Grant telegraphed to Halleck that Fort Henry had fallen, and added: "*I shall take and destroy Fort Donelson on the 8th.*" Badeau says:[2] "This was the first mention of Fort Donelson, *whether in conversation or dispatches*, between the two commanders. Halleck made no reply, but notified Buell on the 7th, "General Grant expects to take Fort Donelson, at Dover, to-morrow."

This statement of Col. Badeau, which is confirmed by Halleck's dispatch, is important to the true personal history of the fall of Fort Donelson, for it is conclusive that Grant was the originator of the attack on Donelson, as C. F. Smith was of that on Fort Henry, by his report of the reconnoissance made by himself and Commander Phelps; but, as he had been

---

[1] Badeau's "Military History," page 33.   [2] Idem.

sent out by Grant, it seems most probable that the original idea of this campaign belonged to Grant. Halleck's instructions, which were given on the 30th of January, were full, but they were given after Grant's urgent solicitations, and made no mention of Donelson.

The news of the fall of Fort Henry was received by the country with universal joy; President, Congress, and people rejoiced together. Nor was it without the best reason. Two weeks before, the battle of Mill Springs had been fought and won by Thomas. That was the first battle we had gained, except the affairs of Western Virginia, and great was the rejoicing. But that battle, it was soon seen, was without consequences. The advance of Zollicoffer was only an inroad from the enemy's general line of defense on the Cumberland into Kentucky. The defeat of his force exhilarated us with the thought of a victory opportune and encouraging; but it accomplished nothing. There was no fortification or strategic point in front, to take which would seriously impair their line of defense; nor did General Thomas attempt any. He was satisfied to coöperate in Kentucky with the army of General Buell. The fall of Fort Henry was an event of totally different character. It was not the gaining of a battle to inspire us with the sounds of victory; but it was vastly more important. It was *the gaining of a strategic point which ultimately involved the permanent breaking of the rebel line.* Let the reader recollect that we were the invading force, and that invasion must be successful and conquest complete, or the unity of the nation

could not be restored, and the war would be a worthless expense of blood and wealth.   Now suppose
(what was the real fact) that the rebels were able to
take and keep a line of defense, which we were continually attacking, but unable to break.   While they
were able to do this, we would never succeed.   But
now comes a time when, even without a battle, *we
have broken that line*, and the sun does not rise in
heaven with more certainty than that, if we can hold
that broken point, *we shall drive the whole line back*,
and make the campaign successful.   The great public
rejoiced because we had evident successes, when, indeed, we needed them much ; but it was only the.
educated soldier, with the *coup d'œil* for military
strategy, who could comprehend what the almost
bloodless fall of Fort Henry really accomplished.
Let the reader now come with me to far bloodier
fields and apparently greater results, but which were
all assured consequences of this success.

CHAPTER IV.

DONELSON.

IT was now near the middle of February, and the
people had rejoiced for Mill Springs, and were
gratified with the successes of Western Virginia; but
for ten long and weary months there was no break
in the rebel lines till Fort Henry came. *"All is quiet
along the Potomac!"* was the head-line of every newspaper, and the burden of every reporter. McClellan's army had been organized, drilled, marched and
countermarched along the Potomac, with a check at
Dranesville, and a bad disaster at Ball's Bluff. The
months of November and December, with beautiful
weather and fine roads, had passed away, with no
action and no movement. The Army of the Potomac had gone 'into winter-quarters, and the year
1861 closed with no real advance in the position of
the armies. The people were impatient and disappointed. But one thing had been done, not very

obvious to the eye, but great in fact. It had been the day of preparation. Lincoln had called, not seventy-five thousand, but half a million of men into the field. They had come with the alacrity of youth going to the dance. Along the great rivers, in the valleys of the interior, in the thronged cities, the flag waved in the breeze and the drum-beat was heard in the air. There was no cessation in the uprising of the people. Armories were preparing rifles, muskets, and pistols, by the tens of thousands. Great founderies were casting enormous cannon. The graduates of West Point, taunted with the treachery of their companions in the rebel army, every-where volunteered, and, like Grant at the head of the Twenty-First Illinois, were commanding regiments or brigades, drilling and organizing for active war. Long after Grant had left Cairo, regiments were still organizing and marching to the field from every part of the Western States. The Confederate Congress no longer laughed. Richmond no longer exulted in a prospective march to Washington. One fact the rebels had learned, that they were to have war, and war with the united energies of the Government and nation against them. They realized at last that, although their line of defense was yet complete, though the Southern people had rallied to the Confederate Government with unexpected zeal, yet they had gained nothing, and the best to be expected for them was not peace and prosperity, but a successful defense, after years of bloody and desolating war. How was that defense to be made against far superior strength and resources? Some of their military ideas may be learned from a speech of Mr. Davis, President of the Confederacy, made at the beginning of the war, at the time of adjourning the Confederate Congress to Richmond. He declared that such were the natural advantages of Virginia that it could be defended for twenty years. The advantages of Virginia, as a defensive ground, are unquestionable ; but what would Virginia be but a besieged and insulated fortification, if the lines of communication, west and south, and with them its resources, were cut off? Here was the real solution of the problem, and Mr. Davis, even to the last moment, failed to see this, and utterly failed to comprehend the elements of the great military question with which he had now to deal. Nor is it very evident that our own Government comprehended it better. For ten weary months, as I have said, no successful attack was made on the rebel lines; but the preparation was making, and perhaps that was all we could then accomplish.

Now we have come to Fort Henry, and it is the first telling blow on the enemy's great defense. If no more was done, it opened the Tennessee River to the gun-boats. But more, much more was to be done. Grant had telegraphed Halleck, that he should attack Donelson on the 8th ; but great armies can not be timed to a day, and so the assault was a little later. Let us first see what Fort Donelson was in February, 1862. Near the town of Dover, on the Cumberland River, two small streams run into that river, whose mouths were about a mile and a quarter apart, but in the rear were separated by three miles. The whole intermediate space, as well as that around

Dover, was a "conglomerate of hills and valleys, knolls and ravines."[1] The little streams formed the right and left defenses of the rebel line, which extended nearly three miles, and was strongly intrenched.[2] Within these were detached works and secondary lines, one of which extended round the town of Dover, and part of which commanded the outer line. Then there were rivulets, gullies, ravines, woods, and natural obstacles of all kinds. On some of the commanding hills were posted light batteries, and on the water side below, where a bend enabled them to command the river, were placed heavy water batteries. The main fort, says Badeau,[3] was built on a precipitous hight, or rather range, cloven by a deep gorge opening to the south ; it was about three quarters of a mile from the breastworks, and overlooked both the river and the interior. It covered one hundred acres of ground, and was defended by fifteen heavy guns and two carronades.

The lower or main water battery, which was built with massive parapets and embrasures, formed of coffee sacks filled with sand, was armed with eight thirty-two pound guns, and one ten-inch Columbiad. The other water battery was armed with one heavy rifled gun, carrying a hundred and twenty-eight pound bolt, and two thirty-two pound carronades.[4]

It is very evident, from this description, that Donelson was one of the strongest fortified points held by the rebels during the war, and at this time altogether the strongest. Its natural defenses were

---

[1] Coppée's description.
[2] Badeau's description.
[3] Badeau's Military History, page 37.
[4] Coppée's Grant, page 50.

very great; the works were extensive, and were fully
armed and manned. In addition to the armament
already described, there were six light batteries, making in all sixty-five cannon; and the garrison was
composed of full twenty-one thousand men.[1] The
five thousand men who left Fort Henry were there,
and strong reënforcements were received from Bowling Green. The garrison was composed of thirteen
regiments from Tennessee; two from Kentucky; two
from Alabama; six from Mississippi; one from Texas;
four from Virginia; two independent battalions of
Tennessee infantry; Forrest's Brigade of Cavalry,
and the artillerists necessary to man all the batteries.
It has since been ascertained, that the total number
was at least twenty-one thousand. Such was Donelson; strong by nature, admirably fortified, and fully
manned. Yet, Donelson wanted one thing, which is
certainly of the greatest importance to an army. It
wanted a General! The commander of the South-
Western Department, for the rebels, was A. Sydney
Johnston, a man who is mentioned by all with respect,
and was supposed to have the best military mind in
the rebel army. Unfortunately for the rebel army,
he did not command at Fort Donelson. Still more
unfortunately, the actual commander was Floyd, who
was respected by few, and died with no better name
than he had lived. He was not only a traitor, says
Professor Coppée, but believed to be dishonest, and
proved to be a coward. But worse than even all this
for the rebels, he was no general, and in truth possessed of little military capacity. The next in com-

---

[1] Badeau, page 51, note.

mand was Pillow, who was more honest, but no less ignorant than Floyd. The third was Buckner, who did know something of the military art, and although an early and persistent traitor, was brave and intelligent. Such was Donelson and its defenders. Let us now follow the attack.

The attack was to have been made on the 8th; but the roads were impassable for artillery, and heavy rains so flooded the country that no movement could be made, and Grant wrote, "We are perfectly locked in." During the days of waiting, reënforcements were brought in from Buell's command, and from Hunter in Missouri.[1] General Halleck, commander of the district in which Grant was, did not seem very much impressed with the possibility of advancing, for his orders were defensive.[2] He said: "Hold on to Fort Henry at all events. Impress slaves, if necessary, to strengthen your position as rapidly as possible. It is of vital importance to strengthen your position as rapidly as possible." It is always of importance to strengthen the position of an army; so much so, that good officers will throw up some light timber, or abatis, before their encampment at night. But the thing to be done just now is to take Fort Donelson, and let us do it. As we march up, let us note, that by Halleck's order, it seems, the *slaves* had ceased to be an object of worship, sacred to treason, and protected by the Constitution. They can now be

---

[1] Halleck, in a complimentary acknowledgment, said, that when he wanted troops to reënforce Grant, he applied to Hunter, who cheerfully supplied them.

[2] Badeau, page 36.

impressed to serve the country; that is one step gained.

But let us go on. Grant stopped for neither reenforcements, nor shovels, nor orders. On the 10th he writes to Foote that he is only waiting for the gun-boats.[1] "I feel that there should be no delay in this matter, and yet I do not feel justified in going without some of your gun-boats to coöperate. Can you not send two boats from Cairo immediately up the Cumberland?" News had now come that the rebels were reenforcing Fort Donelson; every hour was of importance. On the 11th Foote with his fleet started by the Ohio and Cumberland. Six regiments of troops, all that were ready, went with him. On the 11th McClernand's Division moved out on two roads, and on the 12th the main column, fifteen thousand strong, marched from Fort Henry, leaving a garrison of twenty-five hundred there.[2] There were but few wagons and few rations, but the men carried forty rounds of cartridges. To prevent all retreat of the enemy one brigade was ordered to be thrown into Dover. The distance to march was twelve miles, and a little after noon Grant's army appeared in front of the fort. The first line was formed in open fields opposite the enemy's center. The left rested on Hickman Creek, and the line reached round to near Dover on the right. The overflow of waters prevented the completion of the line, but Donelson was practically invested.[3]

Thursday, the 13th, was occupied in reconnoitering, skirmishing, and taking positions. McClernand

[1] Badeau, page 35. .   [2] Idem, page 36.   [3] Idem, page 38.

attempted to capture a battery commanding the ridge road, but without orders, and was unsuccessful. In this day's work about three hundred were killed and wounded. The results were, that on the night of the 13th Grant was "established on a line of hights in general parallel with the enemy's works, and extending for a distance of over three miles."[1] Here we note two things of great interest in the siege, and which might have proved fatal. First, Grant found he was actually inferior to the enemy while besieging him. For some reason, not very obvious, the rebel general had not obstructed his march from Fort Henry, nor endeavored to obstruct his taking his position. Nevertheless, Grant found he had got into that position with a force inferior to that of the enemy. He immediately sent for the garrison of Fort Henry, and anxiously expected the fleet with reënforcements. In the mean while (on Thursday) a single gun-boat undertook a little battle on her own account. The correspondent of the " New York Times" says: " During the time that the land forces were engaged, the iron-clad gun-boat Carondelet went up and singly engaged the rebel batteries. She fired one hundred and two shots, and received no great damage in all the tremendous fire to which she was exposed, save in the case of a single shot. This, a monster mass of iron, weighing at least one hundred and twenty-eight pounds, entered one of her forward ports, and, wounding eight men in its passage, dashed with terrific force against the breast-work of coal-bags in front of the boilers, and there

[1] Badeau, page 40.

was stopped. Soon after this she retired from the unequal contest, having covered herself with glory for having so long singly withstood the enormous force of the rebels' entire water-battery.[1]

But a second event occurred which, if not dangerous to the army, was very severe upon the men. This was extreme cold. It was one of the coldest nights ever known in that region. Some of the men had thrown away their blankets. They could build no fires, for they were obliged to bivouac in line of battle, with arms in their hands, as they were within point-blank musket-range of the enemy.[2] Some of the men on both sides were frozen, while the wounded, who lay between the armies in that midnight cold, made the air resound with their cries. Such were the sufferings of our noble volunteers, who, encamped on the Cumberland, shivering in the cold, and in sight of a superior enemy, yet looked forward to the battle with confidence, and not in vain, to a coming victory.

The night was thus passing, in the cold and gloom of winter, when, before daylight, Commodore Foote with the fleet came up, and the troops from Fort Henry, under Lewis Wallace, arrived, and were put in line. Friday, the 14th, went on with some skirmishing, an irregular fire of sharp-shooters, and the rebel shells falling into our line. At three o'clock, P. M., six gun-boats, four of them iron-clad, attacked the fort, but the batteries were heavy, had complete command of the river, and the attack was disastrous.

[1] Rebellion Record, Vol. IV, page 172.
[2] Badeau, page 40.

The correspondent of the "New York Times" thus describes it:

"I secured a position about half-way between the boats and fort, a little out of the line of fire, and there, for two hours, had the pleasure of listening to a concert of the most gigantic order. At first the roar from fort and boats was unbroken for a single instant, so rapid was the firing, while the air high overhead seemed filled with a million of hissings, as the heavy storm of shells tore furiously ahead on their mission of destruction. In about half an hour the fire from the fort began to slacken, and shortly after was continued from only three guns—the rest apparently having been silenced by our fire. At this time the boats were within some four hundred yards, and were on the point of using grape-shot, when a shot disabled the steering apparatus of the Louisville, by carrying off the top of the wheel-house, and knocking the wheel itself into fragments. There was a tiller aft, and this was instantly taken possession of by the pilot, but he had scarcely reached it ere the rudder was carried away by a shot from the Tylor. Of course the boat became instantly unmanageable, and swung around, receiving a shot in the wood-work toward the stern, which, I believe, wounded several seamen. Under these circumstances it was thought best to retire, and accordingly the whole fleet fell back to the position it had occupied in the morning."[1]

In fact, four of the six gun-boats were disabled; the tiller of one and the wheel of another were shot away; a rifled gun burst upon a third, and a fourth

[1] Rebellion Record, Vol. IV, page 172.

was greatly damaged; and more, Commodore Foote was wounded. At midnight he sent for Grant, and told him that the fleet must put back to Cairo, and advised him to remain quiet till he returned. On that day Grant had himself written: "Appearances now are that we shall have a protracted siege here. I fear the result of an attempt to carry the place by storm with new troops. I feel quite confident, however, of ultimately reducing the place." Even the sturdy and persistent mind of Grant doubted at this time whether Donelson could be immediately reduced. Events were, however, shaping themselves to another and a better result than he had anticipated.

The night of the 14th, Friday, was again severely cold. There was a storm of sleet and snow, and the wearied soldier had to endure the sufferings of another dreary night. In the mean time reenforcements had begun to come, and Grant's army had got to be equal, if not superior, to that of the enemy. Wallace, who had come up from Fort Henry, was put at the head of a Third Division, composed of the troops he had brought, and others coming in. This division was put in the center, just fronting Donelson. Now, if the reader look toward the river, with the fort in front of him, he will see C. F. Smith's Division on the left, or hights above Hickman Creek, which is impassable by fording, Wallace next, in the center, and on the right McClernand's Division. Grant's head-quarters were at Mrs. Crops's, just behind Smith. Such was the situation on the night of the 14th; and it has been justly remarked by a military critic,[1] that

[1] Coppée, page 57.

if the rebel commander had been contented with the defensive, and strengthened his position, we might have been compelled to go through with a regular siege. This was Grant's view the day before, but such was not Floyd's idea. He found himself with forces about equal to Grant's, and with stronger defenses, and knew that our army was constantly being reënforced; so, with the aid of a Council of War, he determined to attack our lines.

At five o'clock on Saturday morning, the 15th, the rebels poured out of Donelson in heavy columns to attack, and, if possible, crush McClernand. If successful, it would have placed our army in a dangerous position, and probably compelled its retreat. The battle which ensued was bloody and decisive. Let us follow its fiery and dreadful scenes, as described by one who saw them.[1]

The columns advanced by the enemy amounted in all to ten thousand men, with thirty pieces of artillery. It seemed as if it must be successful, and, if so, would drive our right and center back upon Smith, on the left, and make it difficult for our army to extricate itself.[2] Reveille was just sounding, the troops

[1] The account given in extracts is from the correspondent of the "New York Times," which is very graphic and interesting.

[2] The statement of force is given by Coppée thus: "Such were Floyd's plans; they were to be tried with the early morning of Saturday, the 15th. Accordingly, at 5, A. M., the rebel column, under Pillow and Johnston moved out from Dover, the advance being taken by Colonel Baldwin's Brigade, composed of the First and Fourteenth Mississippi, and the Twenty-Sixth Tennessee. These were followed by Wharton's Brigade, of two regiments; McCousland's, of two; Davidson's, of three; Drake's, of five; and other troops, amounting in all to ten thousand men, with thirty guns, which were to crush McClernand, and clear a pathway through our right."

were under arms, but in utter ignorance of the enemy's designs. The right was obviously threatened, and the commanders of regiments and brigades, changing front a little, rapidly got their men into line. On the right was McArthur's Brigade; then Oglesby and Wallace; on the left of the Fort Henry road was Cruft's. It was not too soon, for, in a few minutes, the rebel column poured down on McArthur. The eye-witness says:

"The fight raged from daylight till nearly noon, without a moment's cessation, and resulted in the enemy's being driven back to his intrenchments. The battle-ground extended over a space some two miles in length, every inch of which was the witness of a savage conflict. The rebels fought with the most determined bravery, and seemed bent upon breaking through the right wing at any cost. They poured against our lines a perfect flood, and it was only by a bravery that equaled their own, and a resolute determination to conquer that outlasted their efforts, that our gallant soldiers were at length enabled to stay the fierce tide, and finally to hurl it back to its former boundaries. Our men determined that they *would* win, and win they did, with a gallantry that entitles every man to the name of hero.

"The whole of the fight was of the most terrific character. Without a single moment's cessation, the rebels poured into our forces perfect torrents of canister, shell, and round-shot, while their thousands of riflemen hurled in a destructive fire from every bush, tree, log, or obstruction of any kind that afforded shelter. The roar of the battle was like that of a heavy tornado, as it sweeps through some forest on its mission of destruction. Small arms kept up an incessant cracking, mingling with which came up occasionally the roar of company or division firing, while over all came every moment or two the resonant thunders of the batteries."

So raged the battle; and for a time the advantage was with the enemy. Oglesby and McArthur got out of ammunition;[1] they were obliged to fall back; but they retreated between columns of fresh troops, coming to the rescue, and, when they retired, formed a new line facing to the south. But the advancing rebels were all the time terribly received by the light batteries of McAllister, Taylor, and Draper. Posted on the hights, and shifting their positions to suit the circumstances, they continually poured in a heavy fire of grape and canister, and again and again the enemy's lines recoiled. The rebel troops did not display in their first attack the best order and skill. Buckner had come out to attack our new position; his attack was repulsed; and he said his regiments "withdrew without panic, but in some confusion, to the trenches." Nevertheless, the rebels had, in the main, been successful. They had driven back our forces into a new position. Some of our officers were demoralized, and Pillow sent to Nashville a dispatch that the day was theirs; and he thought so. But his new attack failed. He moved upon Thayer's Brigade; "but by their un-

---

[1] This very thing had been foreseen by Grant, and he had written to Halleck for more supplies of ammunition. General Cullum, at Cairo, sent all he could.

flinching stand and deliberate fire, and especially by the firmness of the First Nebraska, and the excellent handling of the artillery, he was now repulsed."[1] We need not pursue in detail the attacks, repulses, movements, and vicissitudes on the right. It was a hard-fought field, and here more strikingly than had yet appeared, shone out the true character and valor of the Western volunteer. In cold, with men freezing on their posts, and the storm of battle raging around, there was no flinching, no impatience.

But where was Grant? What were his plans? What was he doing? Grant's head-quarters, as I have said, were at Crops's house, in the rear of Smith, and a long way from the immediate field of battle we have now been tracing out. But now is the time to bring out his military resources, if he has them. This is no small fight, no Belmont, not even Fort Henry. It is a crushing battle, and if we fail, it may be a long time before we shall break that long line of rebel defense, which stretches from Manassas to Columbus. At two o'clock in the morning, he had been to visit the wounded Foote, and to consult with him on the future operations of the fleet. It had got to be nine o'clock, when he returned to head-quarters, where he was met by an aid-de-camp, galloping up to inform him of the assault on the right, which was the first information he had of it. He next met C. F. Smith, commanding the left, and ordered him to hold himself in readiness to assault the right, with his whole command.[2] This was the decisive order of the day, and the reader will see its true meaning. In any

---

[1] Coppée's "Grant and his Campaigns."   [2] Badeau, page 44.

event, if our right was defeated, it was necessary to hold Smith in readiness ; but, on the other hand, if the enemy were repulsed on our right, then was the decisive moment. The advance of Smith's command to a counter attack on the enemy's right, after the enemy had been repulsed, would in all probability be successful. Grant then rode to the point where the fight was. The rebels had failed to make their way, and were doggedly retiring. Still our troops, also, were disordered ; the ammunition had given out, and the loss of field officers was unusually large. Badeau says :

"There was no pursuit, and the battle was merely lulled, not ended. The men, like all raw troops, imagined the enemy to be in overwhelming force, and reported that the rebels had come out with knapsacks and haversacks, as if they meant to stay out and fight for several days. Grant at once inquired, 'Are the haversacks filled?' Some prisoners were examined, and the haversacks found to contain three days' rations. 'Then they mean to cut their way out; they have no idea of staying here to fight us ;' and, looking at his own disordered men, not yet recovered from the shock of battle, Grant exclaimed, 'Whichever party first attacks now will whip, and the rebels will have to be very quick if they beat me.' "[1]

This illustrates the true point of Grant's military genius. Perfectly self-possessed, even in apparently adverse circumstances, persistent in his purpose, he held it a primary principle to be *constantly pouring*

[1] Badeau, page 45.

his whole force upon the enemy. This possibly might not have been best in some kinds of war, but it was best here, and best always with the rebels. Riding at once to the left, where the troops had not been engaged, he ordered an immediate assault. As he passed along he assured the broken troops that the attack of the morning was only an attempt of the rebels to cut their way out. The troops caught the idea, re-formed, and went to the front.

It was now Smith's turn. He is organizing his columns for a terrible onset. Cook's Brigade is on the left, Cavender's batteries are in the rear to the right and left, so as to fire on the intrenchments ; but the attacking column is Lauman's Brigade, formed in close column of regiments, and it is right to remember these gallant regiments. They were the Second Iowa, the Seventh and the Fourteenth Iowa, and the Twenty-Fifth and Fifty-Second Indiana. While this is going on, Wallace has formed the troops again on the right, and in the end we see has regained all the positions from which we were driven in the morning. And now comes that glorious charge of Smith on the intrenchments of Donelson. Before advancing he rides to the front, and tells the men he will lead them, and that the rifle-pits must be taken by the bayonet. At the signal Smith rides in advance, with the color-bearer beside him. He is near sixty years of age, with gray hair, and commanding figure. His advance is thus described by Coppée:

"Not far has he moved before his front line is swept by the enemy's artillery with murderous effect.

His men waver for a moment, but their General, sublime in his valor, reminds them, in caustic words, that while he, as an old *regular*, is in the line of his professional duty, this is what they have *volunteered* to do. With oaths and urgency, his hat waving upon the point of his sword, by the splendor of his example he leads them on through this valley of death, up the slope, through the abatis, up to the intrench- ment—and over. With a thousand shouts they plant their standards on the captured works, and pour in volley after volley, before which the rebels fly in pre- cipitate terror. Battery after battery is brought for- ward, Stone's arriving first, and then a direct and enfilading fire is poured upon the flanks and faces of the work. Four hundred of Smith's gallant column have fallen, but the charge is decisive. Grant's tac- tics and Smith's splendid valor have won the day."

The battle was won. The rebels now fought only for darkness. That night Grant slept in a negro hut, and Smith, with his troops, on the frozen ground, *within the enemy's works*. But Floyd and Pillow were engaged in a different way. They were both contriving how they could save their necks ; for, although our Government hanged no traitors, they had an anxious fear that somebody might be hanged, and they had a suspicion that they were very fitting persons to be made examples of. So Floyd, in a council of his officers, declared he should desert the troops, and Pillow declared the same.[1] In the

[1] Badeau, page 47. In a Supplementary Report made by Floyd to the rebel War Department he had the audacity to say : "The boat on which I was, left the shore and steered up the river. By this precise mode I effected my escape, and after leaving the wharf, the Depart-

night time both these officers, with some three thousand men, escaped by the aid of boats. Buckner was left to surrender his army, and in the morning hoisted the white flag on Fort Donelson. He told Floyd the garrison could not hold out half an hour, and when that worthy left him in command, he immediately sent a messenger to Grant, asking terms of capitulation. Buckner said that, "*in consideration of all the circumstances*, he proposed to the Federal commander to appoint commissioners to agree upon terms of capitulation." To this Grant made the memorable reply: "*No terms other than an unconditional and immediate surrender can be accepted. I propose to move immediately upon your works.*" [1]

We need not recite the mere details of a victory. Fifteen thousand prisoners, sixty-five cannon, twenty

ment *will be pleased to hear, that I encountered no danger whatever from the enemy.*"

[1] The following is the actual correspondence, which should be preserved in history, as an example of prompt, pointed, and laconic negotiation:

"HEAD-QUARTERS, FORT DONELSON, *February* 16, 1862.

"SIR—In consideration of all the circumstances governing the present situation of affairs at this station, I propose to the commanding officer of the Federal forces the appointment of commissioners to agree upon terms of capitulation of the forces and fort under my command, and in that view suggest an armistice until twelve o'clock to-day.

"I am sir, very respectfully, your obedient servant,

"S. B. BUCKNER, *Brigadier-General, C. S. A.*

"HEAD-QUARTERS, ARMY IN THE FIELD,
"*Camp near Donelson, February* 16, 1862.

"To GENERAL S. B. BUCKNER, *Confederate Army:*

"Yours of this date, proposing an armistice and appointment of commissioners to settle terms of capitulation, is just received. *No terms other than an unconditional and immediate surrender can be accepted. I propose to move immediately upon your works.*

"I am sir, very respectfully, your obedient servant,

"U. S. GRANT, *Brigadier-General U. S. A., commanding.*"

thousand small arms, and the strongest fortification in the West, were the present fruits of the capture of Fort Donelson. The siege had lasted four days, all but one of which were days of fighting. Of the losses, it seems that, comparing both accounts, four thousand, five hundred men were killed, wounded, or disabled, making very nearly one-tenth part of those engaged.

On the morning of the surrender Grant rode over to Buckner's quarters. They had been together at West Point, and now breakfasted together on the banks of the Cumberland, in the most singular and interesting circumstances. Buckner acknowledged it had been the intention of the rebel commander to cut their way out. In the course of the conversation he alluded to Grant's inferior force at the beginning of the siege, and remarked: "If I had been in command you would n't have reached Fort Donelson so easily." To which Grant replied: "If you had been in command I should have waited for reënforcements, and marched from Fort Henry in greater strength; but I knew that Pillow would not come out of his works to fight, and told my staff so, though I believed he would fight behind his works."[1]

The characters of Floyd and Pillow were too well known to our commander to excite any dread of their achievements. Military critics agree, I believe, that Floyd ought to have obstructed Grant's march from Fort Donelson, and to have made the assault on him before Wallace and fresh troops came up. He arrived before the place with only fifteen thousand men, some six or eight thousand less than the

· Badeau, page 50.

rebels had, but on the last day of the fight he had twenty-seven thousand available men, and reënforcements constantly arriving. After that, all idea of an attack upon him was absurd.

Now, what were the results of the capture of Fort Donelson? The capture of Fort Henry was the *key* to the taking of Donelson ; but what did the capture of both do? In the view of the great public, an event like that of Donelson is looked on simply as a victory, so many killed, and so many prisoners, and the place captured. This is ground for triumph ; and so the people did triumph. Flags were raised on every house and hill ; streets were filled with rejoicing people ; thanksgivings were made ; and in the Churches, *te deum laudamus*[1] was sung. The rejoicing was great ; the moral effect was great ; the hearts of the people were strengthened, and the rebels were startled,[2] if not dismayed, by the fact first brought stunningly to their minds, that they had war, bloody war, on their hands, as the result of their awful crime, not only against their Government, but against the common hopes and interests of mankind, all involved in the success of the American Government. Such was the moral result of that conflict, and perhaps no event in the war had in that respect a greater effect. But what was the military result? Relatively, it was even greater. Great battles have often been fought, and produced no practical effect on the contest. But Donelson was decisive of grand results. I have

---

[1] *Te Deum* (Thee, O God, we praise,) was always sung in the French cathedrals, on obtaining a victory.

[2] See "Richmond Dispatch," "Charleston Courier," and other rebel papers.

already traced the strategic line of rebel defense; its right rested on Manassas, and its left on the Mississippi, at Columbus.[1] Intermediate were the Valley of Virginia, Cumberland Gap, Knoxville, Bowling Green, Forts Henry and Donelson. Now, the reader will see that, if any one of the important points in this line was taken, that those on each side would be, in military phrase, "*flanked;*" and if a position is flanked, it compels either a change of front and stronger force, or an abandonment of the position. Donelson flanked Columbus and Bowling Green, two of the most important points in the whole rebel line. It did more; it opened the Cumberland, so that Nashville must fall; and it opened the Tennessee, so that ultimately we could command North Alabama; and rendered it almost impossible for the rebels to hold a second line, which must necessarily be, from Memphis, on the Memphis and Charleston Railroad. What did happen? *Events followed in precisely the logical sequence* of a problem strategically solved. The public looked on, and rejoiced in astonishment, not at all conscious that these events were an inevitable result of the fall of Donelson.

Let us follow these events by dates, and see how beautifully this strategic problem was solved. The battle of Mill Springs, though in itself unimportant, shook the rebels' faith in their power to hold Bowling Green; and when Fort Henry fell they knew, that though there might be a protracted siege at Donel-

---

[1] The Trans-Mississippi War never was of any importance to the rebels, and, below Missouri, of no importance to us. This was the opinion of General Joe Johnston, and will be obvious on a review of the war.

son, yet the probability was it must fall. Buell's army, strong and well organized, was advancing on its front, and now Fort Donelson is besieged. They waited till it was invested, and then, on the 14th of February, they evacuated Bowling Green. On the morning of the 15th, the very day of the bloody battle at Donelson, Mitchel's Division entered Bowling Green,[1] called by the rebels the "Gibraltar of Kentucky."

The city of Nashville was surrendered on the 25th, and occupied by the Fourth Ohio Cavalry, Colonel John Kennett. Columbus was evacuated on March 4th, of which General Cullum (writing to McClellan) justly says: "Columbus, the Gibraltar of the West, is ours, and Kentucky is free, thanks to the brilliant strategy of the campaign by which the enemy's center was pierced at Fort Henry and Donelson, his wings isolated from each other and turned, compelling thus the evacuation of his stronghold of Bowling Green first, and now Columbus."[2] But, stranger still, on March 11th, Manassas was evacuated. Was that caused by the capture of Donelson? In part it certainly was. First, Beauregard was obliged to fly to the West with fifteen thousand of the army of Manassas, *in order to take a new line, and make it possible to defend it.* Thus the old line of rebel defense was abandoned, except in the center, where the Valley of Virginia offered natural defenses, unapproachable till we were ready for a new advance.

---

[1] Y. S., of the "Cincinnati Gazette," describes its capture in a very interesting manner.

[2] Cullum's Report, March 4th.

The rebel right now took the Valley of the Rappahannock in the East, and from Memphis to Chattanooga in the West. It is true that, often during the war, the rebels penetrated, by raids great or small, to the Potomac and the Ohio, but never to stay—never to take an advanced line. Donelson, Nashville, Bowling Green, Columbus, Manassas — all were gone! The rebel line in the West was thrown back two hundred miles, with Kentucky and Tennessee gained to the Union territory. Thus Donelson was a great and a decisive event. I always thought its value in the elements of the war was underrated, both by military critics and by the general public. The public rejoiced most heartily, but, of course, did not fully comprehend the strategic bearings of that event, while military men have been looking at the grander, but not better fought, battles of a later period.

But what is thought of Grant? He is acting under the general supervision of Halleck; but Halleck was not present, and does not seem, by any published evidence, to have conceived the plan. He did all he could to furnish reënforcements, and aided the expedition as much as he could. But Halleck had a very cautious and not very quick mind, and it is curious to see how, when Grant had won Fort Donelson, and the rebel armies were in full retreat from all their great posts, Halleck telegraphs Grant to be cautious. "Avoid any general engagement with strong forces. It will be better to retreat than to risk a general battle."[1] Why, he had just fought the most dangerous battle he could fight, and the rebels

---

[1] Halleck's Telegram to Grant, dated St. Louis, March 1st.

were in hot haste retreating from every point in their whole line! If the ideas of Halleck had prevailed, the war would have lasted ten years, if the parties to it had not died of exhaustion in the mean time. Far different was the view taken by Stanton, the War Secretary, who, with no military education, nevertheless had the true *coup d'œil* of a soldier. He saw that, with the rebel contempt (real or professed) for the North, and their swagger and dash, there must be an earnest, bloody, and persevering war.

On the 20th of February he wrote to some one: "We may well rejoice at the recent victories, for they teach us that battles are to be won now, and by us, in the same and only manner that they were ever won by any people, or in any age, since the days of Joshua, by boldly pursuing and striking the foe. What, under the blessing of Providence, I conceive to be the true organization of victory and military combination to end this war, was declared in a few words, by General Grant's message to General Buckner: 'I propose to move immediately on your works.' This was the beginning of a support bestowed by the Secretary of War on the Western general, which was never intermitted, while the need of that support remained."[1]

"I propose to move immediately on your works." That was, henceforth, the motto of the war. Was it not hard that, in its own bosom, in its own household, among its own children, the nation should be compelled to have this awful conflict, filled with sorrow, darkness, suffering?` It seems to me, even, as I write now, when the scenes of peace have returned,

[1] Badeau, page 54.

and the verdure of prosperity is springing up afresh, that it was a very hard thing for this young nation to have and to do. Why should these scenes exist? Why should the earth be covered with blood? Because it is a law of Providence that the sins of nations should be punished on earth, and in their own growing life. So it has been with every nation, and so it is with Christianity itself. The Gospel announced the law of Peace; but was it to bring peace to the nations? Christ announced that it would bring divisions, and that wars and convulsions would come, till his kingdom was established. Was it not so? Has not every nation in Europe been convulsed with wars in its own bosom? While they retained in themselves antagonistic elements, this was inevitable. We had a vast antagonism of elements, and there was no wisdom to get rid of that antagonism till one of them was destroyed. It was a necessity of nature and a law of Providence. One thing we might have done. We might have destroyed the unity of the nation, and filled this North American Continent with several nations. What would we have saved? One war, to make a hundred. Great calamities are thus, in the order of Divine Providence, made the seeds of a fruitful prosperity. We had come to the time when there must be preached a fiery Gospel, but not a Gospel without its salutary teachings, not without its part in the great campaign of Truth, marching on to an Eternal victory.

"Mine eyes have seen the glory of the coming of the Lord:
  He is trampling out the vintage where the grapes of wrath are stored;
  He hath loosed the fateful lightning of his terrible swift sword:
      His truth is marching on.

I have seen him in the watch-fires of a hundred circling camps ;
They have builded him an altar in the evening dews and damps ;
I have read his righteous sentence by the dim and flaring lamps :
His day is marching on.

I have read a fiery Gospel writ in burnished rows of steel :
' As ye deal with my contemners, so with you my grace shall deal ;
Let the Hero, born of woman, crush the serpent with his heel,
Since God is marching on.' "[1]

The fiery Gospel went on, through stormy battles, and through damp disease, till antagonism ceased, and the star of peace returned. In the mean time, was there no other scene than that of blood? Was there no sound but the trumpet call? Was there no kindly office to be performed, which would lead the mind from the passions of destruction to those of healing and comfort?

Scarcely had the war begun, or the echoes of Sumpter died away, when a gathering of American women asked, " What can we do?" Are there no functions for us to perform, which will encourage or strengthen, comfort or heal? The answer came from their hearts: " We will go to work. We will make gloves, and comforts, and bandages for wounds ; for, by and by, these gallant soldiers will be sick and wounded."

On the 20th of April, 1861, five days after the surrender of Sumpter, the " Soldiers' Aid Society, of Cleveland " was formed by the ladies ; and then began the great Sanitary Commission. Time passed on, and it grew up into a great benevolent institution. It fell to the lot of the Cincinnati Branch of the Sanitary Commission, in conjunction with those of

---

[1] " Battle Hymn of the Republic," by Mrs. Julia Ward Howe.

Louisville and St. Louis, to do most of the sanitary work for the Western armies. The battle of Fort Donelson made not only an era of the war, but an era in the work of the Sanitary Commission. The news of the fall of Donelson was received at Cincinnati, on the morning of February 16, 1862, and the Board of Commissioners immediately met,[1] and ceased not their labors till steamboats had been chartered, surgeons and nurses employed, and every possible means supplied to bring home and provide for the wounded and the sick. The messengers of mercy were continually in motion; and, by the consent of General Halleck, hundreds of the wounded were brought to Cincinnati, and carried to the hospitals. The aid societies provided for the Commission; and the Commission provided for the wounded; and thus the work of mercy went on. The silver lining was seen on the cloud, amid the flashes of the storm and the darkness of the night.

[1] Mansfield's History of the Cincinnati Sanitary Commission.

CHAPTER V.

SHILOH.

THE AMERICAN VOLUNTEER—ATTEMPT TO CENSURE GRANT—ITS FAILURE, AND HIS PROMOTION — PREPARATIONS AT PITTSBURG LANDING—BATTLE OF SHILOH—A GREAT VICTORY — MILITARY CRITICS — GRANT VINDICATED — THE OBJECT OF THE BATTLE—AND THE RESULTS.

THE fall of Donelson, of Nashville, of Columbus, and Bowling Green, made a most brilliant campaign; but the year was just begun, and more work, equally decisive, was to be done, both in the field and in the camps at home. The last, though accompanied by no voice of Fame, was the most important. Lincoln had called for half a million of men, months before, and they were continually gathering to the camps, where they must be organized, drilled, and fitted for the march. This required time. In the mean while the country presented the finest examples of heroic patriotism history had ever recorded. The AMERICAN VOLUNTEER was a being which the modern world had not produced. Such a soldier had been seen in ancient Sparta; but Sparta was only a camp, and the Spartan only an Indian warrior. His mode of life was barbarous, and the hardships at home almost equal to those of the severest war. He was not leaving the refinements of a civilized life, the comforts of a domestic home, and the business which promised individual success. When he marched against the Persian, he was doing what he had been educated to do, and engaging in warfare to which he was already inured. Not so the volunteer in the Union Army. He was leaving civilized life; he was giving up a settled business; he was parting from tearful friends; he was the only son of a widow, or the husband of a young wife; or the father of young children; he was one on whom the happiness of others depended, and for whom tears were shed, even by heroic hearts, and prayers offered up by the most faithful of Christians. Such was the American Volunteer, self-sacrificing, offering his services, it may be his life, on the altar of his country. While such patriotism remains, who can fear for his country? While the memory of it remains, who can cease to believe in human nature, or cease to honor such noble spirits?

Let us now return to the movements of Grant. Soon after the fall of Donelson there occurred one of those curious episodes in military history, which are entirely different from any thing we see in civil life, and which are regarded by people of common sense with great surprise. This was nothing less than the suspension of Grant from his command! What had happened? Certainly his success did not entitle him to immunity from the penalties of military law. But what offense had he committed? The actions at Fort Donelson had been so severe, and the constant arrival of troops during the siege had, made the numbers so uncertain, that Grant had been unable immediately to report the precise losses, casualties, and numbers of his troops. It seems, also, that General C. F. Smith had been sent up the Cumberland to Clarkesville, and Grant, not having heard directly from him, went himself to Nashville on the 27th of February. In the mean time he had written and telegraphed to General Halleck all his movements. That General, however, either did not receive the messages, or thought the offense of leaving his immediate command greater than the merit of watching the enemy's movements, and on the 3d of March, without any explanation, wrote:

"I have had no communication with General Grant for more than a week. He left his command without my authority, and went to Nashville. His army seems to be as much demoralized by the victory of Fort Donelson as was that of the Potomac by the defeat of Bull Run. It is hard to censure a successful general immediately after a victory, but I think he richly deserves it. I can get no returns, no reports, no information of any kind from him. Satisfied with his victory, he sits down and enjoys it, without any regard to the future. I am worn out and tired by this neglect and inefficiency. C. F. Smith is almost the only officer equal to the emergency." The next day, having probably received authority from Washington, he telegraphed to Grant: "You will place Major-General C. F. Smith in command of expedition, and remain yourself at Fort Henry. Why do you not obey my orders to report strength and position of your command?"

This is one of the most extraordinary documents

in military history. Grant had gained a great victory; it was only two weeks after that victory; fortress after fortress had fallen in consequence of it; the army was active at every point; yet Halleck talks of its being demoralized, and wants a daily report of every company and regiment. McClellan was then in command, and probably sympathized profoundly with the genius and sagacity of Halleck.

Grant replied that he was not aware of disobeying orders, and certainly did not intend to, and that he had almost daily reported the condition of his command, and had averaged writing more than once a day since leaving Cairo. Again Halleck rebuked, and twice Grant asked to be relieved. Soon after, Halleck transmitted to Grant a letter of inquiry from Lorenzo Thomas, Adjutant-General (since quite noted) on the subject of Grant's leaving his command, and his own reply, dated March 15th,[1] in which he said there was "*no want of military subordination on the part of General Grant, and his failure to make returns of his forces has been explained.*" This was just on the part of General Halleck, and relieves him from the suspicion of wanton injustice.

This episode was soon over, and Grant restored to his command. In the mean time, General C. F. Smith had been placed in command, while Grant remained at Fort Henry.[2] Smith pushed forward troops to Eastport, on the Tennessee; but ultimately took Pittsburg Landing as the initial point. Halleck still kept up his cautions. On the 13th of March he telegraphs Grant, "Do n't bring on any general

[1] Badeau, pages 63, 64.   [2] Badeau's statement.

engagement at Paris. If the enemy appear in force, our troops must fall back." Evidently Halleck knew that Grant would fight, and had a wholesome fear of any such performance. In a military point of view, he was at that time right. Our volunteers had been gathering from every part of the country; and many of them were very ill disciplined, and not prepared for steady and desperate conflicts in the field. Some delay was, no doubt, needed.

It is necessary here to refer to some incidental affairs, in order to understand the general position. We have seen the rebels had abandoned Columbus; but, near the same time, they fortified Island No. 10, on the Mississippi, and although it was not a strong place itself, they expected to obstruct the navigation of the Mississippi, and for a short time did. General Pope, however, by judicious movements at and from New Madrid, compelled the enemy to evacuate, and on the 6th of April, the very day of the battle of Shiloh, our transports were descending the river.[1] This coöperative movement was absolutely necessary to the success of the advance in the interior; for it is very evident we must reënforce and provision our army from the Mississippi in making any advance beyond the Tennessee.

Let us now return to the initial point of operations at Pittsburg Landing. This field, on which was soon to be fought the battle of Shiloh, was selected

[1] A full account of this affair is given in Professor Coppée's " Grant and his Campaigns." Colonel J. W. Bissell, with his Engineer Regiment, under the direction of General Schuyler Hamilton, actually cut a canal twelve miles long, and fifty feet wide, through heavy woods ! and on the night of the 4th of April, the Carondelet ran by to New Madrid.

by General C. F. Smith. It was on the west bank
of the Tennessee; that is, on the same side with the
enemy's forces, which were in front; and this fact has
been severely criticised on one hand, and firmly
defended on the other. The reasons seem about
balanced. If our army had been defeated, (and
Sidney Johnston, who commanded, and Beauregard,
who succeeded him, were convinced it would be,)
where was its retreat? It is rare that a commander can afford to leave such a question wholly
out of view. The gun-boats Tylor and Lexington
could do something in securing the re-passage of
the river. But it seems to me, and did to Beauregard, that if our army had been defeated, it must
have become an almost total wreck. On the other
hand, the reasons are equally strong. We were the
advancing, not the defending army. A river is a
material defense, and if we permitted the enemy to
hold the other bank, we must have crossed it on
pontoons, in face of a powerful armament. Smith
was a sagacious and well-educated officer, and looking to the fact that we must advance, and that we
had some support from the gun-boats, he was probably right. At any rate, there we were, at Pittsburg
Landing, with the gathering host of the enemy in
front. Beauregard had left the East some time before, with fifteen thousand troops from the Army of
Manassas. Albert Sidney Johnston, considered by
many as the best military mind in the rebel service, commanded the formidable force now concentrated to crush the army of Grant, and defeat what
they well knew was our purpose—the conquest of

the Mississippi Valley. Corinth was the central point of the rebel forces, and Pittsburg Landing that of ours. The fact that we were on the west side of the river, and, if defeated, had small chance of safety, was a great temptation to the rebel commander, and he was right in yielding to it. If successful, he could, in a great measure, destroy one of our finest armies; and if unsuccessful, he could retreat.

Accordingly, on the 3d of April, Johnston issued an address to his army, of which the following is a paragraph:

"*Soldiers of the Army of the Mississippi:* I have put you in motion to offer battle to the invaders of your country, with the resolution, and discipline, and valor becoming men, fighting, as you are, for all worth living or dying for. You can but march to a decisive victory over agrarian mercenaries sent to subjugate and despoil you of your liberties, property, and honor." [1]

This assertion that our troops were "*agrarian mercenaries*," often repeated during the war, was disgraceful to the rebel mind, for, in any event, the time must have come when history would have corrected such a falsehood.

"Accompanying this address were general orders, dividing the Army of the Mississippi into three *corps d'armée.* General Beauregard was proclaimed second in command of the whole force.

"The first *corps d'armée* was assigned to General Polk, and embraced all the troops of his former command, less detached cavalry, and artillery, and

---

[1] Rebellion Record, page 75 of Diary, Vol. IV.

reserves, detached for the defense of Fort Pillow and Madrid Bend.

"The second *corps d'armée* was assigned to General Bragg, and was to consist of the Second Division of the Army of the Mississippi, less artillery and cavalry hereafter detached.

"The third *corps d'armée* was assigned to General Hardee, and consisted of the Army of Kentucky. General Crittenden was assigned a command of reserves, to consist of not less than two brigades."

We now know the rebel plan of attack, and their reasons for it; but, before we trace out the rebel movement, let us take a view of our position and forces. The following is a brief account, by Coppée, of Pittsburg Landing, and the general reason for the battle:

"It was on the west bank of the Tennessee, and for the most part densely wooded with tall trees, and but little undergrowth. The landing is immediately flanked on the left by a short but precipitous ravine, along which runs the road to Corinth. On the right and left, forming a good natural flanking arrangement, were Snake and Lick Creeks, which would compel the attack of the enemy to be made in front. The distance between the mouths of these creeks is about two and a half miles. The locality was well chosen. The landing was protected by the gun-boats Tylor and Lexington. Buell's Army of the Ohio was coming up to reenforce Grant, and, although the river lay in our rear, that was the direction of advance. Just at that time it was the best possible thing for our army to fight a battle, and the moral effect of a victory would be invaluable to our cause."

What if it had not been a victory?

The authority for the rebel plan of the battle is Mr. Preston, brother-in-law, and confidential aid of A. S. Johnston at Shiloh,[1] which was confirmed by accounts from other sources, both on the Union and the rebel side. The rebel army was from 45,000 to 60,000 ; Grant's near 38,000. The Union troops did not take advantage of the peculiar features of the country, and were, therefore, in a more unfavorable situation than they need have been. I have been informed by officers in the battle that some of the divisions had not even axes and shovels to make those temporary defenses which might have been erected. This, however, was no doubt the result rather of the hurry with which the army had been collected at this point than of the officers in command. General De Peyster, criticising the position, says :

"Woods, brush, ravines, and similar obstacles afforded opportunities for surprise, and blinds for attack, without corresponding advantages for resistance. The ground, however, was easily susceptible of defense. With twenty-four hours' work, felling trees, making abatis, throwing up earthworks, and mounting guns to sweep the ravines, the position could have been rendered impregnable to any sudden assault.[2] The natural obstacles, however, which mili-

[1] I take this account from a very interesting little work by J. Watts De Peyster, entitled, "The Decisive Conflicts of the Late Civil War."

[2] Colonel Worthington, of the Forty-Sixth Ohio Regiment, informed me of the same fact at the time, and the omission of that precaution

tary command ignored, were fully taken advantage of by the troops themselves, when they fell back to make their successful individual, irregular defense. When it came to this, and organized resistance had ceased, it realized what Brigadier-General Sweeney said— 'The rebels drove us all day, but it took them all day to drive us.'"[1]

We have now the entire situation before us, and we come to the plan of the battle, as devised by Johnston. I give it in the words of De Peyster, as derived from the best of rebel authorities:

"A. Sidney Johnston's plan of attack was in reality the oblique order of battle—that is, in principle. He saw that the weak point of the Union line was Prentiss's left. He knew the ground well, yes, perfectly well, and intended to amuse and engage the loyal right and center, throw the weight of his force on Prentiss's left, get in its rear, and continually throw off rear and flanking attacks, even as Prentiss fell back, up the ravines which shot out like spurs from mountain ranges, penetrating the Union position. The configuration of the ground or ravines, through which Lick Creek empties itself, can not be better represented than by a section of a 'Silver,' or what they call 'a Ladder Pine,' the main ravine representing the trunk, the spur-ravines the branches.

"As this oblique and then flanking attack progressed, A. Sidney Johnston intended to strip his left and center, passing reënforcements behind the

can only be excused on the ground that there had not been time to complete the arrangements.

[1] De Peyster's "Conflicts."

mask of battle or blind of fire, to his right, leaving only sufficient forces there to occupy McClernand and Sherman's attention, to feed, strengthen, and support the main attack till he had massed his troops on the left, far in the rear of the loyal line of battle; whence, advancing up along the river, he could cut them off completely from it, and 'bag the whole crowd.' Such a conception, carried out as it was as long as A. Sidney Johnston lived, was worthy of the real father of modern oblique attacks, Frederick K., of Prussia. It was in the full tide of success when a bullet (according to one account, according to another a piece of a shell) put an end to the greatest military brain and life of rebeldom."[1]

Such was the plan of the rebel attack. What was the position of our forces to receive that attack?

Grant had arrived at Savannah on the 17th of March; a point from which he could best superintend the operations of the army, place the divisions, and determine on his plans. The forces in the field on the morning of the 6th of April, (Sunday,) were five divisions, thus placed: "Prentiss was on the left, about a mile and a half from the Landing, facing southward; McClernand at some distance on his right, facing south-west; Sherman at Shiloh Church, on the right of McClernand, and in advance of him; Hurlbut and W. H. L. Wallace a mile in rear of McClernand, in reserve; the former supporting the left and the latter the right wing." It will be observed that the whole were within the limits of Lick Creek,

---

[1] Professor Coppée seems to have attributed the plan of the rebels to Beauregard; but such it was not; it belonged to Johnston.

Snake Creek, and Owl Creek, a branch of Snake. A division under General Lewis Wallace lay at Crump's Landing, and was intended as a reserve, to come early into battle, but lost its way, and did not take part till late in the day. Such was the position of our forces on the night of the 5th; the rebel forces at that time lying just behind the shield of woods in front, and hearing the drums of our tattoo beat.

Sunday the sun rose bright, and the morning was beautiful. Nature takes no note of the greatest convulsions of human society, and looks calmly on at the most dreadful scenes of human destruction. The correspondent of the "Cincinnati Gazette" wrote:

"The sun never rose on a more beautiful morning than that of Sunday, April 6th. Lulled by the general security, I had remained in pleasant quarters at Crump's, below Pittsburg Landing, on the river. By sunrise I was roused by the cry: 'They 're fighting above.' Volleys of musketry could, sure enough, be distinguished, and occasionally the sullen boom of artillery came echoing down the stream. Momentarily the volume of sound increased, till it became evident it was no skirmish that was in progress, and that a considerable portion of the army must be already engaged. Hastily springing on the guards of a passing steamboat, I hurried up.

"The sweet spring sunshine danced over the rippling waters, and softly lit up the green of the banks. A few fleecy clouds alone broke the azure above. A light breeze murmured among the young leaves; the blue-birds were singing their gentle treble to the stern music that still came louder and deeper to us from the bluffs above, and the frogs were croaking their feeble imitation from the marshy islands that studded the channel."

On this beautiful morning, and on the verge of a great battle, let us see where the principal commanders and parties to it were. Buell, whose army was marching to join Grant, was anxiously expected; for, although Grant intended to attack the enemy, if they did not attack him, yet it having been discovered that Johnston had been greatly reënforced, and that defeat was possible, it is true that Grant looked with anxiety for the arrival of these reënforcements. On the evening of the 5th Nelson's Division arrived in the vicinity of Savannah. Early on the morning of Sunday, (Grant and his staff were breakfasting, with their horses saddled, not more than six miles distant from Pittsburg, in a direct line,) the heavy firing was heard, and an order was instantly dispatched to General Nelson to move his entire command to the river bank opposite Pittsburg.[1] Grant, at seven o'clock, started in person for the front, having written a note to Buell, which is important here, as indicating clearly what Grant had anticipated, and how little he was surprised by what occurred:

"Heavy firing is heard up the river, indicating plainly that an attack has been made upon our most advanced positions. I have been looking for this, but did not believe the attack could be made before Monday or Tuesday. This necessitates my joining the

[1] Grant's written order to Nelson, on the morning of the 6th, to move opposite Pittsburg. The march began at one o'clock, and the division arrived at four, P. M. Suppose it had arrived at noon, as it might, would not Beauregard have been defeated that afternoon?

forces up the river, instead of meeting you to-day, as I had contemplated.   I have directed General Nelson to move to the river with his division.   He can march to opposite Pittsburg."

Here, then, we have the actual position of all the principal parties to the battle of Shiloh, on the morning of the 6th, (Sunday.)   Sidney Johnston had moved his army close up to our camp, and early in the morning had commenced the attack.   Nelson's Division of Buell's forces had been ordered up.   Grant had breakfasted, and was now galloping to the front. The battle had begun, and the roar of the guns came like the tornadoes of the West, sweeping through the woods and over the plains.   The rebel onset was made with tremendous force.   The advanced Division of Sherman, and the left under Prentiss, received the first shock, and as they were raw troops, many gave way, and the civilians who were at the landing, and the reporters who crowd round the army like birds of prey to the carcass, were in haste to proclaim a rout, and told of the thousands who crowded to the landing as the troops retreated.   There were the skulkers, the civilians, the camp men, who are always numerous in a new army.   But the battle raged on, and, notwithstanding the number of skulkers, never did the volunteers fight better.   Sherman's Division, though driven back, re-formed and retreated, like the lion as he slowly draws his body back, already wounded by the hunter.   McClernand's Division supported Sherman's left; but on Prentiss came the great shock; for, as I have shown, it was Johnston's plan to heap repeated attacks on our left, driving

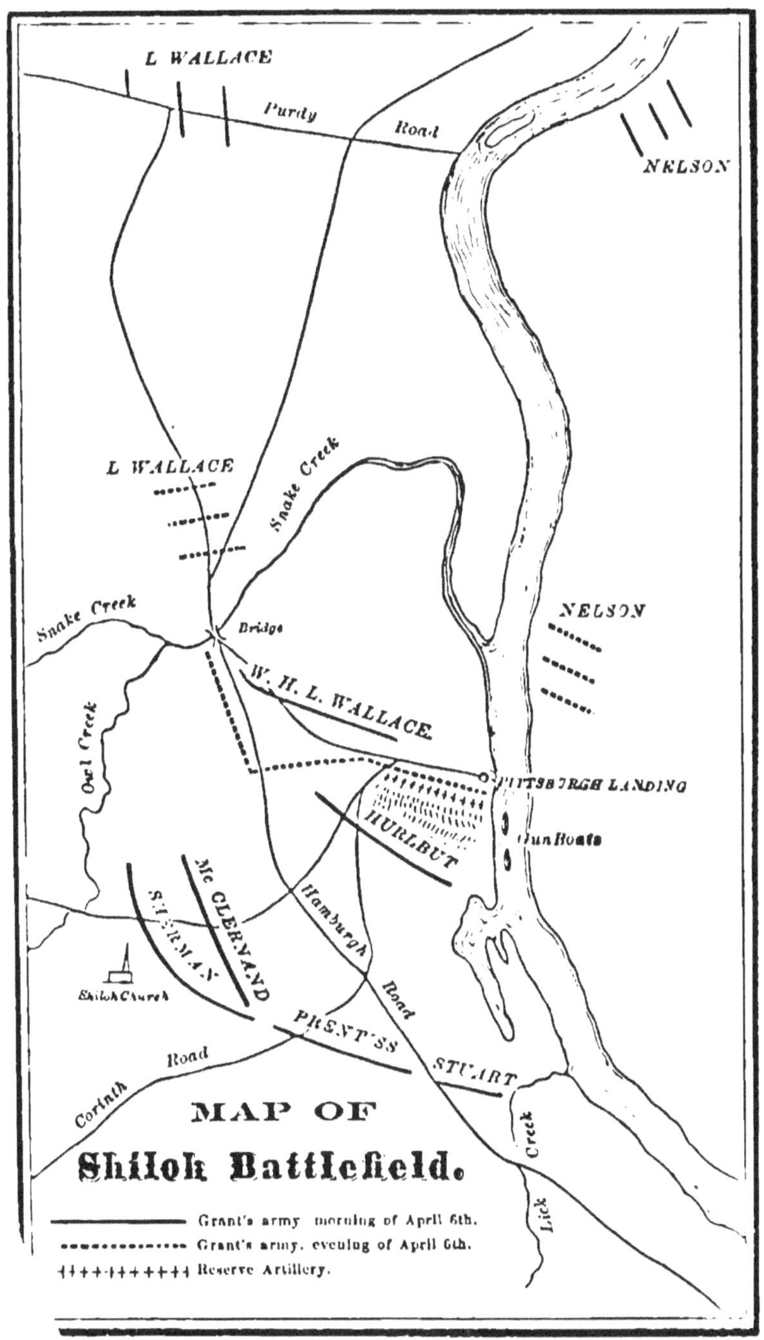

MAP OF
Shiloh Battlefield.

it back, in order to get possession of the landing. Prentiss was not surprised, though totally unaware that a whole army was to be poured upon him. He had pickets out, and had sent four companies to reconnoiter. But this reconnoitering party was suddenly attacked, and the shock came with stunning force. Prentiss is driven back in confusion. Between him and Sherman there is a gap, and into this gap rushes the rebel General Hardee, and he flanks the retreating regiments of Prentiss, and the left of Sherman also. Prentiss has been reënforced by Hurlbut, with the Brigade of Veatch, and endeavors in vain to stem the torrent. In vain, for Bragg has reënforced Hardee, and on the rebel columns push. Prentiss is soon enveloped, his division driven back, part of his field-officers killed; but, after a desperate fight, he and portions of his division are captured. So far, Johnston was succeeding in his plan ; our left was broken, and fast drifting toward the landing, and the day there looked dark. Although broken, it is a mistake to suppose those gallant men were, like the skulkers from the front, out of the fight, or demoralized. They were no longer available as organizations, but they took to skirmishing in masses, and did effective service. The Fifteenth Wisconsin had nine hundred men, of whom four hundred were marksmen, and it is related of one of them that, falling back from tree to tree, his Colonel came up and said, " How many have you finished ?" " Colonel," replied this cool individual, " I have fired thirty-seven cartridges, and I do n't feel certain of six." He had brought down *thirty-one rebels !* So raged the battle, even where our broken and disordered troops fell back.

Let us return to the center. Sherman had been gradually driven back. McClernand had come into line, bearing the brunt of the advancing attack. Hurlbut had endeavored to strengthen the left. Wallace was coming in, and had sent a brigade to reënforce Stewart, on the extreme left, who was attacked by Breckinridge's reserves. Sherman had been forced back more and more; but parts of his division had done most gallant fighting. The regiments of McDowell, and Buckland's Brigade, maintained their lines, fought bravely, and suffered severely.[1] So, all over the field, there was hard fighting and brave conduct; but still, at 10, A. M., the day was evidently going against us; but then, as one aptly said, *we made them take the day to it;* and it was good fighting did it.

The battle was confused; the divisions covered so much space, that we can not follow each regiment, or man, through this terrible day. We must be contented to look at general movements, and mark well results, for many mistaken accounts of that battle have been given.

"As far as mathematical statements and lines can indicate such a confused condition of things," says Professor Coppée,[2] "the order at ten o'clock was the following: Colonel Stewart, of Sherman's Division, who had been posted on the Hamburg road in the

---

[1] See General Sherman's Report, in which particular regiments and actions are named.

[2] "Grant and his Campaigns," page 88.

morning, far to the left, and who had held his position most gallantly against the overwhelming numbers of Breckinridge's reserves, had been slowly driven back to join Hurlbut's left, in spite of the reenforcements of McArthur's Brigade, of Wallace's Division. Next came Hurlbut, who had posted himself to resist the rebel advance; and behind him were the fugitives of General Prentiss. McClernand was on his right and rear; and Sherman's left in rear of McClernand."

Our men had now found out what I have stated was the rebel plan of the battle—the constant attacking and pushing our left. Coppée says:

"As it was now manifest that the fury of the rebel attack was to be directed to our left, General Wallace marched his other brigades over to join McArthur, thus filling the space so threatened upon Hurlbut's left, and took with him three Missouri batteries—Stone's, Richardson's, and Webber's—all under Major Cavender. Here, from ten o'clock till four, this devoted force manfully sustained the terrific fire and frequent attack of the continually increasing foe. Upon Wallace and Hurlbut the enemy made four separate charges, which were splendidly repulsed. At length Hurlbut was obliged to fall back, and, their supports all gone, Wallace's Division were satisfied that they too must retire. To add to the disorder, their commander, General Wallace, fell mortally wounded, and was carried from the field."

Now we are at the crisis of the battle. Prentiss is a prisoner; Wallace is mortally wounded. Regiment after regiment has been broken; division after division has retreated slowly back, till our left is fast approaching the Landing. And still the enemy is thundering on. Weary, cut up, and no little demoralized he is too.[1] For we need not think that, in this bloody field, it is our army alone which has suffered, and has skulkers falling behind. Not so; the rebels had their full share of all those losses; but they had the advantage of the advance, and the appearance of victory. The sun of their glory was, however, soon to sink; and victory, which seemed so sure, was soon to fade away, and be seen no more.

At half-past 2, P. M., Albert Sidney Johnston was borne from the field by his friend, Colonel Preston. With him the true genius of the campaign perished. The battle for a time slackened; not only on this account, but because the rebel army was greatly shattered and wearied. At length, about 4, P. M., Beauregard was ready for the last charge.

On the crest of a ridge on our left, Colonel Webster and Major Cavender had hastily planted batteries[2]—on the crest of a ridge overlooking a ravine, which still intervened between the enemy and our reduced and shortened line. The enemy placed their artillery on the opposite crest, and determined to seize and cross the ravine. Here were the divisions of Breckinridge, and Chalmers, and Withers, embattled for their charge. It was in vain. The fire of our artillery was tremendous; and just then the gun-boats (the Tylor and Lexington) got a chance to pour in their fire. The rebels were attacking on Lick

[1] See Beauregard's Official Report.
[2] See General Hurlbut's Report.

Creek, where our troops had lain in the morning. The gun-boats entered the mouth of the creek, and opened their guns up the ravine. Three times the rebels charged, under the fire of batteries and boats, and each time were driven back, with great loss. Just as this scene was closing, the advance of General Buell's army, the Brigade of General Ammen, arrived, and had no sooner got to the bank than it was *put in position by Grant himself*, who was in that part of the field.[1] This part of Buell's forces fired but a few volleys that night, and, as appears from the regimental reports, lost but three or four men, killed and wounded.[2] In fact, the battle was ended. Johnston had perished, and Beauregard failed to drive Grant's army into the Tennessee. The night was drawing on ; both armies were exhausted ; the enemy retired to his camps ; and our troops, inspired by hope, lay upon their arms, expecting victory on the morrow. Before the last charge of the rebels, when the battle was waning, after Johnston's death, and before Buell's troops had arrived, Grant (then with Sherman's Division) gave orders to renew the battle in the morning. Did that look like defeat ? No! The darkest hour had been in the forenoon, and Grant saw that Beauregard's army had begun to fail. Lewis Wallace's Division was yet fresh for the field ; and batteries and gun-boats were in position. The probability is, that, even left to itself, the Army of

---

[1] Report of Colonel Ammen, and Report of Lieutenant-Colonel Jones, Twenty-Fourth Ohio. These reports prove that Grant directed these movements himself.

[2] Report of Colonel Grose, Thirty-Sixth Indiana.

the Tennessee would have achieved a glorious victory under the morrow's sun.

The scenes of that night, could they have been pictured on canvas, would have been different, but equally interesting with those of the day. It was a dark and stormy night, and even the rebel commanders could not find their troops.[1] The National troops had been driven from all their camps, and with their organizations much broken up, formed more a mass of brave fighting men, stubbornly maintaining their ground, than that of a regularly disciplined army. So sunk the weary to rest; so lay the dead under the dark clouds; so lay and groaned the wounded, where, between two armies, none could attend them. Here they sleep, quiet as the infant; here they lie as quiet, in the arms of death; here they lie, in the pain and agonies of desperate wounds, longing for some refreshing draught, which is only supplied by the rains of Heaven. But yonder is a different scene. All night long the divisions of Buell were being ferried across the river. Grant visited each division commander in the night, and repeated himself the order to attack in the morning; and, amidst the silence of the sleepers on one side, and the movements of troops on the other, and the consultations of Generals, the gun-boats were dropping shell after shell into the enemy's camps. Thus did

---

[1] "Such was the nature of the ground over which we had fought, and the heavy resistance we had met, that the commands of the whole army were very much shattered. In a dark and stormy night commanders found it impossible to find and assemble their troops; each body or fragment bivouacking where night overtook them."—*Bragg's Report.*

nature and man, the storm from the clouds and the wrecks of battle, mingle in that strange scene on the banks of the Tennessee, near the little church of Shiloh, on that memorable Sunday night.

And now, before the drum again wakes the sleepers, before the harvest of death again begins, let us ask where was Grant, and what he had been doing? I have said that Grant expected the attack, but not quite so soon, unless the enemy waited for him to attack them, which he meant to do. On the evening before, (Saturday the 5th,) Nelson's Division of Buell's forces had arrived near Savannah. Grant, anxious to meet Buell, breakfasted early with his staff, and had their horses saddled and waiting. It was then he heard the heavy firing, and leaving an order for Nelson to advance, and a hasty note for Buell, he immediately proceeded to the scene of action, several miles distant. Two hours after this, at ten o'clock, when the battle raged fiercest, and the hour was darkest for us, Grant was with Sherman,[1] on the right of his division, encouraging him to a stubborn resistance, and in answer to an inquiry about cartridges, said he had foreseen and provided for that. So well was this done that "all day long a train of wagons was passing from the Landing to the front, carrying ammunition over the narrow and crowded road."[2] From the front Grant proceeded rapidly to the left, and, at intervals, was engaged in forming new lines and sending stragglers back to their regiments, a work most necessary

[1] Sherman's Letter to the United States Service Magazine.

[2] Badeau, in his "Military History," says that Colonel Pride, of Grant's staff, organized this train.

in the emergency.[1] At half-past four in the afternoon Grant met Buell at the Landing, (for Buell, on hearing of the battle at Savannah, rode up in person,) and explained the situation of affairs to him. Buell inquired: "*What preparations have you made for retreating, General?*" Grant at once said: "*I have n't despaired of whipping them yet.*" Buell then went to hurry up his own troops. A little after, at five o'clock, Grant is seen posting the regiments of General Ammen's Brigade, (Nelson's Division,) to support the batteries, which, I have said, were planted on the ridge to defeat the enemy's last attack.[2] Soon after the enemy is driven back, and about six o'clock (for it was near and before sunset) Grant rode up to General Sherman,[3] explained to him the situation of affairs on the left, ordered him to get all things ready, and *at daylight next day attack the enemy.* Sherman says this was before he knew Buell had arrived. Grant knew it; but at four o'clock in the afternoon, says Sherman, on a deliberate calculation of the available forces, the arrival of Lewis Wallace's Division, and the recovery of the stragglers, Grant thought himself justified in resuming the offensive next morning. Was that a correct judgment? This was before the last grand attack on the left, and before Grant knew the almost fatal force of that attack. It is doubtful whether he or any of our Generals fully

[1] Badeau's "Military History."

[2] Nelson (see Report) says the head of his column marched up the bank of Pittsburg Landing at 5, P. M. And Ammen (see Ammen's Report) says that General Grant directed him, at the top of the bank, to support a battery assailed by the enemy.

[3] Sherman's Letter to the United States Service Magazine.

comprehended on that day the plan of Johnston in his continued oblique attack on our left.[1] But it was there the heaviest attack was made, there the pressure was the greatest, and there the enemy's success was the greatest, and there, but for the admirable arrangement of a circle of batteries by Webster and Cavender, their attack might have been fatal. Whatever *might* have happened, we know that Grant had not despaired of the battle, for so he told Buell; so he thought when he ordered Sherman to assume the offensive in the morning.

Let us now take a glance at the position of the army on the evening of the 6th of April. Our divisions had been partly broken, partly driven back, partly disorganized, but not wholly broken. No part of our line had really been pierced in all its retreat; but it had retreated so that the two wings were just about two miles back from the position of the front line in the morning. The line now extended from Snake Creek bridge on the right to the crest and ravine, a little way from the Landing. This line was nearly two miles long, with an apex projecting toward the right. The gun-boats were on the left, commanding the ravine, and the bridge over Snake Creek made the extreme right. All night long the troops of Buell were crossing the river and forming in position.[2]

"Grant visited each division commander, including Nelson, after dark, directing the new position of each, and repeating in person his orders for an

---

[1] See the testimony of Col. Preston, given in the "Decisive Conflicts," by De Peyster.

[2] See Buell's Report, April 15, 1862.

advance at early dawn. He told each to 'attack with a heavy skirmish line, as soon as it was light enough to see, and then to follow up with his entire command, leaving no reserves.' Before midnight he returned to the Landing, and lay on the ground, with his head against the stump of a tree, where he got thoroughly drenched by the storm, but slept soundly, confident of victory on the morrow."[1]

The battle of the 7th (Monday) was comparatively easy. Indeed, if we suppose the rebel commander to have been fully informed of the arrival of reënforcements, he could have had no object in the battle of the 7th but to cover his retreat. In fact, however, Beauregard was in doubt, and *hoped*, from the preceding rains, that Buell had been delayed.[2] In the mean time, however, three divisions of Buell's army had crossed the Tennessee, and were formed precisely where they would be most effective; for, observe that the enemy's main attack had been persistently on our left, and opposite our position (that on the ravine) lay the main body of the rebel forces. Buell's three corps (those of Nelson, Crittenden, and McCook) were formed from our center to the left; Sherman on the right, and toward Snake Creek bridge, kept the front. At daylight the attack was made, and Sherman says: "I advanced my division by the flank, the resistance being trivial, up to the very spot where the day before the battle had been most severe, and then waited till near noon for Buell's troops to get up abreast, when the entire line

---

[1] This statement is taken from Badeau's "Military History," page 87.
[2] See Beauregard's Report of the 11th April.

advanced, and recovered all the ground we had ever held." The sharp fight was on the left, where the divisions of Buell attacked in fine order, and gradually drove the enemy before them. Here we may let General Beauregard tell the story of the result; for, although he claimed a great victory for the day before, and now considered that he was only defeated by fresh troops, yet, in the concluding facts, he seems to be mainly correct. Beauregard says:

"On the left, however, and nearest to the point of arrival of his reënforcements, he drove forward line after line of his fresh troops, which were met with a resolution and courage of which our country may be proudly hopeful. Again and again our troops were brought to the charge, invariably to win the position at issue, invariably to drive back their foe. But hour by hour thus opposed to an enemy constantly reënforced, our ranks were perceptibly thinned under the unceasing, withering fire of the enemy, and by twelve meridian, eighteen hours of hard fighting had sensibly exhausted a large number; my last reserves had necessarily been disposed of, and the enemy was evidently receiving fresh reënforcements after each repulse; accordingly, about one, P. M., I determined to withdraw from so unequal a conflict, securing such of the results of the victory of the day before as were. practicable."[1]

The *result* was, he made a hasty retreat, with *not half the available strength with which he went into the battle.*[2]

---

[1] Beauregard's Report, 11th of April.
[2] Idem. This admission is important to Grant's military position.

Such was the BATTLE OF SHILOH, the least understood, and the most misrepresented of any battle or event in that war. It was a battle which some military critics have regarded as most decisive, in which more than twenty thousand men (about equally divided in the two armies) were lost; at which the best Generals of the whole rebel armies were defeated, and which, nevertheless, was represented to the country as a battle in which there was no generalship; in which the position was wrongly chosen; in which the General was absent from the field, and at which thousands of men ran away, and thousands of others were slaughtered without a reason! The simple story of its events, as I have related them, from unquestionable evidence, is a sufficient answer to these misrepresentations. A man who has led an army of raw recruits into the field; fought them, without the slightest fortification, against superior numbers;[1] and found himself ready at night for a victory on the morrow, needs no vindication. Success may not be a test of merit; but success there was at least a proof that Grant knew what he was about. Time and victory have vindicated Grant from the criticisms and aspersions cast upon him in relation to his conduct at Shiloh. But it is due to those who wish to know the *truth* of Grant's conduct at Shiloh, whether military or personal, to make a brief review of his position, both at Donelson and Shiloh; for they are connected together. This is especially necessary, as most of the unfavorable criticisms have

[1] Beauregard's Report admits that he had 41,000 men; and, without Lewis Wallace's Division, Grant had not over 35,000.

been made by men totally unacquainted with military affairs, and unfit to make any criticism at all. Such critics, however sincere or earnest, are generally conscious of their deficiencies, and will be found very generous in their quotations of military proverbs, from Napoleon, Frederick, Wellington, and Jomini, all of whom would have found their proverbs totally inapplicable in American warfare. They never carried on war in such an extent of country, or with such numerous armies; and were men of too strong minds, and too much military science, to have marched an American army on European ideas.

The criticisms made on General Grant, at Donelson and Shiloh, were principally these:

1. That the plan of the Donelson Expedition was formed by Buell, for which reference is made to a dispatch from Buell to Halleck, dated January 3, 1862. But what had a letter to *Halleck* to do with it, unless Halleck communicated it to Grant? This he did not do, and no intimation of such a plan was made to Grant, till Grant and Foote had urged it on Halleck. Grant has made no claim to a general plan of that campaign; but, if he had, this dispatch of Buell to Halleck would have been no refutation of it. Most probably, no general plan of that campaign was made by any body.

2. It has been said and assumed by those who seem to have forgot that armies move in reference to an object, and battles are fought to obtain that object, that the *position* of the army on the west side of the Tennessee River, and therefore exposed to an attack, was a blunder. The position was

selected by General C. F. Smith; and not only selected, but every division was placed in position by him.[1] But when General Grant came into command, a few days later, he might unquestionably have removed the army to the other side. If, then, the army was at that time in danger from a bad position, Grant is responsible for it. But he did not think so; and it may be doubted whether any daring General would have thought so. In the first place, the army was already there, placed by General Smith; and to move back was to show a sense of fear, and to perform a doubtful operation. In the next place, the position was *naturally very strong*, and that it was so, ultimately enabled Grant to turn disaster into victory. On either side lay large and deep creeks, heading near together, and breaking the country into rough and difficult ravines; so that the army could be attacked only in front, and was substantially protected on either side. In the third place, the gun-boats afforded no small defense at the river; and, lastly, Buell's army was hourly expected. The position of the army was in fact a very strong one; and the errors committed (and it seems to me there were some) were not in choosing the position, but *in the management of it.* There can, I think, be no doubt, that our troops should have taken possession of the woods in front, or a part of them, and constructed abatis, and light intrenchments in front. There was time enough for this, and the subsequent experience of our armies in the war (when they did do such things)

---

[1] Sherman's Letter to United States Service Magazine.

proved they were necessary.[1] It was said, on the other hand, that, at this period of the war, our men did not believe in such defenses. Perhaps so; but the whole art of war proved that they were necessary to prevent the effect of sudden attacks. Whatever opinion may be formed of that, the position at Shiloh was a strong one; and whether the army ought originally to have been placed on that side of the river is a question not to be settled now, except on general principles. Two arguments are decidedly in favor of this position. The first is, that, in spite of all our danger, *we did succeed.* The other is, that an attacking army *must advance.* Suppose we had not crossed the Tennessee *then*, and Beauregard's army had taken the other side, how long before we would have crossed?

3. Again, it has been said that we were surprised. This is contradicted, both by the facts and the officers. We have seen that Grant said he had expected this; but he did not expect it so soon, by a day or two. Sherman says, there had been skirmishing the two previous days; and Prentiss had pickets a mile in advance, and four companies reconnoitering at 3 o'clock in the morning. Grant was telegraphing to Halleck each day, and on the 5th telegraphed him that there had been skirmishing; that the enemy were apparently in considerable force; that he had no idea a general attack would be made, "*but will be prepared should such a thing take place.*"[2] The

---

[1] Before the Battle of Shiloh was fought, Colonel Worthington, of the Forty-Sixth Ohio, (of Sherman's Division,) wrote me, that these precautions ought to be taken.

[2] Badeau's "Military History."

idea of a surprise arose from the very fact, and fault, I have commented on, the want of abatis and intrenchments. For want of them, the pickets and first lines of troops were very quickly driven and broken; and this gave lookers-on the idea of a surprise. Beauregard, in his report, says: "At 5, A. M., on the 6th instant, a reconnoitering party of the enemy having become engaged with our advanced pickets, the commander of the forces gave orders to begin the movement and attack as determined upon."[1] Bragg, in his report, says substantially the same thing. The idea of not expecting an attack at Shiloh, or of being surprised on the morning of the battle, must therefore be given up.

4. The grossest misrepresentations as to Grant himself were made; that he was far from the battle; that he was negligent; that he made no plan on the 6th, for the battle of the 7th; and other charges more gross and equally false were circulated by those whose imagination was greater than their knowledge. The simple narrative of the facts above stated refutes them all. For four days Grant was in constant activity; every day dispatching to Halleck; on the morning of the 6th, breakfasting early for a start; ordering up Nelson, and riding at once to the front; consulting with Sherman, at 10 o'clock; riding and forming men over the whole field of battle; meeting Buell at 4 o'clock, at the Landing; putting Ammen's Brigade in position, at 5 o'clock; ordering Sherman to be ready for a morning attack; and meeting Buell and Sherman in the evening, to make arrangements

[1] Beauregard's Report, 21st of April, 1862.

for the morrow's battle, (which were made and perfectly carried out,) and at midnight sleeping at the
foot of a tree amid drenching rains. If this is not
care and activity and plan and grit, what is?

5. What was the theory of the battle, and what
was its result? General Sherman may not have been
authorized to announce what was a pre-arranged plan,
in his letter to the "United States Service Magazine,"
but he most certainly stated what was required to be
done and what happened, when he says:

"It was necessary that a combat, fierce and bitter,
to test the manhood of the two armies, should come
off, and that was as good a place as any. It was not
then a question of military skill and strategy, but of
courage and pluck, and I am convinced that every
life lost that day to us was necessary, for otherwise
at Corinth, at Memphis, at Vicksburg, we would have
found harder resistance, had we not shown our enemies
that, rude and untutored as we then were, we could
fight as well as they."

The rebellion was begun and carried on, on the
part of the Confederate States, under several great
delusions, of which it seemed as impossible to unde-
ceive them as it would be to reason a lunatic into
sanity. One of them was, that there was a positive
personal and military inferiority on the part of Northern men. This, like the idea that cotton was supreme
in commerce, had to be destroyed before the rebels
could come to a true perception of their condition.
It is not at all probable that the battle of Shiloh
was deliberately fought on Sherman's theory, but it is
certain that Grant, finding that the rebels rallied as

energetically as ever after Donelson and Shiloh, henceforward believed and acted on the idea that nothing but hard blows and crushing force could conquer the rebellion.[1]

Now, what was the actual result of Shiloh? A very intelligent military critic[2] considered it one of the most decisive battles of the war. At any rate it did produce the *moral* effect, which we see was needed, as testified to by rebel soldiers. The following paragraph sums up the main facts:

"If any battle of the rebellion comes up to the estimate of Creasy as to decisiveness, that battle was Shiloh. In many respects it was the battle of the war. It disposed of the rebels' best General, dissipated their highest hopes, reversed all their life-long-learned theories. By their camp-fires the rebel soldiers discussed, in after days, that conflict—drew conclusions which obliterated all their former traditional beliefs and ideas. With bitter oaths, an ear-witness reports, they were wont to exclaim: 'Do n't tell us the Yanks won't fight; we know how they fought at Shiloh!' The South did not believe that the war really meant killing till after Donelson and Pittsburg Landing."

Shiloh was a military sequel to Donelson, and so it ought to have been, in a well-arranged and successful campaign. But had that campaign any plan? Perhaps we shall be able to answer that hereafter. I think Shiloh was *not* decisive, but that it ought to, and *would* have been, but for the inefficient conduct of

[1] Badeau's "Military History."
[2] The "Decisive Conflicts," by De Peyster.

General Halleck, who subsequently took command. Whether this is a correct opinion we shall see by a comparison of dates and facts. At present we shall leave the victorious Union army resting on the night of the 7th of April, and Beauregard retreating to Corinth. There stands the little log church at Shiloh. It was built in the wilderness. It had, doubtless, seen many a gathering of peaceful people, listening to the messenger of the Cross, and looking with hope to the Shiloh to come. It now realized the declaration of the living Shiloh, that war would attend the preaching of his Word, and destruction wait on its progress.[1] The little church had seen the beautiful light of Sunday morning, heard the birds sing their sweet music, beheld the crash of battle, as it rolled over the living and the dead, saw the dark storm of the night as it rained on the wounded and the dying, and looked out on the victor and the vanquished, as weary they sank to rest! Soon the little church is gone,[2] and now we look into the heavens for the Shiloh which is to come!

[1] Mark xiii.
[2] In a few days Shiloh Church fell and was gone!

CHAPTER VI.

HALLECK TAKES COMMAND OF THE ARMY—GRANT A SUBORDINATE—SHERMAN'S RECONNOISSANCE—GRANT PUT IN THE SHADE—LINCOLN'S SUPPORT—HALLECK GETS TO CORINTH AND INTRENCHES—CORINTH EVACUATED—THE NEW STRATEGIC LINE—BEAUREGARD DISCOVERS·CHATTANOOGA, AND HALLECK SEES IT TOO—THE ARMY IS SCATTERED, AND HALLECK DEPARTS—GRANT AGAIN IN COMMAND—BATTLE OF IUKA—BATTLE OF CORINTH—SANITARY COMMISSION—CHRISTIAN WOMEN.

BY the gallant fighting of the volunteers in the army of Grant, by Grant's own unbroken firmness and inflexible daring, by the effective fire of the gun-boats, and by the arrival and fine conduct of Buell, Shiloh was not only retrieved, but turned into a glorious victory. The nation rejoiced, Congress thanked, and in spite of all misrepresentations, the people began to see the truth, that Shiloh was not planned poorly, nor fought badly,[1] but that it was not only successful, but successful for good reasons, and that Grant was in fact an able and noble soldier. We are now to see Grant in the part of a subordinate, and to trace out a chapter of events, which, containing no very decisive movements, is yet remarkably

[1] Time and truth have at length cleared away both the mystery and misrepresentation of Shiloh.

curious, in both military and personal history. On the 9th of April, (two days after the great battle,) Halleck (who was commander of the Western Department) left St. Louis for the scene of action. Perhaps he thought there might be jealousy between Grant and Buell, who had commanded separate armies, or perhaps had a laudable ambition to share in the glory of the campaign. At any rate he quickly arrived at Pittsburg Landing, and on the 13th of April issued a General Order,[1] "congratulating the troops on their glorious successes," and directing Generals Grant and Buell to retain the "immediate command of their respective armies in the field." If the events following were to happen just as they did, it was well for Grant's reputation that he could prove precisely the date when he ceased to be a commander and became a subordinate. The rebels were retreating with a broken army, reduced on the evening of the 6th (first day's battle) to a half of its available strength.[2] We shall see that, till our delays allowed them to be reenforced, and even then, they did not really expect to hold Corinth. If there be any principle, either of common-sense or military science, it is that a defeated and broken enemy should not be allowed to re-form, reënforce, and recuperate himself. He should be pressed and destroyed, if possible. No doubt our wearied troops should have been allowed some rest, and some reorganization was necessary; but Buell's army was fresh and strong, and it does not appear

---

[1] Halleck's General Order, dated Pittsburg, April 13th.

[2] Beauregard's Report of April 11th, in which he states that his army was 40,350 strong, and that on that evening it could only muster 20,000 availables.

that Lewis Wallace's Division had lost any thing. Here, then, we had an army stronger than that of Beauregard's, even when the first divisions, which fought the first day at Shiloh, were left out of the account. What happened? We shall see. Grant did not lie still. On the 8th Sherman went out on the Corinth road, with two brigades of his fatigued troops ; had a skirmish, but found the enemy had retreated in confusion.[1] Sherman says :

"The roads are very bad, and are strewed with abandoned wagons, ambulances, and limber-boxes. The enemy has succeeded in carrying off the guns, but has crippled his batteries by abandoning the hind limber-boxes of at least twenty guns. I am satisfied that the enemy's infantry and cavalry passed Lick Creek this morning, traveling all last night, and that he left behind all his cavalry, which has protected his retreat. But the signs of confusion and disorder mark the whole road."

But, in spite of all weariness, and losses, Grant was not idle a day. On the 12th, he sent out an expedition of four thousand men, on five transports, with the gun-boats Tylor and Lexington, to Eastport, Mississippi, where they landed, proceeded to Bear Creek Bridge, and destroyed two bridges over the Mobile and Ohio Railroad. The expedition returned in the evening, and the army was now ready to renew the campaign. On the morning of the next day (13th) Halleck assumed the command, and, for the next three months, Grant was a subordinate to Halleck ; and for the two months of that time seems to have

---

[1] Sherman's Report, dated 8th of April.

known nothing of any general plan of operations, and only once to have made a suggestion of an important movement, when he was informed by the commander, that he might keep his advice till it was asked.[1] In fact, with the misrepresentations made of Shiloh, and Halleck's evident belief that Grant was a second-rate sort of a person, the victor in the greatest of battles was as much under a cloud, as if he had been the defeated general, very mercifully treated if he es-_caped censure! There was one man in the country who thought Grant had the qualities most available in war, and fortunately that man had the power to sustain him. Abraham Lincoln was seldom mistaken in his judgment of men, and although having no military study or education himself, was several times, during the war, compelled to order movements and make changes in defiance of the conservative military, as well as civil, leaders about him. It is quite probable that Grant would more than once have been sacrificed to military jealousy, if it had not been for the firmness of Lincoln. In addition to this, Grant's own good qualities saved him from any collision with his superior officers. He was eminently a soldier, truly loyal to his country, and put that loyalty above any considerations of private feeling. Besides, he was calm in temperament, and self-confident. So now he told Halleck he was only intent on his duty, and should perform any service assigned him.

I need not go into many details about Halleck's march to Corinth, and the imaginary siege of that place. It can all be told very briefly.

[1] Badeau's "Military History," page 102.

The distance from Pittsburg Landing direct to Corinth was nineteen miles. Perhaps, by the road taken by the army, it may have been more. At any rate, it was not a two days' march. Then the question was a very simple one. Ought our army to move immediately on, and attack the broken forces of the enemy at once? or ought we to wait for reënforcements, and by that loss of time to allow the enemy to be reenforced and intrench? General Halleck seems to have preferred the latter course; for, with nearly fifty thousand men in the armies of Buell and Grant, he seems to have made no move whatever in more than two weeks! On the 1st of May, he issued a general order, transferring Thomas's Division from the Army of the Ohio to the Army of Tennessee, and giving Thomas the command of Grant's Army, Grant retaining the command of the District of Tennessee. Having made this extraordinary expenditure of intellectual vigor (and being reënforced by twenty-five thousand men under General Pope) the Commanding General thought it was time to begin. On the 1st of May, Monterey, a little town about half way to Corinth, was occupied; and on the 3d of May, General Paine, of Pope's Corps, occupied Farmington, another little village, from which the rebels hastily retired to Corinth; but, on the 9th, they recaptured it, with a large force under Van Dorn and Price. We hear no more till we learn that, on the 17th, Sherman had carried a position called " Russell's House," [1] where he could hear distinctly the drums beating in Corinth. At last, we are before Corinth; and now

[1] Sherman's Report, dated May 19th.

let us see what we have done, and what the enemy has done. Halleck assumed command of the army on the 13th of April; he has been reënforced twenty-five thousand men, and he has now, on the 17th of May, (thirty-five days,) arrived in front of Corinth. He has averaged just *half a mile per day*, without meeting any serious resistance. In the mean time, the enemy, seeing we had lost the real advantage of the victory at Shiloh, began to take courage, reënforce, intrench, and make a bold front. Beauregard was an engineer officer, and he laid out and began to arm fortifications at Corinth, large enough and strong enough to have covered an army of a hundred thousand men; and he came near getting them. Van Dorn and Price, from Arkansas and Missouri, and the garrison of New Orleans, (for we had taken New Orleans in April,) came gathering in, and the supposed strength of the rebel army was not less than seventy-five thousand men; but, one half this great army had come there *after we ought to have been in Corinth*. But, in this sort of business, Halleck was not to be outdone. He had an immense department, and he gathered more than a hundred thousand men in front of Corinth. If we had failed to use the spade at Shiloh, no such charge could be made against us now. The more Beauregard fortified, the more we fortified; and it seemed as if the generals of the two armies were making an experiment on the possibilities of unlimited digging. The position of affairs is thus described by Badeau, who was present:[1]

"The National army moved slowly up toward

[1] Badeau's "Military History," page 101.

Corinth, from the battle-field of Shiloh, after Halleck arrived, making no advance except when protected by intrenchments. This was greatly to the dissatisfaction of both officers and men, to whom such operations were new, and seemed to savor of timidity. But Halleck had derived a lesson from the assaults of Shiloh, and the outcry in consequence; he was determined not to be attacked unawares, and collected his forces from every quarter of his immense department, concentrating a hundred and twenty thousand bayonets; yet it took him six weeks to advance less than fifteen miles, the enemy in all that while making no offensive movement; on the contrary, the rebels constructed defenses still more elaborate than those behind which Halleck advanced. Beauregard's strength was estimated at seventy thousand; he himself reported it at forty-seven thousand, and the officers and men of the National army were anxious to avail themselves of their vast superiority in numbers."

There must, however, be an end of such performances, and at length, on the 30th, Halleck reports to Stanton,[1] that our divisions are in the enemy's advanced works; and sure enough the siege of Corinth is at an end. This was not, however, till good opportunities of fighting and destroying the rebel army had been lost.

But what has become of the enemy? It was believed, by Grant and other officers, that Beauregard did not intend to remain at Corinth, but was only endeavoring to gain time. This was well established

[1] Halleck's Dispatch to Stanton, May 30, 1862.

13 .

by a reconnoissance of General T. W. Sherman, on the 15th of May.[1] Corinth entered, and the rebels already far away, Halleck sent out strong forces in pursuit ; but it is not to be supposed Beauregard intended to be taken, and he was not. He got to Tupelo when our men got to Baldwin, on the 10th, and here the siege and flight of Corinth ended.

In the mean time, Halleck's Reports were magnificent. On the 4th of June, he reports Pope thirty miles from Florence, Alabama, with forty thousand men, and making great numbers of prisoners. On the 9th of June, he dispatches, that " the enemy has fallen back fifty miles, and that the rebel losses are estimated at forty thousand." Time, however, proved that considerable deductions had to be made from these accounts.

We may now ask, where was Grant? He was quietly remaining with his troops ; not charged with any expedition, or responsible for any conduct of the army. Whatever may have been the cause, Grant and Buell seem to have been left to their own reflections, with the least possible to do with any active operations. Grant might be likened to Achilles resting in his tent, while Agammemnon led the forces of the Greeks ; only that, unlike Achilles, he was not inactive by his own will. Once, he ventured to sug-

---

[1] T. W. Sherman says : " The result of this reconnoissance was reported to your head-quarters," [those of Major-General Thomas, commanding right wing,] " together with the information obtained from the prisoners, among which was the important fact that the rebel commander had issued orders the day before, that all baggage of the troops, except what could be carried in knapsacks, was to be immediately sent by the Mobile and Ohio Railroad to Okolona."

gest a movement on the enemy's lines; but his advice being scouted, he never offered it again. Time passes on. It was two months before the termination of Halleck's Corinthian movement, and now we may ask, what is the sum of the results of Shiloh? What is our present situation?

On June 6th, Memphis was surrendered to Commodore C. H. Davis,[1] who in an engagement with the rebel flotilla had destroyed or captured it. Memphis, as I have observed, was the left or Mississippi point of the second line formed by the enemy after Donelson. Corinth was a principal railroad point on that line: hence it followed inevitably that, if those points were taken and held by us, the enemy's line must fall back and be re-formed. They would not like to give us Northern Mississippi, nor was it a territory very important to us; but its fall was inevitable, and the rebel left wing must fall back on a new defensible line. Henceforward, therefore, the rebel left wing rested on Vicksburg, its right stretching east to Jackson and Meridian, on the Mississippi Railroad; thence to Selma, bearing up to the Memphis and Charleston Railroad, and resting at the center on Chattanooga. The right wing of the rebel defenses remained unchanged, resting at the east on the Rappahannock, passing down through the Valley of Virginia, and pivoted on Chattanooga, with Knoxville and Cumberland in front of it. Their line ran north from Chattanooga just as long as we permitted it, and that was till Rosecrans took Chattanooga, which was the *most important single event*, in a strategic point of

<hr>

[1] Commodore Davis's Report, dated June 6, 1862.

view, during the war.   From the time the rebel army fell back from Manassas, (March, 1862,) till Grant passed the Rapidan, (May, 1864,) more than two years, we had marched and countermarched grand armies, fought bravely and nobly in twenty battles, had victories and defeats, lost one hundred thousand men, *and not advanced one mile in the actual line of attack* on the enemy's right or east wing.   The reason was not in the conduct of the armies, but an error in the strategic plan, if plan there was.   A vital and successful attack on the enemy's line of defenses *could only be made from the West*, and no such a one was made till the Mississippi was taken, and the whole left wing and center of the rebel forces turned, driven back, and the right wing at Richmond *cut off from its resources.*

But we need not consider this now.   It is enough to note that the rebel line, first driven back from Columbus, Donelson, and Bowling Green, was now driven back from Memphis and Corinth.   The first line was broken; the second is now broken, and the third line is formed through Vicksburg, Jackson, Meridian, Selma, and Chattanooga.   In the mean time the brilliant and energetic Mitchel (in these particulars unsurpassed) had left Buell at Nashville, and dashing down over the Tennessee, had arrived at Huntsville,[1] North Alabama, and astonished the people on both sides of the line very much as if a meteor had fallen from the skies; but meteors are not

[1] Mitchel occupied Huntsville May 2d and Rogersville May 14th. He remained a few days longer, when he was ordered to South Carolina, and died at Beaufort.

permanent bodies, and this brilliant expedition had
no permanent results. It was only a raid. Nothing
short of a hundred thousand men could have maintained Mitchel at Huntsville. The art of war does
not permit raids to be turned into conquests; and
so, whether it was Mitchel or Morgan, Grierson or
Pleasanton, Bragg or Lee,[1] nothing was made by
raids which pass *through* the enemy's line of defense without holding it. But this raid of Mitchel's,
and the driving back of the rebel line from Memphis
and Corinth, evidently gave the rebel leaders a new
idea of the importance of Chattanooga,[2] and as evidently impressed the same idea upon us. Why did
we not seize Chattanooga in the summer of 1861?
It matters not. We began to see now what it meant,
and the rebels saw it clearer than we did. But let us
hasten to events. Halleck saw Chattanooga looming
up in the distance, and in the middle of June sent off
Buell with four divisions, stretching along the Tennessee, and trying to see if they could not get ahead
of Bragg, who was going in the same direction. Here
occurred the first great error of this campaign. We
had been successful at every point, and now Halleck
had the finest army which had been assembled,
greater than that which McClellan led on the Peninsula. What was its object? It should have accom-

---

[1] The several marches of Lee across the Potomac, and of Bragg in
Kentucky, were mere raids across the lines, and resulted in nothing
but loss, except the capture of provender.

[2] I was at the Suck of the Tennessee twenty-five years before, when
Chattanooga was not yet built. I marked the extraordinary defensi-
bility of the country, and wondered why we did not seize it in the beginning of the war.

plished some great thing, and· that great thing lay before it. Vicksburg was at that time comparatively weak, and if it could be taken at all from the land side, then was the time to do it. But the army was divided and scattered, and on the Mississippi a year of precious time was lost.

On the 17th of July Halleck was called to the chief command at Washington, and left the command of the Army of Tennessee to Grant.[1] On the fall of Memphis, Grant had been ordered to make his head-quarters there, and was then removed to Corinth. Now he is left in command of the Army of Tennessee. He has got into his element again, and he will not get out of it soon. With five divisions of the grand army of Halleck sent away, for such was the fact, he is left in a difficult and trying position ; for the rebels very soon see that error, and forthwith begin to try whether they can not break through, and get back their lost line. Grant is greatly annoyed, and for several months he is to travel a hard road. Leaving Memphis in command of Sherman, and held strongly enough, Grant remained at Corinth, fortify-ing as well as he could these points, (on two leading railroads,) Corinth and Jackson, (at the Junction,) on the Mobile and Ohio Railroad, and Bolivar, on the Mississippi Central. Every man that Grant could possibly spare was sent to Buell, who had already

---

[1] A singular story is told about this, that when Halleck received the appointment of General-in-Chief, he offered the command of the army in Mississippi to a Colonel Allen, who was a quarter-master, (supersed-ing Grant,) but that Allen had more sense than Halleck, and rejected it. I was always skeptical about this, and it may not be true ; but it rests on the authority of a letter from Allen himself, quoted by Badeau in his "Military History."

been out-marched and out-bragged by General Braxton Bragg, who had already reached Chattanooga. Grant had comparatively few troops, and was held so insignificant at the time, that he was troubled with few orders. The magnificent march on the peninsula of Virginia had been turned into the magnificent raid of Lee into Maryland; both of them, in the end, of little importance. Van Dorn and Price, however, felt that in such an active state of society they ought to take some part. Accordingly, Van Dorn commenced a movement to the east of Grant, either with a view of crossing the Tennessee, or of making some ulterior operation to the east. This move was made by the division under Price, who, on the 13th of September, advanced from the South and seized Iuka, a point on the Memphis and Charleston Railroad, and twenty-one miles east of Corinth. On the 15th, Grant telegraphed Halleck: "If I can, I will attack Price before he crosses Bear Creek. If he can be beaten there, it will prevent the design either to go north, or to unite forces and attack here." He had been collecting his forces, and when the enemy struck Iuka, cutting the railroad and telegraph wires between them and Corinth, Grant began operations. Van Dorn was far to the south-west, threatening Corinth, and he meant to divide them and destroy Price. Rosecrans, (who then commanded Pope's troops,) moved south of the railroad, to cut off the roads by which Price could retreat; and Ord, with a corps of eight thousand, was moved out on the railroad, (and a train of cars ready,) so that he could move up to help Rosecrans, or back to defend Corinth, (for Van

Dorn *might* attack Corinth.)   The arrangement was a good one ; but bad roads (as is often the case) delayed Rosecrans, so that he got up only in the afternoon instead of the morning.   The result was, the enemy were prepared, and attacked him.   There was a hard fight,[1] but the rebels, finding themselves likely to be cut off, retreated on the only road left.   The rebels were foiled entirely in their plans, and escaped destruction only by treachery.[2]   The rebels were foiled, but not crippled.   Price moved back and joined Van Dorn, and the same old game of annoyance to Grant was continued.

It seems, from what followed, and the new rebel officers who appeared on the scene, that the enemy was largely reënforced, probably from Arkansas and Louisiana.   They had over thirty thousand men, (Rosecrans said thirty-eight thousand,) and were bent on striking a blow.   The object was soon perceived to be Corinth.   About this time, Grant telegraphed to Washington : "My position is precarious, but I hope to get out of it all right."   Rosecrans then com-

---

[1] "HEAD-QUARTERS ARMY OF THE MISSISSIPPI, TWO MILES SOUTH OF IUKA, *September* 19, 1862—10 1-2, P. M.

"MAJOR-GENERAL U. S. GRANT:

"*General*—We met the enemy in force just above this point. The engagement lasted several hours. We have lost two or three pieces of artillery. Firing was very heavy. You must attack in the morning and in force. The ground is horrid, unknown to us, and no room for development. Could n't use our artillery at all ; fired but few shots. Push in on them till we can have time to do something. We will try to get a position on our right which will take Iuka.

"W. S. ROSECRANS, *Brigadier-General.*"

[2] Badeau says, that Colonel Thompson, a Confederate officer, told General Ord, that a Dr. Burton had passed himself on Rosecrans as a Union spy, and then returned to Price, and gave him the information he required.

manded at Corinth,[1] and Grant immediately directed him to call in his troops, and ordered McPherson, with a brigade, to his support. On the 2d of October, Van Dorn, with the Confederate Generals Price, Lovell, Villipigue, and Rust, appeared in front of Corinth, to fight again for Northern Mississippi. A month before, as I have said, Grant had been fortifying, as far as he could, Corinth, Jackson, and Bolivar, and we now see the end gained by it. Rosecrans, having about nineteen thousand men, had pushed out to see whether he could not be the one to attack ; but he was mistaken in that, for, on the afternoon of the 3d of October, Van Dorn attacked, and drove him back to the town. New dispositions were made, and the line of our forts was far stronger than the enemy supposed. General Van Dorn, having driven our forces, telegraphed to Richmond a great victory! In the art of prophetic telegraphing, the rebel Generals seem to have had a remarkable faculty. Most probably they thought every battle must be a Bull Run. Never were they more disastrously disappointed than now. We had inner works,[2] with strong forts. There was Fort Robinette on the left, and Battery William, and Battery Powell.

On the 4th of October a great battle was fought. The rebel lines were closed within a thousand yards

---

[1] Rosecrans had arrived at Corinth, from Iuka, on the 26th.

[2] Coppee says : " Immediately upon General Halleck's departure for Washington, these works were pushed forward with energy, and by the 25th of September, when Rosecrans took command, they were nearly completed. To Major Prime, under General Grant's orders, belongs the credit of laying out and constructing the fortifications against which the enemy was now about to hurl his masses, with impetuous but unavailing valor."

of our works, and during the night they had thrown up some batteries in our front. In the morning they began with an artillery fire, which was soon silenced; then, at half-past nine, A. M., they stormed the right, at Battery Powell, where Generals T. A. Davies and Hamilton were posted. Here they made some impression, but the fight was terrific. The account of it is thus given by Professor Coppée:

"The battle raged upon Davies and Fort Powell. The Bolivar road, by which they came, was swept by our guns; huge gaps were made in their column, but, without halting, they opened out in a loose deployment, encircling our lines, and losing fearfully as they came up. Nothing stopped them. 'They came up,' (writes an eye-witness to the 'Cincinnati Commercial,' October 9th,) 'with their faces averted, like men striving to protect themselves against a driving storm of hail.' They reach the broad glacis; our troops are on the rude covered way, and will certainly repel them, were it not for an unaccountable panic which struck a portion of Davies's Division. This will never do. Davies struggles manfully to check it. Rosecrans flies into their midst, fights like a simple grenadier, and, with entreaties, threats, and the flat of his saber, puts an end to the 'untimely and untoward stampede,' which was but partial after all."

Davies's men rally. Sullivan comes to his aid; they retake Battery Powell, (into which a few of the enemy had got,) and Hamilton sweeps the avenues of approach. Price has lost the fight, and on his side it is over.

On our left, (the enemy's right,) says Coppée,

"the attack was conducted by Van Dorn in person. Under cover of a cloud of skirmishers he had formed his men in column of attack, and twenty minutes after Price moved forward he launched four columns upon Battery Robinette and our adjacent lines. His heavy guns are disposed in rear. Then began those 'gorgeous pyrotechnics of the battle,' spoken of by General Rosecrans, the description of which he leaves to 'pens dipped in poetic ink.' The fighting was indeed Homeric. From the moment they came in sight, till they were within fifty yards of the work, they were mowed, and torn, and shattered by grape, shell, and canister; and when, after a gallant advance, these brave Mississippi and Texas troops pause for a breathing space, before a final charge, the Ohio and Missouri regiments, which have been lying flat, rise at a signal, and pour in a volley, before which the enemy reel and fall back in horror. But even this does not keep them long dismayed. They came to take Corinth, and they are not going to give it up so easily."

Again and again the rebel columns charged, and again and again were routed. At length they gave way and retired. They had lost the battle; a battle to them at least of immense importance; for, had they succeeded, we should have lost all we had gained by the battle of Shiloh. But their star in the West had sunk, and sunk darkly on their fortunes. They never did regain any thing which they lost at Donelson and Shiloh. Raids, from Bragg's down to Morgan's, they did make; but never again did they win back the great battle-field of the West. The sun of victory continued to shine gloriously on Grant, and he won in the West more than enough to counter-balance the failure on the Potomac. The rebels, in addition to their defeat, lost heavily,[1] and were glad, by a rapid retreat, to save themselves from destruction.[2]

Rosecrans well deserved all the applause which followed him for this battle, which, *as* a battle, was fought by him; but Grant had directed the movement and combination of forces which resulted in victory. After the end he issued an Order, of which the following is a paragraph:

"It is with heart-felt gratitude the General commanding congratulates the armies of the West for another great victory won by them on the 3d, 4th, and 5th instant, over the combined armies of Van Dorn, Price, and Lovell.

"The enemy chose his own time and place of attack, and knowing the troops of the West as he does,

---

[1] I see no rebel account of losses, and it is said our Government has no detailed account of the battle, but Rosecrans made a full Report, from which I take the following account of rebel loss:

"The enemy's loss in killed was 1,423 officers and men; their loss in wounded, taking the general average, amounts to 5,692. We took 2,248 prisoners, among whom are one hundred and thirty-seven field officers, captains, and subalterns, representing fifty-three regiments of infantry, sixteen regiments of cavalry, thirteen batteries of artillery, and seven battalions, making sixty-nine regiments, six battalions, and thirteen batteries, besides separate companies.

"We took also fourteen stands of colors, two pieces of artillery, 3,300 stand of arms, 4,500 rounds of ammunition, and a large lot of accouterments. The enemy blew up several wagons between Corinth and Chewalla, and beyond Chewalla many ammunition wagons and carriages were destroyed, and the ground was strewn with tents, officers' mess-chests, and small arms. We pursued them forty miles in force and sixty miles with cavalry."

[2] A letter in the "Grenada Appeal," in the Rebellion Record, Vol. V, page 505, praises their Generals for making their escape on the Hatchie.

and with great facilities for knowing their numbers, never would have made the attempt, except with a superior force numerically. *But for the undaunted bravery of officers and soldiers, who have yet to learn defeat*, the efforts of the enemy must have proven successful."[1]

Badeau, in his "Military History," intimates that Grant was dissatisfied with Rosecrans, and that the latter was not quick to obey. This is zeal without discretion. There was no officer of the army whose military career will bear criticism better than that of Rosecrans, and probably not a General in command during the war who was more competent to his place. Grant made no complaint of Rosecrans, and his military character needs no support from the glossing of prejudice or partiality. Since the departure of Halleck, Grant had been left free to pursue his own judgment, and though compelled by the reduction of his forces to keep on the defensive, we see that his defensive was in reality offensive by becoming victory. After the second Corinth, Grant combined the divisions of Ord, Hurlbut, and Rosecrans, in pursuit of the enemy, so that Price barely escaped in crossing the Hatchie. When, however, the forces of the enemy had got beyond the Hatchie, Grant recalled his divisions, and for a few weeks there was comparative quiet.

On the 8th of October, Lincoln congratulated Grant, in a dispatch, and asked, "*How does it all sum up?*"[2] Certainly, this is a very pertinent question.

[1] Grant's Order, October 2d.
[2] Rebellion Record, Vol. V, page 500.

The sum of those operations was twofold. First, we *secured* what we had got, by Shiloh and the first Corinth. We maintained North Mississippi, and opened the way to Vicksburg. I said, that as each line of rebel defense was broken, it was never regained, nor even passed, except by mere raids. But, suppose the battle of Corinth had been lost, what then? Why, we should have inevitably lost the whole ground we had got after the battle of Shiloh. Grant directed all the *movements* by which we were successful; but, suppose a less skillful and less determined commander than Rosecrans had fought that battle, defeat would have been very possible, and the results might have been very different.[1] But the enemy was defeated and driven back, with another effect, not less important. This was the *moral effect.* Throughout the war this was of the greatest importance. The war was largely the result of a conflict of moral ideas. I have stated how profoundly impressed the rebel mind was with the fighting of our soldiers at Shiloh. It was scarcely less impressed with the fighting at Iuka and Corinth. The rebel generals were inferior in capacity; their loss very great, and their shattered forces retreated, with a salutary conviction that Western men were brave, daring, and enduring.

We have a month before us now in which to look round and consider our condition. The armies came

---

[1] A very fine account of the battle of Corinth was given at the time, by Mr. Bickham, correspondent of the "Cincinnati Commercial," now editor of the "Dayton Journal," who gives the whole credit to Rosecrans. Badeau gives it all to Grant. The *battle* of Corinth was due to Rosecrans, and the general *movement* to Grant.

from the people; and as the rivers can not live without springs, so the armies were continually recruited and refreshed from the people. I have described how, when Sumpter was fired on, the American women asked, "What shall we do?" how the Sanitary Commission was formed; and how, when the Cumberland ran with the blood of Donelson, the Sanitary Commission of Cincinnati flew, with healing on its wings, to comfort the weary and the wounded soldiers. The guns of Shiloh had scarcely ceased their roar, when the Sanitary Commission entered the field. The Commission at Cincinnati chartered the Tycoon and the Monarch, two large vessels, furnished them with volunteer physicians and nurses, supplied them with all the necessaries, comforts, and delicacies which suffering men might need, and proceeded at once to the scene of action.[1] To this work General Halleck gave his full authority,[2] and requested boats to be sent, and Camp Dennison to be fitted up for the wounded. The Tycoon, the first boat, left Cincinnati with fifteen surgeons, twenty-four medical students, thirty-eight citizen nurses, and two druggists. She was fitted with every thing the body of man could need, contributed in a few hours by the citizens of Cincinnati. As she passed down the river, the *moral victory* of Donelson and Shiloh was everywhere evident. A gentleman, who had been down the river the year before, remarked that there was a great change. Then, both sides of the Ohio seemed to show the signs of disloyalty. The flag of the

---

[1] Mansfield's "History of the Cincinnati Sanitary Commission."
[2] Halleck's Dispatch, 10th of April, 1862.

Union was seldom seen,[1] and the people were declaiming against the Government. Now the scene was changed. As the boat descended the river, on her mission of patriotic charity, she was constantly greeted with the waving of flags and handkerchiefs from either shore. On the 17th the "Tycoon" returned, loaded with wounded soldiers. On the Commission went in its noble work. The people spared no offerings. The Commission spared no labor or zeal. How many of the wounded and the suffering must have owed their lives to this noble work of the Christian patriot!

As the army still pursued its course to the South, the Sanitary Commission was more needed, and more zealously put forth its energies. In the summer of 1862 the Cincinnati Commission put forth an appeal to the women.

"Women of the North-West! Your husbands, brothers, sons, your and our dearest, are, or soon will be, in the field. If one of them, by any want of effort, suffers, it will be your and our irremediable fault. The business of the men of the country is now war. Let it be also the business of her women. The former are to march, toil, and fight; let the latter work with equal energy and patriotism in their own sphere, and labor for the common good. Then will the march be bereft of half its fatigue, the battle of more than half its danger, and the blessings of generations to come shall rest upon you."

Such was the ardent appeal of the Commission

---

[1] A lady in Kentucky told me, that for three miles on one side of her home, and eight on the other, there was not a loyal man! This shows what Kentucky neutrality was worth.

to the women of the West, and most nobly did they respond! Hundreds of villages, scattered over the North-West, heard and answered that appeal. Aid societies of every kind were formed. Church circles met and sewed garments for the soldiers, with all the zeal which they would have put forth in the holy cause of missions. Daily the contributions came in from every quarter of the land; daily the Commission met, and sent forth its charities; daily the wounded and sick returned from the far-distant battle-fields; daily they were put in hospitals and camps, and often did the delicate lady and the young girl volunteer to watch by the soldier's side, and nurse his sick form and beguile his weary hours. It seems to me, as I look back upon the scenes of that war, that nothing in it was more beautiful or glorious than this work of Christian charity. Shall we despair of the Republic, when patriotism nerves to such heroism, and Christianity impels to such noble benevolence? It was not merely Republicanism, it was Christianity, whose strength was illustrated by that war. The Republic stands not only on the strength of the people, but on the strength of Christianity. If it did not, we might well despair; but, with it, the gates of hell shall not prevail against it. The Christian at home thought of the soldier in the field:

> "No base ambitions quickened these;
> They saw but Freedom's need;
> No dreams of flow'ry paths of ease,
> No bribe but valor's meed;
> And some shall win the hero's grave,
> The battle-smoke their pall;
> But honor dwells where fall the brave,
> And God is over all!"

CHAPTER VII.

VICKSBURG.

AFTER the battles terminating with the 6th of
October, Grant felt a strong desire to advance,
and if possible seize Vicksburg, by a land route. But
this seems to have been subsequent to the determination of Mr. Lincoln to proceed immediately with the
Mississippi campaign. This appears from the following "*confidential*" Order, issued by Mr. Lincoln, and
dated October 21, 1862:

"ORDERED, that Major-General McClernand be, and he is directed
to proceed to the States of Indiana, Illinois, and Iowa, to organize
the troops remaining in those States and to be raised by volunteering
or draft, and forward them with all dispatch to Memphis, Cairo, or
such other points as may hereafter be designated by the General-in-
Chief, to the end that, when a sufficient force, not required by the
operations of General Grant's command, shall be raised, an expedition may be organized under General McClernand's command, against

Vicksburg, and to clear the Mississippi River and open navigation to New Orleans."

Indorsement: "This order, though marked 'confidential,' may be shown by General McClernand to governors, and even others, when, in his discretion, he believes so doing to be indispensable to the progress of the expedition. I add, that I feel deep interest in the success of the expedition, and desire it to be pushed forward with all possible dispatch, consistently with the other parts of the military service.   A. LINCOLN."

This Order[1] evidently aims at an expedition down the river, and independent of Grant's command. The result proved, that, as an independent expedition, it was ill-advised, and, we shall see, by Grant's subsequent movements, that an independent land expedition was equally so.

On the 26th of October, Grant wrote to Halleck, making the bold proposition to abandon Corinth and the inferior posts about it—destroy all the railroads leading to and from Corinth—and (said he) "with small reënforcements at Memphis, I would be able to move down the Mississippi Central Road, and cause the evacuation of Vicksburg. I am ready, however, to do with my might whatever you may direct, without criticism." Grant was a little mistaken in this plan; but the close of this letter shows one of his greatest virtues—his perfect willingness to do what he was directed to do, without jealousy, and without criticism. Grant assumed nothing. He was not vain enough to believe he was the only man of sense in the world, and he had none of that impulsive, or rather thoughtless, spirit, which took fire at some small or imaginary slight. He was above all

---

[1] I am indebted to Badeau's "Military History" for this Order, which I have not found elsewhere.

such weakness. Mere vanity, self-importance, and jealousy cost some of the really able generals of the war their places and their means of usefulness. Whether it was temperament or self-command, Grant gained by a want of these weaknesses, and hence was perfectly willing to follow Halleck's plan, if his own was rejected. Halleck, however, before receiving Grant's letter, had coolly telegraphed him, " Be prepared to concentrate your troops in case of attack." The commanding General at Washington was always prepared to resist attacks. In the mean while, Grant had been exercising his administrative ability to great advantage. He limited the number and kinds of trains, baggage, etc., cutting down *impedimenta* to the smallest amount ; and, it has been humorously said, reducing his own baggage to a—*tooth-brush !* There is no question that almost all armies carry too much baggage ; and, as I have read the accounts of the comfortable provisions, and even luxuries, in the tents of some of our officers, I have felt that a commanding general, who knew his duty and the true science of war, would suffer no such things. A republican army should be a Spartan army, filled with the fire of patriotism, and willing to endure all hardships for love of country. Grant had divided his army into four corps : the first, under Major-General Sherman, had its head-quarters at Memphis ; the second, Major-General Hurlbut, at Jackson ; the third, under Brigadier-General C. S. Hamilton, at Corinth ; and the fourth, General T. A. Davies, at Columbus. On the 2d of November, Grant, having received no orders to the contrary, moved with three divisions

from Corinth and two from Bolivar, writing this to
Halleck. Halleck approved of his advance, but did
not authorize the abandonment of the position;
so Grant moved with three divisions. His army
amounted to about thirty thousand men, McPherson
commanding the right wing, and C. S. Hamilton the
left. He knew the enemy was about equal to him,
but felt perfectly confident.[1] In a few days he had
made a rapid and successful advance. On the 4th
he occupied La Grange, (near Grand Junction,) on
the Memphis and Charleston Railroad; and on the
13th Colonel Lee, Chief of Cavalry, took possession
of Holly Springs, (Miss.) ; and on the morning of the
29th Grant passed that place with the main body.
In the mean time the cavalry were far in advance,
keeping up a constant skirmishing. Holly Springs is
about twenty-five miles from Grand Junction, and in
the richest part of Mississippi. In the next five or
six days several skirmishes took place, and, on the
17th of December, Grant had his head-quarters at
Oxford, Mississippi, about twenty-five miles in advance
of Holly Springs and fifty miles from Grand Junction. The cavalry had penetrated to Coffeeville.
This was the situation of Grant on the 18th of December, and, leaving him there, we must return and
try to find out what he had planned, and what this
campaign means. I have already stated that the war
could only end by a campaign carried on *from the
West.* Hence the Mississippi River was the *axis* on
which the war turned; and when we fully possessed

---

[1] He wrote Sherman that the enemy was thirty thousand, and he
could handle him without gloves.—*Badeau.*

the Mississippi, it was the *grand base* from which our columns poured east, cutting off resources and lines of communication as we went. In the progress of the campaign on the Mississippi we had taken New Orleans, (April, 1862,) and previously Columbus, Island No. 10, and Memphis, driving the rebels from both their first and their second line of defense, resting on the Mississippi ; and now, their third and only line from the Mississippi rested on Vicksburg ; and below that, they held Port Hudson, making a reach on the Mississippi, which they had perfect command of, and which was of vast importance to them. Nothing they had was of more importance. Through that they brought their beef cattle from Texas, the only portion of the Confederacy which had a surplus ; through that they kept communication with the important States of Arkansas and Texas, receiving reenforcements of men and provisions. The Trans-Mississippi (except Missouri) was of no consequence to us, (and the Banks raid up Red River was an absurd expedition,) but of the greatest consequence to them. Hence, about the time that Grant was getting up his combined attack on Vicksburg, (that is, his first one, of which we are now speaking,) the rebels clearly foresaw the absolute necessity of holding Vicksburg and Port Hudson. They accordingly fortified them in the strongest manner. We have the testimony of Jefferson Davis precisely to this point. In his speech before the Legislature of Mississippi, on December 26, 1862,[1] he says : " Vicksburg and Port Hudson are the real points of attack. Every

[1] See " Rebellion Record," Vol. VI, page 297.

effort will be made to capture those places, with the view of forcing the navigation of the Mississippi, of cutting off our communications with the Trans-Mississippi Department, and of severing the Western from the Eastern portion of the Confederacy." He dwelt largely upon the defenses of Vicksburg. After stating the failure of the attack by the fleet, (which had been made some time before,) he says, "a few earth-works were thrown up, a few guns were mounted," and Vicksburg received the shock of both fleets. The important point made, and which must be remembered in considering the movement now going on, is this : " Now, we are far better prepared in that quarter. *The works, then weak, have been greatly strengthened ; the troops assigned for their defense are better disciplined, and better instructed ; and that great soldier who came with me has been pouring in his forces to assist in its protection."* Who was this great soldier ? This was Joseph E. Johnston. Davis says he brought him with him. Pemberton had been in command ; but, as early certainly as the 26th of December, Johnston took command of the Department, and Pemberton of the particular forces at Vicksburg.

This being the situation of the rebels, and the condition of their defenses, let me ask, What was Grant's plan ? It seems, from numbers of letters and dispatches,' that Grant wanted to move forward by land in connection with the river expedition, which, as we have seen by Lincoln's order, had been previously directed. This was fully assented to by Halleck, who firmly supported Grant at this time,

---

' These are quoted in Badeau's " Military History."

and fully approved by General Sherman, who was to take part in it. Accordingly, the plan agreed upon was this : Grant was to move down by Holly Springs and Oxford to Grenada, there to hold Pemberton in check, while Sherman was to descend the Mississippi and attack Vicksburg. At the same time a force under General Washburn was to land at Delta (Yazoo Pass) and strike for Grenada, with a view of cutting Pemberton's communication. Sherman stated the case thus :[1] "Grant moved direct on Pemberton, while I moved from Memphis, and a smaller force under General Washburn struck directly for Grenada ; and the first thing Pemberton knew the depot of his supplies was almost in the grasp of a small cavalry force, and he fell back in confusion, and gave us the Tallahatchie without a battle."

It would have been better if Pemberton had not been scared back. It was Grant's idea to fight, and, if possible, to destroy the enemy's armies ; but Pemberton's retreat gave no opportunity to fight, while the prolongation of Grant's line did give opportunity, as we shall presently see, for a very different feat on the part of the enemy. This combined movement on the part of Grant, Sherman, and Washburn has been called by a military critic a very brilliant piece of strategy.[2] Whatever it might have been in theory, it was disastrous in fact. Besides, it had one essential defect. To move an army parallel with the Mississippi without supports on it, could only be done with overwhelming forces, able to garrison and

---

[1] Sherman's speech at St. Louis.
[2] See criticism in Coppée's "Grant and his Campaigns."

hold each depot beyond the power of assault. Grant's forces were not large enough for this. This might easily have been done and Vicksburg captured, in my opinion, if Halleck had pushed promptly on from Corinth. The defenses of Vicksburg were then weak, and it would have inevitably fallen. But the time for this was now passed.

This combined movement being planned, let us now see what actually happened. On the night of the 18th of December the telegraph wires in the rear of Grant were cut at several points, and on the 20th Van Dorn, who had moved round Grant's army in a well-devised and well-executed raid, captured Holly Springs, with Grant's main depot of supplies, and millions of dollars in property. It is true, this attack at Holly Springs might have been resisted, and that the place was unnecessarily and disgracefully surrendered. But, whether taken or not, the plan of Grant's expedition had this essential fault, that it was prolonging a land line without water supports, which was at any time liable to this very misfortune. Here, I must remark, that this was Grant's only failure,[1] and there is no great military commander who has been without failures. General Sherman embarked at Memphis, on a hundred transports, with thirty thousand men, on the same day, (20th of December,) and at Helena was reënforced with twelve thousand more, making an army of forty-two thou-

---

[1] Trenton and Humboldt were entered and captured by the rebel forces on the same day by Forrest, showing that it was not merely the capture of Holly Springs which made the difficulty; it was that the communications *could* be cut at any time.

sand men. For one week Grant's communications with the Mississippi were entirely cut off, and Sherman heard nothing of him, so that this grand river expedition was entirely independent of any support from Grant, and, in fact, needed none. On the 24th Sherman reached Milliken's Bend, and on the 26th successfully disembarked near the mouth of Yazoo River. Vicksburg lies on a bluff, which is part of a long line of bluffs and hills, nearly three hundred feet in hight, and touching the Yazoo at Haines's Bluff, which was strongly fortified, and from which down the fortifications extended. These fortifications Sherman attacked on the 27th with four divisions, and utterly failed. He lost heavily,[1] and the enemy but little, and on the 30th raised the siege, (if an assault can be called a siege,) reëmbarked, and sailed out of the Yazoo. This was the end of the grand land and water combined attack on Vicksburg. Grant had all his communications cut, his main depot of supplies destroyed, and, for one week, was isolated. On the 23d he was back at Holly Springs. Sherman sailed the very day Grant's communications were destroyed, was defeated at Vicksburg, and on the 30th was back again. Sherman very naively says that his failure was owing " to the strength of the enemy's position, both natural and artificial." Very probable! Vicksburg was strong naturally, but what made it so strong artificially? I have already quoted (page 167) Davis's statement, in his speech to the Legislature, made on the 26th of December, that, after the fall

---

[1] He lost 175 killed, 930 wounded, and 743 missing, making 1,848, being eightfold the loss of the enemy.

of Corinth, Vicksburg had been strongly fortified, and that J. E. Johnston had been put in command. The time had passed when Vicksburg was to be taken by a *coup de main*. The truth is very simple, and now evident to all, that the long delays of Halleck after Corinth, and his subsequent division of the army for fear of Bragg's movement, (which actually took place,) were the cause of losing the golden opportunity of capturing Vicksburg in July or August.

In the mean time Grant had learned a very important fact, (which was afterward successfully applied by Sherman,) that our army *could subsist itself in the South.* For a week Grant had to get his supplies as he could from the country. The enemy were rejoicing that he would have to starve or retreat ; but he soon informed them, to their astonishment, that he should live on *their* provisions. These he found were more than enough ; and he found out that when there was need of it, *the army could subsist in the enemy's country without depots;* for at that time Mississippi, and indeed all the South, was rich in food.

On the 4th of January, 1863,[1] McClernand assumed the command of the whole Mississippi expedition. To understand this it is only necessary to read Lincoln's Order, at the head of this chapter, which McClernand claimed, and Lincoln subsequently admitted and indorsed, gave him the command of the Mississippi expedition. It has been said that Sherman hurried the expedition off out of jealousy of McClernand. It was hurried off to get rid of McClernand, but for a very different reason. The fact was, that neither

[1] Sherman's Order, January 4th. Rebellion Record, Vol. VI, p. 317.

Halleck, Grant, Sherman, nor the officers generally, had any confidence in McClernand's military abilities.[1] Lincoln had given him the command, against the advice of all the regular officers, for McClernand had been a friend, and I believe partner, of Lincoln's in Illinois. At any rate, here is McClernand at Milliken's Bend, in command. What next is to be done? One good thing McClernand did immediately. Up the Arkansas was Fort Hindman, or, as generally called, "Arkansas Post." This was of very little military consequence, but had, at that time, a large body of the enemy's forces, and considerable artillery. Against this post McClernand immediately moved his forces, by White River and a cut-off, into the Arkansas. The fort, artillery, and thousands of prisoners were taken. It was a fair set-off against the failure at Vicksburg, and answered the purpose of inspiriting the people, who, at that time, were discouraged by several reverses.[2]

On the 10th of January, 1863, Grant established his head-quarters at Memphis, writing to McClernand that he had heard nothing from the expedition since Sherman left, and adding, that "if there is force enough within the limits of my control to secure a certain victory at Vicksburg, they will be sent there."

On the 17th of January Grant paid a visit to the transport fleet lying at Napoleon, and there he seems to have intimated his first conviction of the plan,

[1] A full statement of this affair is given in Badeau's "Military History," pages 128–130, and it is fully sustained by the letters, telegrams, orders, etc., at the time.

[2] See General McClernand's Report, dated January 20, 1863. Rebellion Record, Vol. VI, page 360.

which, after various trials, was at last fully successful. He wrote to Halleck: "*Our troops must get below the city to be used effectually.*" After his return from Napoleon, he wrote, on the 20th, that "the work of reducing Vicksburg *will take time and men, but can be accomplished.*" Here, then, Grant seems to have arrived at a full comprehension of the nature of the problem, and of the means of solving it. He was to get *below* Vicksburg, and then cut off its supplies, and invest it from the interior. But the problem for the time seemed literally impossible. Not only Vicksburg and its bluff, but from Haines's Bluff, on the ridge of hills some twelve miles above, to Warrenton, six miles below, was almost a continued line of batteries, so that it did not seem possible to get supplies, with provisions and munitions, to say nothing of troops, below. Then, as for going round, while the whole country was intersected with rivers, bayous, swamps, and the low grounds overflowed at high water, *that* seemed impracticable. The problem was a hard one; and we shall soon see that Grant had his own ideas on the subject, and was not much indebted to any plans at Washington.

Grant now commenced operations. He ordered the whole army lying at Napoleon to Young's Point, where they arrived on the 21st. Young's Point is on the western side of the Mississippi, about nine miles above Vicksburg, and nearly opposite the mouth of the Yazoo. Grant's own army was moved to Memphis, and embarked on one hundred and twenty-five transports. These were the veteran soldiers of the West. To the vast army now concentrating at

Young's Point was added a large number of gunboats—the Chillicothe, Indianola, Lafayette, Eastport, and a number of others, many of them ironclads, formed a most formidable river navy. Soon this vast armament was assembled. On the 29th Grant himself arrived, and on the 30th assumed command. The old difficulty with McClernand remained, but was soon settled. Grant was commander of the Department, and, therefore, had a right to command. But he and Halleck, who was now supporting Grant most effectually, at last prevailed with Lincoln, and Grant received authority to put whomsoever he pleased in command. Accordingly Grant issued a General Order, which put McClernand in command of the Thirteenth Army Corps. McClernand inquired if it was the intention of that Order to limit his command to that Corps? To which Grant emphatically replied it was.[1] So that matter was settled; but Grant wrote to Halleck he was not ambitious of the command, and with the same discreet prudence he had heretofore displayed, said he was willing to do all he could *in any position assigned him;*[2] but he determined to go with the expedition himself.

Grant saw that the long line of fortifications in front, at, and around Vicksburg, could not be assaulted with success, and, therefore, the problem was, how to *get below.* Here we must remember that Port Hudson below shut up the river there, else Banks and his army, which, in the mean time, were to coöperate

---

[1] McClernand's letters of January 30th and February 1st, and Grant's, January 31st.

[2] Grant's Letter to Halleck, February 1, 1863.

with Grant, (but which never did,) might have come up and helped. But Banks and his flotilla were completely cut off, and the problem for Grant was, not to join Banks below Port Hudson—that would do no good—but to get on the Mississippi, between Vicksburg and Port Hudson, so that he could be fed there long enough to invest Vicksburg and complete his communications. It did not, as we shall see, make much difference as to the particular point, provided it was low enough to flank the Vicksburg outworks. But how to get below, *that* is the question. Grant's first idea, as a possibility, was a *cut-off* of the peninsula in front of Vicksburg, or, an approach by a succession · of water-courses from Yazoo Pass ; in one word, some water communication, by which he could transport his men and stores. On the 22d he wrote to McClernand, " I hope the work of changing the channel of the Mississippi is begun ;" and also, " On the present rise it is barely possible that the Yazoo Pass might be turned to good account in aiding our enterprise."[1] This was his first thought ; but it does not seem ever to have impressed his mind with any conviction of success. Indeed, for three months, the army and the public were amused with a succession of efforts to make canals and cut-offs on the Mississippi. I shall not trace out these various operations, which are really interesting only to the engineers and soldiers employed on them. The first was "Williams's Canal," which had been begun before Grant went there. The river, several miles above Vicksburg, turned nearly north-east, and run in that

---

[1] Badeau's "Military History," page 154.

direction till it struck the Vicksburg Bluffs, and, seemingly turned by them, ran in almost a contrary direction ; so that nearly opposite Vicksburg was a long, narrow peninsula, at the narrowest part of which it was only necessary to dig a canal about a mile long to make a new channel for the Mississippi, (provided it was willing to go there,) which would leave Vicksburg high and dry. The work progressed very well till, all at once, the river objected to this proceeding, carried off the lower end or mouth of the canal, and came near flooding out the soldiers, who escaped in great haste. Grant said the canal had the small difficulty of being perpendicular at both ends to the river, which, of course, had no idea of going into it. So ended that scheme, which the rebels laughed at, and Grant cared but little about.

The next fancy with projectors of internal navigation in the army was the Lake Providence route. The lake was seventy miles to the north of Vicksburg, and but one mile from the Mississippi ; that mile was cut through, and if we could have employed a year upon it, we should probably have got through Red River to a point near Port Hudson ; but the Bayous Bertie and Macon, which made the communication, were filled with timber, and overflowed into swamps, and, in one word, no steamboats went through. But it was a fine field of enterprise for the ingenuity of engineers and speculators in rich lands.

The next scheme was Yazoo Pass, which is far above Vicksburg, but which goes into Moon Lake, and from that into Coldwater River, and thence into the Tallahatchie River, which is one branch of the

Yazoo. This made an actual opening to the Yazoo above Vicksburg, and was navigable. Here was something which was tangible and possible. Grant did hope something from this route. The enemy were building gun-boats on the Tallahatchie, and it was very desirable to destroy them. He hoped to get the gun-boats through and down the Tallahatchie so as to coöperate with a land force in attacking Haines's Bluff. Accordingly, a division of troops, under General Ross, embarked on twenty-two transports, preceded by two gun-boats, and accompanied by a squadron of light craft. By working away at the outlet, and removing obstructions, they got into the Yazoo Inlet; but when there, the difficulties encountered were almost incredible. The Pass was in most places not more than a hundred feet wide; the trees met across it; fallen timbers were in the way; the channel turned and twisted in every direction. The enemy put all possible obstructions in front, and when the fleet passed, renewed them behind, so that the passage was a continual struggle of labor and skill, and not of fighting. Nevertheless, the expedition got through, and finally emerged into the Coldwater, and from the Coldwater into the Tallahatchie. In the mean while a great deal of time was lost, of which the rebels availed themselves. In the Yazoo, just below the Tallahatchie, was Greenwood, and there the rebels had built Fort Pemberton, well-placed, armed, and fortified. Ross, with his troops and gun-boats, got there, made an assault, and failed completely. So they retired, and the Yazoo expedition was ended.

While this was going on Grant found another

pass. This was by Steele's Bayou, which, after going through a dozen bayous and rivers—in all only about a hundred and fifty miles—led finally to a point above Haines's Bluff, and consequently flanked both that and Greenwood. This was altogether the most promising of these wandering enterprises. Grant saw this, and went there reconnoitering himself. The greatest difficulty was the continual obstruction of the trees. He returned, and hurried up Porter with his flotilla and Sherman with a division of troops. They got into the bayou, and through half a dozen streams, till they actually got within a short distance of the Yazoo. But the rebels found out the course and object of the expedition, and made such preparations that Grant thought it prudent to abandon the plan.

Here we are, then, on the 23d of March, after having failed in several attempts at internal navigation for war purposes, at Milliken's Bend, just about as well off as when we began, six weeks before. The nation was impatient, and people wondered what Grant was about, and why he did not attempt some decisive blow. But Grant was not impatient. That was not in his nature; and now was the time for him to show that determined will and firmness of purpose which, with his calm temperament, made the chief elements of his character. The time was not lost, for who that knows the Mississippi expects that an army can move with facility on its banks in February and March? The troops, however, were used to labor, marches, and endurance. Luckily they kept in good health in what is generally an unhealthy region. So the grand army of Grant and the river fleet of Porter are now at Milliken's Bend; while there the spring is just opening out, and the ground will be soon available for the march and encampments of troops. Now we are ready, and soon we shall enter upon one of the most admirable and successful campaigns, not only of this war, but of any which modern history can exhibit.

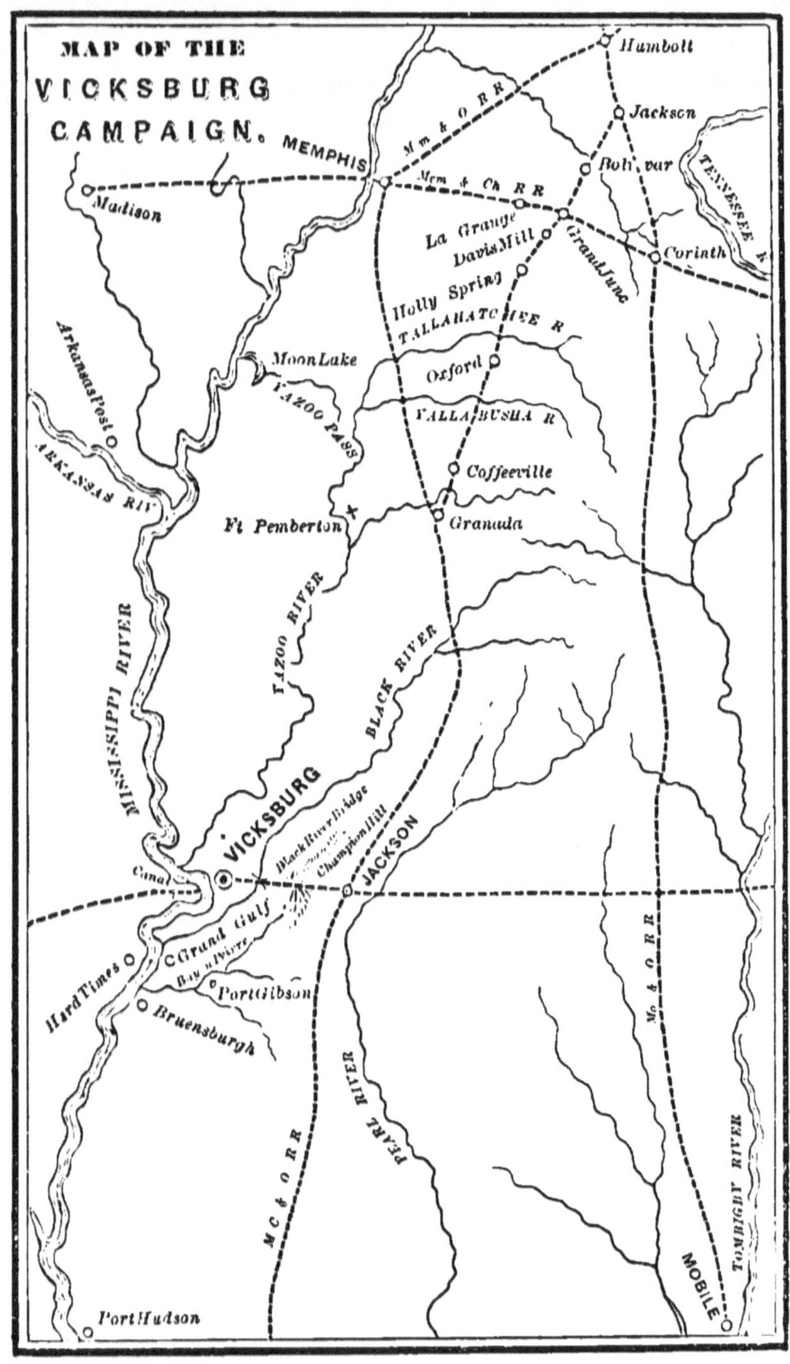

MAP OF THE
VICKSBURG
CAMPAIGN.
MEMPHIS
Humbolt
Jackson
Boli var
Mem & O RR
Mem & Ch RR
La Grange
Davis Mill
Grand Junc
Corinth
TENNESSEE R.
Madison
Holly Spring
TALLAHATCHEE R
Arkansas Post
Moon Lake
YAZOO PASS
Oxford
YALLA BUSHA R
ARKANSAS RIV
Coffeeville
Ft Pemberton
Granada
YAZOO RIVER
MISSISSIPPI RIVER
BLACK RIVER
VICKSBURG
Black River Bridge
Champion Hill
JACKSON
Canal
Grand Gulf
Bayou Pierre
Port Gibson
Mc & O RR
Hard Times
Bruensburgh
Mc & O RR
PEARL RIVER
TOMBIGBY RIVER
Port Hudson
MOBILE

CHAPTER VIII.

VICKSBURG.

THE GOVERNMENT HAS NO GENERAL PLAN—GRANT MAKES A PLAN FOR HIMSELF—ACTS CONTRARY TO THE ADVICE OF HIS GENERALS, AND TAKES THE RESPONSIBILITY—ARMY MOVES TO NEW CARTHAGE—MIDNIGHT PASSAGE OF THE GUN-BOATS—ARMY CROSSES THE MISSISSIPPI—BATTLE OF PORT GIBSON—FALL OF GRAND GULF—BATTLES OF RAYMOND, OF JACKSON, OF CHAMPION'S HILL, AND OF BIG BLACK—GRANT'S MILITARY GENIUS—REBEL ERRORS—VICKSBURG INVESTED—INEFFICIENCY OF JOHNSTON—SURRENDER OF VICKSBURG.

THE Government had planned a coöperative expedition, under Banks, to proceed up the Mississippi, capture Port Hudson, and unite with Grant in an investment of Vicksburg. This plan had two essential defects: one, that it divided our forces without any probable advantage ; and the other, that Port Hudson was in the way of the coöperation, which place Banks might not find easier to take than Grant did Vicksburg. This turned out to be the fact. Banks had forty thousand, with all of Farragut's fleet. On the 14th of March Farragut attacked the rebel batteries at Port Hudson, and after a terrible bombardment, of several hours' duration, was compelled to retire.[1] How was Banks to coöperate?

[1] "Rebellion Record," Vol. VI, page 55.

The fact was, that Banks, at a subsequent period, attacked Port Hudson and failed ; that place fell only as a sequel to the capture of Vicksburg. The Government, however, thought a good deal of this idea.

On the 2d of April, Halleck wrote to Grant, using these words : " What is most desired (and your attention is again called to this object) is, that your forces and those of General Banks should be brought into coöperation as early as possible. If he can not get up to coöperate with you on Vicksburg, can not you get troops down to help him at Port Hudson, or, at least, can you not destroy Grand Gulf before it becomes too strong ?"

If Grant had sent troops down to Banks, it would have been a clear loss of men and time. The rebels *had* fortified Port Hudson, and it could only be taken by investment, or, as actually happened, by the fall of Vicksburg. In all this time Grant had in his view only *the destruction of the enemy's forces.* After Shiloh, this became his one leading military idea. He found the enemy re-rallying after defeat, even when the strong strategic lines were broken, and, therefore, concluded that they would continue to rally, in such an extensive country, unless their armies were destroyed ; and this was the rebel idea also. Davis said they could defend themselves twenty years in Virginia. Grant's idea was correct, but he seems to me never to have fully understood *the necessity of a comprehensive strategy* to the execution and success of his own idea. Nor is he to be blamed for this ; for he was not Commander-in-Chief, and, strange as it may seem, *there is no evidence whatever that the*

Government had, up to this time, any general plan of conducting the war.[1] The attacks in the East and in the West were isolated. Different commanders had formed different plans; and Mr. Lincoln himself at one time took command. Then McClellan—then Halleck—and, long subsequent to this time, Grant. McClellan seems to have cast no eye beyond the mountains at all. Halleck, in command of the Western Department, had a plan; but, at Washington, seems to have had no general scheme of strategic operations. But we must return to Grant. Whatever ideas were revolving in his mind, it is plain he can only be held responsible for his department. The old problem, how to get behind or below Vicksburg, is still before him, and now it is to be solved.

On the 4th of April we have the germ, the initial, of the true idea of taking Vicksburg. On that day Grant wrote to Halleck: "The discipline and health of this army is now good, and I am satisfied the greatest confidence of success prevails." He thus described to Halleck the plan he now proposed:

"There is a system of bayous running from Milliken's Bend, also from near the river at this point, [Young's Point], that are navigable for large and small steamers, passing around by Richmond to New Carthage. There is also a good wagon-road from Milliken's Bend to New Carthage. The dredges are now engaged cutting a canal from here into these

---

[1] I have tried to find any general plan or system of strategy adopted by the Government in the first three years of the war, and am satisfied none existed. Particular generals claimed merit for particular plans, and controversies have arisen on this subject; but a general system of the war for the whole vast field of strategy did not exist.

bayous. I am having all the empty coal-boats and other barges prepared for carrying troops and artillery, and have written to Colonel Allen for some more, and also for six tugs to tow them. With them it would be easy to carry supplies to New Carthage, and any point south of that. My expectation is for some of the naval fleet to run the batteries of Vicksburg, while the army moves' through by this new route. Once there, I will move to Warrenton or Grand Gulf, probably the latter. From either of these points, there are good roads to Jackson and the Black River bridge, without crossing Black River. I will keep my army together, and see to it that I am not cut off from my supplies, or beat in any other way than a fair fight."[1]

There was one objection to this plan, which, however, I think more apparent than real. This was, that Grant would cut himself off from his supplies, and seemingly put himself where he would put the enemy. Colonel Badeau states, in his " Military History," that Sherman, McPherson, Logan, Wilson, and others, *opposed this plan*, and considered it a fatal error. Sherman said that the only way to take Vicksburg was from the north. " Then," said Grant, " that requires me to go back to Memphis." " Exactly so," said Sherman, " that is what I mean." Grant thought a retrograde movement would be disastrous to the country, which would not endure another reverse ; and he declared *he would take no step backward.* Sherman sent,

---

[1] This letter of Grant's is taken from Badeau's " Military History ;" but all these military letters, reports, and telegrams are in course of publication by the Government, but will not be out in time for this work.

through Colonel Rawlins, a written communication, urging him to take the line of the Yallabusha. Grant read it in silence,[1] but made no change of plan. Onward! was Grant's command. It has been said that Grant's successes were *accidents!*[2] Can any body inform me where the accident was here? Grant, with determined will—if you please, obstinacy—went on, in spite of the opinions and judgment of his military advisers. If he failed, it was ruinous; if he succeeded, no one can share the credit with him. But the fact is, Grant was right in every view of the case. It would not do to retrograde. Nor was there any great danger in the movement as to his supplies. He had learned (what Sherman afterward learned in Georgia) that the central portions of the South were full of food, and that, if necessary, he could support his army there. Then a rapid march would enable him to join Banks, if such a movement were desirable; and, finally, what was to prevent supplying his army by the route he came? In all aspects of the case he was right. But let those who talk of accidents remember that he made his grand move round Vicksburg against the opinion of such men as Sherman and McPherson.

On the 29th of March the grand march began. McClernand's Division took Richmond, a point below, and made a march of twenty-seven miles to New

[1] Badeau's "Military History."

[2] In an article in the "Southern Home Journal," recently, the notorious Pollard, who is no military authority, and speaks only rebel opinions, says that Grant has risen only by "accident." It is a most extraordinary series of accidents, which always run one way, and that, too, in opposition to the opinions and judgments of able men!

Carthage. But the last point was not occupied till the 6th of April. The country was in many places deluged, the levees were broken in places, and the road but a few inches out of water. Grant wrote: "The embarrassment I have had to contend against on account of extreme high water can not be appreciated by any one not present to witness it."

Bridges had to be built, round-about roads taken, and the distance marched by the army was doubled. Indeed, the labor, exposure, and difficulties of this route were almost incredible. At length McClernand's Division is safe at New Carthage. But of what use is this advance without transportation? The Mississippi is a mighty river; to cross in small bodies would be dangerous, for the enemy is strong. Porter's fleet and transports are above Vicksburg. What is to be done? Grant had solved the problem in his own mind, and told Halleck, "My expectation is, that some of the fleet will run the batteries of Vicksburg." Was that possible? Now we are to answer that question.

The night of the 16th of April was fixed upon for the enterprise. Seven gun-boats and four transports formed the squadron, under Commodore Porter, which was to pass under the fire of the tremendous batteries, and, if possible, reach New Carthage with supplies and means of transportation. Such enterprises had failed heretofore, and, to the minds of even sailors, the idea was surrounded with horrors. A call for volunteers was made, and what the fleet could not supply the army did, for in the army were pilots, engineers, and craftsmen of all descriptions. The fleet is manned; the transports are piled up with cotton on the sides; the gun-boats on the Vicksburg side are lined with chains, timbers, or whatever will resist the shock of balls. The gun-boats take the side of the batteries, and the transports hug the other shore. And now it is night, a dark night, for no moon shines above. The sun had set beautifully, and the stars came out; but the night deepened, and the boats are only seen as dark masses in the water.[1] All were anxious. Grant stood on the shore; Sherman was there. Officers and men were on board boats, gazing in almost breathless silence.[2] At eleven o'clock the Benton, with the gallant Porter on board, noiselessly goes into the dark waters. Another and another follow, and for a little time all is quiet; the enemy were unsuspicious. The boats pass on, and, stealing slowly along, are scarcely distinguishable from the foliage on the opposite bank. The crowd on our side of the river had been full of talk and noise; but now all is hushed. The boats are passing into the darkness of the opposite shore. "Will they get by?" and quick beats every heart.

"Three-quarters of an hour passed. People heard nothing save their own suppressed breathings; saw nothing save a long, low bank of darkness, which, like a black fog, walled the view below, and joined the sky and river in the direction of Vicksburg. And all watched this gathering of darkness, for in it were thunders, and lightnings, and volcanoes, which at any instant might light up the night with fierce

[1] Letter to "New York Tribune," dated April 17, 1863.
[2] Badeau's "Military History."

irruptions. So long a time passed without any thing occurring that people began to believe the enemy had determined, for some malevolent purpose, to allow the fleet to pass below without obstruction."

Ah, no! The rebels knew too well what was meant, and would have given half their hopes to have sunk that fleet. It is sixteen minutes past eleven, and the alarmed sentinel on Vicksburg bluff has seen the dark ships. In a moment the scene lights up, the sullen thunder of the first gun is heard, and crash after crash roars through the midnight air— and Porter joins in with a rapid and tremendous fire from the gun-boats. It is now past twelve, and they are just passing the little city, and the shot and shell are thick in the air.[1] It is dark, but the rebels set fire to houses and beacons, and the streets of Vicksburg can be seen. The Henry Clay (transport) is on fire, and soon sends up its lurid blaze. The boats are all struck, and one of the transports, disabled, floats down to Carthage.[2]

"The currents were strong, and dangerous eddies delayed the vessels ; the lights glaring in every direction, and the smoke enveloping the squadron, confused the pilots ; the bulwarks, even of the iron-clads, were crushed ; and the uproar of artillery, reëchoing from the hills, was incessant. One of the heaviest guns of the enemy was seen to burst in the streets of Vicksburg, and the whole population was awake and out of doors, watching the scene on which its destinies depended. For two hours and forty min-

[1] Grant was in the midst of the fire, anxiously looking on.
[2] The Forest Queen was disabled, and towed down by a gun-boat.

utes the fleets were under fire. But, at last, the transports and the gun-boats had all got out of range, the blazing beacons on the hills and on the stream burned low, the array of batteries belching flame and noise from the embattled bluffs had ceased their utterance, and silence and darkness resumed their sway over the beleaguered city, and the swamps and rivers that encircle Vicksburg." [1]

Thus ended one of the most remarkable scenes which occurred in that terrible war, and one of the most interesting which has occurred in any war.

One scene told by Badeau is worth repeating, to show the effect on the rebel mind, and the sad incidents of such a war. One of the finest plantations of the South was the head-quarters, at that time, of General McClernand. It was clad in the beauty of the sunny South, surrounded with lawns, and planted with the fruits and flowers of a balmy clime. The fig-tree, the magnolia, and the oleander grew and bloomed there. But its unfortunate owner was possessed with the demon of rebellion. The " Yankee " was to him the spirit of evil. Perhaps, if he had known a Yankee better, or even known his country better, he would not have so hated him. Perhaps ignorance was his misfortune, as it is of countless multitudes who are the hapless victims of an ill-lot, not perhaps of altogether their own making. But here is a Yankee on his plantation, and here are the Yankees coming on in their midnight passage of Vicksburg. He is as anxious as Grant. He do n't believe they will get by ; and the first thing that does

<hr>

[1] Badeau's " Military History," page 192.

come is the burning fragment of the Henry Clay; and then the barge cut loose comes floating down; certainly this does not look like Yankee success, and the rebel planter is rejoicing. He shouts, "The Yankees are defeated;" and he comes up and says: "Where are your gun-boats now? Vicksburg has put an end to them all;" and the National officers feared lest his elation might prove well-founded. By daylight, however, the wrecks had all passed by; and, after awhile, a gun-boat appeared below the bend; and then a transport; then, one after another, the whole fleet of iron-clads and army steamers hove in sight from their perilous passage. The "Yankees" now had their turn of rejoicing, and thanked the rebel for teaching them the word. "Where are your gun-boats now?" they said. "Did Vicksburg put an end to them all?" But the old man was too much exasperated at the National success to endure the taunts he had himself provoked, and rushed away in a rage. The next day he set fire to his own house, rather than allow it to shelter his enemies. This may be Spartan, but it was not civilized, and seems sad to look upon in the light of our American institutions.

On the 17th Grant telegraphed Halleck that seven gun-boats and three transports passed the Vicksburg batteries last night, and, "if it is possible, I will occupy Grand Gulf within four days." He did *not* get there in four days, but still in time for the great object.

On the 2d of April six boats and a number of barges ran the Vicksburg batteries, and Grant said they were all more or less injured,[1] and the Tigress sunk, but concluded, " I look upon this as a great success." And well he might, for he had now got gun-boats and transports enough below Vicksburg to transport and manage his army ; and this was the first thing to be done in the solution of the great problem. Grant had said he would take Grand Gulf, but it was not to be quite in the way he imagined. Two corps (McClernand's and McPherson's) had arrived when he thought to attack Grand Gulf in front. In fact, the navy did attack the forts, and, for several hours, rained upon them shot and shell, disabling part of the batteries, but in vain, for they could not reach the top batteries, and found the forts were not to be taken in that way.

What next ? Now comes the development of the idea, which Grant held tenaciously to the end of the war, *to flank the enemy till he brought him to battle, and then destroy him.* Grand Gulf was not taken by the navy, and could not be by landing ; so he looks below, and finds he can land below Grand Gulf and flank it. In one word, he now determines to *turn* the enemy's left, which would result in cutting the Jackson Railroad and reducing the rebel commander to the alternative of either shutting himself up in Vicksburg, or of abandoning it. No finer tactical movement on a large field was ever made. It was the most admirable of Grant's operations, and the most admirable made during the war; yet let us recollect that this whole movement was made in opposition to the opinions of his Generals, and looked upon at

---

[1] Grant's telegram to Halleck.

Washington with fear and anxiety. It was Grant's own plan, and no result either of accident or advice. "Once at Grand Gulf," says Grant, "I do not feel a doubt of success in the entire driving out of the enemy from the banks of the river."

In the mean time Grant superintended every thing personally. His orders were given in detail, so that the commanders could make no mistakes unless they disobeyed orders. In the commissary, the quarter-master's, the adjutant's departments, everywhere, Grant was the chief administrator. We see here exactly what gave Grant success; not merely sagacity in military enterprise, but that cool, persevering, energetic, administrative ability, which enabled him to keep every thing in its place, and direct every thing to its proper end. I copy from Badeau's "Military History" the following paragraphs, which fully illustrate this point in his character. Badeau was his secretary, and can testify to what no one else can. On the 30th of April he issued a variety of orders, of which the following are part:

"The same day the chief commissary of the Thirteenth Corps received the following directions: 'You will issue to the troops of this command, without provision returns, for their subsistence during the next *five* days, *three* rations;' and corps commanders were instructed to direct their 'chief quarter-masters to seize, for the use of the army in the field during the ensuing campaign, such land transportation as may be necessary, belonging to the inhabitants of the country through which they may pass.'

"These orders and dispatches were all written in

Grant's own hand, and nearly all signed with his own name. Like most of the important papers emanating from his head-quarters during the war, they were his own composition, struck out at the moment they were needed by the emergency of the moment, and sent off without emendation or change. Dates and names, and matter of that description, in the larger reports were, of course, often supplied by others, but the gist and the text were Grant's own. None of his staff-officers ever attempted to imitate his style."

On the 30th of April, from early day, gun-boats, transports, barges, every thing which could be used for transportation, were busy ferrying McClernand's Corps across to Bruinsburg, below Bayou Pierre. The Seventeenth (McPherson's) followed as fast as possible. Four miles below Port Gibson they were met by the rebel General Bowen. His force was posted where two roads meet, upon ridges, with a broken country on each side. The action was a serious one, and Grant came on to the ground aware of all its importance. The result was not doubtful. With heavy forces continually coming up, Grant drove the enemy from their position with heavy loss,[1] and they fled over the Bayou Pierre, destroying the bridges. Next day McPherson built a new bridge, and the pursuit of the enemy was continued. Thus ended the battle of Port Gibson, the first step in Grant's turning the enemy and driving him in.

These movements compelled the evacuation of Grand Gulf, which, on the 3d of May, was taken possession of by Admiral Porter; and on the evening

---

[1] The rebels lost 150 killed, 300 wounded, and 600 prisoners.

of the same day Grant rode in with his staff. Porter and Grant were both surprised at the strength and defenses of that place, Porter describing[1] them as the strongest on the Mississippi, except Vicksburg. Fortunately the rapid advance of Grant reduced the enemy to the necessity of abandoning Grand Gulf immediately, and a large amount of heavy artillery and ammunition were taken there. Fortunately, also, no time was left to complete the new defenses. One grand point was now gained. The enemy abandoned all the country from Bayou Pierre to Big Black, and Pemberton, who commanded that particular district, dispatched to Johnston that Grant was turning their defenses below, and intended to inclose them in Vicksburg. The enemy, as well as our Government, was surprised. Grand Gulf was now made the base of supplies, and the army lay at Hawkinson's Ferry of the Big Black, waiting for wagons, supplies, and Sherman.

At this place let us look at two or three incidental points in the drama. What was the condition of the army at this time? for it has been much exposed, and I recollect that every body thought there would be much sickness. Grant says, writing to Halleck, on the 3d of May:

"My force, however, was too heavy for his, and composed of well-disciplined and hardy men, *who know no defeat, and are not willing to learn what it is.* This army is in the finest health and spirits. Since leaving Milliken's Bend they have marched as much by night as by day, through mud and rain,

---

[1] Porter's Report, May 3, 1863.

without tents or much other baggage, and on irregular rations, without a complaint, and with less straggling than I have ever before witnessed. Where all have done so well, it would be out of place to make invidious distinction."

This is certainly extraordinary, and equally fortunate. In fact, Grant was now coming into the active campaign, with a large army in admirable order.

Another incident to be noticed, and one of much importance at this time, is Grierson's raid. This expedition originated with Grant himself. His idea was to dispatch Grierson, with about five hundred men, and cut the railroad beyond Jackson. He said to Hurlbut, it would be hazardous, but would pay well if successful. This was two months before his present movement. Delays and obstacles (as it turned out luckily for us) prevented the start of this expedition till the middle of April. On the 17th of April, Grierson set out from La Grange, with some fifteen hundred cavalry, and, after seventeen days of most extraordinary performance in riding and hard work, arrived at Baton Rouge, on the Lower Mississippi. He broke up railroads, destroyed stores, and paroled prisoners, making an almost marvelous raid through an enemy's country, fresh in the memory of the people and to be memorable in history. It accomplished all that was expected, and was very opportune. I mention it here, because it was one element—although a minor one—in the general plan which Grant had formed for himself.

Grant sat up the night of the 3d, writing dispatches, letters, orders. First, in the order of busi-

ness, is the supply question ; and so he writes off to
Sullivan above, and to Sherman, detailed directions
as to the quantity of supplies, and how they must
be furnished.

Having gained the grand object of four months'
operations—dry ground on the enemy's interior line—
the army felt encouraged, and Grant inspirited. But
there was still something to be determined as to immediate movements. There were really but two lines
of advance, and they were quite obvious. Grant
might move directly on Vicksburg, and he might
also move on Jackson, cut the railroads, and effectually prevent the enemy's reënforcing Pemberton. He
took the last course. But it turned out afterward
that Halleck had issued a positive order for Grant to
join Banks, if possible, *between Vicksburg and Port
Hudson*, and that Lincoln himself feared Grant had
made a fatal mistake in turning north from Port
Gibson.[1] Such was the strange fatuity—the night-
mare of fear—which prevailed at Washington during
the greater part. of the war. Luckily Grant did not
know any thing of all this, and boldly pushed on to
success and victory. Finding Pemberton very strong
in front and hearing, from every quarter, that Johnston was advancing troops from the East, so that it
was quite obvious, if the forces of Pemberton and
Johnston were united, they would be greater than his
own,[2] and there might be a failure of his plan, he

---

[1] Lincoln subsequently wrote a letter to Grant acknowledging his error.

[2] The field reports of Pemberton proved that he had in all 52,000
men. Grant's three corps, then *available*, did not amount to more than
that number.

came at once to the conclusion that he would anticipate this and advance on Jackson *between* the forces
of the enemy. This required an abandonment of
Grand Gulf, and consequently his base of supplies
from Hard Times and Milliken's Bend. Sherman,
who was on the other side of the river hurrying up
supplies, was alarmed, and wrote to Grant that if
they were to come by that single road, the road
would soon be choked. Grant immediately replied
that he did not expect to rely on that road, but
merely wanted to get up coffee, hard bread, and
salt ; for all the rest he would rely on the country,
in which there was plenty of beef and corn. In
fact, Grant had then more rations on hand than
he had when he left New Carthage.' He had cut
away from his base at Milliken's Bend, and he was
now about to cut away from his new base at Grand
Gulf. The Government at Washington was astonished, and the rebel Government at Richmond more
so. But on the night of the 3d of May, Grant arrived at Hawkinson's Ferry, with his total amount of
baggage—a tooth-brush! He had lodged and eaten
where he could, and his staff had done the same.
And now the army cuts loose from Grand Gulf to
practice that great military principle—*forage on the
enemy.* He had learned, as I said, in his march to
Oxford (Mississippi) and return, after his communications were cut off, that the enemy had abundance
of food. He wanted coffee and salt ; for the rest he
could get along well enough without a base.

And now he has formed the plan of a short but

' Badeau's "Military History."

decisive campaign, which, if it did not capture Vicksburg, must inevitably result in shutting up Pemberton. Two things were absolutely necessary, if possible : to deceive Pemberton with the idea that Grant was advancing immediately on Vicksburg, and then to cut off his communications, so that he could receive neither provisions nor reënforcements. For the first, he advanced bodies of troops to within six or seven miles of Vicksburg. The Big Black River, in its course to the east of that place, runs nearly parallel with the Mississippi, as far as Hawkinson's Ferry, and then soon enters the Mississippi, at Grand Gulf, where that river makes a bend to the east. The railroad from Vicksburg to Jackson crosses the Big Black about fifteen miles from the town ; Edwards's Station is eighteen, Clinton thirty-five, and Jackson forty miles ; but on the roads traveled by the troops the distances were longer. Leaving Hawkinson's Ferry, there were two roads leading to the north, east of Black River. One was near the river, leading up to Edwards's Station, and the other considerably to the east, through the villages of Utica and Raymond, to Clinton, on the railroad, ten miles from Jackson. Grant put McClernand's Corps on the first, hugging Black River, and threatening to cross its bridges in an advance on Vicksburg. This perplexed Pemberton, and masked, in a good degree, the movement of McPherson's Corps, which took the Raymond road, with the design of taking Jackson and cutting the communications. The plan worked with entire success. In the mean time Sherman had crossed the Mississippi with his corps, and advanced up to support

either McClernand or McPherson. On the 12th
of May Grant was with Sherman, encamped on the
road to Edwards's Station, seven miles west of Raymond, and on the day previous (11th) Grant wrote
Halleck, " I shall communicate with Grand Gulf no
more." On that same day Halleck had telegraphed
to Grant that he must unite with Banks. In the
meanwhile McPherson moved on, and, on the 12th,
was encountered by the enemy near Raymond. The
rebels, under the command of General Gregg, made
a brisk and determined battle, but in vain. They
were defeated ; and on the 14th Grant telegraphs
Halleck from Raymond, " McPherson took this place
on the 12th, after a brisk fight of more than two
hours."[1] McPherson is now at Clinton, Sherman on
the direct Jackson road, and McClernand bringing
up the rear. Now we can see the most important
part of these grand tactics have succeeded. Grant is
at Clinton, *on the Jackson road.* On the 13th Mc-
Pherson reached Clinton, and began tearing up all the
railroad tracks, burning bridges, and destroying telegraphs. Finding that Johnston, who had now taken
command at Jackson, was trying to hold on while he
could get reënforcements, Grant at once ordered up
McClernand and Sherman's Corps to join McPherson
in his attack on Jackson. At the same time Johnston directed Pemberton to bring up his forces to
attack Grant in the rear ;[2] but it was too late—Pem-

[1] The loss on our side was 69 killed, 341 wounded, 30 missing ; on
the enemy's, 100 killed, 305 wounded, and 45 prisoners.

[2] "I have lately arrived, and learn that Major-General Sherman is
between us with four divisions at Clinton. It is important to reëstab-
lish communications, that you may be reenforced. If practicable, come

berton had been deceived, and his forces were at Edwards's Station on the 14th.

On the 14th of May Jackson was, in fact, well fortified with long lines of intrenchments; but, unlike Vicksburg, it had no great natural defenses, and required more troops than Johnston had. He had now the troops driven back from Raymond, the garrison of Jackson, and some reënforcements from Georgia and South Carolina, altogether a considerable body, but unequal to the veteran corps of Grant. Johnston was attacked in his defenses by the Corps of McPherson and Sherman, and defeated. The result is told by Grant, writing from Jackson: "This place fell into our hands yesterday, after a fight of about three hours. Joe Johnston was in command. The enemy retreated north, evidently with the design of joining the Vicksburg force. I am concentrating my force at Bolton, to cut them off, if possible."[1]

The night before, Johnston had passed a gay evening in the house now occupied by Grant. It is quite common, however, for men to appear most gay, when in fact most sad.

Johnston could not have expected to defeat Grant, but he evidently did expect to save Pemberton's army. But that was a vanity. We have gained another great step in this decisive campaign. Jackson, as a *railroad center, and the roads leading to it, are destroyed.*[2]

up in his rear at once. To beat such a detachment would be of immense value. All the troops you can quickly assemble should be brought. Time is all-important."—*Johnston to Pemberton, May 13th.*

[1] Grant's telegram from Jackson, May 15th.

[2] Sherman's Corps took charge of Jackson, and Badeau says: "He set about his work in the morning, and utterly destroyed the railroads

It is no longer possible to unite the rebel forces. It is no longer possible to save Vicksburg; but it may be possible to save Pemberton's army. What shall be done with it? Johnston went to Canton, and thence dispatched two brigades forty miles from Jackson; and this he did, as he said in his report, to prevent the *enemy in Jackson* from drawing provisions from the East. Johnston was as much deceived as Pemberton; for Grant had no idea of remaining in Jackson. He did not dream that Grant had cut his own communications, and got plenty of provisions where he was. He told Pemberton that when the reënforcements were up, the rest of the army must be united with him. But that was just what Grant did not mean to have done. There was, however, danger of it; but Grant had got possession of Johnston's dispatches. He instantly converged all his forces on Bolton's Station, which was twenty-eight miles from Vicksburg, and seventeen from Jackson. This was, in fact, placing himself where he separated and cut off from each other all the enemy's forces; for Pemberton, utterly deceived, as well as Johnston, disobeyed the order of Johnston to move toward Clinton, and

in every direction, north, east, south, and west, for a distance, in all, of twenty miles. All the bridges, factories, and arsenals were burned, and whatever could be of use to the rebels, destroyed. The importance of Jackson, as a railroad center and a depot of stores and military factories, was annihilated, and the principal object of its capture attained. A hotel and a church in Jackson were burned without orders, and there was some pillaging by the soldiers, which their officers sought in every way to restrain." This was not all. Pictures were shot through, pianos broken up, and a great deal of private property destroyed. This was not the work of the officers, but of men who had been insulted and injured by rebels, and were determined to make rebels *feel* the consequences of their own conduct.

actually went to Dillon's, south of Edwards's Station, in order, as he said, to cut Grant's communications! Both of them were evidently deluded with the idea that Grant depended on his communications. So, if we look on the map, we shall find Johnston running to Canton, (north,) Gregg, east, and Pemberton at Dillon's, (south,) and Grant concentrated at Bolton's Station, central between them. No general could desire a better position than this. Pemberton, however, soon finds out his mistake, and at once moves up to Champion's Hill, west of Bolton, determined to make a stand. Grant is delayed somewhat by the necessity of renewing bridges, which had been destroyed, over Baker's Creek. But, during the 16th, the work was done, and the enemy now in complete force, (Pemberton, Bowen, and Loring all being there,) were brought to battle, without being entirely conscious of their situation, or with whom they had to deal.[1] This delusion of Pemberton and Johnston was one of the great advantages we had; but it must be remembered that this delusion was a direct consequence of Grant's movements. It was the excel-

[1] "When General Johnston, on the 13th of May, informed me that Sherman was at Clinton, and ordered me to attack him in the rear, neither he nor I knew that Sherman was in the act of advancing on Jackson, which place he entered at twelve o'clock on the next day; that a corps of the enemy was at Raymond, following Sherman's march upon Jackson; and that another corps was near Dillon's, probably moving in the same direction; and, consequently, that the orders to attack Sherman could not be executed. Nor was I myself aware till, several hours after I had received and promised to obey the order, that it could not be obeyed without the destruction of my army; but on my arrival at Edwards's depot, two hours after I received the order, I found a large force of the enemy at Dillon's, on my right flank, and ready to attack me in the flank or rear if I moved on Clinton."—*Pemberton's add. Rep.*

lence of Grant's plan that it must deceive the enemy, and that it must almost inevitably be successful.

McPherson was in front, and outranked by Mc-Clernand, under whom he was unwilling to risk the battle. The position of the enemy is thus described by Badeau:

"At six and a half o'clock McPherson dispatched to Grant: 'I think it advisable for you to come forward to the front as soon as you can.' Grant started at once, at forty minutes past seven, for the advance. On the way he found Hovey's Division at a halt, and the road blocked up with wagon trains. Grant soon cleared a way for the troops, and the battle was evidently coming on.

" The enemy was strongly posted, with his left on a high, wooded ridge, called Champion's Hill, over which the road to Edwards's Station runs, making a sharp turn to the south, as it strikes the hills. This ridge rises sixty or seventy feet above the surrounding country, and is the highest land for many miles around; the topmost point is bald, and gave the rebels a commanding position for their artillery; but the remainder of the crest, as well as a precipitous hill-side to the east of the road, is covered by a dense forest and undergrowth, and scarred with deep ravines, through whose entanglements troops could pass only with extreme difficulty. To the north the timber extends a short distance down the hill, and opens into cultivated fields. The enemy's line extended over ridge and hills for two or three miles. McPherson commenced the attack, with Hovey's Division, and two brigades of Logan, and steadily drove the enemy back till our troops approached the hill. The road over the hill was a natural fortification. It was cut through the crest of the ridge at the steepest part, the bank on the upper side commanding all below; so that even when the National troops had apparently gained the road, the rebels stood behind this novel breastwork, covered from every fire, and masters still of the whole declivity. These were the only fortifications at Champion's Hill, but they answered the rebels well."

The enemy, seeing that they lost ground, sent reënforcements rapidly. Grant, who, standing on a spur of a hill, saw this, sent forward Crocker's Division. But the tide of battle ebbed and flowed. Hovey's exhausted troops were at one time compelled to fall back. In fact, the National line was in danger. Grant was fighting the battle with one-third of his army, for he had tried to hurry up McClernand in vain. On the right, however, Stevenson's Brigade, of Logan's Division, made a successful charge, fairly cutting off the enemy's retreat to Edwards's Station; and the enemy, seeing this, abandoned his position in front, and Hovey and Crocker pressed on, and the rebel line rolled back. The rebels fled; Logan's charge precipitated the rout, and the battle of Champion's Hill was won at four o'clock in the afternoon. The battle had been fought with McPherson's Corps and Hovey's Division of the Thirteenth Corps. In all, Grant had in the *actual* battle about fifteen thousand men, and of these he lost heavily. It was the bloodiest field since Grant commenced operations around Vicksburg.[1] We took about three thousand prisoners, and about thirty pieces of artillery. The battle was very disastrous to the rebels in every way. Loring's Division of the rebel force, which held their right, got separated by the rapidity of Grant's advance, fled to the southward, and, after making a wide circuit, and losing many men, at length succeeded in joining Johnston at Jackson, with about five thousand troops. Thus this division was cut off from the defense of Vicksburg. At this time Johnston was resting, in utter ignorance of what either Grant or Pemberton was doing. On the same day, also, Sherman left Jackson, marched twenty miles, reached Bolton, and was informed of the battle of Champion's Hill. He was immediately ordered north to Bridgeport, on the Big Black, obviously with the view of preventing any attempt of Pemberton to escape.

In the mean time, McClernand's Corps is moved forward, and, arriving at the Big Black Bridge, finds the enemy in a very strong position. The river makes a bend to the east. On the west side were high bluffs ; on the east, a wide bottom, surrounded by a deep bayou, making a natural ditch. The bridge was fortified in front by a *tete-de-pont*, (bridge-head,) with twenty pieces of artillery, and four thousand men. The struggle was not long, however ; a successful charge drove the enemy from his intrenchments, in confusion and dismay, over the river. All the battles round Vicksburg are now ended—Grand Gulf, Raymond, Jackson, Champion's Hill, Big Black—all are

---

[1] Our army lost 426 men killed, 1,842 wounded, and 189 missing. Hovey alone lost 1,200, being nearly one-third of his command.

over. The dreams of the enemy are vanished. On the night of the 17th of May his broken, dispirited troops enter the little city of Vicksburg. The inhabitants are dismayed and astonished. The Avenger of crimes seems, to their excited imaginations, to be rushing on for their destruction! On the 22d of May Grant drew his own lines round Vicksburg, with a grasp which none could escape. Some time was to elapse, and many a man sank in the darkness of death, but the end was certain. The strategy with which Grant moved from Milliken's Bend to Carthage, from Carthage to Bruinsburg, thence to Grand Gulf, and thence (cutting himself clear of his base) to Jackson, Champion's Hill, and Vicksburg, is as brilliant as any to be found in military annals.

Some writers say, "*Grant had no genius.*" They look upon him as a sort of hard-headed, pounding machine, who, with a strong will and a hard hammer, hammered the enemy to death. The rebel historian says he is an *accident!* Our own writers, *civilians*, (for no military man says such things,) say Grant has not genius. Why, what would they have? What is genius? Especially, what is military genius? Do they know? The best definition of genius is, *strong natural faculties, fully put forth on some one subject.* Had not Grant strong natural faculties, and did he not put them forth to the utmost degree? The campaign around Vicksburg was *his own*, emphatically his own, in opposition to the views of the Government, and the advice of his generals. Can the captious critics of Grant's career show me any plan in the movements of the greatest generals more

original, better performed, or more far-sighted, than
the campaign of Vicksburg? Let us now turn to
the rebel mind. What did the rebel generals think?
What did they intend?

It is quite evident that Johnston, who seems to
be much admired as an officer, by both rebel and
Union writers, was completely outgeneraled by Grant,
and defeated in every purpose. We have the correspondence and reports of Johnston and Pemberton,
which show that both were bewildered, and that
when the game was lost, Johnston was intent only
to put the blame on Pemberton. But how does he
clear himself? Where was he in the thirteen days
from the 3d to the 16th of May? He made a pretense of defending Jackson, but if he had any (as he
must have had) correct information about Grant's
forces, he must have known that to be impossible.
Why did he scatter himself and Gregg off in different directions? If he could be of any use to Pemberton, he had an opportunity, in those thirteen days,
of uniting with him, or provisioning Vicksburg, if it
could be done. The truth is, Johnston did not then,
or at any time in the war, vindicate the reputation
he had acquired. One thing he did, which, at first
sight, seems sound judgment. He told Pemberton
to leave Vicksburg, and save his army.[1] But, if he
left Vicksburg, he left the Mississippi. The whole
of it must at once fall into our hands, and the sun

---

[1] Pemberton was actually moving to join Johnston when Grant
attacked him at Champion's Hill. He dispatched to Johnston particularly about his route, when he added, "Heavy skirmishing now going
on in my front." Grant had been too quick for him.

did not shine more certainly than that the loss of the Mississippi was the loss of the war. They did not clearly see this either at Washington or Richmond; but it was not the less a fact.

But let us pursue our march. Vicksburg was invested fully on the 22d of May, and, to all practical purposes, this must be the end of Vicksburg. There was the possibility that the rebel Government could get another army together and raise the siege. There was great reliance at Richmond on Johnston. There were constant rumors in the Northern newspapers of rebel armies coming to the relief of Pemberton, and endangering Grant. But let us see what did happen. The events of any decisive importance in the siege are few. Haines's Bluff, that most formidable post, had been abandoned by the enemy, and its garrison withdrawn to Vicksburg. It was no longer worth any thing. Strategy had done what Sherman, with forty thousand men, had been unable to do by storm. It is said that on the 18th—six long months after Sherman's attack—Grant and Sherman met on the farthest hight of Walnut Hills, and looked down on the Yazoo River, and the very bluff which Sherman had stormed in vain; and Sherman acknowledged that he could not see the end till then; but now the campaign was a success, if they never took the town.[1] Grant smoked his cigar and said nothing. To him the campaign was a success when he crossed the Mississippi and turned the enemy's left, so as to command the Jackson road.

[1] This statement rests wholly on the authority of Badeau in his "Military History."

We are now before Vicksburg, cutting the unfortunate Pemberton off from any possibility of escape. And here we come to one of Grant's characteristics, in this case quite remarkable. The critics say he had no genius. I have shown he had a genius for war. But there was one sort of genius he had not a bit of. He had no genius for brag and bluster. Indeed, he was singularly deficient in the art of boasting. It never struck him, when standing on the bluffs of Walnut Hills, what a wonderful proclamation he might have made. In this he was something like the great Frederick, whose proclamations were the briefest possible, and whose brag was nothing. But what a genius Napoleon had for it! Napoleon is the great admiration of young writers, and such imaginative critics as read Jomini, and Thiers, and Napoleon's Conversations, and then think they know the whole theory of the art of war, and are able to pronounce at once that Grant had no genius, that he was himself an accident, and that a long line of uninterrupted successes are all due to a series of happy accidents! I leave such people to the judgment of posterity, at whose bar they will appear no more ridiculous than have many of the historians of past ages. But let us read Grant's proclamation as Napoleon would have written it. Here it is:

"Soldiers of the Army of the Mississippi! From the hights of Vicksburg you look down upon your defeated enemy, and share in the joy of glorious victory! In a campaign of twenty days you have marched two hundred miles, beaten the enemy in five successive battles, taken eighty-eight pieces of field and heavy artillery, captured six thousand, five hundred prisoners, and put six thousand *hors de combat!* You have seized the capital of the enemy, destroyed his railroad communications, and driven him into his last refuge, whence he can not escape! Soldiers, your commander congratulates you, and the Republic is grateful!"

Such would have been the proclamation of Napoleon, with the advantage, in Grant's case, that every word would have been true. But, alas! for the soldier who wants either the stimulus of vanity, or the genius of imagination! He will be contented with success, and allow facts to make history, and historians to proclaim that he was deficient in genius, in manners, and in humanity.[1]

On the 22d of May, Grant, either from misinformation or misapprehension of the enemy's strength, ventured on an assault, which proved to be a mistake. Vicksburg was naturally and artificially strongly fortified, and fortified places are never attempted by assault in European warfare, and ought not to be any where. When we come to set down with an army before a strongly fortified and fully garrisoned place, we can have no resource but regular approaches. Here the engineer is the real commander, and by his skill alone can the place be taken, unless starved out. Grant had not hesitated to depart from all European precedents in his strategy over our great plains, and forests, and rivers. No precedents were applicable to

---

[1] All these charges are brought against Grant by intelligent men, both rebel and Union. It is disgraceful to their information and to their intellect.

such a case, and he followed none. But here was a
new experience. He was not an engineer officer, and
knew nothing about fortified cities. So he made a
furious assault, and the Corps of Sherman, McPherson, and McClernand bravely, but uselessly, assaulted
parapets and forts, manned with an army inside. It
was in vain ; and we lost, in one form and another,
nearly three thousand men. This was rather a sad
comment on our victories. But it could make no
difference in the result. It only taught Grant he
must take another course.

In the mean time Grant had a personal trouble,
which gave him much uneasiness,[1] and which he now
got rid of. This was General McClernand, who with
the most patriotic motives, and good service in the
war, seems to have been very unfit to command a
corps, and who now, by misinformation to Grant on
the field, caused a large part of the loss in the assault.
The difficulty with McClernand was still further increased by his congratulatory order to his troops,
dated May 31st,[2] by which those who read it, and know

---

[1] This will be best understood by a paragraph from Grant's Report
to Halleck, dated May 24th : " The loss on our side was not very heavy
at first, but receiving repeated dispatches from Major-General McClernand, saying that he was hard pressed on his right and left, and calling
for reënforcements, I gave him all of McPherson's Corps but four
brigades, and caused Sherman to press the enemy on our right, which
caused us to double our losses for the day. They will probably reach
fifteen hundred killed and wounded. General McClernand's dispatches
misled me as to the facts, and caused much of this loss. He is entirely
unfit for the position of corps commander, both on the march and on
the battle-field. Looking after his corps gives me more labor and infinitely more uneasiness than all the remainder of my department."

[2] See McClernand's Order, "Rebellion Record," Vol. VI, p. 637.
The paragraph in relation to Champion's Hill, in which he speaks of

no more, would learn that the battles had all been fought, and the work all done, by McClernand's Corps. He seems to have been very nervous, easily excited, and not fully to have comprehended military positions. With all this, he had much merit, and had done much service. He was, however, removed, and General Ord put in command of his corps.

I need not enter into the details of the siege of Vicksburg. They will interest few except engineers. Grant found that the place was to be taken only by ordinary approaches, and he must have reënforcements. Lammon's Division from Memphis, and two divisions of the Sixteenth Corps, came ; on the 11th of June, General Kinney's Division, from the Department of Missouri, arrived ; and on the 14th of June, two divisions of the Ninth Corps, under General Parke. Thus we see that Grant was soon reënforced enough to put him beyond any possibility of danger from an attack on his rear—the east. Johnston was compelled to look on at a distance, and see his enemy's success. Grant raised counter-fortifications to the rebels, and drew his lines closer and stronger. He made mines, and blew them up ; but there is only one case in which mines are useful—that is, when they are actually under the enemy's ramparts, and blow open a passage. They are the last things to be used previous to the assault. So they went on mining till the 25th of June, when a grand mine exploded, and they prepared for a storm of the intrenchments. The

winning the battle, "*with the assistance of McPherson's Corps,*" is most extraordinary. Hovey's Division *did* belong to McClernand's Corps, but it was the only one in the battle, and was directed that day by Grant.

parallels of Grant's army had got so near, in some places, that the Union and the rebel soldiers talked to each other over the parapets, and even went so far as to interchange supplies of tobacco and crackers. This is very much like gleams of sunshine in the midst of a storm. Poor human nature will speak out its human sympathy in the midst of the terrors of war. Alas! is there no remedy for the ills of Government but these terrible ills of war? At last, when our men were almost near enough to the enemy to touch them—when they were just peeping over the parapets—when the citizens and rebel soldiers had been for days living on mule flesh—when the last hope had expired in Pemberton's breast, and he had vindicated to the world that he was not a traitor to his cause, (for they had charged him with being one,) on the 3d of July he asked for terms of surrender. The terms were agreed upon, the delivery of the place to be made next day. So, at 10 o'clock on Saturday, the glorious 4th of July, the garrison of Vicksburg marched out and stacked their arms in front of their conquerors.

"All along the rebel works they poured out, in gray, through the sally-ports and across the ditches, and laid down their colors, sometimes on the very spot where so many of the besiegers had laid down their lives ; and then, in sight of the National troops, who were standing on their own parapets, the rebels returned inside the works, prisoners of war. Thirty-one thousand, six hundred men were surrendered to Grant. Among these were two thousand, one hundred and fifty-three officers, of whom fifteen were generals.   One hundred and seventy-two cannon also fell into his hands, *the largest capture of men and material ever made in war*."[1]

Logan's Division entered first, and the Forty-Fifth Illinois placed its battle-flag on the Court-House of Vicksburg.   Two thousand officers were surrendered ; and their temper and behavior is thus described in the concluding scene by Badeau, who, I suppose, was present :

"Grant rode into the town, with his staff, at the head of Logan's Division.   The rebel soldiers gazed curiously at their conqueror, as he came inside the lines that had resisted him so valiantly, but they paid him no sign of disrespect.   He went direct to one of the rebel head-quarters : there was no one to receive him, and he dismounted and entered the porch where Pemberton sat with his generals ; they saluted Grant, but not one offered him a chair, though all had seats themselves.   Neither the rank nor the reputation of their captor, nor the swords he had allowed them to wear, prompted them to this simple act of courtesy.   Pemberton was especially sullen, both in conversation and behavior. .Finally, for very shame, one of the rebels offered a place to Grant.   The day was hot and dusty ; he was thirsty from his ride, and asked for a drink of water.   They told him he could find it inside ; and, no one showing him the way, he groped in a passage till he found a negro, who gave him the cup of cold water only, which his enemy had

[1] Badeau's "Military History."   At the surrender of Ulm only thirty thousand men and sixty pieces of cannon were captured.   Pemberton had thirty-two thousand.

almost denied. When he returned, his seat had been taken, and he remained standing during the rest of the interview, which lasted about half an hour."

I suppose it is not easy for human nature to feel pleasant under the circumstances in which Pemberton and his officers were placed. But it was not the conduct which a Bayard or a Washington would have displayed, nor one which we should have expected from Southern chivalry. So ended the drama of Vicksburg; and though the war lasted nearly two years longer, they were years, on the part of the rebels, of hopeless controversy. Port Hudson immediately fell. We turned back the whole left line of rebel defenses, and folded their armies back on Chattanooga and Richmond. Vicksburg was decisive, and Grant came out of that campaign with the congratulations of a nation, and victorious over the opinions of the Government, as well as the armies of the rebels.

CHAPTER IX.

THE PREPARATION.

GRANT ORDERS SHERMAN TO ADVANCE—JACKSON RETAKEN,
AND THE CAMPAIGN ENDED—GRANT IS OPPOSED TO TRADE
ON THE LINES—PROTECTS NEGRO SOLDIERS—WANTS TO
MOVE ON MOBILE—FAILURE OF THE POTOMAC CAMPAIGNS
AND SUCCESS OF ROSECRANS—GOVERNMENT FAILS TO RE-
ENFORCE HIM—LINCOLN'S PROCLAMATION AND ITS MORAL
EFFECT.

> "HAIL, Father of Waters ! again thou art free !
> And miscreant treason hath vainly enchained thee ;
> Roll on, mighty river, and bear to the sea
> The praises of those who so gallantly gained thee !
> 　From fountain to ocean, from source to the sea,
> 　The West is exulting—'Our river is free !'
>
> Fit emblem of freedom ! thy home is the North !
> And thou wert not forgot by the mother that bore thee ;
> From snows everlasting thou chainless burst forth,
> And chainless we solemnly swore to restore thee.
> 　O'er river and prairie, o'er mountain and lea,
> 　The North is exulting—'Our river is free !'" [1]

> "SHE comes from St. Louis !　Away with the plea
> That river or people divided may be !
> One current sweeps past us, one likeness we wear ;
> One flag through the future right proudly we 'll bear ;
> All hail to the day without malice or jar !
> She comes from St. Louis !　Hurrah and hurrah !" [2]

[1] From "Opening of the Mississippi," by Captain R. H. Crittenden.

[2] On the 16th of July, 1863, the steamboat Imperial arrived at New Orleans from
St. Louis, and this verse is taken from a spirited Ode, written for that event, by Edna
Dean Proctor.

THE Mississippi was free, indeed, and the tide of war ebbed back from its banks. Grant did not sleep upon his achievements. Before the prisoners were paroled (on the evening of the 3d of July) Grant wrote to Sherman: "Make all your calculations to attack Johnston, and destroy the road north of Jackson." For Johnston, on the investment of Vicksburg, had taken possession of Jackson, had been reënforced by several divisions of troops, and had been making vain efforts to attack Grant on a weak point, or get Pemberton to do so. He now lay at Jackson, in a sullen humor, brooding over what he called Pemberton's blunders and his own ill-fortune.[1]

Sherman promptly obeyed the order to march. Ord and Steele, with their corps, followed, and by the 12th of July the army was again in front of Jackson. This place was on Pearl River, and on the 13th both flanks of our army touched on the river. Johnston was well fortified, and got the idea that Sherman meant to attack him, in which case he hoped to succeed behind his defenses; but this General would make no such mistake, and quietly began to throw up intrenchments. Johnston is again outgeneraled.

---

[1] I have already stated my conviction, founded only on his own orders, reports, and movements, that Johnston was an overrated man. His true course was, even if he had but small force, to keep up an incessant attack on Grant, and keep near him, to give Pemberton some chance of escape. He did exactly the contrary. He kept as far off as he could, and talked of cutting off Grant's supplies. He says in his report: "On the 12th I said to him, 'To take from Bragg a force which would make this army fit to oppose Grant, would involve yielding Tennessee. It is for the Government to decide between this State and Tennessee.'" They had no part of Tennessee but Chattanooga, and all they did with Bragg's army was to make worthless raids.

He writes to the rebel President: "If the enemy will not attack, we must, at the last moment, withdraw;" and he did. Again, Jackson is made a scene of desolation. Railroads, locomotives, cars, and bridges are destroyed on every side for many miles. The campaign is at an end; the capital of Mississippi is a second time occupied; all the rebel fortifications on the river captured or destroyed, and the army of Pemberton, which had exceeded fifty thousand men, taken, destroyed, or scattered.[1]

It is most fortunate for Grant that his merit (and no critic or historian can think it small) in the Vicksburg campaign can be shared with no other generals, nor with the Government itself. Nor was there wanting proof to establish this, nor generosity in the Administration to acknowledge it. The nation rejoiced, and Lincoln was surprised. On the 13th of July he wrote that memorable letter to Grant— one of the curiosities of literature, for its magnanimity, and as characteristic of the man:

"*My Dear General,*—I do not remember that you and I ever met personally. I write this now as a grateful acknowledgment for the almost inestimable service you have done the country. I wish to say a word further. When you first reached the vicinity of Vicksburg, I thought you should do what you finally did—march the troops across the neck, run

---

[1] I have said that the army of Pemberton numbered on the rolls, at the beginning of the campaign, 52,000 men. The following statement is the nearest I can come to the losses of Pemberton: Surrendered at Vicksburg, 31,600; captured at Champion's Hill, 3,000; captured at Big Black and Port Gibson, 3,000; killed and wounded, 10,000; escaped under Loring, 5,000. Aggregate, 52,600 men.

the batteries with the transports, and thus go below; and I never had any faith, except a general hope that you knew better than I, that the Yazoo Pass expedition and the like could succeed. When you got below and took Port Gibson, Grand Gulf, and vicinity, I thought you should go down the river and join General Banks; and when you turned northward, east of the Big Black, I feared it was a mistake. I now wish to make a personal acknowledgment that you were right, and I was wrong."

Halleck also was liberal in his praise—compared his campaign to that of Napoleon at Ulm, and spoke of his report as "brief, soldierly, and in every respect creditable and satisfactory." I have said Grant did not know how, and has not yet learned how, to *proclaim* his own merits, or even that of the army; so his report was "brief and soldierly"—nothing more.[1] Grant's last words in the campaign of Vicksburg were sent in the telegram of the 18th of July, announcing the retreat of Johnston. And now, looking out for new preparations, he said: "It seems to me now that Mobile should be captured, the expedition starting from some point on Lake Pontchartrain." He was looking from the ruins of Vicksburg into the future of the drama, as its scenes drew toward the end.

And now, before we turn our eyes toward Chattanooga, let us turn to some points in the conduct of the war which concern Grant's administrative ability,

---

[1] Some newspaper said: Grant neither made a speech to his soldiers, nor marched at the head of a column! The last is false, but the former is true.

in which he has shown himself superior to any man of the day, and, therefore, fully competent to take charge of the most extensive executive duties. As soon as we got possession of Kentucky and Tennessee on the Cumberland and the Mississippi, it was perfectly natural that the commercial public should immediately want to trade there. The war had straitened trade, especially that in the Mississippi Valley. The merchants panted to renew it, and the speculators more than the merchants; the vultures who follow in the track of the eagle are ever watchful for the carcass; the jackal is waiting for the prey left by the lion.[1] One of the most disgraceful chapters in the history of modern civilization is that which describes the attempt to trade over the dead bodies of fallen men, and make profit out of the sufferings of a country! This conduct is natural, and perhaps human nature is not to be blamed for its instincts. However this may be, a body of traders in the wake, or near the camps of an army, is hostile, if not fatal, to its success ; and Grant, who had all the qualities of a good soldier, was utterly opposed to it. The traders were continually pressing the Secretary of the Treasury to open trade, and he wrote to Grant that "this rigorous line" gives rise to "serious, and some well-founded, complaints." The Secretary suggested bonds to be given by parties having permits. Grant replied, with truth and sound judgment: "No matter what the restrictions thrown around trade, *if any whatever is allowed, it will be made the means of*

---

[1] Every body remembers the story of John Hook entering the camp of the Revolutionary Army, crying, "Beef! beef!"

supplying the enemy with all they want." All history proves this, and it is only surprising that the Government could have thought of permitting it. There is no doubt that this border trade did a great deal of mischief during the war. Grant said, however, that, whatever he thought, *he would obey.* Badeau quotes this passage from him: "*No theory of my own will ever stand in the way of my executing in good faith any order I may receive from those in authority over me;* but my position has given me an opportunity of seeing what could not be known by persons away from the scene of war, and I venture, therefore, great caution in opening trade with rebels."

Such was Grant's sound judgment on the question of trade with enemies. He was equally sound and judicious on the question arising out of the employment of negro soldiers. When the history of these times is read by posterity, nothing will appear so strange, so fatuitous, as our hesitation to employ negro soldiers, or our doubts about emancipation. A large part of the American people seemed laboring under awful delusions. In the South, we know they were; and we were scarcely less so in the North. What is the object of war? Destruction—certainly so far as to subdue your enemy! Do you use a gun to kill with? then why not a negro, if he can be made a soldier? Is the negro your enemy's property? then why not destroy that property by emancipation? All this was plain to true military men, but it came slowly to the country. Gradually we accepted the negroes as soldiers, and finally Lincoln's glorious emancipation destroyed property in them. Grant looked upon the negro simply as a soldier. When we enlisted negroes in our defense, he knew they must be protected. It would demoralize the Government, the army, and the nation not to protect the negro soldier. The rebels, however, thought they could punish the negro, and not the white soldier. Not so thought Grant, and so he taught them. He went into no physiology or metaphysics about whether the negro was a man or a baboon—whether he was a slave or a freeman—he knew him as an American soldier, entitled to all the rights of other soldiers; and he meant those rights should be protected.

"The rebels at first refused to recognize black troops as soldiers, and threatened that, if captured, neither they nor their white officers should receive the treatment of prisoners of war; the former were to be regarded as runaway slaves, the latter as thieves and robbers, having stolen and appropriated slave property. Grant, however, was determined to protect all those whom he commanded; and when it was reported to him that a white captain and some negro soldiers, captured at Milliken's Bend, had been hung, he wrote to General Richard Taylor, then commanding the rebel forces in Louisiana: 'I feel no inclination to retaliate for the offenses of irresponsible persons, but, if it is the policy of any general intrusted with the command of troops to show no quarter, or to punish with death prisoners taken in battle, I will accept the issue.'"[1]

The rebels made a pretense of referring the matter to the State authorities, but took care to do noth-

[1] Badeau's "Military History," page 408.

ing which would bring upon them the retaliation with which Grant had threatened them.

On the 24th of July Grant again urged the attack on Mobile, and suggested, what was true, that it would make a diversion from Bragg's army. But one of the finest opportunities of the war was lost, and that for reasons which had no force whatever. Rosecrans was left without sufficient forces, and, as a consequence, to lose the battle of Chickamauga ; and we failed to take Mobile, at an inviting moment, because Banks, with a large army, had been sent to Texas.[1] And what became of Banks ? No part of all our military movements in Louisiana and Texas was worth one-fourth part the men we lost there. It was the weakest part of all the military conduct of the Government. Washington was continually counteracting all that Grant, or Rosecrans, or any good officer could do, and its treatment of Rosecrans was what no honest man can regard without pain.[2]

Mobile was not attacked. Banks was sent to Louisiana and Texas, to waste a fine army in useless expeditions ; Rosecrans was left without reënforcements ; and Bragg allowed, uninterrupted, to collect an immense force in front of Chattanooga, and almost, but happily not altogether, to succeed in taking that key-point in the strategy of the war. In fact, from

---

[1] Lincoln and Halleck both wrote to Grant that this was the reason.

[2] I am glad that the evidence, both oral and documentary, shows that Grant was entirely innocent of the wrong done Rosecrans. What that wrong was, and who did it, will be seen in the next pages. Grant seems to have had none of that malicious weakness which strives to elevate himself by putting other people down. He was just to his generals, and willing to obey.

the middle of July to the middle of October, three precious months were wasted, illustrating one great principle of war, that to take advantage of a victory is as important as to gain it. In the last days of August, Grant went to New Orleans, and, at a review there, unfortunately was thrown from his horse, which confined him to one position for a month, and for two months he had to use crutches. To understand what now became the part of Grant and of the Western armies, we must glance for a single moment at what had been done in other parts of the battle-field, in the long time since Grant left Cairo for the conquest of the Mississippi.

McClellan had made his grand march on the Peninsula, fought a dozen battles, and fought them well, but had been compelled to return to the Potomac to drive Lee out of Maryland ; had won victories at South Mountain and Antietam, and at last terminated his career by inglorious delay. Then Burnside had made his disastrous assault on Fredericksburg, losing thousands, and nothing accomplished. Then Hooker had crossed the Rapidan, and made masterly dispositions, fought a great battle, and retired, because the water was high ! Such, for two years, had been the proceedings on the Potomac ; armies after armies marching and fighting *with no result whatever*, except the loss of more men than Grant was charged with losing in his grand campaign for the conquest of Richmond.[1] Nor had the

---

[1] One of the gravest charges made against Grant is, that, to obtain success, he sacrificed a vast number of men before Richmond. Let such critics count up the losses of two years of failures, and see whether they are any less than Grant's loss in one year of success.

rebel general done any better. Lee had made two grand raids with his whole army into Maryland and Pennsylvania, each time losing thousands of men he could not afford to lose, and accomplishing nothing. At length, in his last raid, on the same 4th of July on which Vicksburg surrendered, he met with our army at Gettysburg, and suffered a most disastrous defeat. But even Gettysburg was decisive in only a negative sense. It was what we were saved from, and not what we gained, which made it important. We did not advance to Richmond by Gettysburg. In one word, *all the military schemes and strategy of the Potomac campaigns had been indecisive and worthless.*[1] The reason was obvious. The whole idea of the Richmond campaign *at that time* was wrong, because, if we had taken Richmond, the mountains and valleys of Virginia, as Davis had declared, would have been easily defended. Armies in the field, as well as fortified towns, are only successfully attacked *when they are turned, and their resources are cut off.* The army of Lee, even if beaten in the field, must be practically successful till his resources in the South-West were cut off, and the Mississippi became our base of operations. It was not till Grant had conquered the Mississippi that the conquest of Virginia became possible, and then it was .only possible by enabling us to hold and operate from Chattanooga.

Now let us turn to another field of the West. We have seen Rosecrans in the successful battles of Iuka and Corinth, exhibiting the qualities of a brill-

---

[1] The only way to disprove this verdict is to show that in October, 1863, we were nearer Richmond than in October, 1861.

iant and brave soldier. It is evident he was one of
the men the Government wanted. Accordingly, in
the autumn of 1862, he was appointed to command
the army forming in Middle Tennessee to act against
Bragg, and with Chattanooga as the objective point.
Soon after, he fought the great battle of Stone River,
in which he showed the talent of a great general.
Following this up with successful strategy through
Tullahoma, he drove Bragg back, and, on September
9, 1863, triumphantly entered Chattanooga. This
was the key-point of the rebel line of defense, without which, any attempts to defend the South-West,
or prevent the fall of Richmond, would be in vain.
The captures of Vicksburg and Chattanooga were
twin events. At the time this happened, it will be
remembered, Grant was confined to his bed with a
fall from his horse at New Orleans, and that Sherman had just closed up the campaign with Johnston,
and that for some reason—which did not lie at the
door of Grant, but was clearly the offspring of Washington management—the troops were scattered in
various directions, and *not* sent, as they ought to
have been, to Rosecrans. The consequence was,
the battle of Chickamauga, called a defeat, but which
was only partially so, (for nothing is a defeat where
the enemy gains nothing,) by which Rosecrans fell,
for a time, under a shadow. It was only a shadow,
for a careful examination of the facts by any impartial mind will prove that the most charged against
Rosecrans was only some temporary indiscretion
Was this ground to dismiss a successful and a popular general? In the West it was a very unpopular

act of the Government, nor can I get rid of the impression that it was equally unjust. But with its policy or its injustice Grant had nothing to do. He was far distant from Chattanooga, and unmixed with the personal or political intrigues which in our war, as in all others, mingled in the operations of the army, as in the proceedings of the Cabinet. It happened, fortunately for himself as well as the country, that Grant's temperament, as well as disconnection with party intrigues, enabled him to arrive at calm and impartial judgments without doing any thing unjust to individuals, or contrary to the policy of the Government. When, therefore, Grant was offered the command of the army at Chattanooga, he accepted it on grounds of duty and policy, without reference to the particular position of Rosecrans, or the plans for the Potomac. He was simply aiming at the success of the whole military system.[1]

The Secretary of War had gone to the West, and met Grant at Indianapolis for a conference. The Secretary gave Grant the command of the armies of the Ohio, the Cumberland, and the Tennessee. On this Colonel Badeau makes the following extraordinary statement:

"The Secretary of War accompanied him as far as Louisville; there both remained a day, discussing the situation of affairs, and Grant gathering the views

---

[1] It is proper to say that, on the 13th of September, Halleck had telegraphed that Grant's available force should be sent to Memphis, and thence to Rosecrans. This dispatch did not arrive till after the battle of Chickamauga was fought; and for this long and unnecessary delay of *two months* in sending Rosecrans reënforcements, Halleck, as it appears, is responsible.

of the Government. During this day the minister received a dispatch from Mr. C. A. Dana, his subordinate, at Chattanooga, intimating that the danger of an abandonment of Chattanooga was instant; that Rosecrans was absolutely preparing for such a movement. The Secretary at once directed Grant to immediately assume his new command, and to relieve Rosecrans before it was possible for the apprehended mischief to be consummated."

There is *no evidence* whatever that Rosecrans had the least idea of abandoning Chattanooga at any time. Why should he want to? Chattanooga was the fruit of his own success; the laurel which adorned his own brow. Why should he give it up? No man has charged Rosecrans with want of resolution or of courage. The dispatch from Dana arrived several days after Chickamauga, when there was no immediate danger whatever; nor did Grant set out till the 19th of October, nearly a month after. It is difficult to see what business Mr. Dana had in the army at that particular time, or from what quarter he derived his information. He did not get it from General Rosecrans, and it looks like a figment of his own imagination.

One other event (memorable in the affairs of men and nations) I must mention before we proceed. This was the Proclamation of Emancipation, issued as Order No. 1, on the 1st of January, 1863. Whatever legal effect might, on the return of peace, (in case slavery had not been abolished by the States,) attach to this docmuent, three consequences followed of vast importance. As a military order, it was conclusive on the army, and at once did away with the absurd idea of many officers, that property in slaves was to be respected. It was most absurd and most mischievous, that, in the beginning of the war, some commanders in the army actually believed and acted on the idea that they must respect property in man! War, of necessity, abolished slavery in all that concerned war. I have already shown that Grant compelled the rebels to respect the rights of negro soldiers. Fremont, in Missouri, had proclaimed them free, and the Government was so frightened that it instantly repealed the order! Such is the terrible effect, even on the strongest minds, of a moral insanity, which seems to corrupt even the constitution of the human soul. But this order, if it did not destroy the moral delusion, became the law of the army, and Grant was very willing to live up to it. Another effect was, a decided reaction on the public opinion of Europe, especially that of England. France was ready to declare against us, conquer Mexico, and extend, as Napoleon expressed it, the limits of the Latin race. But Napoleon had not the moral courage to act without England, and the English aristocracy (naturally detesting republicanism) dared not act with the workingmen against them. Such was the situation of affairs when Lincoln's Proclamation threw the whole antislavery people of England (and that was a vast number) in our favor. Thus England was held fast, and France dared not act alone.

But a greater effect was produced on the opinion of this country. Perhaps very few people, if any, were added to the numerical strength of the Government, and in the South the majority of Unionists were carried over to the rebels. But the moral effect was of far greater weight than all that. A moral idea of tremendous force now impelled and stimulated the supporters of Government, while, on the other hand, the moral depression on the rebel mind was equally great. They saw clearly that all hope of help from Europe was gone, and that nothing but a miraculous military success could save the thousands of millions in slave property from utter destruction. In fine, the MORAL CRISIS of the war was passed when Lincoln issued his Emancipation Proclamation, though Vicksburg and Gettysburg had not yet come. Of all the heroic acts which live in history, none was nobler than that of Lincoln; and of all the laurels which adorn the memories of heroes and of statesmen, none are greener, or will live longer, than those of the great American President.

CHAPTER X.

CHATTANOOGA.

THE SWITZERLAND OF AMERICA—THE SUCK OF THE TENNES-
SEE—CHATTANOOGA—GRANT TAKES COMMAND—BRAGG
BOASTS—ROSECRANS'S PREPARATIONS—HOOKER MOVES ON
LOOKOUT—ROADS SAFE—BRAGG DETACHES LONGSTREET—
GRANT MAKES ALL ARRANGEMENTS—SENDS ORDER TO
BURNSIDE—BATTLE ABOVE THE CLOUDS—HOOKER STORMS
LOOKOUT MOUNTAIN—SHERMAN ATTACKS MISSIONARY
RIDGE—THOMAS BREAKS THE ENEMY'S CENTER—GREAT
VICTORY—SIEGE OF KNOXVILLE—CAMPAIGN ENDED.

" The day had been one of dense mists and rains, and much of General Hooker's
battle was fought above the clouds, which concealed him from our view, but from
which his musketry was heard."—*General Meigs to Secretary Stanton.*

" By the banks of Chattanooga, watching with a soldier's heed,
In the chilly autumn morning, gallant Grant was on his steed ;
For the foe had climbed above him with the banners of their band,
And the cannon swept the river from the hills of Cumberland.

Like a trumpet rang his orders : ' Howard, Thomas, to the bridge !
One brigade aboard the Dunbar ! storm the hights of Mission Ridge,
On the left the ledges, Sherman, charge and hurl the rebels down !
Hooker, take the steeps of Lookout, and the slopes before the town !'
"T. B."

———

" 'T was the legion so famed of the White Star, and led on by Geary
    the brave,
That was chosen to gather the laurel, or find on the mountain a grave.

  .   .   .   .

O ! long as the mountains shall rise o'er the waters of bright Ten-
    nessee,
Shall be told the proud deeds of the White Star, the cloud-treading
    host of the free !

> The camp-fire shall blaze to the chorus, the picket-post peal it on
> high,
> How was fought the fierce battle of Lookout—how won THE GRAND
> FIGHT OF THE SKY!" [1]

THIRTY years ago I descended the Tennessee River in a little steamboat. At Knoxville I had attended a railroad convention, whose object was to unite the South and the West. Had the original plan been successfully carried out, who can tell whether the mutuality of interests and acquaintance might not have even prevented the terrible struggle which, twenty years after, took place? Such was not the purpose of Providence. A great crime had to be avenged; a great evil to be abolished; a nation to be disciplined, and a great experiment to be tried on the possibility of self-government in a state of uninterrupted freedom. At Knoxville I saw the Holston coming from the valley of Virginia to join the Tennessee, and both together roll toward the Father of Waters. The mountains stood around to sentinel the land, and as we passed below Kingston we came to the Suck of the Tennessee, where the river breaks through the Cumberland Ridges. There are but two other spots which compare with this: one is the passage of the Hudson, through the mountain ridge, at West Point; and the other that of the Potomac, at Harper's Ferry. They are very much alike in the main feature. The Tennessee was compressed at the Suck into so narrow and rocky a channel that it seemed impossible to pass by steamboat. To me, standing on the deck, it seemed scarcely as broad as

---

[1] "Lookout Mountain," by Alfred B. Street.

the steamboat itself. On the south of the Suck was the grand Lookout Mountain, since so memorable in history. Above Lookout was Chattanooga Valley, and where it opens on the Tennessee was formerly Ross's Landing. This spot is the present Chattanooga; but, when I was there, there was no town whatever; that is of recent creation. On the other side of Lookout, between that and Raccoon Ridge, was Lookout Valley. Chattanooga Valley was between Missionary Ridge and Lookout. It will be seen there were three ridges—Mission, Lookout, and Raccoon; that between the first two was Chattanooga Valley, and between the last two Lookout Valley. The main ridge was Lookout Mountain, over two thousand feet in hight, which looked down upon the winding Tennessee in rugged and gloomy grandeur. It was winding round its base that the Tennessee made the "Suck," so called from the rapid whirl of the waters, tumbling over rocks, and compressed to a narrow breadth. On the opposite side were ridges also, but with broader valleys. Passing through these mountain gorges, in our little steamboat, I was forcibly reminded of West Point, and its almost impregnable defenses. This was a Switzerland, which hardy freemen might defend against half a world. When the war broke out, in 1861, I urged upon General Mitchel the necessity of occupying East Tennessee and its principal points. He actually got an order to do that, when, soon after, it was countermanded, and he ordered to join Buell. McClellan said that he was anxious to occupy East Tennessee. Why did he not do it? The fact is, the Government had no

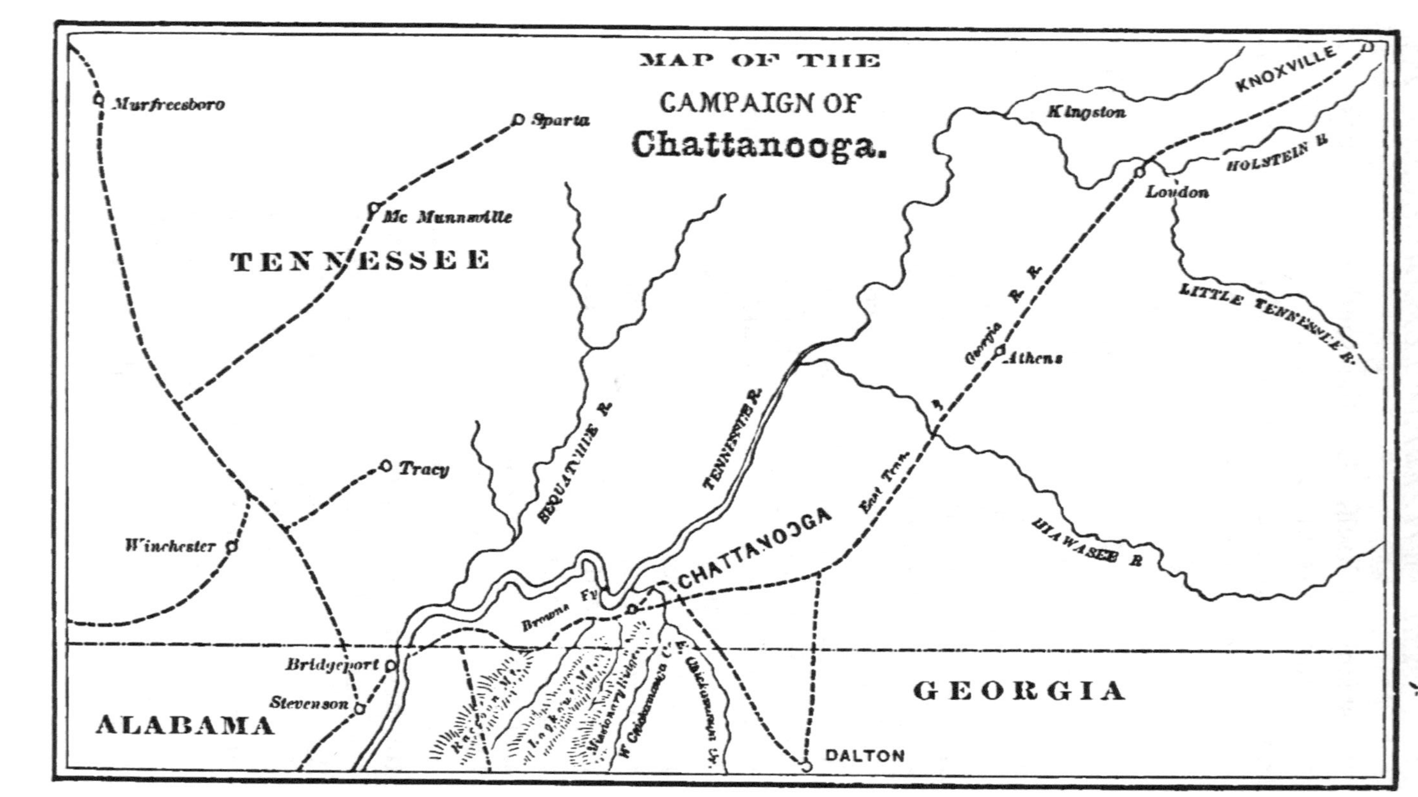

MAP OF THE
CAMPAIGN OF
Chattanooga.
Murfreesboro
Sparta
Kingston
KNOXVILLE
HOLSTEIN R.
Loudon
Mc Munnville
TENNESSEE
LITTLE TENNESSEE R.
Georgia R. R.
Athens
SEQUATCHIE R.
TENNESSEE R.
HIAWASEE R.
Tracy
East Tenn.
Winchester
CHATTANOOGA
Browns Fy.
Bridgeport
GEORGIA
Stevenson
Raccoon Mt.
Lookout Mt.
Missionary Ridge
W. Chickamauga Cr.
Chickamauga Cr.
ALABAMA
DALTON

general plan of strategy, and constantly suffered itself to be diverted from its true objects by the raids and threatenings of the enemy.

Grant took command of the army on the 19th of October. He telegraphed to Thomas, (who was that day put in command,) who replied: "I will hold the town *till we starve!*" This was the answer of a brave soldier, but it had been the decision of Rosecrans also; and there was no great merit in it, for no good soldier would abandon Chattanooga while it was possible to hold it; and the question was precisely the same to Rosecrans, to Thomas, and to Grant. That question was, simply, to starve or not to starve. The case was fairly stated by Bragg, who said: "Possessed of the shortest route to his depot, and the one by which reënforcements must reach him, *we hold him at our mercy, and his destruction is only a question of time.*"[1] So Bragg thought; but he was very apt to be mistaken; and we shall see how it turned out.[2] The position of Rosecrans at Chattanooga was this: Partially defeated at Chickamauga, with very heavy losses of men, he was compelled to shut himself up in Chattanooga, and draw his line of defense around it, so that *its safety should be made*

---

[1] Bragg's Report.

[2] I have said Chickamauga was not a defeat, and so said the rebels. The following is from a writer in the "Richmond Whig:" "That the campaign, so far, is a failure, and the battle of Chickamauga, though a victory, is not a success, are propositions too plain for denial. We have not recovered Chattanooga as yet, much less Tennessee, and it may be well for the country to inquire, whether the fault lies with a subordinate officer, or is to be traced to the inefficiency and incompetency of one higher in rank—one who is presumed intellectually to direct the operations of the Army of Tennessee."

certain. In doing this he lost, as Bragg said, his short communication by the Tennessee, and was compelled to carry his provisions by a circuitous route of *sixty miles* over Walden's Ridge. The result was, that in the very bad state of the roads, and only wagons to rely on, that this became almost impossible, and the army really was near starvation. The phrase of Thomas, that he would remain till he was starved, was very significant, though not very remarkable. On the 23d of October, Grant, having gone part of the way by rail and part on horseback, over almost impassable roads, (over which, being lame, he had sometimes to be carried,) arrived at Chattanooga. Here he saw, at once, that the first object was to regain the short line of supplies by Lookout Mountain and Valley. This was so obvious that Halleck had written him three days before to this effect, and Rosecrans had foreseen and made the arrangements by which it was to be done.[1] Colonel

[1] Halleck wrote to Grant on the 20th, (which Grant did not get, probably,) that the communication must be opened. That Rosecrans had made the arrangements, which (mainly) Grant adopted, is proved by the sworn testimony of Rosecrans, uncontradicted by any body. I take the following paragraph from Mr. Whitelaw Reid's "Ohio in the War:"

"General Rosecrans, in testimony under oath before the Committee on the Conduct of the War, specifically stated that he had formed these plans, had made reconnoissances preliminary to carrying them out, and had explained them (fifteen days, in fact, before his removal) to Generals Thomas and Garfield, and, some time later, to General William F. Smith. Grant afterward acknowledged, in terms, his indebtedness to General William F. Smith for the crossing below Chattanooga, and the connection with Hooker.

"In the course of his testimony, just referred to, General Rosecrans said: 'As early as the 4th of October, I called the attention of Generals Thomas and Garfield to the map of Chattanooga and vicinity,

Badeau, after stating, as I have previously related, that Dana informed the Government that Rosecrans was about to abandon Chattanooga, on which Grant sent his hasty order of the 19th to Thomas, admits, in his "Military History," that Rosecrans had determined to hold Chattanooga. "When Rosecrans discovered the extent of his misfortune, he determined, if possible, to hold Chattanooga, but thought himself unable to do more. The whole army was at once withdrawn into the town, and in two days a formidable line of works was thrown up, so close that some of the houses were left outside."

This is the fact, and it is not necessary to the clear and just fame of General Grant, to misrepresent or diminish the merits of Rosecrans. This officer, relieved of his command, returned to Cincinnati, where, in the winter months, he served as President of the Sanitary Commission—a service whose laurels are as green, and whose memory will be longer than those won on the battle-field, for they will live among the immortals.

On the 23d of September, Halleck ordered the Eleventh and Twelfth Corps from the Army of the

and, pointing out to them the positions, stated that, as soon as I could possibly get the bridge materials for that purpose, I would take possession of Lookout Valley (the point on the south side, reached by the march across the peninsula) and fortify it, thus completely covering the road from there to Bridgeport. . . . To effect this General Hooker was directed to concentrate his troops at Stephenson and Bridgeport, and advised that, as soon as his train should arrive, or enough of it to subsist his army, ten or twelve miles from his depot, he would be directed to move into Lookout Valley. . . . On the 19th, I directed General William F. Smith to reconnoiter the shore above Chattanooga, with a view to that very movement on the enemy's right flank, which was afterward made by General Sherman.'"

Potomac, and sent them by rail to the support of Rosecrans, just three weeks too late. They came to Bridgeport, for, had they gone into Chattanooga, they would only have made bad worse by consuming provisions. In October, Burnside, with a large number of troops and the Ninth Corps, had taken Knoxville, and held the greater part of East Tennessee, but made no connection with Rosecrans. Here, then, was the position : Rosecrans in Chattanooga, with his army approaching starvation, and two corps at Bridgeport, ready to join him, and Burnside to the East, who ought to connect with him. The problem to be solved, as I have remarked, was very obvious. A junction must be made with Hooker, and the direct communication opened. Brown's Ferry was near the foot of Raccoon Mountain, near Lookout Valley, and opposite the Suck, or west side of Lookout Mountain. Near the foot of Lookout, and at the outlet of the valley, the rebels held position with a brigade. Now that was the very position to be taken ; for the distance from Brown's Ferry to Chattanooga, across Moccasin Point, was not very great. The plan was to send down a body of men in pontoons to Brown's Ferry, seize it, and build a bridge there. At the same time Hooker was to advance from Bridgeport by a wagon road, through a gap of Raccoon, to Wauhatchie, in Lookout Valley ; to seize the position of the enemy on the sides of Lookout Mountain ; all of which, if successful, would result in our getting a short communication by Bridgeport and Brown's Ferry.[1]

[1] "Rosecrans had contemplated some movement of this sort, and had ordered a pontoon bridge to be prepared, but had been content

The plan was successful. On the night of the 26th, dark and foggy, Hazen descended, with eighteen hundred men, in sixty pontoon·boats, rounded Lookout, and, by five o'clock, had seized the hills covering the ferry. Another body, with materials for a bridge, was moved across Moccasin Point, and, in two or three hours more, the hights rising from Lookout Valley were secured, and made safe from attack. On the same day, (the 26th,) Hooker crossed the Tennessee on pontoons, at Bridgeport, with the Eleventh and part of the Twelfth Corps, under Howard and Geary; descending through a gorge of Raccoon Mountain, he arrived safely in Lookout Valley, and encamped at night within a mile of Brown's Ferry. The next night he was furiously attacked by Longstreet, who, after a severe battle, was repulsed. The enemy had attempted to dislodge Howard's Corps from hights considerably above him; but he not only repulsed them, but seized the hights. Thus Lookout Valley and Brown's Ferry were seized and held, and, come what may, the army would be provisioned, and Bragg's boast be in vain. At the same time General Johnson marched from Chattanooga, with a part of the Fourth Corps, to hold the road passed over by Hooker, and command the hights near Kelly's Ferry, (a ferry between Brown's and Bridgeport,) and thus, by these ferries and a part of the river, the supply line was reduced to a comparatively small distance. Thus one of the main parts of the strategic movement in the Chattanooga

with such remote preliminaries." He had done all he could, and was then building two steamboats at Bridgeport.

campaign was well and most successfully completed.

Grant now formed the design of attacking the rebels on Missionary Ridge; for Bragg's army lay in an arc, with its right resting on Missionary Ridge, its center in Chattanooga Valley, and its left on Lookout Mountain. The strength of the position was on Missionary Ridge, about four hundred feet above the valley of Chattanooga, and extending back for miles. Here lay the best part of the rebel army. The immediate object of the attack was to relieve Burnside's army in East Tennessee. To understand this, we must return for a moment to the position of Burnside. He had, as I have said, gone into East Tennessee with a large body of troops, and been reënforced with the Ninth Corps. Failing, however, to connect with Rosecrans's army at Chattanooga, he was now in danger of being cut off, and of suffering, if not of being absolutely captured, for want of food. A considerable body of rebel forces were coming down against him from Virginia, (which, however, turned out not to be very important,) and he was threatened with serious attack from Bragg. This last attack turned out, in the order of Providence, (as many other things did,) very contrary to the rebel expectations, and very advantageous to Grant and Burnside. On the 4th of November, Longstreet, one of the best generals in the rebel army, received orders to take a corps and move into East Tennessee as rapidly as possible, give sudden blows, and, if possible, drive Burnside out, or better, capture or destroy him.[1]

---

[1] Bragg's order to Longstreet, on the 4th of November.

Longstreet accordingly set out, with about twenty thousand men, of which part were cavalry, under Wheeler. Bragg and Longstreet, who planned this expedition together, were both utterly mistaken as to the true position of affairs. Longstreet told Bragg that he had overestimated our army, that it would be no greater than his, after the proposed force was withdrawn. Perhaps, at that day, it was not. But Sherman, with the Fifteenth Corps, and all the troops he could collect, was then marching in the Valley of the Tennessee for Chattanooga. Grant was fully aware that he must have a large army to drive Bragg back; and, therefore, had made arrangements for all the men and all the provisions he could get, to be hurried on to Chattanooga. He had anticipated this very movement, and was afraid that Bragg would burst through to the east of him, and so he wrote Sherman to hurry up. When, therefore, Bragg came to send twenty thousand men from his army on the chase for Burnside, Grant saw his advantage, and, writing to Burnside to hold on, even if he lost half his army, immediately prepared for the final shock at Chattanooga. We can now understand the posi- tion: Bragg sending off Longstreet to the east, and thus greatly weakening his own army, while Sherman (already arrived at Huntsville) is hurrying up to Grant with an entire corps and several divisions; Long- street rushing furiously after Burnside, and most sig- nally failing in the storm of Knoxville; Sherman soon coming up; and Bragg resting in security, while Grant is preparing the storm to overwhelm him.

This is the real position on the 7th of November, although Sherman had not arrived.

On that day (the 7th) Grant telegraphed Halleck that Longstreet was moving against Burnside, and said: "I have ordered Thomas to attack the north end of Missionary Ridge, and when that is carried to threaten or attack the enemy's line of communication between Cleveland and Dalton."[1] But this was not to be quite so soon. The artillery was in the mud; there were not horses to draw it; things were not ready. In fine, the army could not move. Grant was compelled to do what was for the best under any circumstances, wait for Sherman to come up. No doubt Burnside was in great danger. Halleck was in great anxiety about him, and kept up a succession of telegrams to Grant. Grant saw all this, and had already told Burnside to do the only thing possible, and which, in fact, did save him. First, to rely on the loyal Tennesseans for provisions; which he did, and got enough; and to fight to the last at Knoxville; which he did, and was victorious. In fact, there was not so much real danger to Burnside as had been apprehended. It turned out, by comparing his dispatches to Grant and Halleck, in the middle of November, that, though the men might suffer in the winter, if Longstreet remained on the railroad south of him, yet there was no danger of starvation. He had plenty of beef, and kept the mills round grinding for him. He was on the Tennessee, between Knoxville and Kingston, and had no idea of

---

[1] This, if successful, was to cut the communications between Bragg and Longstreet.

falling back. He was ready for fight, if fight was necessary. In the mean time, during the first half of November, Grant was making every possible preparation for the support and movement of troops. Never was his administrative ability more strikingly exhibited. He was constantly dispatching all the commanders in his wide department to collect troops, munitions, provisions, and transportation. From every quarter they were coming. He got Porter to convey transports up the Cumberland. He ordered the Louisville and Nashville Railroad to be put to its utmost capacity of transportation, in order to supply the depots at Nashville, and got all the locomotives and steamboats possible to carry the supplies to Bridgeport. From every quarter troops and materials were concentrating to make the grand move from Chattanooga effective and decisive.

At last, on the 16th, the Corps of Sherman arrived at Bridgeport,[1] and on the 18th at Chattanooga. On the 20th, Bragg performed a little maneuver which, if such deception were not justifiable in war, would be extremely ridiculous. He sent a note to Grant, that, as there were some non-combatants in Chattanooga, he would recommend their speedy withdrawal! Grant at once inferred that Bragg meant to withdraw his own forces. Accordingly, he immediately ordered a grand reconnoissance toward Missionary Ridge, which was performed by General Thomas and four divisions. This was done on the 23d of November, and was remarkably successful;

---

[1] The reader should examine the little map, and get an idea of the localities.

for General Wood's Division charged up and took Orchard Knob, a rather important spur of Missionary Ridge, and drove the enemy from their advanced intrenchments. This encouraged the troops, and was a good beginning for the great conflict. It was discovered that the enemy actually were sending troops to Longstreet, and thus this movement was most opportune.

The great object of attack was the north end of Missionary Ridge, an attack to be made by General Sherman ; but other attacks and arrangements were to be made before that came. So, on the next day, (24th,) came Hooker's decisive assault on Lookout Mountain. The enemy's whole line (altogether too long, as they knew) extended from Lookout Valley (holding the top of Lookout) to Chickamauga Valley, east of Missionary Ridge. This was an arc of some six or seven miles in length, altogether too much for Bragg to hold. Around the foot of Lookout, and commanding the river, lay Hooker with his force. The present object is to take the summit of Lookout, and then be able to attack and turn the enemy's left. Bragg, in his official Report,[1] says the resistance was made by only one brigade ; but also adds, that the commander on that field (General Stevenson) had *six brigades available*, and one would think that was enough to defend a mountain cliff. But we shall get a clearer view by turning to Hooker's account of it. He says :[2]

"At this time the enemy's pickets formed a con-

---

[1] Bragg's Report, dated Dalton, November 30th.
[2] Hooker's Report, dated February 4, 1864.

tinuous line along the right bank of Lookout Creek, with the reserves in the valleys, while his main force was encamped in the hollow, half-way up the slope of the mountain. The summit itself was held by three brigades of Stevenson's Division, and these were comparatively safe, as the only means of access from the west, for a distance of twenty miles up the valley, was by two or three trails, admitting of the passage of but one man at a time, and even these trails were held at the top by rebel pickets. For this reason no direct attempt was made for the dislodgment of this force. On the Chattanooga side, which is less precipitous, a road of easy grade has been made, communicating with the summit by zig-zag lines running diagonally up the mountain-side ; and it was believed that before our troops should gain possession of this, the enemy on the top would evacuate his position, to avoid being cut off from his main body, to rejoin which would involve a march of twenty or thirty miles. Viewed from whatever point, Lookout Mountain, with its high, palisaded crest and its steep, ragged, rocky, and deeply furrowed slopes, presented an imposing barrier to our advance, and when to these natural obstacles were added almost interminable well-planned and well-constructed defenses, held by Americans, the assault became an enterprise worthy of the ambition and renown of the troops to whom it was intrusted."

After various arrangements had been made of divisions and corps for the general assault, Hooker says : " The troops on the mountain rushed on in their advance, the right passing directly under the muzzles of the enemy's guns on the summit, climbing over ledges and bowlders, uphill and downhill, furiously driving the enemy from his camp, and from position after position. This lasted till twelve o'clock, when Geary's advance heroically rounded the -peak of the mountain." The enemy were driven panic-stricken from their positions. The success was uninterrupted and irresistible. Hooker again says:

"It was now near two o'clock, and our operations were arrested by the darkness. The clouds, which had hovered over and enveloped the summit of the mountain during the morning, and to some extent favored our movements, gradually settled into the valley, and completely vailed it from our view. Indeed, from the moment we rounded the peak of the mountain, it was only from the roar of battle, and the occasional glimpse our comrades in the valley could catch of our lines and standards, that they knew of the strife in its progress; and when, from these evidences, our true condition was revealed to them, their painful anxiety yielded to transports of joy, which only soldiers can feel in the earliest moments of dawning victory."

General Meigs described this assault as " Hooker's battle above the clouds," and it had all the elements of poetic grandeur. The clouds were seen far below, while, from the summit of that hoary mountain, the deep boom of cannon came, and occasionally the red flash of its fire could be seen from below; and then the clouds, bursting away, disclosed to their friends below the heroes of Lookout Mountain. As the night came on, the falling fire of musketry could be heard, and away in the valley below, those on the mountain could behold the camp-fires of the hostile armies stretching far away.

This movement was decisive of all the coming operations. Bragg did not underrate it, although he was in hopes to defend successfully what he deemed the almost impregnable position of Missionary Ridge. He says, in his report:

"Arriving just before sunset, I found we had lost all the advantages of the position. Orders were immediately given for the ground to be disputed, till we could withdraw our forces across Chattanooga Creek, and the movement was commenced. This having been successfully accomplished, our whole forces were concentrated on the Ridge, and extended to the right, to meet the movement in that direction."

Any one can see that, with the command of Lookout Mountain and Chattanooga Valley, the enemy's positions on Missionary Ridge must be eventually turned, (as they really were,) and finally fall. There might be hard fighting and much loss, but Missionary Ridge must fall. And, beyond doubt, it was the conviction of this fact which caused the moral defection of the rebel army, of which the rebel writers from the field all complain. They said, the veteran troops of Bragg did not fight as well as usual. From Missionary Ridge, looking upon Lookout Mountain, they could see clearly enough the hopelessness of their condition. And yet Bragg hoped on, and wondered why his troops faltered. But still the battle is to be fought, and we must return to Missionary Ridge.

The position of our army on the morning of the 25th of November has been very well described by Colonel Badeau, and I extract it from his "Military History:"

"The morning of the 25th of November broke raw and cold, but the sun shone brilliantly from a cloudless sky, and the great battle-field was all disclosed. To the north and east was the railroad junction of Chattanooga, which gave the position so much of its value; the roads by which Grant sought communication with Burnside, and those along which the rebel general was drawing his supplies. Behind the National forces, the impetuous river made its tortuous way, never for a mile pursuing the same course; while the Cumberland Mountains and Walden's Ridge formed the massive background. Grant's main line faced south and east, toward Missionary Ridge, now not a mile away. Lookout Mountain, on the National right, bounded the view, Hooker marching down its sides, and through the valley of Chattanooga Creek, to Rossville Gap. Sherman had gained the extreme left of the Ridge, but immense difficulties in his front were yet to overcome; and, all along the crest were the batteries and trenches, filled with rebel soldiers, in front of the Army of the Cumberland. Bragg's head-quarters were plainly visible, on the Ridge, at the center of his now contracted line, while Grant's own position was on the knoll that had been wrested from the rebels the day before. From this point the whole battle-field was displayed; trees, houses, fences, all landmarks in the valley had been swept away for camps."

Grant, Thomas, and the Division officers of the Army of the Cumberland stood on Orchard Knoll, surveying the field, and ready for the combat. On the east side of Missionary Ridge the two Chickamaugas (North and South) ran. As the north end of the Ridge was the main point to be attacked, Grant had assembled there pontoon bridges, and a steamboat, to transport men and artillery, ready for Sherman's attack. Grant, in his official report, describes this operation thus:[1]

"On the night of the 23d of November, Sherman, with three divisions of his army, strengthened by Davis's Division of Thomas's Corps, which had been stationed along the north bank of the river, convenient to where the crossing was to be effected, was ready for operations. At an hour sufficiently early to secure the south bank of the river, just below the mouth of South Chickamauga, by dawn of day, the pontoons in the North Chickamauga were loaded with thirty armed men each, who floated quietly past the enemy's pickets, landed, and captured all but one of the guard, twenty in number, before the enemy was aware of the presence of a foe. The steamboat Dunbar, with a barge in tow, after having finished ferrying across the river the horses procured from Sherman, with which to move Thomas's artillery, was sent up from Chattanooga to aid in crossing artillery and troops; and by daylight of the morning of the 24th of November, eight thousand men were on the south side of the Tennessee, and fortified in rifle-trenches.

[1] Grant's Official Report, dated December 23, 1863.

"By twelve o'clock, M., the pontoon bridges across the Tennessee and the Chickamauga were laid, and the remainder of Sherman's forces crossed over, and at half-past three, P. M., the whole of the northern extremity of Missionary Ridge, to near the railroad tunnel, was in Sherman's possession. During the night he fortified the position thus secured, making it equal, if not superior, in strength to that held by the enemy."

It was the 25th when the brilliant sun and cloudless sky looked down on the great battle of Missionary Ridge. Sherman's charge was on the front of and up Missionary Ridge. Bragg saw the danger, and charged heavily upon him, committing the error of weakening his center to strengthen his left. Grant, who stood on Orchard Knoll, saw the weak place, and at once threw in Thomas, with four divisions, among which were Sheridan and Baird. It was decisive, and henceforward the enemy, broken and dispirited, had no more to do than to make the best of their retreat.

Here I leave the scene to be described by Mr. Furay, the able and interesting correspondent of the "Cincinnati Gazette." After describing the charge of Granger and Palmer, Wood and Sheridan, (of Thomas's Corps,) he says:

"Here, according to original orders, our lines should have halted; but the men were no longer controllable. Baird had carried the rifle-pits in front of his position, and the shout of triumph, rousing the blood to a very frenzy of enthusiasm, rang all along

the line. Cheering each other forward, the three
divisions began to climb the ridge,

'A fiery mass
Of living valor rolling on the foe!'

"The whole Ridge blazed with artillery. Direct,
plunging, and cross-fire, from a hundred pieces of
cannon, was hurled upon that glorious band of heroes scaling the Ridge, and when they were half-way
up, a storm of musket-balls was flung into their very
faces. In reply to the rebel cannon upon the Ridge,
Fort Wood, Fort Negley, and all our batteries that
could be placed in position, opened their sublime
music.

"The storm of war was now abroad with super-
natural power, and as each successive volley burst
from the cloud of smoke which overspread the con-
tending hosts, it seemed that ten thousand mighty
echoes wakened from their slumbers, went groaning
and growling around the mountains, as if resolved to
shake them from their bases, then rolled away down
the valleys, growing fainter and fainter, till ex-
tinguished by echoes of succeeding volleys, as the
distant roar of the cataract is drowned in the nearer
thunders of the cloud.

"And still the Union troops pressed on, scaling
unwaveringly the sides of Missionary Ridge. The
blood of their comrades renders their footsteps slippery; the toil of the ascent almost takes away their
breath; the rebel musketry and artillery mow down
their thinned ranks; but still they press on! Not
once do they even seem to waver. The color-bearers
press ahead, and plant their flags far in advance of

the troops; and at last, O moment of supremest triumph! they reach the crest, and rush like an avalanche upon the astonished foe. Whole regiments throw down their arms and surrender, the rebel artillerists are bayoneted by their guns, and the cannon, which had a moment before been thundering on the Union ranks, are now turned about, pouring death and terror into the midst of the mass of miserable fugitives who are rushing down the eastern slope of the Ridge.

"Almost simultaneously with this immortal charge Hooker threw his forces through a gap in the ridge upon the Rossville road, and hurled them upon the left flank of the enemy, while Johnston charged this portion of their line in front. Already demoralized by the spectacle upon their right, they offered but a feeble resistance, were captured by hundreds, or ran away like frightened sheep."

Such was the battle of Chattanooga, well planned, well fought, and entirely decisive in its results. Bragg had to fall back at once to Dalton, (Georgia,) and never again advanced to the front. The tide of war had ebbed back upon the rebels, and all that remained was to fight with the desperation of a dying gladiator. The drama might have, and did have, some other scenes, but they were all tending, as if drawn by the Omnipotent hand of Providence, toward one complete, perfect, and final catastrophe. No tragedy, drawn out by the highest skill of poetic art, could be more perfectly directed toward an inevitable end than had been the campaigns of Grant, from the time he assumed command at Cairo, till the victory of Chattanooga.

The true view of Chattanooga and its results was taken by the rebels as quickly as by ourselves. The "Richmond Dispatch" contained an interesting letter from the battle-ground, written at Chickamauga, November 25th, midnight, from which I take the following paragraphs:

"The Confederates have sustained to-day the most ignominious defeat of the whole war—a defeat for which there is but little excuse or palliation. For the first time during our struggle for National independence, our defeat is chargeable to the troops themselves, and not to the blunders or incompetency of their leaders. It is difficult to realize how a defeat so complete could have occurred on ground so favorable, notwithstanding the great disparity in the forces of the two hostile armies. . . . .

"The day was lost. Hardee still maintained his ground; but no success of the right wing could restore the left to its original position. All men—even the bravest—are subject to error and confusion; but to-day some of the Confederates did not fight with their accustomed courage. Possibly the contrast between the heavy masses of the Federals, as they rolled across the valley and up the mountain ridge, and their own long and attenuated line, was not of a character to encourage them."

Certainly not. A Spartan would have fought just the same against any odds. But an American is not a Spartan, and has a moral and an intellectual sense, which enables him quickly to perceive and weigh results. The rebel soldiers saw and knew well the consequences of Hooker's march down the sides of

Lookout Mountain upon Rossville, and folding up, as he moved, their whole rear guard. The time for retreat had come, and the sun of that rebel army set forever!

It is now necessary for us to take a glance at Burnside. Grant, Halleck, and Lincoln had all been in anxiety about him. Halleck could-get no peace of mind, and the burden of his dispatches to Grant was—Burnside. He scarcely overrated the importance of a disaster there; but, in fact, Burnside was in a better condition than he was supposed to be. As I have said, he found plenty of beef, and had mills to grind flour. But at length he was shut up in Knoxville, and when there, was reduced to half rations. Longstreet had been, as happened to our forces at Chattanooga, delayed. On the 14th of November, Burnside was between Knoxville, Kingston, and London. On the 15th, he withdrew from London, slowly, toward Knoxville, with the view of drawing Longstreet on, for, at this time, Longstreet had not got up to him. The rebel commander crossed the Tennessee at London, and came up with our men at Campbell's Station, south of Knoxville, where there was a smart fight, and Burnside fell back to Knoxville; but Longstreet did not immediately follow, and Burnside went to work with great vigor and skill in fortifying, and getting troops and provisions. In all this he succeeded very well, and on the 20th of November he considered the line of defenses perfectly secure. He availed himself of all possible fortifications, from creeks turned into ditches, abatis, and wire-works, up to regular forts. The

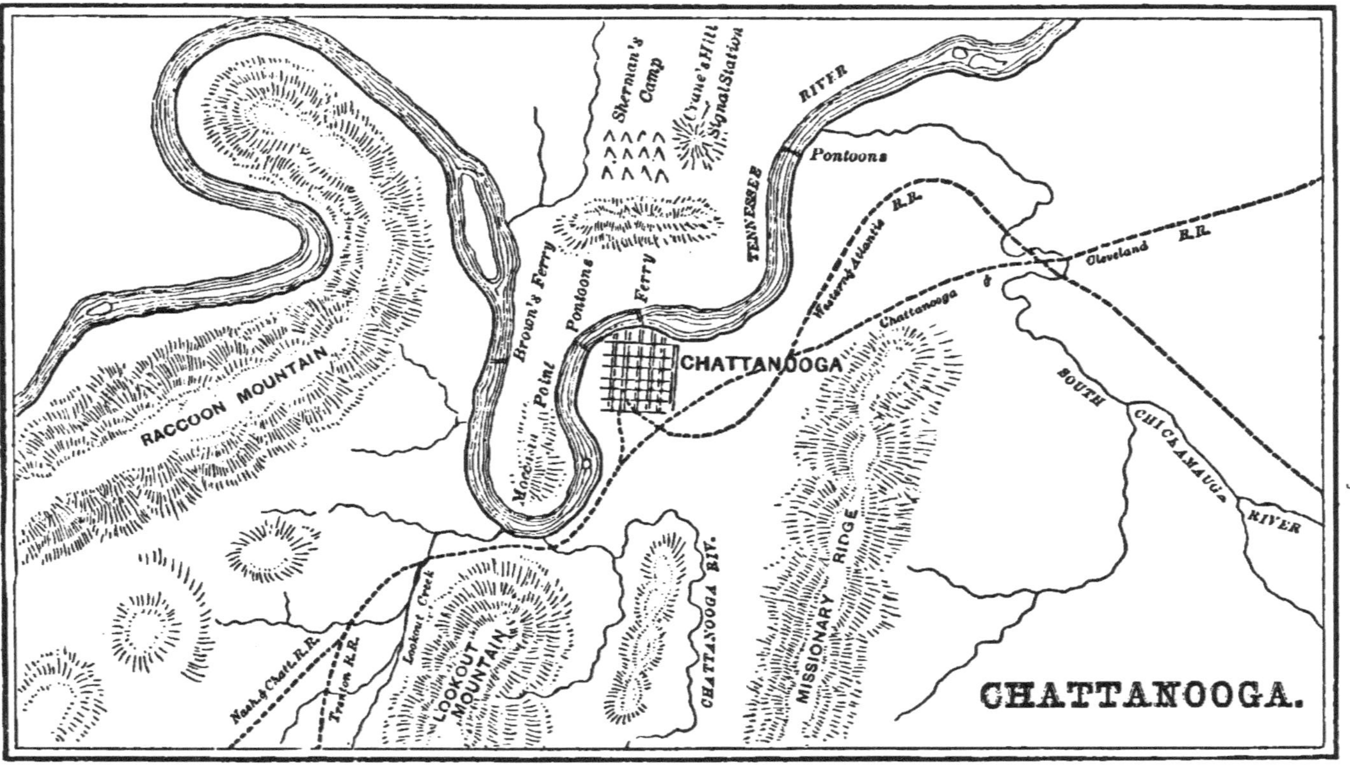

RACCOON MOUNTAIN
Sherman's Camp
Crane's Hill Signal Station
TENNESSEE RIVER
Pontoons
Western & Atlantic R.R.
Cleveland R.R.
Chattanooga
Brown's Ferry
Pontoons
Ferry
Moccasin Point
CHATTANOOGA
SOUTH CHICKAMAUGA RIVER
Nash. & Chatt. R.R.
Trenton R.R.
Lookout Creek
LOOKOUT MOUNTAIN
CHATTANOOGA RIV.
MISSIONARY RIDGE
CHATTANOOGA.

principal of these was Fort Sanders, on the north-west of the town, which was a commanding position. He had a pontoon bridge over the Holston, which facilitated his operations, and which the rebels tried vainly to break with a floating raft. For some reason, not apparent, Longstreet lost his usual sagacity and energy, engaging himself in establishing his own lines, reconnoissances, and skirmishes. It got to be the 27th of November, two days after the battle of Chattanooga, when Buckner (detached from Bragg most foolishly) reached him, with two brigades. Longstreet, however, began to hear of Bragg's defeat, and heroically resolved on an assault. Accordingly, on the 29th, he stormed Fort Sanders, which was very strong, having a deep ditch and high parapet. The assault was most furious, and the rebels fought with desperate valor, but in vain. In attempting to cross the ditch and carry the parapets, they lost heavily, and the garrison but little. Longstreet then received a dispatch from the rebel President, stating that Bragg was defeated, and he should withdraw to his assistance. Longstreet, however, continued the siege, in hopes of withdrawing a large body from Grant, which he did; for Grant, like Halleck, was very anxious about Burnside, and, after the battle of Chattanooga, sent Sherman with a large force to his relief. Foster was also coming to him from the north side, and Grant was in some hope of disorganizing or capturing Longstreet. But he heard of this plan, and, on the 3d of December, put his troops in motion, crossed the Holston at Strawberry, and transferred his army to the east side, unmolested by

Burnside. On the 5th, Sherman had arrived near enough to communicate with Burnside. This ended the siege of Knoxville, and for the present the campaign in the West. The grand concentration of forces in the American Switzerland had not been in vain. The rebel armies had been most signally defeated, Burnside's force saved from what seemed inevitable disaster, and, far more important than either, Chattanooga and its mountain defenses made the *point d'appui*—the strategic base of future movements, which should conquer and sever from the rebel Confederacy all the broad fields of the South-West. The hour of destiny was near at hand, and the news from Chattanooga came like the music of glorious song to the hearts of the people.

"Widows weeping by their firesides, loyal hearts despondent grown,
Smile to hear their country's triumph from the gate of heaven blown,
And the patriot poor shall wonder, in their simple hearts to know,
In the land above the thunder their embattled champions go."

22

CHAPTER XII.

PREPARATION.

GRANT'S PERSONAL CONDUCT—HIS PRESENCE IN BATTLE—
REJOICINGS OF THE PEOPLE—HONORS TO GRANT—DINNER
AT ST. LOUIS—HIS CIGAR-CASE—PLANS FOR THE FUTURE—
SHERMAN'S RAID ON MERIDIAN—RESULTS—AN INCIDENT—
REBEL BOASTS—GRANT MADE LIEUTENANT-GENERAL—
GIVEN COMMAND OF ALL FORCES—TAKES COMMAND, AND
MAKES A NEW PLAN.

IS it a law of our nature that the more conspicuous,
useful, or successful any man may become, he is,
therefore, the more to be assailed by the shafts of
envy and malignity? It seems so, and history seems
scarcely to have found an exception.[1] But even if this
must be, it seems almost incredible that the defamer
should select points of attack which to people of common-sense must appear almost impossible; yet, while I
write these pages, various incredible charges are made
against Grant. It is not at all necessary to exhibit
him as a very extraordinary man in order to defend
him against them. It is only necessary to show that
he does not fall behind other people in the common
qualities of human nature. One of these charges I
will notice here, because he had now arrived at the

---

[1] At this distance of time we may suppose Washington to have been
an exception; but he was not. He was libeled severely by those whom
his success had injured, and whose schemes he had disappointed.

hight of military fame; and, one would think, to acquire that required some courage in conduct, coolness in command, and self-possession of mind. These are qualities which Grant actually has in a high degree; and yet he has been represented as not exposing himself to danger, and intoxicated on the field of battle! I feel ashamed to notice such things, and should be ashamed to notice them if they were said of General Lee. But *some* truth on this subject ought to be told. I have already related that Grant stood with General Smith in the terrible assault on the enemy's right at Donelson. I have traced him through the day at Shiloh, from sunrise at Savannah, through the whole field of battle, to sunset; leading Ammen's Brigade to the defense of the batteries; sleeping till midnight, in the rain, at the foot of a tree; and I have also shown him standing with Thomas on Orchard Knob, at Chattanooga. This is enough; but I find, in Professor Coppée's "Grant and his Campaigns," the statement of a staff officer, which is conclusive on this subject. It should be remembered that a general commanding ought not, except in urgent cases, to lead troops himself; for the loss of a commander may occasion the loss of an army, as Sidney Johnston's death at Shiloh did very much to derange, and ultimately defeat, Beauregard's army. I quote here the staff officer's evidence. It was written of the battle of Chattanooga:

"It has been a matter of universal wonder in this army that General Grant himself was not killed, and that no more accidents occurred to his staff; for the General was always in the front, (his staff with him, of course,) and perfectly heedless of the storm of hissing bullets and screaming shell flying around him. His apparent want of sensibility does not arise from heedlessness, heartlessness, or vain military affectation, but from a sense of the responsibility resting upon him when in battle. When at Ringgold we rode for half a mile in the face of the enemy, under an incessant fire of cannon and musketry; nor did we ride fast, but upon an ordinary trot; 'and not once do I believe did it enter the General's mind that he was in danger. I was by his side, and watched him closely. In riding that distance we were going to the front, and I could see that he was studying the positions of the two armies; and, of course, planning how to defeat the enemy, who was here making a most desperate stand, and was slaughtering our men fearfully."

After this no more need be said of Grant's personal conduct in battle. The part of a great general is not to be a cavalier of romantic gallantry, but to be the skillful and prudent commander, to whom is committed the lives of an army and the interests of a country.

Grant had now reached the culmination of his military success; for, even though greater battles might be fought, the rebellion ended, the Government restored, and a new career opened to him, it was improbable that greater campaigns, or occasion for more successful strategy, would ever come to him than those of Vicksburg and Chattanooga. Accordingly the rejoicings of the people, and the honors bestowed by the Government, could scarcely be exceeded. Illumination lit up the cities, salutes were fired, and, on the 7th of December, the President issued his Proclamation for a general thanksgiving to God "for this great advancement for the National cause." The next day he sent to Grant the following brief and characteristic dispatch, which Grant embodied in orders to the army:

"WASHINGTON, *December* 8, 1863.

"MAJOR-GENERAL GRANT:

"Understanding that your lodgment at Chattanooga and Knoxville is now secure, I wish to tender you, and all under your command, my more than thanks—my profoundest gratitude—for the skill, courage, and perseverance with which you and they, over so great difficulties, have effected that important object. God bless you all!

"A. LINCOLN."

December 17th, a joint resolution of thanks to Grant, and to the officers and soldiers of both armies, passed both Houses of Congress, which also directed that a gold medal, with suitable emblems and devices,[1] be struck and presented to Major-General Grant. Professor Coppée makes the following enumeration of the honors conferred upon him:[2]

" Learned, religious, temperance societies elected him honorary or life member. Cigars, revolvers, and gifts of various kinds were showered upon him. To none of which does he revert with so much pleasure as to a brier-wood cigar-case, made with a pocket-knife by a poor soldier, and presented to him with feelings of veneration and regard, but with no desire for any return. The Legislatures of Ohio and New

---

[1] On one side was the profile of Grant, surrounded by a wreath of laurels, with his name, the year 1863, and a galaxy of stars. On the reverse, a figure of Fame, with a trump and a scroll, bearing the names of his victories. The motto was: " Proclaim Liberty throughout the Land."

[2] "Grant and His Campaigns," page 250.

York voted him thanks. Mothers call their children
after him, and a large generation of little U. S.'s and
Grants date their birthdays at this time."

In the mean time, Grant made a tour to Knoxville, and a general inspection of his troops and posts.
This led him to a very curious journey, which was
a visit to Cumberland Gap, and thence to Louisville,
on horseback, in mid-winter. This was so severe a
route that he had to walk in some places. On the
11th he was in Louisville, and on the 13th in Nashville, ordering on immense bodies of stores for the
depot at Chattanooga, in readiness for the future
grand movement from that point. Thence he quickly
returned to Chattanooga. Soon after, one of his sons
being dangerously ill at St. Louis, he went there and
spent a few days among old friends. He had lived
there in former years. No sooner was " U. S. Grant,
Chattanooga," plainly written on the hotel book than
St. Louis went into general commotion. The news
flew, and speedily an assembly of gentlemen got
together at short notice, invited him to a public dinner, and, rather strangely for him, it was accepted
for the 29th of January, 1864. He had been an
almost unknown citizen there, at one time engaged
in selling wood from his farm, and it is not surprising that he was willing to receive honor from a people among whom he had lived obscure, now that he
was risen to fame and prosperity. He was received
by two hundred gentlemen, at the Lindell Hotel, and
after a complimentary toast, returned the briefest
possible thanks. The common Council of St. Louis
presented their thanks in glowing terms ; he was

serenaded at night, and the crowd gathered round his door to see the extraordinary man, who, at St. Louis, nobody guessed to be a hero, but who had now become renowned. To all these demonstrations, Grant is said to have exhibited the philosophy of the inveterate smoker—who takes refuge from calamities in the exhaustless resources of a cigar-case—and resolutely smoked away!

We must now return for a moment to Grant's view of the future campaign, and his arrangements for some great and important raids. In the middle of January he had written to Halleck, that he looked upon the next line to be taken to be *that from Chattanooga to Mobile*, Montgomery and Atlanta being the important *intermediate* points.[1] He then proposed to establish large supplies on the Tennessee River, *so as to be independent of the railroads*. This is a general idea of what was actually done by Sherman. In order to do this, he had planned an expedition by Sherman to Meridian, on the east side of the State of Mississippi, which was not understood by the general public, and was very much misunderstood by the rebels, till they subsequently felt the effects of it. Grant had found that the interior of Mississippi and Alabama was full of food and provisions, and he knew that the railroads running through the sea-board States in the South, carried thence supplies, in any quantity, to the rebel armies. Hence, in operating from the line of the Mississippi, one of the

---

[1] It is plain that the march from Atlanta (which was to be a common point) to Mobile was by no means as good a plan as that which was performed by Sherman to Savannah.

advantages would be to cut off and destroy the supplies and railroads of the South-West. As early as December 11th, he wrote to McPherson, in command at Vicksburg : "I shall start a cavalry force through Mississippi in about two weeks, to clear out the State entirely of all rebels." And on the 23d, he wrote Halleck that he was collecting a large cavalry force at Savannah, to cross the Tennessee, clear out Forrest, and destroy, as far as possible, the Mobile and Ohio Railroad. It is very obvious, no permanent occupation was intended by such a force ; and when, subsequently, the rebels rejoiced at what they supposed the compulsory return from Meridian, and disappointment of Sherman, they were very much mistaken in the object, and in what was really done, as we shall soon see.

Sherman set out from Vicksburg on February the 3d, reached Jackson, February the 6th, and arrived at Meridian on the 14th. In the mean time, however, Smith, with seven thousand cavalry, had set out from Memphis, to coöperate with Sherman, but, in consequence of delays and difficulties, did not meet him. Sherman, however, remained a week at Meridian, and, as he said, "made the most complete destruction of the railroads ever beheld—south below Quitman, east to Cuba Station, twenty miles north to Lauderdale Springs, and west all the way back to Jackson."[1] He thus sums up the destruction made by his own and Smith's raids—and it is certainly enough to make a perfect success in the objects proposed :

"The general result of the expedition, including

[1] Sherman's dispatch, February 27, 1864.

Smith's and the Yazoo River movements, are about as follows: One hundred and fifty miles of railroad, sixty-seven bridges, seven thousand feet of trestle, twenty locomotives, twenty-eight cars, ten thousand bales of cotton, several steam-mills, and over two million bushels of corn were destroyed. The railroad destruction is complete and thorough. The capture of prisoners exceeds all loss. Upward of eight thousand contrabands and refugees came in with various columns."

This was really the greatest "raid" of the war, and the stories and incidents told of it were innumerable. The following is told of the Mayor of Brandon:

"Before I had dismounted I was somewhat amused, and a little sorry, for a venerable-looking Southern gentleman, who came riding with great dignity into our camp on a very fine horse. He had scarcely got into the yard when three cavalrymen rode up to him and demanded his horse; he refused at first, but finally succumbed, dismounted, and one of the soldiers got off an old, poor, jaded-looking animal, handed the venerable gentleman the reins, mounted the old fellow's blooded steed, and all three rode off in a hurry. Seeing the old gentleman looking rather distressed, I rode up and asked, 'What 's the matter, neighbor?' 'Why, sir,' he answered, 'I am the Mayor of the town; I came here in search of General McPherson, to make some arrangement by which we could be protected, and they have taken my horse from me.' 'Bad enough,' we replied; 'these Yankees are terrible fellows, and you had better watch very closely, or they will steal your town before morning.' As he turned and rode away on his poor, old, worn-out cavalry-horse, looking like the personification of grief, seated on a very badly carved monument of the equine race, we thought it about the best instance of stealing a horse and selling a mare (mayor) on record, and was worthy of being kept among the archives of the Southern Confederacy."[1]

In this expedition Sherman had subsisted the army a month on the country, and done incalculable mischief; yet the rebels had so utterly misconceived its object, and knew so little of the real results, that, on the retreat of Sherman, they boasted of great success! Nothing could be more ridiculous, or illustrate more forcibly the actual condition of the rebels at that time than the Order[2] issued by Lieutenant-General Leonidas Polk. He talked of our defeat and rout, and losses of men, arms, and artillery! This General Polk had been a Bishop of the Episcopal Church, but having graduated at West Point, thought himself justified in exchanging his ecclesiastical robes for the epaulets of a general. It is to be hoped that in the judgment of Heaven he was found better qualified for the first than the last, and that the mantle which covers a multitude of sins may be broad enough to cover his in the cause of secession.

The winter had now passed away, and there was no 'more campaigning for Grant till the opening of that grand campaign which terminated the war by the surrender at Appomattox Court-House.

---

[1] F. McC., Sixteenth Iowa Volunteers.
[2] Order No. 22, issued from Demopolis, (Ala.,) February 26th.

We have now arrived at an altogether new stage in Grant's career. He had heretofore acted a first part in results, but a second part in command. The time had come when the Government felt that, if Grant could perform a first part in the field, it was well to give him a choice of positions and the direction of operations. Accordingly, on the 26th of February, the very time Sherman returned to Vicksburg, and terminated the last of Grant's minor campaigns, Congress passed an act creating (or rather reviving) the office of Lieutenant-General, and authorizing the President to put the person appointed in command of the armies of the United States. This office had existed, and still existed, in the person of Lieutenant-General Winfield Scott.[1] It was originally created for General Washington, who commanded the army in 1798, when war with France was threatened. It was conferred also on Scott, who still survived, but was retired from active service. In regard to the grades of generals, the rebel government was wiser than ours, for it had created two new grades, those of General and Lieutenant-General. The commander of an army ought to be simply General, and if we had Lieutenant-Generals, they would be the commanders of corps.

On the creation of the grade of Lieutenant-General, Lincoln immediately appointed Grant, who was confirmed by the Senate, on the 2d of March, 1864. Halleck immediately telegraphed Grant to come to Washington, where, on the 8th of March,

---

[1] General Scott was on the retired list, and was Lieutenant-General by brevet.

he arrived at Willard's Hotel, almost unknown to any one present, as that city had by no means been a fashionable resort with him. That renowned place is thronged much more by those who want to do without work than by those who, like Grant, are hard workers in the service of their country.

Grant had come to Washington, but had nothing to ask before he came, and nothing to seek after he arrived. Mr. Washburn, the representative of the Galena District in Congress, makes the following statement, as remarkable as it is honorable. Speaking of Grant, he says:

"*No man, with his consent, has ever mentioned his name in connection with any position.* I say what I know to be true, when I allege that every promotion he has received since he first entered the service to put down this rebellion, was moved without his knowledge or consent. And in regard to this very matter of Lieutenant-General, *after the bill was introduced, and his name mentioned in connection therewith, he wrote me, and admonished me that he had been highly honored already by the Government, and did not ask or deserve any thing more in the shape of honors or promotion; and that a success over the enemy was what he craved above every thing else; that he only desired to hold such an influence over those under his command as to use them to the best advantage to secure that end.*"

No Roman triumphal procession awaited Grant at Washington; for, except what Grant himself had done in his successful campaigns, there was nothing to triumph over. The whole line of the rebel defense, east of the Alleghanies, remained intact. Lee was encamped on the Rapidan, as calm and audacious as ever. The Shenandoah Valley remained in possession of the rebels. The South-Western Valley, down nearly to Knoxville, was theirs also. Their great defenses at Mobile, Charleston, and Wilmington were still theirs. In fine, notwithstanding the rebels had lost the Mississippi and Chattanooga, the Government at Washington, looking over its fruitless and yet destructive campaigns on the Potomac, felt a sort of mournful joy instead of a hopeful confidence. Hence there was no ecstasy on the appearance of Grant. The Americans are neither Romans nor Frenchmen ; so, when Lee looked at them from the Rapidan, with a bold and taunting defiance, and had looked at them so for three long years, they got up no triumphal procession, as Romans or Frenchmen might have done, even for the victories of Grant. But Lincoln quietly presented him with his commission :

"*General Grant,*—The nation's appreciation of what you have done, and its reliance upon you for what remains to be done in the existing great struggle, are such that you are now presented with this commission, constituting you Lieutenant-General in the army of the United States. With this high honor devolves upon you, also, a corresponding responsibility. As the country herein trusts you, so, under God, it will sustain you. I scarcely need to add that, with what I here speak for the nation, goes my own hearty personal concurrence."

The words of General Grant are few and far between; but now he did reply briefly:

"*Mr. President,*—I accept the commission, with gratitude for the high honor conferred. With the aid of the noble armies that have fought on so many fields for our common country, it will be my earnest endeavor not to disappoint your expectations. I feel the full weight of the responsibilities now devolving on me, and I know that if they are met, it will be due to those armies, and, above all, to the favor of that Providence which leads both nations and men."

On the 10th of March, an order assigned the new Lieutenant-General to the command of all the armies of the United States. To understand the prompt manner in which things were done, and the readiness with which Grant put himself to the work, I transcribe his first order:

"HEAD-QUARTERS OF THE ARMIES OF THE UNITED STATES, }
"*Nashville, Tenn., March* 17, 1864. }

"In pursuance of the following order of the President:

"'EXECUTIVE MANSION, WASHINGTON, *March* 10, 1864.

"'Under the authority of the act of Congress to appoint to the grade of Lieutenant-General in the army, of March 1, 1864, Lieutenant-General Ulysses S. Grant, United States Army, is appointed to the command of the armies of the United States.

"'ABRAHAM LINCOLN.'

I assume command of the armies of the United States. Head-quarters will be in the field, and, till further orders, will be with the Army of the Potomac. There will be an office head-quarters in Washington, to which all official communications will be sent, except those from the army where the head-quarters are at the date of their address.

"U. S. GRANT, *Lieutenant-General.*"

"*Head-quarters will be in the field.*" That is the first announcement, and it was a joy to hear it; for certain it was that the 'atmosphere of Washington was exceedingly uncongenial to genius in war. Stanton was energetic; Lincoln had the fervor of warlike patriotism; but there was one dark phantom rose to their minds, and was drawn like a pall over the faces of the generals—fear for Washington! In a moral and political sense, this was just. For a long period of the war we had a difficult task to prevent the interference of England and France; and, undoubtedly, if Washington was taken by the rebels, (although of little importance in a military point of view,) it would have a disastrous moral and political effect. But now Grant has a new scheme of tactics. He will defend Washington in the field. *Head-quarters in the field—* that means hard fighting; it means continuous and fearful blows; and if the enemy can not meet them, they will be smashed; that is all of it, and there is no more to be thought of. But these blows are not to fall only on Lee's Virginia Army; they are to fall at all points where there is an enemy's army, or fortification. We had come to the time when we really had greatly superior forces, and the great point of generalship was *to make superior forces available.* Grant set about it in the true way. First, we must oppose superior armies to the enemy's armies; and, secondly, we must organize coöperative armies against their fortresses and commercial points; so that while our armies were breaking up their armies, our coöperative forces should cut off or destroy all the resources by which new armies might be formed. While we had strong enough armies in the field, we should also attack other important points; so that when the final blow was struck, every thing would be ended. This is the task Grant now set himself to perform; and as we trace his career on the broad theater of events, we must recollect that he is now to be responsible for the whole conduct of the war, and not for single armies or departments. It had become obvious to all minds that we must have some general and unitized plan; and this could only be done with one commander. I have already said there is *no evidence* that, up to this time, the Government had *any general plan* of the war. No general in one department could form one, and there is no evidence that any was ever formed at Washington. This is a remarkable feature of the war, and one which military critics should hereafter carefully consider. It was certainly by no means creditable to the statesmanship of the country.

CHAPTER XII.

THE WILDERNESS.

THE GENERAL PLAN OF THE CAMPAIGN—ORGANIZATION OF THE GRAND ARMY—LEE'S POSITION—HUNDRED DAYS' MEN—OFFER OF THE GOVERNORS—MEADE'S ADDRESS—GRAND ARMY CROSSES THE RAPIDAN—THE WILDERNESS—LINE OF BATTLE—TWO DAYS' FIGHT IN THE WILDERNESS—LEE'S DISPATCHES—CAN NOT SUCCEED, AND MARCHES BY THE RIGHT FLANK—GRANT'S GENERALSHIP—HIS POSITION IN THE BATTLE.

" Down by the rushing Rapidan, hark ! how the muskets crack !
The battle-smoke rolls up so thick, the very heavens are black !
No blossom-scented winds are there, no drops of silver rain ;
The air is thick with sulphurous heat, and filled with moans of pain.

O ! let us not forget them—our brave, unselfish boys—
Who have given up their loved ones, their happy household joys,
And stand to-night in rank and file, determined to a man,
To triumph over treason, down by the Rapidan !

And let our hearts be hopeful ; our faith, unwavering, strong ;
Right must be all victorious when battling with the *Wrong*.
Let us bear up our heroes' hands !   Pray, every soul that can,
'God bless our boys who fight to-night, down by the Rapidan !'" [1]

THE war clouds were now gathering from every point of the horizon ; but most they gathered round the army on the Rappahannock.   This army lay, during the winter, near the Rapidan, and was commanded by General George Gordon Meade—an

[1] "Rebellion Record," Vol. VIII—last page.

officer to whom the country owes a profound debt of gratitude, not only for the greatest successes, but for the most constant, earnest, and devoted services to his country. Grant, with good sense and sound judgment, left him in the immediate command of the grand army in its march on Richmond. A knowledge of men, and especially of military men, is one of Grant's characteristics, and we shall see that his selections for the staff of the army were admirable; but we have not got quite to that point. We must first take a glance at the general situation, in order to see where the enemy are, what we have done, and what we mean to do.

What was beyond the Mississippi—the rebel army under Kirby Smith, and the Union army under Banks, we may disregard; for neither of them had any important bearing on the war. If Banks had been entirely successful in Louisiana, by capturing Shreveport, it would have been of no practical use to us; and, to the rebels, their armies in Louisiana and Texas were entirely useless. The points in the rebel defenses we were to reach were these: The armies of Lee, in Virginia, of Johnston, in Georgia, and the cities of Mobile, Wilmington, Savannah, and Charleston, together with the supplies in the South-West and the Shenandoah Valley. Having these objects before us, it is easy to comprehend the general scheme of Grant's campaign. It was, 1. To find and crush the rebel armies. Lee's Army of Virginia was to be attacked, and crushed by as many blows as might be necessary, by the army of General Meade, with which Grant went himself. Johnston's army was to be crushed in the same way by Sherman, whose troops and supplies were now collecting at Chattanooga, and who, when arrived at Atlanta, was to move against Mobile, Savannah, or Augusta, as seemed most judicious to the commander. 2. The ports of Wilmington, Charleston, etc., were to be attacked by subsidiary forces; and, in fine, by attacks on the interior of the rebel States, all their forces were to be employed in such a manner that no reënforcements could be spared to Lee and Johnston. 3. The Shenandoah Valley was to be occupied, so that the supplies Lee's army was constantly drawing from thence should be cut off. In addition to these general plans there were certain auxiliary expeditions to be made. Early in April, Grant had informed Butler of the plan of the campaign, and directed him to move on to the south side of the James, seize City Point, and close on Richmond, as far as he could, with the view to coöperate with Grant, when he should drive back Lee, and finally unite with him on the south side of the James. A large expedition, under General Crook, was also to move for the Kanawha, in order to cut communications in the Valley of Virginia. General Sigel also had a Corps in the Shenandoah Valley. All these movements come, when we consider them together, to two points: 1st. To destroy the enemy's armies; and, 2d, by lateral movements, to prevent the possibility of reënforcing and supplying them. I shall now confine myself to the army of Grant in the march on Richmond, and to the part he performed. It must be left to other writers, in other times, to present a complete and critical history of the grand transactions, military and civil, which terminated the war of the rebellion.

In the conflict with Lee—so fierce, bloody, and protracted—upon which Grant was now about to enter, the first thing we must notice is the strength and the organization of the forces. I shall not relate the military details of the campaign, for they would only confuse the unmilitary reader, and are unnecessary to a correct view of Grant's acts, character, or generalship. It *is*, however, necessary for us to distinguish between the several Corps of the Army, their line of march, and principal actions, in order to see clearly the strategy which he adopted, and the degree of its success.

The Army of the Potomac—I should say more properly the Army of Richmond—was reorganized, at the close of March, in the following manner:

SECOND CORPS, commanded by General Winfield Scott Hancock, of the infantry, who had exhibited great gallantry and good conduct in previous campaigns with the Army of the Potomac. This corps had four divisions, commanded by Barlow, Gibbon, Bisney, and Barr.

FIFTH CORPS, commanded by Gouvernuer K. Warren, originally an officer of engineers, promoted for his valor and skill. This corps also had four divisions, commanded by Wadsworth, Crawford, Robinson, and Griffin.

SIXTH CORPS, commanded by Major-General John Sedgwick, a very popular officer, originally of the artillery. This corps had three divisions, commanded by H. G. Wright, Getty, and Prince.

THE CAVALRY CORPS was commanded by General Philip H. Sheridan, originally an officer of regular infantry, and whose dashing qualities had made him distinguished at Chattanooga and various other points.

THE PARK OF ARTILLERY was under the general direction of General Henry J. Hunt, and the immediate command of Colonel H. S. Benton.

THE ENGINEER TROOPS AND PONTOONS were under the command of Major J. C. Duane, of the engineers.

THE QUARTER-MASTER'S DEPARTMENT was under the command of General Rufus Ingals.

THE STAFF OFFICERS were principally General John A. Rawlins, Chief; Colonel Bower, Adjutant-General; Colonel Duff, Inspector-General; Colonel Badeau, Secretary, with numerous aids, adjutants, quarter-masters, and inspectors.

THE NINTH CORPS, commanded by General Ambrose E. Burnside, consisted chiefly of colored troops, and had been recruiting and drilling at Annapolis, but in the latter part of April was suddenly marched to join the Army of Meade, at Culpepper. The entire aggregate of *available* men in the Army of the Potomac on the 1st of May, 1864, was (120,384) one hundred and twenty thousand three hundred and eighty-four men,' the largest army which had ever been collected at one spot in the United States. It is said by some writers that Lee's Army, which lay near Orange Court-House, was but (52,000) fifty-two thousand men. This may have been the case in the winter, but was evidently incorrect at this period, for, in the next thirty days, Lee lost twenty thousand

' Secretary of War's Report, November, 1865.

men, disabled in some way, and yet was able to fight a battle with Grant. History should not attempt to contradict probabilities. The fact was, Lee was continually reënforced from the day the campaign opened till his communications with the South were mainly cut off, and the South, exhausted, refused to furnish men. We had a great superiority of forces, then numbering (in all quarters) 622,000 availables,[1] and the rebels (in all) over 350,000.[2] But to make this superiority available was the very thing in which Grant's skill and administrative ability was to be exercised. It was for this he was made commander of the army, and in this he achieved the successes which terminated the war.

Here we must note one of those outbursts of patriotism which signalized our arms at that time, and, in fact, made one of the glorious features in the conduct of the loyal people, and one of the most successful instruments in putting down the rebellion. We made many errors and blunders in our practical conduct of the war, but we made none of the heart. The heart of the loyal people beat fervently, warmly, heroically for their country. From first to last there was no faintness of the heart, no yielding of the mind, no cessation of hope and faith. Knowing this, and relying upon it, the Governors of Ohio, Indiana,

---

[1] This is the number of availables on the Returns of the Army, May 1, 1864.

[2] The rebel army was much underrated, but it was not all available to them. For example, we held at that time 88,000 prisoners; and there were 70,000 men under Kirby Smith and Taylor, which were entirely useless to them. Under Lee and Johnston, at Mobile, Charleston, Wilmington, etc., were about 200,000 men.

Illinois, and Iowa offered the Government one hundred thousand men for one hundred days, independent of, and not to be counted in, any regular calls or drafts made by the President. The object of this was to supply the place of veterans sent to Grant's army, and taken from garrisons, posts, lines, etc., where the veterans had been employed. Many of the troops with Grant were raw troops, and it was very important not only that he should have enough men, but that he should have those experienced and inured to war. If Lee's army was inferior in numbers, it was composed of veteran troops, who would not be easily vanquished, even with twice their numbers of raw men. The tremendous magnitude of the campaign was well known to the patriotic Governors of the States, and the danger of relying wholly on raw troops equally obvious. To avoid this danger, the Governors of Western States offered to relieve thousands of veterans in posts and garrisons by volunteers from their States. Accordingly, a proposition to furnish hundred days' men for this purpose was made by Governors Brough, of Ohio, Morton, of Indiana, Yates, of Illinois, and Stone, of Iowa, and was promptly accepted by President Lincoln. Ohio had at that time an enrolled militia, called the "National Guard," composed of nearly forty regiments. Governor Brough immediately called these into the field, and Ohio actually furnished the Government 36,000 of these men. The Governors of Indiana, Illinois, and Iowa called for volunteers, and many thousands were furnished, though I have no account of the whole number. No more patriotic act was done during the war than this of the hundred days' men. Many of them, like Putnam in the Revolution, left their plows in the field, and their wives to till the farm. These men went right to the front, and some of the regiments were engaged in battle, and suffered severely. Thus it was that Grant's army was filled up and moved on to its conquests—brave men in reserve, and self-sacrificing women at home. The march of armies and the crash of battle-fields I can relate, but where shall I find the pen to record these triumphs of the heart, these heroic emotions, which kindled souls with the love of country, and fired them with energy for successful achievement?

I must leave these scenes for the field down on the Rapidan. Head-quarters is in the field. The army is organized, and, on the 3d of May, General Meade issued a stirring address to the soldiers. A part of his address is worthy to be remembered:

"*Soldiers!* The eyes of the whole country are looking with anxious hope to the blow you are about to strike in the most sacred cause that ever called men to arms. Remember your homes, your wives, and children, and bear in mind that the sooner your enemies are overcome, the sooner you will be returned to enjoy the benefits and blessings of peace. Bear with patience the hardships and sacrifices you will be called upon to endure. Have confidence in your officers, and in each other.

"Keep your ranks, on the march and on the battle-field, and let each man earnestly implore God's blessing, and endeavor by his thoughts and actions to render himself worthy of the favor he seeks. With clear conscience and strong arms, actuated by a high sense of duty, fighting to preserve the Government and the institutions handed down to us by our fore-fathers, if true to ourselves, victory, under God's blessing, must and will attend our efforts."

The blessing of God did attend them! For, though they were to march where McClellan had marched in vain—where Burnside had lost his thousands—and where Hooker, after a brilliant advance, had re-treated—where Lee had made his bold advances on the capital of the country—where, in every field, was buried the dead, and where thousands of his own number were soon again to wet with their blood those fatal fields—yet, with all this before them, they marched with the confidence of hope to the music of victory! Grant was their leader, the country their supporter, and God, our all, was looking down upon them, and from the mid-heaven inspiring them with the smiles of His favor, and pointing to the unfading star of their glorious destiny! The Army of the Po-tomac was no more to be beaten—no more to re-treat—no more to despond!

So rose the sun on the morning of the 3d upon the Army of the Potomac, which, by midnight, was to be crossing the Rapidan:

"O! let us not forget them—our brave, unselfish boys—
  Who have given up their loved ones, their happy household joys,
  And stand to-night in rank and file, determined to a man,
  To triumph over treason, down by the Rapidan!"

Before we cross the river, let us take a glance at the position of the rebel army under Lee. Lee had been bivouacked all winter near Orange Court-House, and had made an intrenched camp of nearly twenty miles in length, to cover the crossings of the Rapidan. His army, like Grant's, was divided into three main corps, commanded by Ewell, Hill, and Longstreet, with a Cavalry Corps, under the command of General J. E. B. Stuart. Lee's army lay on each side of Orange Court-House, on the left, (as we look north to the Rapidan,) to Gordonsville, near which Longstreet's Corps lay, and on the right to Mine Run, (a creek emptying into the Rapidan,) about twelve miles from Orange Court-House. Stuart's Cavalry lay on the south side of the river, and Ewell and Hill's, in succession, after him. The general idea of Lee was to defend the line of the Rapidan, by intrenchments extending from near the fords on the right, through and beyond Orange Court-House, in front of the Rapidan. It was, unquestionably, a well-chosen position; but he could not guard the whole line, from Fredericksburg to the mountains, and, therefore, there must be an opportunity to cross the Rapidan, either to the right or to the left. Grant chose to *turn* Lee's army (if he could) by Lee's right—that is, between Lee and Fredericksburg. If he could not succeed fully in this, then he intended pushing him by his own left (Lee's right) flank, in the oblique movement, which, if Lee could not drive him back, would result in making Lee retreat on a curve, and carry Grant round him to the East, in a more extended curve, till Grant swung round Richmond on to the James. *As this actually happened*, it is well for us to note the plan in advance. The *head-quarters* of the army leaves Culpepper, ten miles north of the Rapidan, crosses that river, proceeds to Spottsylvania; then eastwardly, crossing the Mattapony; then to the Pamunkey, at Hanover; then to Mechanicsville; then round Richmond to the James. An examination of any common map will show that this march was a curve, at first turning slowly, and then, at Richmond, narrowing more rapidly. It is very evident that if Grant could have beaten Lee in a great battle, Lee must have gone at once into Richmond, and been besieged, terminating the campaign much more speedily. On the other hand, if Lee could have beaten Grant, he would, of course, have arrested the campaign there, as it had been arrested in the case of Hooker and Burnside. But he could not do this, and the most he could do was to fight his way slowly back to Richmond. Let us see how he was driven back. To the right of Lee's defenses, at Mine Run, (looking north,) and about six miles from each other, were Germania and Ely's Fords, over the Rapidan. The road from Culpepper, through Stevensburg, led over Germania Ford; east of that, a road branched off, through Richardsville, to Ely's Ford. These were the roads through which Grant's army passed the Rapidan. Nearly opposite these fords (south) was a singular district of country, called the "Wilderness." As this little district has become memorable, and might, with great propriety, be called "the dark and bloody ground," I give here a brief description of it, from the pen of Professor Coppée:"[1]

"The Wilderness is a broken table-land, covered over with dense undergrowth, with but few clearings,

[1] "Grant and His Campaigns," page 288.

in which the rebels could conceal themselves, which proved a formidable obstacle to our advance. It was intersected by numerous cross roads, generally narrow, and bounded on either side by a dense growth of low-limbed and scraggy pines, stiff and bristling chincapins and scrub oaks. The undergrowth was principally of hazel. There were many deep ravines, but not sufficiently precipitous to offer us much trouble on that account, the principal difficulty being in the almost impenetrable undergrowth, which would impede our advance in line of battle, and render the artillery almost useless. Besides the cross roads mentioned, numerous narrow wood roads pass through the Wilderness in all directions."

Such was the "Wilderness," and in the midst of it stood the "Wilderness tavern," and to the right of that, some six miles toward Fredericksburg, was the now noted "Chancellorsville." At the Wilderness tavern two roads, the "plank road" and the "turnpike road" from Orange to Fredericksburg, intersected. It will be easy to find these localities on a tolerable map, and thus the movement of the several corps of our army will be understood.

At night, on the 3d of May, two cavalry divisions moved down the roads from Culpepper (one on each) to Germania and Ely's Fords. They carried pontoon trains and engineers with them, laid the bridges, and a division of cavalry moved at once to the Wilderness tavern and Chancellorsville without opposition. Now the reader sees that the Wilderness tavern was an important strategic point, for there the two roads from Orange met, and thence went a branch-road to Spottsylvania. It was Grant's intention and wish to gain the Wilderness roads, and secure them in advance of Lee. In that case, he would have *turned* Lee entirely, if not cut him off from Richmond; but that he was not destined to do entirely, though enough of it to compel Lee to oblique, and pursue a curve to Richmond. The cavalry, as I said, secured the pontoons, and marched to the Wilderness without opposition. At three, A. M., the Second Corps (Hancock's) moved by Stevensburg and Richardsville to Ely's Ford. At the same time the Fifth Corps (Warren's) marched through Stevensburg to Germania Ford. This was closely followed by the Sixth Corps, (Sedgwick's.) During the day the whole army had crossed the Rapidan, the Second Corps encamping on the old battle-field of Chancellorsville, the Fifth at the Wilderness tavern, and the Sixth from the tavern to Germania Ford. The Ninth Corps (Burnside's) did not cross, but followed to the Rapidan, and remained as a reserve. So far the movement was entirely successful, and if Lee continued on the defensive, his communications were likely to be cut off. This would not do, and he commenced a rapid movement to prevent it. Lee immediately left his position and intrenchments behind him, moving Ewell on the old turnpike and Hill on the plank road.[1] Our line was formed, it will be seen, on several miles, extending from Chancellorsville by the Wilderness tavern to the Orange road and Germania Ford. The attack really came from us; for when Ewell came up on the

[1] Lee's dispatch, May 5, 1864.

Orange turnpike, Warren (Fifth Corps) was ordered to halt and attack the enemy's front furiously, when he could find it, which he did at twelve o'clock (on the 5th.) Having got into line, he attacked Ewell with the divisions of Griffin and Wadsworth. At first, he drove back Ewell, but the Sixth Corps was not up in time, and the left of Warren was exposed, because Hancock had not got in from Chancellorsville. Then Hill's Corps of the enemy came down on the plank road, and there was great danger for Warren, till Hancock's Corps came in and checked the enemy's attack. And so the battle went on in the afternoon of the 5th, furious and bloody, on broken ground and thick undergrowth, where little artillery could be used, and where the enemy, knowing the ground, had greatly the advantage. It was a bloody day, and two of the most signalized men of our army fell on that field—Wadsworth and Hays.

What Lee thought of that day he very candidly expressed in his dispatch of the 5th. He says: "By the blessing of God, we maintained our position against every effort till night, when the combat closed. We have to mourn the loss of many brave officers and men."

Maintained his position! Yes, and had it been a contest for a battle-field, this would have been very well, but *to do no more* in the Wilderness was fatal. The very thing in question was, Whether *we* could cross the Rapidan and stay there? But we are not through. To-morrow is to be bloodier yet, and we shall see whether Lee can stand there.

On the night of the 5th Grant saw clearly that the

great shock of the battle would be on Hancock, who, with the Second Corps, had come up from Chancellorsville to the Wilderness tavern, as he was ordered by Grant, not a minute too soon, for Hill was coming down on that vital point, and Longstreet following him. Still there was, on the day before, a gap there, through which the enemy at one time penetrated, and, with desperate exertions, were driven back. Now we are, on the night of the 5th, preparing for the battle of the 6th. Grant had no idea of standing on the defensive. His word was, always, attack, attack! And attack it must be, at five o'clock in the morning. As I said, Hancock could not fill the whole space to Warren, and there Grant knew the storm was coming. So Burnside now crossed the river, and took post in the gap, between the Second and Fifth Corps, and between the plank road and the turnpike, which, as I have said, converged till they intersected at the Wilderness tavern. Getty's Division, of the Sixth Corps, and Wadsworth's, of the Fifth, were near the same place, to reënforce and strengthen Hancock's right, for there was to be the struggle. Ewell was still in front of Warren and Sedgwick, and Longstreet had come up to the help of Hill. Hancock began, at five o'clock, with a furious attack on Hill, and drove him back in some confusion; but just then Longstreet came up, with the best corps of Lee's army, and, driving Hancock back, threatens the left of our army with being turned and driven back on the river. But Lee is no Sidney Johnston, nor is this the field of Shiloh. Lee, like Beauregard, is an engineer officer, and, by the very element which makes him a good engineer, loses that tact in strategy, and that brilliancy of movement, which is necessary to the success of a great battle. This idea of pouring the strength of his army on Hancock's left is a good one; but, after succeeding for a moment, he is successfully resisted by the very divisions (Wadsworth's and Getty's) which Grant had provided for that purpose. Wadsworth, a noble spirit, is killed, but the work is done, nobly done, and Hill is brought to a stand, as if by a rampart of rocks. Here the battle, for a time, stops. Like Beauregard, on the field of Shiloh, Lee takes time to think, and gather up his strength. This is good engineering, but bad tactics. At four o'clock he has massed his troops, and is ready again, and it is evident the main struggle is again to be with Hancock. Grant, with the same accurate sagacity and true military discernment, had seen the whole of it, and threw in, at the weak point, between Hancock and Warren, a large part of Burnside's Ninth Corps, and thus was prepared. Hill and Longstreet came down, with heavy lines, and all their available men. They came as with the shock of the tornado. It seemed as if every thing would be swept away, and, for a moment, it was so. Two whole divisions of Hancock were driven back; but two other divisions came in, and with such force as made the rebel lines shake and retreat. It is said that at this time Lee rushed forward, and was about to head the charge of a brigade himself, but was restrained by his officers. If true, as it may be, it shows that Lee thoroughly comprehended that to drive back Hancock and seize that position was essential to his success in the battle and the campaign. But let us go on. His attack failed, and all the military objects of the battle were to him lost. In the mean time other attacks were made by Ewell, on our right, which were apparently more successful, but which, in no event, could be decisive. Lee and Grant were both too good generals to rely much on the event of these collateral affairs. General Gordon, toward night, moved from the enemy's left, outflanked our right, made a furious charge, captured two generals, and the greater part of two brigades, which afforded Lee an opportunity to boast a little, but which he, of all men, knew best was a worthless success. Sedgwick, of the Sixth Corps, soon drove Gordon back, and the battle of the Wilderness was, to all practical intents, closed. Night closed around the weary and exhausted armies. They slept on one of the bloodiest fields America had ever seen.' In that dark and tangled wilderness, how many slept the sleep of death! how many groaned in anguish! how many tired sleepers, in dreams, looked through those shadows of the night, to the far-off home they were to see no more! For again and again the fields were to be crimsoned, and again the brave were to fall. In dreams only will thousands of the wearied sleepers see their homes again.

> " Our bugles sang truce, for the night-cloud had lowered,
> And the sentinel stars set their watch in the sky;

¹ The losses in the battles of the Wilderness were estimated, at the time, at 15,000 ; but they were much more, and probably the greatest in any one conflict of the war. In the final reports of the War Department the return of losses is thus given, including all to the 12th of May : Killed, 3,288 ; wounded, 19,278 ; missing, 6,844.

> And thousands had sunk on the ground overpowered—
>   The weary to sleep, and the wounded to die.
>
> .   .   .   .
>
> At dead of the night a sweet vision I saw,
>   And thrice ere the morning I dreamt it again.
>
> Methought from the battle-field's dreadful array,
>   Far, far I had roamed on a desolate track:
> 'T was autumn—and sunshine arose on the way
>   To the home of my fathers, that welcomed me **back.**
>
> .   .   .   .
>
> Stay, stay with us! rest, thou art weary and worn;
>   And fain was their war-broken soldier to stay;
> But sorrow returned with the dawning of morn,
>   And the voice in my dreaming ear melted away." [1]

The morn returned but to renew the fight. The orders were still to advance; but soon it is apparent that Lee wants no more fight *there*. He could not drive Grant away, and knows that we are on the road to Richmond. So he is moving off to the right flank in his retreat by curve lines. On the 8th, his dispatch to Richmond was: "The enemy have abandoned their position, and are marching toward Fredericksburg. I am moving on the right flank." [2] Yes, we are *in* Fredericksburg; that is no longer an objective point, and General Lee will keep moving by his right flank for a good while. He will be fond of curvilinear movements!

But where was Grant in this grand fight? How did he carry himself? What he did as General we know. Not one of his movements failed. Every corps, division, and regiment went into its place. The Army of the Potomac was no more to know retreat. *Now* it had a general, and Lee learned the

---

[1] "Soldier's Dream," by Campbell.
[2] Lee's dispatch to Seddon, May 8, 1864.

greatest lesson he ever learned. McClellan, and Hooker, and Burnside he knew how to deal with, and, notwithstanding Gettysburg, he stood in no great awe of Meade. But now we may imagine he did not feel quite sure of the future. Dark clouds gathered round him. The twenty years' war in Virginia, which the short-sighted Davis had predicted, was evidently drawing rapidly to a close. Armies, States, rebellions, all want mind as well as men. Mind moves them, and mind alone can give them success. Sidney Johnston was killed at Shiloh; the dashing Jackson was dead; and here is Longstreet, the best of corps commanders, wounded in the Wilderness, so that he can no longer head the battle. The position of Hancock in the Wilderness is *not* carried, and here is Lee moving to the right flank! How delusive to the great public is the battle-field! Here is Lee, dispatching to Richmond that he has taken thousands of prisoners. Here is a critic on Grant, denouncing him for the slaughter of men; and here is another critic saying it is a drawn battle. But look again. Why are our troops in Fredericksburg? Why is Grant in full march for Spottsylvania? and why is Lee moving by the right flank? The battle is gained; but where was Grant? The head-quarters of General Grant, says Coppée, were in the rear of the center, near the plank road, and most of the time he was on a piny knoll with Meade, in the rear of Warren. "Those who observed him during the actions were struck with his unpretending appearance and his imperturbable manner. Neither danger nor responsibility seemed to affect him; but he seemed at times lost in thought, and occasionally, on the receipt of information, would mount his horse and gallop off to the point where he was needed, to return with equal speed to his post of observation."[1]

Such was Grant in the Wilderness—the same firm, sagacious, calm, unpretending, and imperturbable being that he had been at Donelson, at Shiloh, and at Vicksburg. This sort of character is not easily understood at first, because we are continually looking out for something extraordinary, something uncommon, brilliant, and striking in a great commander. But when the people do understand such a character, they soon learn to regard it with confidence, and to admire it the more for its unconscious simplicity.

[1] Coppée's "Grant and His Campaigns," page 301.

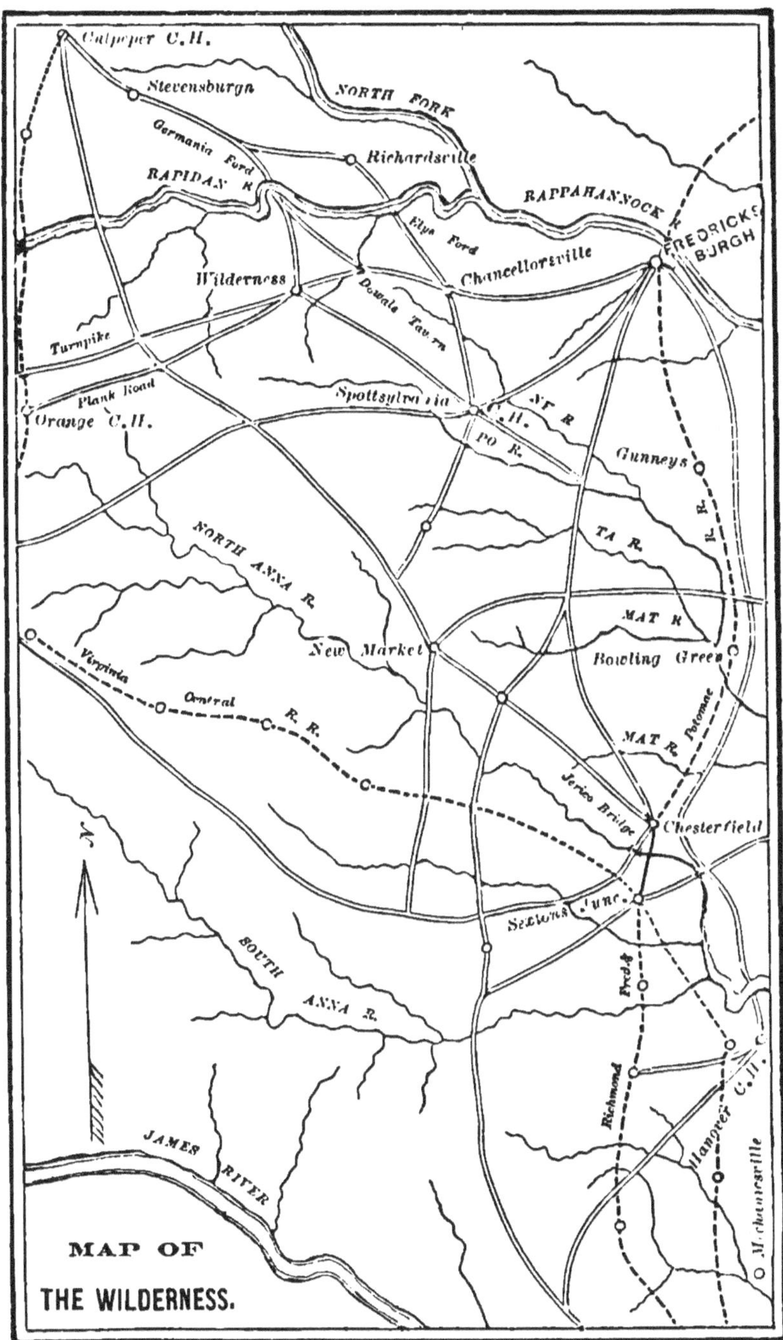

Culpeper C.H.
Stevensburgn
NORTH FORK
Germania Ford
Richardsville
RAPIDAN R.
RAPPAHANNOCK R.
Elys Ford
FREDRICKS BURGH
Wilderness
Chancellorsville
Dowals Tavern
Turnpike
Spottsylvania C.H.
NT R
Plank Road
Gunneys
Orange C.H.
PO R.
R. R.
TA R.
NORTH ANNA R.
MAT R
Virginia
New Market
Bowling Green
Central
R. R.
MAT R.
Potomac
Jerico Bridge
Chesterfield
SOUTH
Settons Junc.
ANNA R.
Fred.&
Richmond
JAMES
Hanover C.H.
RIVER
Mechanicsville
N.
MAP OF
THE WILDERNESS.

CHAPTER XIII.

ON TO RICHMOND.

OF all our blunders in the war, (and we made many,) "On to Richmond" had been the greatest; because Richmond, taken in the early period of the war, would have been of no practical advantage. It would have given us éclat, but not success. Let the reader suppose General Lee to have been driven from Richmond into Lynchburg—would he not have been as defensible there as in Richmond? He would have lost some advantage in defending the sea-board, but he would have gained more in defending the Valley of Virginia, and covering the approaches to Chattanooga. But we already had Norfolk, securing Chesapeake Bay. Whatever opinions may be formed of that matter, it is certain that we had lost three years, and nearly three armies, in a useless attack on the defenses of Richmond. The critics who complain of the losses sustained by Grant's army should remember this, and consider whether it was not better to finish the work in one vigorous campaign, however bloody, than to take three years, and slaughter three armies?

But here we are moving out of the Wilderness, (and we shall all be glad to get out,) and we are not going to Fredericksburg, for we have got Fredericksburg. We are obliquing to Lee's right. He was not quick enough to get in front of us; and if he had got there, and could have successfully resisted us, we should have turned his left. He was not strong enough to prevent the movement, which was inevitable. On the 8th our army is on the road to Spottsylvania—Second, Fifth, Sixth, and Ninth Corps—all of them, with the cavalry and trains. Two of our corps took the road to Todd's tavern, half a dozen miles west of Spottsylvania, and others the plank-road toward Fredericksburg. Lee took another road on the south, and, in general, parallel to the course of our troops. Saturday night and Sunday morning, (the 9th,) the Second and Fifth Corps passed on toward Spottsylvania. In the next five days Lee made repeated attacks laterally, endeavoring to flank and drive back our columns, and, at Spottsylvania, fought a hard and bloody battle. On Sunday there was an engagement with a part of Warren's Corps, and on Monday, one with Hancock; during which day General Sedgwick, a good and much admired officer, was killed in a skirmish.

On Tuesday, the 10th of May, Grant's army lay along the Po, (one of the small streams which make the Mattapony,) near Spottsylvania Court-House. The enemy held a fortified position directly opposite, partly on the Ny, (another little branch of the Mattapony,) on a rising ground, with breastworks, and the marshy ground of the Ny in front.　And now it is very plain we are to have another battle.　Lee had got into Spottsylvania a little ahead of us, and if we are to go on, we must fight him; and, moreover, my reader, the more he fights the better for us.　We shall lose gallant men, but we shall win the campaign.

On the 10th a gallant charge was made by the Fifth Corps, with part of the Second, under Gibbons and Birney.　Repeated charges were made, till the enemy was driven to his rifle-pits.　In the mean time Barlow's Division, on the right, had been turned, and suffered some loss; but, in the afternoon, General Upton, of the Sixth Corps, made a successful charge on the enemy, scaling his works, capturing a thousand prisoners and several guns.　So closed the 10th of May, with heavy losses, but with no decisive results.　Spottsylvania was not taken, but we were there to begin again.　So far it was nothing but fighting, and so it was likely to continue.　We commenced fighting on the 4th, and it is now the morning of the 11th, when Grant sent to the War Department a very celebrated dispatch:

"HEAD-QUARTERS IN THE FIELD, *May* 11, 1864. 8, A. M.

"We have now ended the sixth day of very heavy fighting.　The result, to this time, is much in our favor.

"Our losses have been heavy, as well as those of the enemy.　I think the loss of the enemy must be greater.

"We have taken over five thousand prisoners by battle, while he has taken from us but few, except stragglers.

"I PROPOSE TO FIGHT IT OUT ON THIS LINE, IF IT TAKES ALL SUMMER.　　　　　　　　　U. S. GRANT,

"*Lieutenant-General, Commanding the Armies of the United States.*"

I remember when that dispatch came to Cincinnati.　It was noon of a bright day—a glorious May day. "I PROPOSE TO FIGHT IT OUT ON THIS LINE, IF IT TAKES ALL SUMMER." Some persons have criticised this, by saying Grant did not go on *that* line. He *did* go on that line precisely, for the line he was on was after Lee and his army,[1] whether that was a straight line or a curved line. It did take all summer, and all winter too, but it was the same line, and the Army of the Potomac never again retreated. When the people heard that Grant was determined to "*fight it out on that line*" they rejoiced, for they knew that was the line which would lead to victory and peace. All was *not* quiet on the Potomac, but all *was* the march of armies and the shock of battles.

On the 11th there was no fighting. The positions of the armies were the same, and Lee covered Spottsylvania in a crescent-shaped line.

On the 12th, (Thursday,) the dawn of day came on with a dense fog, and in this dim light Hancock again advanced to the attack. The noble Second, led by its dashing commander, was again to be crimsoned with blood. The Second Corps was formed in two heavy lines, with double columns of battalions, Barlow and Birney in the first line, and Gibbon and Mott in the second. The attack was on the enemy's right center, at a salient angle of earthworks held by Johnson's Division of Ewell's Corps. Our columns moved silently, and, from what followed, it seems unseen by the enemy. Professor Coppée thus describes what followed :

"They passed over the rugged and densely wooded

---

[1] This was distinctly stated in Grant's Order to Meade, (in March,) that Lee's army was the objective point, and where Lee went he was to go.

space, the enthusiasm growing at every step, till, with a terrible charge, and a storm of cheers, they reached the enemy's works, scaled them in front and flank, surprising the rebels at their breakfast, surrounding them, and capturing Edward Johnson's entire division, with its general, two brigades of other troops, with their commander, Brigadier-General George H. Stuart, and thirty guns. The number of prisoners taken was between three and four thousand. It was the most decided success yet achieved during the campaign. When Hancock heard that these generals were taken, he directed that they should be brought to him. Offering his hand to Johnson, that officer was so affected as to shed tears, declaring that he would have preferred death to captivity. He then extended his hand to Stuart, whom he had known before, saying, 'How are you, Stuart?' but the rebel, with great haughtiness, replied, 'I am General Stuart, of the Confederate Army; and, under present circumstances, I decline to take your hand.' Hancock's cool and dignified reply was: 'And under any other circumstances, General, I should not have offered it.'"[1]

An hour after the column of attack had been formed, Hancock sent to Grant a pencil dispatch, which went over the country like electric fire: "I have captured from thirty to forty guns. I have finished up Johnson, and am now going into Early." His going into Early was not quite so successful; still he pushed on to the second line of rifle pits, stormed and took it. The enemy now rallied with desperate energy, and for fourteen long hours, weary

[1] Coppee's "Grant and His Campaigns," page 313.

and bloody, the armies fought on, with various fortune. Burnside and Hill had a furious fight; but the success of Hancock was the main achievement of the day. We had taken part of the enemy's intrenchments, and, on the night of the 12th, Lee again advanced backward, and gave evidence of having beaten Grant by taking the road to Richmond! Lee was both too sensible and too honest a man to make more of the thing than there was in it. It is not easy to make Lee a great general, but we may readily admit he was fair and candid; so, in his General Order of May 14th, he announced a series of successes; but what were they? Imboden had driven somebody back on the Potomac; Jones had driven back Averill, (who, by the way, had done immense damage on the Virginia and Tennessee Road); Banks had been defeated in Western Louisiana, and Grant's Cavalry had been repulsed at Richmond. At Richmond! How came they there? The fact was, Grant's Cavalry had ridden into the suburbs of Richmond; the alarm bells were rung; but, being only cavalry, they thought it safer to ride round the city, and finally arrived on the James!¹ But what of Lee and his army? Here he becomes quite modest, and is justly thankful and grateful that his army has not been destroyed, and that he has checked the principal army of the enemy. How did he check it? On the night of the 12th he retreats; and on the 13th General Meade issues a

---

¹ Perhaps this brief notice of these expeditions is enough. They were all side expeditions, to keep the enemy busy, and from reënforcing Lee. Banks was miserably defeated in Louisiana; but his army was of no use there. Averill had been successful.

different kind of an Order. He congratulates the army on its successes, and says:

"For eight days and nights, almost without any intermission, through rain and sunshine, you have been fighting a desperate foe in positions naturally strong, and rendered doubly so by intrenchments. You have compelled him to abandon his fortifications on the Rapidan, to retire and to attempt to stop your progress, and now he has abandoned the last intrenched position, so tenaciously held, suffering in all a loss of eighteen guns, twenty-two colors, eight thousand prisoners, including two general officers. Your heroic deeds, noble endurance of fatigue and privation, will ever be memorable. Let us return thanks to God for the mercy thus shown us, and ask earnestly for its continuance."

For several days nothing important was done. The rains had been heavy, the roads almost impassable, and great numbers of the wounded had to be provided for. We now held Fredericksburg, and most of the wounded were carried to the hospitals at Washington. In these eight days' fighting the army had lost enormously ; but so had Lee's army, and so it must be till the end. Up to May 21st, (when the army was moving on the Anna,) the losses were, killed, 5,434 ; wounded, 27,234 ; and missing, 6,915. Of these, 27,000 were in the Second, Fifth, and Sixth Corps. It was found, however, that a very large proportion of the wounded were but slightly injured, so that probably more than half the wounded were returned to the army in a few weeks. The actual losses were never so great as they were represented to be. They were losses, for the time being, from the army; but of all that 39,000 returned among the losses, not more than one-third (13,000) were killed, died, or were permanently injured. General Grant, in a subsequent report, (July, 1865,) left it to the calm judgment of the country, and especially of those who mourned, whether better plans might have been conceived or better executed; but for himself, he said, he had acted conscientiously and faithfully.

When Lee left Spottsylvania, the heaviest battles of the Richmond campaigns were over. Other battles and other tragedies were enacted for nearly a year to come; but I do not propose to recite their details, for they amount to but little more than the wearisome processes of a siege. I shall hasten on to the last scene of the drama. But, in the mean time, two or three incidental enterprises must be mentioned. First, on the same day on which Grant crossed the Rapidan, (the 4th,) Butler moved up the James, was joined by a division under Gilmore, and, on the 5th, occupied both City Point and Bermuda, having completely surprised the enemy. He intrenched himself here, and made an attack on the railroad, but was not entirely successful in cutting off the enemy's approaches. Beauregard arrived from the South, and Butler was really held fast at Bermuda. In this position, his force was of no use, except as a garrison for Bermuda—a position from which to operate in the future. But the losses of both Grant and Lee made reënforcements necessary. Breckinridge was sent up from the South-West to Lee, and Beauregard sent forward part of his army from Petersburg; and thus

Lee was heavily reënforced, and so was Grant. Stanton announced, from the War Department, that it was the purpose of Government to keep Grant reënforced to the end. And so he was. Thus matters stood on the 19th of May, when we recommenced our march to Richmond. All the night of the 20th, the troops were moving to new positions. The cavalry were near Gaines's Station, on the Fredericksburg Railroad, and the Second Corps on the way, near Spottsylvania; and at 6, A. M., of the 21st, the Fifth Corps (Warren's) took up its line of march, and all was again motion. Forward! is the order. Grant was marching to the North Anna, and Lee was going there too; and it seems, from what took place, that Lee had prepared intrenchments at all these places. The advance of the army reached the North Anna on the morning of the 22d of May. The bridge over the North Anna was defended by a redan, and commanded by batteries; but a brilliant charge of Berry's Division carried it. The army crossed the Anna on the 24th; but Grant was rather surprised to find Lee's army drawn up in strong intrenchments in a triangle, with the apex toward the Anna, and the wings very strongly defended. So Grant continued his plan—the oblique—flanking the enemy's right. He recrossed the Anna on the 27th, under cover of a false attack on Lee, and took his march easterly to the Pamunkey. So poor Lee lost all his labor on intrenchments. His position was admirable, but he was flanked! On the 28th, Sheridan entered Hanovertown, on the Pamunkey River, fifteen miles from Richmond. The infantry divisions began to arrive that day. The crossing of the Pamunkey was secured, and transports were already arriving by York River for the support of the army. On the 29th, the whole army crossed the Pamunkey, and took position about three miles from it. On Tuesday, the 31st, the army was reënforced by the Eighteenth Corps, (General C. F. Smith,) from Bermuda. On that day Grant ordered the cavalry to take possession of Cold Harbor, and hold it, which it did, but not without a hard fight. Cold Harbor was a very important position, and the enemy did not mean we should hold it, if possible to prevent it; so, on the 1st of June, a division under Hoke made a furious attack on Sheridan, which was repulsed; but Hoke was soon reënforced heavily, and on our side the Sixth Corps (now Wright's) and the Eighteenth (C. F. Smith's) came in, and the enemy was defeated in all attempts to dislodge us. And thus we held complete possession of Cold Harbor, which was to us quite important. But now came an affair (very bloody) in which we had nothing to boast of. Grant thought he could drive the enemy over the Chickahominy by an assault, which he accordingly made, on the 3d of June, but without success. His own account of it, and his view of the situation, was given in his report, as follows:

"On the 3d of June we again assaulted the enemy's works, in the hope of driving him from his position. In this attempt our loss was heavy, while that of the enemy, I have reason to believe, was comparatively light. It was the only general attack made from the Rapidan to the James which did not inflict upon the enemy losses to compensate for our own losses. I would not be understood as saying that all previous attacks resulted in victories to our arms, or accomplished as much as I had hoped from them; but they inflicted upon the enemy severe losses, which tended, in the end, to the complete overthrow of the rebellion."

This was the battle of Cold Harbor, of which Grant dispatched, on June the 5th, that he thought the killed, wounded, and missing, in three days' operations, would be about seven thousand five hundred. In fact, it was much greater, the total losses amounting to about thirteen thousand. For the next seven days there was intrenching and counter-intrenching, by both armies, on lines near and nearly parallel to one another. But Grant had, long before, determined to take the James River as his base, *unless* he could succeed in a forward attack on Lee; but Lee's defensive movements prevented this, and he now determined to leave the base of York River, and the line of Chickahominy, and swing round upon the James. Now, let it be observed, that *he did this on his own responsibility, and against the opinions of other generals,*[1] as he did at Vicksburg. If, therefore, there be any merit in his campaigns, I say he is fully entitled to it, and unquestionably he is willing to take the responsibility for his errors.

The enemy had fortified Bottom's Bridge, and lay from that along the Chickahominy. Below that (six miles) was Long's Bridge, and below that Jones's.

[1] See Halleck's letter to Grant, dated May 27, 1864, in which he gives the opinions of McClellan and other generals on the best mode of attacking Richmond.

On the 12th, the grand army began to move. The Second and Fifth Corps moved over Long's Bridge; the Sixth and Ninth over Jones's, and the Eighteenth marched to the White House, embarked in transports, and went to Bermuda Hundred by water. On Tuesday, the 14th, the army began crossing the James, on pontoon bridges, and on Wednesday had completed its magnificent movement. And now Grant's army is where McClellan ought to have put his in the first place, on the James, with our navy for its base. For the next four or five days, there were attacks on Petersburg, and skirmishes in various directions; but the enemy had now arrived in force, and it was vain to expect any thing from a mere assault. We must now sit down to a regular siege, and yet not quite a siege, because the enemy's communications to the west and south were kept open, mainly by three railroads; one to Weldon, North Carolina; one to Danville, on the Roanoke; and one to Lynchburg. These supplied Lee's army with men and provisions; and now the reader must understand that the great object of the siege was to cut off these communications. I shall not now detail the various assaults, maneuvers, enterprises, and raids which, for the next eight months, occupied Grant's army. It is unnecessary to understand the movements which brought about success, and uninteresting to the general reader. Deep Bottom, only ten miles from Richmond, was occupied on the 21st of June, and immediately connected with Bermuda Hundred by a pontoon bridge. In the latter part of June, Wilson and Kautz (cavalry officers) made great and important raids on the

Weldon and Danville Railroads, destroying a great many miles of road, and doing immense damage. All this, however, was not decisive. The army had done much, but now had to rest for a time.

In the mean while a great expedition had been sent up the Shenandoah Valley, under Hunter, whose object was Lynchburg. It was very successful till it got before Lynchburg, when it was found that Lee, with his communications all open, had thrown forward nearly a corps of troops for the support of that place, and that Hunter was nearly without provisions. The consequence was, that Hunter retreated, and failed in his main object. In truth, looking to the objective points, our half dozen lateral expeditions had accomplished little ; but, in another point of view, they had accomplished very much. They held fifty thousand good troops from joining Lee, and they had destroyed an immense amount of supplies, which had been accumulated at various points for his army.

It had now got to be the beginning of July, the atmosphere scorching hot, the ground parched, and the troops wearied out, greatly needing rest ; so Grant ordered no more marches or battles just then, but left the troops to rest for a time, while the officers were preparing various episodes to the campaign, some of which were neither very successful nor very commendable.

But here let us rest, glad to know that no more such battles as those of the Wilderness and of Spottsylvania are to be fought again till our war-worn troops return in victory and peace.

CHAPTER XIV.

CLOSE OF THE WAR.

THE PETERSBURG MINE—GRANT'S LETTER ON THE REBELS—TAKES THE WELDON RAILROAD—SENDS SHERIDAN AFTER EARLY—BATTLES OF WINCHESTER, OF FISHER'S HILL, AND OF MIDDLETOWN — EARLY'S FORCES DESTROYED — HOOD GOES TO NASHVILLE AND SHERMAN GOES TO SAVANNAH—SHERMAN'S CHRISTMAS PRESENT—MOBILE AND WILMINGTON TAKEN—SHERMAN MARCHES TO RALEIGH—STORM OF PETERSBURG—BATTLE OF FIVE FORKS—SURRENDER OF LEE—SURRENDER OF JOHNSTON—GRAND REVIEW AT WASHINGTON.

THE army was now comparatively at rest, in the hot days of a Southern summer; but the officers wanted something to do; so they proceeded to dig a mine. Now a mine can be useful only in one case—when the enemy has a strong rampart, perhaps a bastion, strongly defended, which you can not then storm. If you can manage to blow up a part of that work, and storm the breach instantly, you can probably make a lodgment in the enemy's works, and that is what you want. But such an operation was not applicable to the case of Petersburg, and probably would not have succeeded if no accident or misunderstanding had occurred in the arrangements. However that may be, the mine at Petersburg did

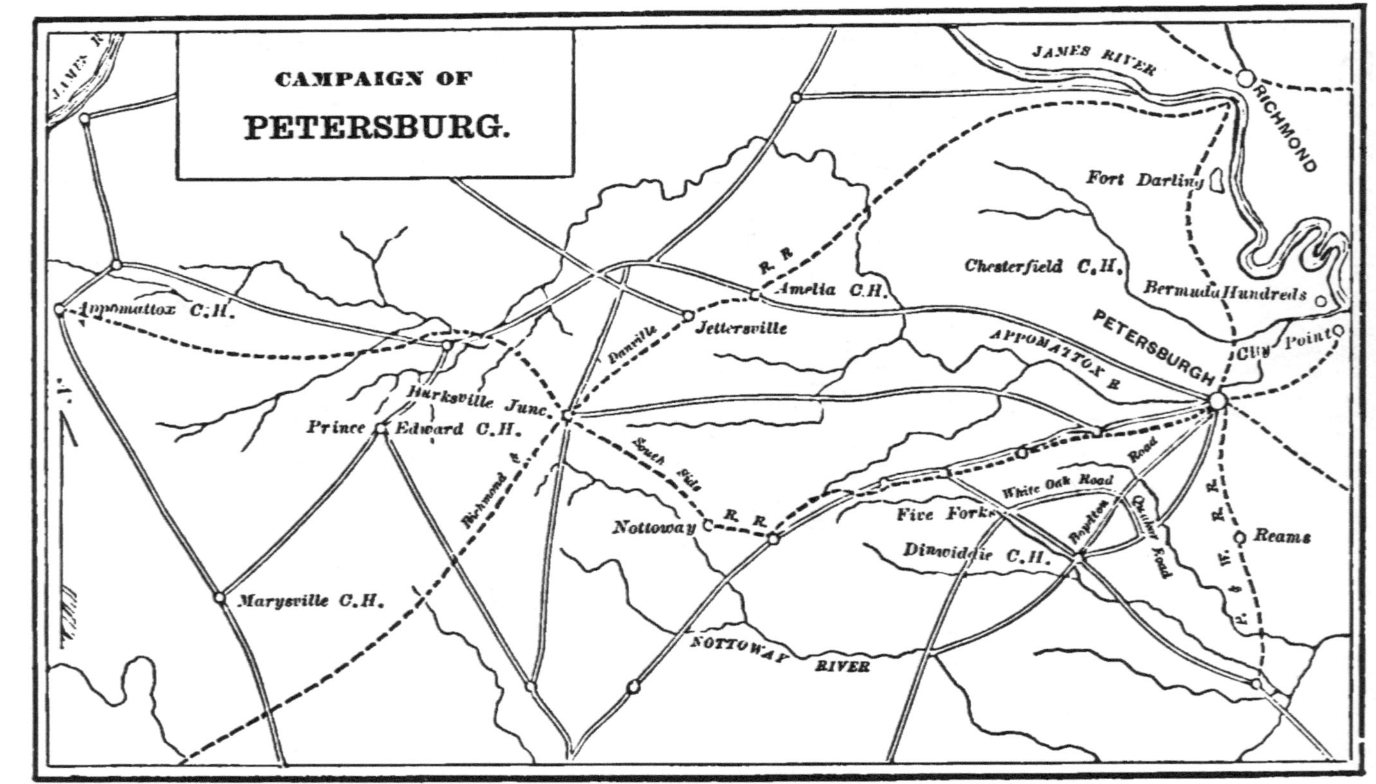

CAMPAIGN OF
PETERSBURG.
JAMES R.
JAMES RIVER
RICHMOND
Fort Darling
Chesterfield C.H.
Bermuda Hundreds
PETERSBURGH
City Point
Appomattox C.H.
R. R.
Amelia C.H.
Danville
Jettersville
APPOMATTOX R.
Burksville Junc.
Prince Edward C.H.
South Side
White Oak Road
Road
Richmond &
Nottoway
R. R.
Five Forks
Poplton
Quaker Road
Reams
Dinwiddie C.H.
R. W. & R. R.
Marysville C.H.
NOTTOWAY RIVER

not succeed. It exploded on the 30th of July. The storming party failed to be on time; the enemy enfiladed the breach with the fire of artillery, and had a second line in the rear. The result was, we lost heavily, and the mine was, in fact, a great disaster. The memory of it brings to my mind the loss of many fair and promising young men, needlessly cut down in the bloom of their youth.

The summer was now closing, and it is not to be disguised that our operations from the middle of June till September had been unfortunate. All was successful till we arrived on the James; but when there, it seems to have taken several months to arrive at the true conception of what was to be done. It was a simple thing, but hard to do. It was to *cut off the three railroads which supplied Lee's army with men and food.* Till then, there was no need of making bloody assaults on the enemy's works—digging mines and canals, and dreaming of the surrender of Richmond. Grant saw all this; but his enterprising generals wanted employment. Grant saw more than this. He saw the rebellion was exhausted, and he expressed this very well in a letter, written on the 16th of August, to Mr. Washburn, his representative in Congress. He says:

"The rebels have now in their ranks their last man. The little boys and old men are guarding prisoners, guarding railroad bridges, and forming a good part of their garrisons for intrenched positions. A man lost by them can not be replaced. They have robbed the cradle and the grave equally to get their present force. Besides what they lose in frequent skirmishes and battles, they are now losing from desertions and other causes at least one regiment per day."

This was true and terse. They had robbed the cradle and the grave, and no more men could be got. This was not wholly for the want of men, for, in fact, the South had double as many men able to take the field as were in the armies; but the Southern people saw and knew, as well as we did, that the war was practically drawing to a close, and that the rebel Confederacy could in no possible event succeed. The people, therefore, no longer supported the war with any heart, and the rebel Government could no longer get reënforcements except by force.

In the months of autumn no really important operation was performed by Grant's army, after that of taking and holding the Weldon Railroad, which was done by Warren's Corps, on the 20th of August. Over and over again had this been attempted in vain; but our lines were gradually extending to the left, and now we got and kept the Weldon Railroad, which was one of the main lines of supply to the rebel army. That gained, little was done for several months.

In the mean time, let us briefly trace out the collateral movements—one of them, at least, on a grand scale—which, although not under the immediate command of Grant, were, nevertheless, parts of the magnificent plan he had formed to destroy the rebellion. We have seen that Hunter's expedition up the Shenandoah to take Lynchburg was a failure. In consequence of the withdrawal of his troops, (part

of them were sent in other directions,) Early, with a
corps of the rebel army, moved down the Shenandoah, carrying all before him—entered Maryland,
robbing and plundering in every direction, and finally
arrived near the fortifications of Washington. This,
of course, threw the Government into consternation;
but Grant did not, like Frederick to his queen, write,
"Remove the archives!" Nor was he to be moved
from his own position; but he quietly sends the
Sixth Corps (Wright's) and the Nineteenth to Wash-
ton by water. He could afford this, for his army had
been heavily reënforced. He had now the Second,
Fifth, Sixth, Tenth, Eighteenth, and Nineteenth
Corps. He sent the Sixth and Nineteenth to Washington, who quickly drove back Early, and kept on
driving him back, till he got to near Winchester.
But now something new must be done. To the disgrace of our military genius, this see-saw operation
up and down the Shenandoah Valley had been going
on all through the war. It ought to have been
stopped in the beginning; but, I have already said,
the Government had no general plan, which should
cover the country, and be persistently carried out, till
Grant was put in complete command; and now there
was a plan. Hunter's expedition was to have taken
and kept the Shenandoah Valley, but failed; and in
the mean while, Grant had hoped to have brought
Lee to a final battle, and destroyed his army, which,
with our superior forces, could have been done, sooner
or later. But Lee assumed the defensive, and continually fought behind intrenchments; hence he was
able to keep Early in the Valley. But it was time

to stop this, and Grant put a man at the head of the army in the Valley who would fight, and whose ceaseless energy would leave the enemy no opportunity for their customary raids. This man was General Philip H. Sheridan, a native of Ohio, who has well earned the reputation of the American Murat.

On the 7th of August, West Virginia, Washington, and the Susquehanna and the Shenandoah were formed into a new department, called the "Middle Military Division," and General Sheridan assigned to its command. The divisions of cavalry under Torbert and Wilson were sent to him from the Army of the Potomac. The latter part of August and beginning of September were occupied in skirmishes and preparations, and by the middle of September the two armies were in position near Winchester. The enemy, under Early, lay on the west bank of Opequan Creek, covering Winchester; and our army, under Sheridan, lay in front of Berryville. From Berryville south were two roads, one leading directly to Winchester, and the other leading more easterly to White Post. Early lay across the Winchester road on the Opequan, in order to cover Winchester and command the roads south. Grant, who had the direction of all movements, hesitated about giving Sheridan permission to move on the enemy, for, if defeated, it certainly would not be very comfortable. There were Maryland and Washington right before the enemy; so he went to see Sheridan, and was so well satisfied that all the order he gave was, "Go in." Grant asked, if he could be ready Tuesday? Sheridan said, "Yes, Monday." Grant said, in his report,

"He was off promptly to time, and, I may here add, that the result was such that I have never since deemed it necessary to visit General Sheridan before giving him orders."[1] Sheridan's campaign lasted about five weeks, and it was decisive. On the morning of the 19th of September he attacked Early at the crossing of Opequan Creek, and, in a hard-fought, sanguinary battle, utterly defeated him, capturing five pieces of artillery and several thousand prisoners, driving him through Winchester to Fisher's Hill. There Early again made a stand, and was again defeated. Sheridan pursued him to the gaps of the Blue Ridge, and, after stripping the country of its provisions, returned to Strasburg. In the beginning of October, Early, reënforced, returned. On the 9th his cavalry was totally defeated; but, on the 19th, near Middletown, while Sheridan was in Winchester, he succeeded in surprising and turning our army, which retreated some distance. A messenger had informed Sheridan of the enemy's attack, and, just at the crisis, he arrived on the field, having galloped hard from Winchester. The effect was instantaneous. The army was at once re-formed—at once attacked the enemy, who was defeated, with great slaughter, losing his artillery and trains. Early escaped in the night, with the wreck of his army, and no more returned. The brilliant poet of Ohio, T. Buchanan Read, embodied the memory of this battle in the Ode, called "Sheridan's Ride:"

> "He dashed down the line, 'mid a storm of huzzas,
> And the wave of retreat checked its course there, because

[1] Grant's Report, July 22, 1865.

> The sight of the master compelled it to pause.
> With foam and with dust, the black charger was gray;
> By the flash of his eye, and the red nostril's play,
> He seemed to the whole great army to say,
> 'I have brought you Sheridan all the way
> From Winchester, down to save the day!'"

We shall see Sheridan once more, in the last decisive battle, when the war-clouds pass away.

In the mean time Sherman was carrying on a most brilliant campaign in Georgia. On the 6th of May he moved from Chattanooga, with the armies of the Cumberland, Tennessee, and Ohio, commanded respectively by Thomas, McPherson, and Schofield, upon Johnston's army, at Dalton. After battles and skirmishes of various character at Resaca, New Hope, Dallas, Kenesaw, and Atlanta, steadily forcing Johnston's army back from point to point, he took and occupied Atlanta, on the 2d of September. In the bloody battle of the 22d of July, in front of Atlanta, was killed the "brave, accomplished, and noble-hearted" McPherson, who had been with and near Grant in nearly all his long and successful campaigns in the West, and whose loss was lamented by the whole country.

The rebels were so displeased with the ill-success of Johnston that Davis was compelled to put Hood, a Texas officer, in command. This officer had more fight and less skill than Johnston; so he (after fighting, with great loss, the battles round Atlanta) thought he would cut Sherman's communications, and thus drive him back. He did cut the communications for a time effectually, but was himself driven off. After that he devised a new plan, which he thought would certainly succeed—moving to the West, with a view of moving on Middle Tennessee and destroying our great storehouse of supplies at Nashville. At the same time Sherman conceived the counterpart of this. If General Hood chooses to amuse himself in going to Tennessee, why not let him? Nashville can be defended, and I can move on Savannah, Augusta, or Charleston. It is perfectly clear, from what followed, that the rebel Government never imagined what actually happened. "Cutting communications" was a great idea with them throughout the war. Hood thought that if he got a clear road to Nashville, Sherman would follow him, or detach a large part of his army, and the rebel Government never dreamed that Sherman would venture on marching through the country without supplies or communications with our depots. But Grant had learned in Mississippi the great lesson that he could subsist an army in the interior of the South; and he had since then learned another great truth, that *the South could raise no more armies.* Hence, if Hood could be induced to do the very thing he did do, (get out of the way,) it was quite obvious Sherman would have an unobstructed march. To my mind, at the time, there was not a doubt on the subject. I did not see the slightest danger in Sherman's march to the sea. It seemed to me a very easy thing. But what better could the rebels have done? If Hood had kept in front of Sherman, it would have varied the movement only in this: Hood could not then have cut Sherman's communications, and Sherman would have driven him back, just as he had done Johnston.   In fact, the rebel generals were blamed for not doing impossibilities.   They could not raise new armies, and the war was drawing to an inevitable close.   All they fought for, after Vicksburg, was to secure some advantages by negotiation which they would not have by a surrender.   This was proved by the escapade at Niagara, at which poor Clay and Holcomb endeavored to draw Greeley into a negotiation on the part of the Government.   Mr. Lincoln very happily answered them, in his brief answer, "To ALL WHOM IT MAY CONCERN," which it gave them much concern to receive.

Fighting in this desperate way, without a gleam of real hope, Hood rushed off to Nashville, and Sherman took advantage of it.   He had already burned Atlanta, and now, destroying all the railroads about it, he turned his face toward the capital of Georgia. But I here remark, that this plan of Sherman's was formed at a late hour, as is proved by the dispatches between Sherman and Grant.   About the beginning of October, Sherman sent a letter to Grant, proposing that, if Hood went West, he should march on Augusta, Columbia, and Charleston.   Grant believed a good deal more in fighting than he did in a mere march through the country, and, moreover, did not believe in leaving an enemy's army at liberty to go on its own way:

"If he does this, he ought to be met and prevented from getting north of the Tennessee River. If you were to cut loose, I do not believe you would meet Hood's army, but would be bushwhacked by all the old men and little boys, and such railroad-guards as are still left at home. Hood would probably strike for Nashville, thinking that, by going north, he could inflict greater damage upon us than we could upon the rebels by going south. If there is any way of getting at Hood's army, I would prefer that; but I must trust to your own judgment."

This whole scheme will be best understood by the following dispatches between Grant and Sherman, on the 11th of October:

"We can not remain here on the defensive. With the twenty-five thousand men, and the bold cavalry he has, he can constantly break my roads. I would infinitely prefer to make a wreck of the road, and of the country from Chattanooga to Atlanta, including the latter city— send back all my wounded and worthless, and, with my effective army, move through Georgia, smashing things, to the sea. Hood may turn into Tennessee and Kentucky, but I believe he will be forced to follow me. Instead of my being on the defensive, I would be on the offensive; instead of guessing at what he means to do, he would have to guess at my plans. The difference in war is full twenty-five per cent. I can make Savannah, Charleston, or the mouth of the Chattahoochee.

"Answer quick, as I know we will not have the telegraph long.

"W. T. SHERMAN, *Major-General.*
"LIEUTENANT-GENERAL GRANT."

"CITY POINT, VA., *October* 11, 1864—11.30, P. M.

"Your dispatch of to-day received. If you are satisfied the trip to the sea-coast can be made, holding the line of the Tennessee River firmly, you may make it, destroying all the railroad south of Dalton or Chattanooga, as you think best. U. S. GRANT, *Lieutenant-General.*

"MAJOR-GENERAL W. T. SHERMAN."

Most fortunately for Sherman's plan, Hood acted precisely as he should, if he was in the council, and favored the scheme. He marched off toward Nashville; and Sherman, leaving the Fourth and Twenty-Third Corps, under Thomas, to meet Hood, took up his march on the 14th of November. There was, in fact, nothing in his way. The rebels had no army but Hood's which was available, and that had deliberately marched out of the way. Sherman had nothing to do but to take the main roads to Augusta and Savannah, keep his army in good order, and send out his cavalry and bummers to gather provisions from the surrounding country. A few guerrilla cavalry hovered about him, doing but little harm. Johnston was again called upon to resist the invader; but to what purpose, without an army? Sherman went regularly and easily on, with a skirmish here and a skirmish there, keeping the main road to Augusta to the point where the highway to Savannah turned off, and then as steadily on that. Passing along between the Ogechee and the Savannah, Sherman reached Savannah at Christmas; presenting, as he said in his letter, Savannah, with its artillery, munitions, and twenty-five thousand bales of cotton, to the Government, as a Christmas present! It was well done, and was one of the conclusive evidences the rebels were now constantly receiving that the Confederacy was in a dying condition.

Let us now turn to General Hood. This person had a great deal of energy, courage, and determination. When Sherman left Atlanta, he kept on his way toward Nashville. So did Thomas, who had the Fourth Corps, under Stanley, and the Twenty-Third, under Schofield, and a large body of reënforcements, daily arriving from various parts of the West. In December, Hood arrived before Nashville, having occupied Columbia on the 26th of November, and on the 30th advanced to Franklin. Hood having divided his forces into two heavy columns, one of which was intended to flank our troops at Franklin by moving round east of it, attacked that place on the evening of the 30th with his main column. General Schofield commanded at Franklin, and managed to maintain his position there during the day, beginning his retreat at night. It was·a most fortunate retreat; for the enemy's column to the east had nearly succeeded in getting to our rear, and actually marched for some distance near and parallel to our army on the turnpike. The result was, our forces were all driven back to within three miles of Nashville. Great alarm prevailed, and the Government laborers were armed. Hood then seems to have formed the bold plan of cutting off Thomas, in Nashville, from his communications with Louisville and Bridgeport—actually investing him. In the mean while our army was constantly reënforced, and in a few days Thomas became strong enough to take the offensive. Hood occupied the Overton range of hills. On the 15th of December, Thomas made a feint on his right, and a real attack on his left, driving him back from the river below the city, a distance of eight miles, capturing many prisoners, and sixteen pieces of artillery. Hood contracted his lines on the Brentwood hills; but, on the morning of the 16th, was again attacked by Thomas, and totally defeated, losing most of his artillery, and several thousand prisoners. That night General Thomas reported to the War Department a complete victory. Hood retreated with the wreck of his army into North Alabama. The battle of Nashville was complete and decisive. It ended the war in the West, and no more military events of any importance occurred there. In fact, the capture of Chattanooga by Rosecrans, and the capture of Vicksburg and the opening of the Mississippi by Grant, had made any successful defense in the South-West by the rebels impossible. And now the march of Sherman to Savannah, and the final destruction of Hood's army, had utterly destroyed the rebel power in the whole West and South-West. There remained in the once strong and haughty Confederacy, east of the Mississippi, only the three States of Virginia, South and North Carolina, in which the rebels had any strength. In one word, it was reduced to Lee's army, and the fortifications of Wilmington and Charleston. The year 1864 closed with the moral certainty, apparent to all intelligent men, that the Confederacy was conquered; yet there seemed at Richmond the same blind fatuity which, in all history, seems to actuate those whom God has destined to destruction. The rebel Congress continued to deliberate on their plans and resources, in the same style of defiant folly which they had manifested from the beginning. Lee called for more men. Where were they to be had? Conscript and arm the negroes; but the rebel Congress refused to do this till the last moment. The wiser and more sagacious members of the rebel Assembly refused, probably for reasons which history will fail properly to record. They saw that the Confederacy was dying, and if, to save its existence for a few months, (all that was possible,) they raised a negro army, *that negro soldiery would be ready* (when peace returned) *to keep them in subjection.* They were looking to ulterior results, and were wise in so doing; for there can be no doubt that if the negroes had been armed to defend their masters, they would have used those arms against their masters when the war ended.

We must now return to the great field at Richmond, and see what became of Lee and his army, and the few remaining fortresses of the rebels.

After driving Lee from the Weldon Railroad, little had been done in Grant's army. Large forces, as I have already described, had been detached to Sheridan, and it was necessary to destroy the possibilities of Early's movements North, and, as Sheridan did, destroy the grain crops of the Valley, and thus cut off Lee's resources in that quarter, before any thing more decisive could be done. In the mean time, Lee tried to use the Weldon road by wagoning supplies through the country from a certain point on the road; but, in December, an expedition from Grant's army destroyed twenty miles of the road, and thus cut off that resource. The new year, 1865, opened with the moral certainty that the great work of the war would soon be over, and the rebel Confederacy be numbered among the lost things of history. Early's army in the Valley had been destroyed; so had Hood's before Nashville. Mobile had been taken, the Shenandoah Valley had been devastated, and cavalry expeditions from Vicksburg, Baton Rouge, and other points had laid waste the lower part of Mississippi, and carried terror through the South. Grant had declared that the Confederacy was hollow, and wasted of its resources; that the rebel commanders had robbed the cradle and the grave to supply the army. And so they had. But the South had lost its will, its hope, and its courage. It was useless to prolong a desperate conflict only to end in destruction. But the last scene must be gone through with, however bloody, however disastrous.

In the beginning of February, General Grant marched a large part of his army on to Hatcher's Run, to the enemy's right, there threw up intrenchments, and was able to maintain them, after a most furious attack by Lee. This was an advanced position, and one step farther in the direction by which we were to turn the enemy's right.

In the beginning of March the line of Grant's army was thirty miles in length, the right resting at Chapin's farm, on James River, thence crossing the James at Bermuda Hundred, extending round Petersburg as far as Hatcher's Run. This whole line was intrenched, but the greater part of the army lay on the left, for it was necessary we should be continually pressing toward the Southside Railroad, in order to cut off Lee's last communication. In the mean time, Grant had sent orders to Sheridan to take his cavalry and go on toward Lynchburg, destroying, if he could, the canal and railroad, and finally, if he chose, join Sherman in North Carolina, as Grant was afraid Sherman was deficient in cavalry. Sheridan did not do exactly that, but he did, on the whole, quite as well, if not better. He proceeded rapidly up the Valley to Staunton, routed the remnant of poor Early's forces, and then, proceeding to the James River canal and the Lynchburg Railroad, destroyed a large portion of the canal and an immense quantity of provisions and munitions. It was found that the James River canal was the great feeder of Lee's army. Grant's order to Sheridan contains a paragraph which shows how completely the rebel country was now at our mercy, and how fully Grant realized that to cut off their supplies would put an end to the rebel forces. He says:

"This additional raid, with one now about starting from East Tennessee, under Stoneman, numbering four or five thousand cavalry, one from Vicksburg, numbering seven or eight thousand cavalry, one from Eastport, Mississippi, ten thousand cavalry, Canby from Mobile Bay, with about thirty-eight thousand mixed troops—these three latter, pushing for Tuscaloosa, Selma, and Montgomery, and Sherman, with a large army eating out the vitals of South Carolina, is all that will be wanted to leave nothing for the rebellion to stand upon."[1]

To use a common expression, the rebellion was on its last legs, and nothing can be conceived of more hopeless or useless than the struggle the rebels made now, or had made from the fall of Vicksburg.

Sheridan finally arrived at the White House, and joined Grant's army. At this time, in the siege of Richmond, the final destruction of Lee, if he remained in Richmond, seemed inevitable, and the real question was one for Lee's solution. Was he to remain, and there surrender to Grant? or was he to march out, and try to gain Lynchburg, and prolong the war a little while? The last, to be sure, was useless ; but the beaten do n't like to surrender. They look round the whole horizon, to see whether there are any means

---

[1] Grant's dispatch to Sheridan from City Point, February 20th.

of escape. From what followed, it seems that Lee was in a state of irresolution. He could not bear to leave Richmond, and yet he would rather leave it than to surrender there. He thought he would try one desperate assault. A happy turn of fortune, an unforeseen accident, might give a temporary success. So he resolved on storming a portion of our intrenchments. On the right of our line, investing Petersburg, was Fort Steadman ; on the west of it, Fort Haskell; and still further on the extreme right, was Fort McGilvry. All these were mutually enfilading, which was necessary to their defense, in case any one of them should be captured. On the morning of the 25th of March, two rebel divisions, under General Gordon, rushed over our intrenchments and captured Fort Steadman, and the batteries immediately adjoining it. It was a brilliant movement, but only for a moment successful. The guns of Fort Haskell were immediately brought to bear upon them. The division of Hartrauft rush forward and push the enemy out of Steadman into the open space, where our batteries have a cross fire upon them, and the battle ends, with our capture of two thousand prisoners. Of this sudden and brilliant affair, President Lincoln was a spectator, and had the satisfaction of seeing the victory of the Union troops. At the same time that Gordon was repulsed, the left of our line (the Second and Sixth Corps) moved forward, captured the enemy's intrenched picket line on their right, with several hundred prisoners. The day ended with the signal success of the Union army. Lee had now lost his opportunity. A week or two sooner he could have left Richmond ; but now it was too late. He seems to have been wholly irresolute what to do, and so held on.

We must now return for a moment to General Sherman. He left Savannah about the 1st of February, on his march through South Carolina. The rebel commanders supposed it absolutely impossible to cross the swamps of lower Carolina with a large army; and, in fact, this was the main difficulty. But our army had thousands of all sorts of craftsmen in it—lumbermen, engineers, steamboatmen, mechanics of every description, and capable of doing or devising any kind of work. Many miles of the worst swamps were corduroyed, and many streams and rivers were bridged. Thus the army moved on in parallel columns. On the 17th of February, Howard's Corps, with General Sherman, entered Columbia, the capital of South Carolina. The enemy had piled up cotton and lint in the streets, which, by some means, took fire, and destroyed the largest part of Columbia. General Hampton complained very much, and charged it upon the Union troops. Sherman had, in fact, given orders to the contrary, but it was hardly worth a controversy, and probably few Union people regretted that such a retribution should fall on the people of a State which had caused so useless and bloody a war.

In consequence of the march of our army on its rear, and the necessity of preserving, if possible, its garrison, Charleston was evacuated and surrendered on the 18th. The garrison, under General Hardee, marched to the East, to join the scattering bodies of troops now assembling under Johnston. The army crossed the Pedee near Cheraw, (South Carolina,) and, on the 11th of March, reached Fayetteville, on Cape Fear River, (North Carolina.) Here, again, every thing which could be made use of by an enemy was destroyed. Heretofore, Sherman had really no enemy in front of him, except light cavalry and guerrillas. But he was now made aware that there was really a large army gathering in around him.[1] Beauregard's shattered troops at Columbia had gone on. The remains of Hood's Corps had crossed the Savannah at Augusta, and were proceeding rapidly to the front. Hardee had left Charleston with about 15,000 men, and now Sherman had to move cautiously.

In the mean time, General Thomas, who no longer had need of his army at Nashville, had sent round the Twenty-Third Corps, under General Schofield, to join in the operations round Wilmington. These were entirely successful, and, on the 22d of February, General Cox's Division entered that city. The whole coast, with its towns and fortresses, was in our possession. General Sherman knew this, and sent twenty messengers to Schofield, to inform him that he would move on Goldsboro, and that he wanted Schofield and Terry to join him from Newberne.[2] He commenced his own march from Fayetteville on the 15th. On the 18th, Slocum's Corps encamped on the Goldsboro road, five miles from Bentonville. Here a severe battle occurred, but the result was that Sherman held possession of Goldsboro, with the two railroads to Wilmington and Beaufort. We may

[1] Sherman's Report.　　　　[2] Idem.

here leave the Army of Sherman, which, after a series of signal successes, went into camp at Goldsboro, and performed no more active service.

All had now come, on the rebel part, to depend entirely on the fate of Lee, and that was, to discerning eyes, in no way uncertain.

On the 27th of March, Sherman made a hurried visit to Grant at City Point. There was a meeting which can never more be made on earth; for Lincoln, who was the chief personage of the scene, was soon made the victim of that dark and malicious spirit which brought on and still actuated the rebellion. There at City Point, consulting together, were Lincoln, Grant, Sheridan, Meade, and Sherman. Sherman said he could move on Johnston by the 10th of April, with twenty days' supplies; but that did not suit Grant, who was afraid Lee would get away, and somehow join Johnston. So he fixed a grand movement for his army on the 29th of March, and, if unsuccessful, intended to throw his cavalry on their communications, prevent the junction of Lee and Johnston, and beat them in detail. In fact he had issued orders for this movement on the 24th of March, prior to Sherman's arrival.[1]

On the 28th of March, General Sheridan had orders to move next morning, and was informed that the Fifth Corps would move at 3, A. M., on the Vaughn road; the Second at 9, A. M., having only three miles to march to get on the right of the Fifth. Sheridan had nine thousand cavalry, and was to move

[1] Grant's Order to Generals Meade, Ord, and Sheridan, dated March 24, 1865.

at his discretion on the enemy's right—the object being to reach the Danville or Southside road, and not
to attack the enemy in his intrenchments. "Should
he come out," says Grant, "move in with your entire
force, in your own way, and with the full reliance
that the army will engage, or follow, as circumstances
will dictate. I shall be on the field.' After having
accomplished the destruction of the two railroads,
which are now the only avenues of supply to Lee's
army, you may return to this army, selecting your
road farther south."

Sheridan pushed out, on the morning of the 29th,
to Dinwiddie Court-House, where he arrived at 5, P.
M. Our position then was, Sheridan on the extreme
left; Warren, with the Fifth, next; the Second Corps
next; then the Twenty-Fourth, Sixth, and Ninth,
covering Petersburg.

On the afternoon of the 29th Grant sent a dispatch to Sheridan, stating the position of affairs, and
closing with this significant and decisive paragraph:

"I now feel like ending the matter, if it is possible to do so, before
going back. I do not want you, therefore, to cut loose and go after the
enemy's roads at present. In the morning, push round the enemy, if
you can, and get on to his right rear. The movements of the enemy's
cavalry may, of course, modify your action. We will act all together
as one army here, till it is seen what can be done with the enemy. The
signal officer at Cobb's Hill reported, at 11.30, A. M., that a cavalry
column had passed that point from Richmond toward Petersburg,
taking forty minutes to pass.

"U. S. GRANT, *Lieutenant-General.*
"MAJOR-GENERAL P. H. SHERIDAN."

On the 30th, when rain had made the roads too
muddy for infantry, Sheridan started forward with his

' Grant's Order to Sheridan on the 28th.

cavalry. He went on the White Oak road for Five Forks, where he knew the enemy was in force. Warren, with the Fifth, was directed to cross the Boydtown road, and hold it. Sheridan seized the Five Forks, but was driven back to Dinwiddie Court-House. Grant, who was at Gravelly Run, watching all these movements, immediately put the Fifth Corps (Warren's) under the command of Sheridan, and thus reënforced, Sheridan again moved forward, while the other Corps attacked in front. Sheridan was also strengthened with McKenzie's Division of Cavalry; and now he began a series of capital maneuvers. He directed General Merritt to make a feint on the enemy's right flank, while the Fifth Corps struck their left. In the mean time the sun was declining, and Sheridan rode over to the Fifth Corps and hurried it up. The Fifth Corps advanced gallantly, routed the enemy, and pursued him. As soon as Merritt heard the firing he assaulted the enemy's right and carried it. Sheridan said: "The enemy were driven from their strong line of works, and completely routed, the Fifth Corps doubling up their left flank in confusion, and the cavalry of General Merritt dashing on to the White Oak road, capturing their artillery and turning it upon them, and riding into their broken ranks, so demoralized them that they made no serious stand after their line was carried, but took to flight in disorder."

So ended the battle of Five Forks, which was entirely decisive. We took five or six thousand prisoners, and the enemy were entirely demoralized.

On the morning of April 2d, a general assault

was made on the lines of Petersburg, and "General Wright penetrated the lines with his whole corps, sweeping every thing before him, and to his left toward Hatcher's Run." This, also, was decisive. Lee immediately telegraphed Davis that the lines were broken, and Richmond could no longer be held. The rebel President was in church, and immediately packed up, and, with his pretended Cabinet, left the capital that night on the railroad, for Danville. Lee rushed off, with the utmost speed, and Sheridan and Ord after him. Sheridan struck the Danville road in time to head off Lee. We need not trace the few remaining military operations. On the 7th, Grant addressed a note to Lee, stating that farther resistance was vain, and asking the surrender of the Army of Northern Virginia. Lee asked, before considering the proposition, the terms of surrender. To this Grant replied, saying that *peace* was his great desire, and there was but one condition of surrender, "that the men and officers surrendered" shall be disqualified for taking up arms against the Government of the United States till properly exchanged. On the 8th, Lee replied that he would meet Grant on the old stage-road to Richmond, between the pickets of the two armies. Grant declined that; but, on the 9th, (his situation in the mean time having become worse,) Lee asked an interview in accordance with Grant's offer. It was short and decisive. On the 9th of April, at Appomattox Court-House, Lee surrendered the Army of Northern Virginia to General Grant, and thus ended the war; for all that followed was a mere sequel to this main fact.

The description of the surrender of Lee from a rebel pen is worth recording. It is true, and almost draws sympathy—certainly pity—from loyal hearts:

"There is no passage of history in this heart-breaking war which will, for years to come, be more honorably mentioned, and gratefully remembered, than the demeanor, on the 9th of April, 1865, of General Grant toward General Lee. I do not so much allude to the facility with which honorable terms were accorded to the Confederates, as to the bearing of General Grant, and the officers about him, toward General Lee. The interview was brief. Three commissioners upon either side were immediately appointed. The agreement to which these six commissioners acceded is known.

"In the mean time, immediately that General Lee was seen riding to the rear, dressed more gayly than usual, and begirt with his sword, the rumor of immediate surrender flew like wildfire through the Confederates. It might be imagined that an army, which had drawn its last regular rations on the 1st of April, and, harassed incessantly by night and day, had been marching and fighting till the morning of the 9th, would have welcomed any thing like a termination of its sufferings, let it come in what form it might. Let those who idly imagine that the finer feelings are the prerogative of what are called the 'upper classes,' learn from this and similar scenes to appreciate 'common men.' As the great Confederate captain rode back from his interview with General Grant, the news of the surrender acquired shape and consistency, and could no longer be denied. The effect on the worn and battered troops—some of whom had fought since April, 1861, and, sparse survivors of hecatombs of fallen comrades, had passed unscathed through such hurricanes of shot as, within four years, no other men had ever experienced—passes mortal description.

"Whole lines of battle rushed up to their beloved old chief, and, choking with emotion, broke ranks, and struggled with each other to wring him once more by the hand. Men who had fought throughout the war, and knew what the agony and humiliation of that moment must be to him, strove, with a refinement of unselfishness and tenderness which he alone could fully appreciate, to lighten his burden and mitigate his pain. With tears pouring down both cheeks, General Lee at length commanded voice enough to say, 'Men, we have fought through the war together. I have done the best that I could for you.' Not an eye that looked on that scene was dry. Nor was this the emotion of sickly sentimentalists, but of rough and rugged men, familiar with hardships, danger, and death, in a thousand shapes, mastered by sympathy and feeling for another which they never experienced on their own account. I know of no other passage of military history so touching, unless, in spite of the melo-dramatic coloring which French historians have loved to shed over the scene, it can be found in the Adieu de Fontainebleau."[1]

The officers and men were all paroled, not to take up arms till regularly exchanged. As Grant knew

---

[1] I copy this from Coppée's "Grant and His Campaigns," as I do not know from what paper it was taken.

there was no probability that they ever would be exchanged, but, on the contrary, that this was, in fact, the end of the war, he provided, in the paroles, that while they remained peaceful, violating no law of the United States, they should be protected. This was the basis of all the paroles given to the Confederate troops; and it was claimed by Grant, and has been conceded by the Government, that the rebel soldiers could not, under this parole, be seized, tried, or punished, for military offenses, during the war. They have not been; and this immunity from punishment, and, in fact, protection by the Government, they owe to the generous and liberal conduct of General Grant. No man was more determined to put an end to the war, by the destruction of the rebel armies, than General Grant; but he had no particle of personal or unkind feeling to the people; and, while maintaining and enforcing, as far as he could, the reconstruction acts of Congress, he has wished to see peace, order, and humanity prevail in the conquered States.

In consequence of these events, a correspondence was entered into between Generals Sherman and Johnston, which resulted, on the 18th of April, in an agreement for the suspension of hostilities, and a memorandum for a treaty of peace. How General Sherman, or any General, came by power to make terms of peace, we have never been informed; but the sagacity and common-sense of Grant avoided this difficulty in the beginning. Lee, in his letter to Grant, sought to bring him into a treaty of peace; but Grant explicitly informed him that he had no power to make peace, but would treat for a surrender. This *memorandum*, signed by Sherman and Johnston, is the most extraordinary document which was ever put forth in this country;[1] but the war gave rise to extraordinary acts and delusions, and the errors of gallant soldiers should be set down rather to the distemper of the times than to any intentional disrespect of the Government. General Sherman said, in his report, that Mr. Lincoln having been assassinated, he thought to pay respect to his memory by following the policy he felt certain Lincoln would have approved. How very much he was mistaken may be known by the following copy of instructions from Lincoln to Grant:

"War Department, Washington, *March* 3, 1865.
"To Lieutenant-General Grant:

"The President directs me to say to you that he wishes you to have no conference with General Lee, unless it be for the capitulation of General Lee's army, or on some minor and purely military matter. He wishes me to say that you are not to decide, discuss, or confer upon any political question. Such questions the President holds in his own hands, and will submit them to no military conferences or conventions. Meantime you are to press to your utmost your military advantages.
"Edwin M. Stanton, *Secretary of War*."

That was Lincoln's policy; and nothing could better prove his good sense and sagacity. Grant hurried off to see Sherman, while Stanton issued a peremptory order, disapproving the agreement. Soon after, Johnston surrendered, by a military convention; so did Kirby Smith, in the West, and Taylor, in Louisiana. In a few days more, Davis, having

[1] A copy of that "basis of agreement" may be found in the American Encyclopedia for 1865, page 68. It undertakes to settle the status of the States, the people, and the armies of the Confederates, between two Generals!

escaped into Georgia, accompanied by two or three of the miserable men who had followed his fortunes at Richmond, was also taken by a squadron of cavalry. The last acts of this unhappy being would be supremely ridiculous, if they had not occurred in the midst of a tragedy. On the 5th of April, after leaving Richmond, he issued one of those bombastic Proclamations,[1] so entirely characteristic of his career. He represented Lee as having been trammeled by "watching over the approaches" to the capital, but now free to move, and strike the enemy, and said he (Davis) would never make peace with the infamous invaders of Virginia! Could folly go any further, or delusion be greater? By the 1st of June the last armies of the Southern Confederacy had surrendered. After all its terrible crimes and sanguinary battles, its loud boasts and real valor, its dream of imperial greatness, and its visions of morbid ambition, the Southern Confederacy, which had sent its embassadors to claim the support of foreign powers, which had startled the world, as with the sudden appearance of some gigantic creation of the night, as suddenly vanished away! The laugh of scorn, which had issued from the demoniac Congress at Montgomery, had been reëchoed from the gloomy vaults of despair, and was now heard only in dying groans from the distant horizon. Were it not for its too dreadful realities, we might imagine it to have been a creation of Prospero's wand:

> "*These our actors,*
> *As I foretold you, were all spirits, and*

[1] Davis's Proclamation, dated Danville, April 5, 1865.

> *Are melted into air, into thin air;*
> *And, like the baseless fabric of this vision,*
> *The cloud-capped towers, the gorgeous palaces,*
> *The solemn temples, the great globe itself,*
> *Yea, all which it inherit, shall dissolve;*
> *And, like this unsubstantial pageant faded,*
> *Leave not a rack behind."*

With the dispersion of armies ended, also, that work of beneficence which had raised war in our country from the condition of barbarism which, in most periods of the world, it has held to the condition of civilization, attended with the Christian charities. The Sanitary and the Christian Commissions had given evidence of substantial progress in the very elements of society. They had gone into the very midst of disease and danger to comfort the soldiers, carry balm to the wounded, and consolation to the dying. They will make an illuminated page in the histories carried down to posterity, and be remembered with gratitude by thousands of hearts when the storms of war have long been past.

Grant, I said, was utterly deficient in a genius for proclamations, and when Vicksburg was taken—certainly one of the most decisive events of the war—made no proclamation, and quietly went on doing his duty. But now something must be said, and he said it well. He issued Order No. 108, the great point of which was its truth. The concluding paragraph is this. Addressing the soldiers of the army, he said :

"Your marches, sieges, and battles, in distance, duration, resolution, and brilliancy of results, dim the luster of the world's past military achievements, and will be the patriot's precedence in defense of liberty and right in all time to come. In obedience to your country's call, you left your homes and families, and volunteered in its defense. Victory has crowned your valor, and secured the purpose of your patriotic hearts; and, with the gratitude of your countrymen, and the highest honors a great and free nation can accord, you will soon be permitted to return to your homes and families, conscious of having discharged the highest duty of American citizens. To achieve these glorious triumphs, and secure to yourselves, your fellow-countrymen, and posterity, the blessings of free institutions, tens of thousands of your gallant comrades have fallen and sealed the priceless legacy with their lives. The graves of these a grateful nation bedews with tears, honors their memories, and will ever cherish and support their stricken families.   U. S. GRANT, *Lieutenant-General.*"

It may be interesting to know how many men composed the rebel armies in the last year of the war. The following facts, taken from authentic sources, will show nearly the truth. The number of men surrendered in the different armies amounted to 174,223, as follows:

Army of Northern Virginia, commanded by Gen. Lee,	27,805
Army of Tennessee, and others, commanded by Gen. Joseph E. Johnston,	31,243
Army of Gen. Jeff. Thompson, in Missouri,	7,978
Miscellaneous paroles in the Department of Virginia,	9,072
Paroled at Cumberland, Md., and other stations,	9,377
Paroled by Gen. McCook in Alabama and Florida,	6,428
Army of the Department of Alabama, under Lieut.-Gen. Taylor,	42,293
Army of the Trans-Mississippi Department, under Gen. E. K. Smith,	17,686
Paroled in the Department of Washington,	3,390
Paroled in Virginia, Tennessee, Georgia, Alabama, Louisiana, and Texas,	13,922
Surrendered at Nashville and Chattanooga, Tenn.,	5,029

In addition to those surrendered at the close of the war, there were in the Federal custody, between January 1st and 20th of October of the same year, 98,802 prisoners of war.

But to these must be added the killed or disabled by wounds. We will suppose only one-third of the wounded to be disabled or kept from the field, and, taking the estimate, results are as follows :

	Killed.	Disabled.
In Lee's Department, ...	14,650	20,500
In Georgia "	7,660	4,200
In Tennessee "	6,250	5,800
In all other "	4,310	4,100
Total, ...	32,870	34,600

Here are no less than 67,470 men of the rebel army killed or totally disabled after Grant crossed the Rapidan, in May, 1864. This includes only the great battles or sieges. There are, no doubt, some thousands of others omitted. Taking the above data, we have this result :

Surrendered in the different armies, . . .	174,323
Prisoners, ...	98,802
Killed and disabled in the last year, . . .	67,470
Total, ...	340,595

This corresponds very well with the statements made in one of the last debates of the rebel Congress, in which the *available* men were stated at various numbers, from 200,000 to 500,000. I suppose that, including their guerrillas, they had 300,000 men available in the last year of the war.

But now we must close the scene with what I consider one of the finest lessons which the history of our country can carry down to posterity. The army was an army of volunteers. It was no mercenary army. It was no army of some ambitious conqueror. It could be made to fight for no cause not its own. When the cause was gained, when the enemy left the field, the army had no more to do.

It was composed of citizens. It dreamed of no foreign conquests, and no leader dared to ask its aid for any other than a patriotic object. It wanted only home. And now the battalions of Sherman, and the grand Army of the Potomac, wearied with war, march quietly to the capital, to be reviewed by the Chief Magistrate. Gay pennons, bright uniforms, brilliant dresses, beautiful women, grave senators, and noble chiefs receive the war-worn defenders of their country. The glorious flag of the nation waves in triumph. Shouts rend the heavens. The President feelingly thanks the army, and the army peacefully returns to the quietude of home. The soldier's dream is now true, and he again sees wife, children, and home.

CHAPTER XV.

GRANT IN PEACE.

WE have now pursued the career of Grant through long years of war—through weary marches and bloody fields—till we find him victorious over enemies, and applauded by friends. It is time now to review his conduct, as far as we properly may, and consider his character as a citizen. It is an old adage, *de mortuis nil nisi bonum*—to say of the dead nothing but good—and of the living one would think it was almost equally a practice to say, *de vivendis nil nisi malum*—nothing but evil. The severest criticism upon public men may safely be allowed, in a free country; but it is evidence, not merely of coarse manners, but of positive injustice, when criticism degenerates into abuse. I said, in the beginning of this volume, that it was not necessary to make General Grant either more or less than he is, in order to commend him to the favor of his countrymen. Saints and heroes are rarely found in history; and, certain it is, that I have found them very rare in our time—

so rare that I think they have not been very common in any age of the world. But, however we may suspect the most eminent men of faults and weaknesses, it will be admitted, by all just minds, that they are entitled to be treated fairly, and if their faults are severely condemned, their virtues should be frankly admitted. General Grant has been charged with some serious faults, both as a general and a citizen. So far as it may be done with propriety, I shall make a brief comment on these criticisms.

It has been said, (which, if true, is no crime,) that Grant had no genius, and succeeded only by pounding. If he had sense to see that pounding was necessary, that was more than his superiors or his critics seem to have had. Genius, in the popular sense, is a rare quality, and, when possessed, is often more destructive than it is useful. It is a very dangerous quality, and it is one which a republican Government seldom needs, and, however strange it may appear, seldom tolerates. The genius of *administration* is what a republican Government needs, and that Grant exhibited in a remarkable degree.

It is said, again, that Grant, especially in his Richmond campaign, caused an unnecessary loss of men, and succeeded by slaughter. This was exactly what the rebels said; and I remember well that the Richmond papers boasted that Grant had lost one hundred thousand men in getting to Richmond, and exclaimed against his inhuman butchery. This rebel horror was caught up with avidity by the enemies of Grant, and has been adopted by ignorant critics. Was it true? Had the charge any such foundation as should condemn Grant's military conduct? In the first place, it was not true; and in the next, it is impossible for any one to say that more or less loss was necessary to the capture of Richmond. War is, in all its forms, a bloody (I may say most cruel) necessity—necessity, I say, because, in this period of the world, no war should exist without necessity. There was but one alternative presented to the American Government—either to dissolve the American Union or to maintain its unity by war. The American people judged the Union a necessity to freedom and civilization, and, therefore, chose war, as a cruel, but an inevitable necessity. In this judgment Grant perfectly agreed. From his peaceful home in Galena he rushed into the ranks of the volunteers, and rose, by a series of unceasing labors and successes, to the highest military rank the nation had ever conferred. He succeeded by skillful, and, at the same time, unceasing pursuit of the enemy from post to post, from camp to camp, from army to army, till the last armed traitor was compelled to surrender. That this was done by fighting, by pounding, and by carnage, no one denies. Did any sensible man expect to succeed by any other means? These statements were not true.

The actual losses of life or limb were greatly exaggerated, and were no greater in our army than in that of the rebels. If we can ascertain what the losses of killed or wounded in Grant's Virginia campaign were, and then see what the losses were in McClellan's, Burnside's, and Hooker's, we shall have the means of making an accurate comparison, and determining whether Grant's successful campaign was

any more destructive than their unsuccessful ones.
This is the true way to determine what was, and
what was not, necessary to success. In the General
Reports of the Army, and in a tabular statement in
the "American Cyclopedia," we have the statistics
of losses sufficiently accurate. The summary of
Grant's losses in the Virginia campaign is:

	Killed.	Wounded.
Wilderness,	3,288	19,278
Spottsylvania,	2,296	9,086
Cold Harbor,	1,705	9,042
Petersburg Mines,	419	1,679
Hatcher's Run,	232	1,062
Five Forks,	1,200	3,800
Miscellaneous,	3,375	7,294
Petersburg assault,	1,198	6,853
Aggregate,	13,713	58,094

This may fall short a little; but it is near the
whole loss. Certainly we did not have more than
80,000 men killed and wounded in Grant's campaign,
from the 3d of May, 1864, on the Rapidan, to the
surrender of Lee at Appomattox Court-House, nearly
a year after. Undoubtedly it was a great loss, though
full half the whole number of wounded recovered
entirely.

Now let us examine the losses of previous campaigns:

	Killed.	Wounded.
McClellan's campaign,	5,291	23,909
Burnside's campaign,	1,028	9,105
Hooker's campaign,	4,800	10,200
Pope's campaign,	2,100	4,000
Meade's campaign,	2,837	13,718
Aggregate,	16,056	60,932

Here we see that the commanders of the Army of the Potomac had lost more men (and if we include sickness a great many more) in two years' useless expeditions than Grant did in the grand and final campaign, which terminated the rebel Confederacy. Here I leave this branch of military criticism. I do not think success a test of merit; but then, no man ought to be condemned because he is successful. If any one thinks that we ought to have spared the army more, and made the war longer, I think the country will not agree with him. It would have saved some lives on our side, and added incalculably to the burdens of the loyal and the destruction of the rebels. We may safely leave the military conduct of Grant to the judgment of posterity.

Other criticisms (or, rather, abuse) have been made upon Grant. He is said to want education, sobriety, and polish. It is positively certain that he did not receive a university education ; that he sold wood in St. Louis market; and that he smokes cigars. But let us look seriously at this charge. Our only right to comment upon it at all, (for we hold all private life to be sacred to all honorable minds,) is that his acts have made him conspicuous, and that, in the Government of the country, he is a public and responsible man. The real question, in looking at the character of Grant, (the one that concerns the country,) is, "What are his *qualifications*, morally and intellectually, for high and important public duties?" Any other question than that, we have no right to consider. The principal traits of his mind have already been brought out by his actions and decisions in the army; but it is well to inquire into his early training and known habits, in order to form a just judgment on his public character. His earliest training was by a Christian mother; and there is no evidence that that training has ever lost its weight and influence. He was also trained to habits of business; and his life at St. Louis and Galena, as well as his ceaseless care and watchfulness in the army, prove that he never sought for pleasure or for idleness where there were duties to perform. His early intellectual discipline was far better than some persons have supposed. Long before he went to West Point he had studied the best arithmetics then in use, and was fond of mathematics. His father had sent him to the best academies; and it is very evident that he had received a good moral and intellectual training before he went to West Point. There is nothing uncommon in this; but I mention it to contradict authoritatively the idea that he was an illiterate boy. It was not so. What he was at West Point I have related. And here let it be said, that in all the solid parts of a good education, West Point is not excelled by any institution in the world. The department in which West Point is deficient is the classical and literary, for the reason that the object of the Military Academy is to make men good officers, and not classical scholars; but there is teaching enough in the department of history and ethics not to leave the graduates wholly destitute of literary acquirements. We find, therefore, that when we look into Grant's orders, letters, and dispatches, they show no want of common literary ability. He has at least that command of language which enables him to express himself clearly. Colonel Badeau states that Grant's orders and letters were mainly written by himself, and that none of his staff could imitate his style.[1]

In Badeau's " Military History" will be found copies of numerous orders, directions, and letters to division commanders and quarter-masters, with constant correspondence with the War Department. These prove not only that he formed plans of all his own operations, but that he kept a continual watch over the details of his army. Read the dispatches to his officers at Vicksburg, and his correspondence with Halleck, and you can not fail to see that Grant possesses great administrative ability; and this is the very kind of ability most necessary to republican government.

Notwithstanding all these evidences of skill, talent, and discretion, Grant is spoken of as being poor in intellect and acquirements! How many of the public men of our country have had more intellect and acquirements than Grant? How much better was the education of Washington or Jackson? Neither of them, as young men, was as well educated as any cadet at West Point. But they, as well as all really great men, acquired a vast deal by experience, and had the original vigor and good sense to apply the knowledge acquired by experience to the best advantage. I admire science and love letters, but I can not conceal from myself the fact that it is not by such acquirements only that our country has attained to freedom and greatness. Washington was a Virginia

<hr>

[1] Badeau's "Military History."

surveyor ; Adams a poor lawyer of Boston ; Putnam a farmer in the field ; and Hamilton a young adventurer from the West Indies. There were other and more highly cultivated men than these in the American Congress, but none that did more service. We shall always have in our Congress men of high cultivation ; but the *men of affairs*, those who have the practical administration of public business, need not be men of great science or of refined literary tastes.

The moral qualities of a public man are, in my opinion, of more importance to the country by far than the most shining abilities or the most courtly manners. In the stern virtues of integrity, of true loyalty, of justice, of prudence, of frugality, and of obedience to law, the country can have more reliance than in the eloquence of Cicero or the genius of Napoleon. It is to these homely virtues that God has given more of success to men and nations than to all the other talents of the human race. These were the real talents which gave success to our Revolutionary ancestors, and founded this Government on principles of justice and of freedom. How far has General Grant exhibited these virtues ? He has never been charged by any one with want of integrity, which, in these latter times, is evidence that he is not suspected of any. Loyalty, obedience to law, prudence, were all exhibited by him in the conduct of the war. A sense of justice was proved by his treatment of the negro, and his uniform kindness to his officers. Nor does he seem to have exhibited bad temper, or made unreasonable demands, which is rather uncommon among officers of the army. I say these things because, having gone over the history of his conduct in the service of the Government, these are the impressions left on my mind, and seem characteristic of one with whom I am personally unacquainted.

Grant seems to have been considerate and generous to his officers, but not at all convivial in habits. Notwithstanding so many rumors were circulated to the contrary, yet all the evidence we have from those who knew him best, to those who were lookers-on in the army, agrees that he was rather serious in his deportment—simple and temperate. The following article is written with so much circumstantiality as to bear the air of truth, and may serve, in place of numerous stories told of him, to illustrate his manners in the army. It is from a lady correspondent of the " Philadelphia Press:"

"During the first three years of the war I was actively identified with the Western branch of the Sanitary Commission, and had abundant opportunity of judging for myself in regard to the character and ability of our generals. During the entire campaign of the opening of the Mississippi it was my privilege to aid in caring for our noble patriots, both in hospital and camps, and I have been for weeks together where I saw General Grant frequently, heard his name constantly, and never did I hear intemperance mentioned in connection with it. Facts are stubborn things. I will relate a few of the many that came directly to my knowledge. In the winter of 1862–63, when the army arrived at Memphis, after long, weary marching, and trials that sicken the heart to think of, two-thirds of the officers and soldiers were in hospitals. General Grant was lying sick at the Gayoso House. One morning Mrs. Grant came into the ladies' parlor, very much depressed, and said the medical director had just been to see Mr. Grant, and thought he would not be able to go any further if he did not stimulate. Said she, 'And I can not persuade him to do so. He says he will not die, and he will not touch a drop upon any consideration.' In less than a week he was on board the advance boat on the way to Vicksburg.

"Again, a few months after, I was on board the head-quarters boat at Milliken's Bend, where quite a lively gathering of officers and ladies had assembled. Cards and music were the order of the evening. General Grant sat in the ladies' cabin, leaning upon a table covered with innumerable maps and routes to Vicksburg, wholly absorbed in contemplation of the great matter before him. He paid no attention whatever to what was going on around, neither did any one dare to interrupt him. For hours he sat thus, till the loved and lamented McPherson stepped up to him, with a glass of liquor in his hand, and said, 'General, this won't do; you are injuring yourself. Join with us in a few toasts, and throw this burden off your mind.' Looking up, and smiling, he replied, 'Mac, you know your whisky won't help me to think. Give me a dozen of the best cigars you can find, and, if the ladies will excuse me for smoking, I think, by the time I have finished them, I shall have this job pretty nearly planned.' Thus he sat, and, when the company retired, we left him there, still smoking and thinking.

"When the army lay around Vicksburg, during that long siege, the time that tried men's souls, I watched every movement it was possible for me to do, feeling almost certain that he would eventually succumb to the custom, alas! too universal among the officers. I was in company with a gentleman from Chicago, who, while calling upon the General, remarked, 'I have some very fine brandy on the boat, and, if you will send an orderly with me to the river, I will send you a case or two.' 'I am greatly obliged,' replied the General, 'but I do not use the article. I have a big job on hand, and, though I know I shall win, I know I must do it with a cool head. Send all the liquor you intend for me to my hospital in the rear; I do n't think a little will hurt the poor fellows down there.'

"At a celebration on the 22d of February before the surrender of Vicksburg, while all around were drinking toasts in sparkling champagne, I saw General Grant push aside a glass of wine, and, taking up a glass of Mississippi water, with the remark, 'This suits the matter in hand,' drink to the toast, 'God gave us Lincoln and liberty; let us fight for both.'"

Lincoln and Liberty! In that toast much of the real character of Grant is shown. Lincoln and liberty were the ideas of the war. Lincoln represented the sovereignty of the nation, and liberty was its object. When Grant adopted these as his text, he entered fully into the spirit, the objects, and the principles of the war for unity and freedom.

The war had closed, but a great work remained to be done. Nearly a million of men were in some way enrolled in the service of the country. The expenses were immense. The burdens upon the people were unprecedented, and the public debt had grown to enormous proportions. The problem before the Government was no longer to win battles and subdue rebels, but to disband the army, to reduce expenses, and reconstruct loyal States from the ruins of the lost Confederacy. The task was not easy, the labors great, and the patriotism required scarcely less than that needed for the most arduous duties of war. On the first of March, 1865, there were 602,593 men present and available for duty. There were, in general and field hospitals, 179,147 sick. Those on detached duty, on furlough, or absent, were 180,000. In all, there were 965,591 men in service, and recruiting still going on. The Government commenced instantly the work of depletion and reorganization. In this work Grant had, as chief of the army, much to do, and probably no important arrangements were made without his advice. On April 28, 1865, twenty days after the surrender of Lee, Secretary Stanton issued an order for the reduction of the expenses of the army, and from that day the work of reduction went on, till, on the 7th of August, 640,806 men had been discharged from service. No country of Europe has ever witnessed a scene like this, and, if we were to select something from the history of our country to illustrate the strength and excellence of republican government, we could take nothing so characteristic and striking as the raising and reduction of the army.

The first blow of rebellious arms against the country brought half a million of men into the field, not recruited for a regular army, not brought out by arbitrary power, not seeking the paths of ambition or of glory, but simply VOLUNTEERS for the love of country. And now the last scene has come, and these vast armies, returning from the field where their valor has conquered rebellion, are reviewed by the Chief Magistrate of the nation, and peacefully return to their homes. Such is the result of republican institutions in bringing out the strength of a nation.

One of the most striking traits of Grant's character exhibited in the war was his *knowledge of men;* and in the administration of armies, or of governments, there is no talent more valuable than this. In recording what I have endeavored to trace of his military conduct, I see that there were very few instances in which he complained of the conduct of his subordinates, or had reason to. Where he had his choice he almost invariably selected the best materials for his work, and was seldom disappointed in them. A more enthusiastic, impulsive man, might have had many more personally attached followers; but, on the other hand, would have made more enemies, and committed greater mistakes. In the reduction of the army, in which he must have had a large share, it is singular how few complaints were made, and how little injustice was done. The great body of the army was very willing to return home; but there were, also, many ambitious aspirants for preferment, and still more urged forward by their friends.

Officially this work of reduction fell chiefly on Mr. Stanton, who did it well; but for two years this reduction and reorganization of the army was going on, and in that time there were four persons on whom, more than upon any others, the labor fell, and to whom the country is greatly indebted for accomplishing this great business well and thoroughly. These were Mr. Stanton, (Secretary of War,) General Grant, and the Chairmen of the Military Committees in the House and the Senate.[1]

And now we bid farewell to these scenes of bloody war, and return to those of peace and prosperity. God has favored this nation as no country was ever favored; and I seem to see visions of restored unity, of a happy people, and of a successful example to other nations of the possibility of a permanent Christian Republic.

[1] The Chairmen of these Committees were General Schenck and General Wilson.

CHAPTER XVI.

GRANT IN POLITICS.

POLITICAL QUESTIONS OF THE DAY—WHAT THEY ARE—GRANT'S PUBLIC CONDUCT IN THEM—HIS VIEWS ON THE GREAT ISSUES—ON CONGRESS AND THE PUBLIC—HIS ADMINISTRATIVE ABILITIES—VIEWS OF THE FATHERS ON THE PRESIDENCY—CORRESPONDENCE WITH THE PRESIDENT.

IT has been said of Grant, first, that he is ignorant of politics ; second, that he has no politics ; and third, that he has no opinions. This could not be said with truth of any man in the United States, much less of an intelligent, educated man, who had fought for the Government through the whole of the last war. Every man has influences about him, social, religious, commercial, and political, which incline him to one or the other side of the great questions which concern the community in which he lives. Grant, therefore, has politics, and he knows something of political matters. The questions are, What are the politics on which he has opinions? and what are his opinions upon them? There is no uncertainty upon these in regard to any of the great issues before the country. Let us analyze the subject. What questions of politics do we mean? Those of Europe or America? Those of the old Federal and Democratic parties? Those of the Whigs and Democrats? Or those of the Unionists and Rebels? A moment's thought will show any intelligent man that, in regard to the party politics of this country, old things have passed away, and all things have become new. The war made a revolution, and the results of that revolution are accomplished facts. No revolution in Europe made such fundamental changes as the abolition of American slavery. Slavery entered into the social and political life of fifteen States. It was related in politics and commerce to all the others. It was imbedded in the American Constitution. Its abolition has torn it out of the Constitution, out of society, and out of commerce. That is the first great fact of the revolution ; but it is by no means all. The slaves became free ; became, by that fact also, constituent elements of political society. With or without suffrage, the fact remains that they are a part of the free population, which is the basis of representation and of popular government. Nor was this all. The war, maintained for the defense of slavery, left an immense debt, which the nation owes both to the citizens of our own country, and to the citizens of other countries. Contingent on that fact is the obligation to pay that debt justly, and to raise taxes to meet the interest. To do this, there is the further obligation to raise those taxes as justly and expend them as frugally as is consistent with the necessities and the honor of the country. Lastly, there remains the great ruins left by the war. The country was united in territory and population, but disunited politically. These being immutable facts, which no state of politics could change, there arose from them. certain political issues. These issues can not be avoided, and they can not be put aside for any old party divisions. The questions are mainly these: 1. That of accepting and faithfully recognizing the result of the war; 2. That of reconstruction; 3. That of the faithful payment of the principal and interest of the public debt; and 4. That of an economical and rigid administration of the public finances. These are the great questions of the day. Our foreign policy is settled. No American will permit foreign interference on this continent such as was attempted by France. No honest American wishes to interfere in the affairs of other nations. No American will permit any wanton insult to the flag or people of the American republic. Such are the questions of domestic and foreign policy, which are important at this time; and on which of these questions do the opponents of General Grant suppose him ignorant? The great issue of the war was to conquer the rebels, and into that Grant went with his heart and soul. But some persons who had well and fairly fought for the war, with the whole Democratic organization, thought it was entirely right to conquer rebels in the field, but was not right to conquer them politically; and on that arises the political conflict of the day. Is there the least doubt about Grant's position upon that subject? Has he not bowed to and faithfully obeyed all the acts of Congress on reconstruction? Did he not sustain Sheridan? Did he not sustain Stanton? Does he not sustain the Tenure of Office Act? If there be an honest man in this country, who is noted for his obedience to law, and who strictly and consistently adheres to the policy of Congress, it is Ulysses S. Grant. He does not follow that policy so much because it is or is not, in his opinion, the best policy, but on the higher and better ground that it is the ACT AND POLICY OF THE LAW-MAKING POWER. This is the great issue of the day. Shall we have a government of the people or of the President? Again: Grant's whole conduct since the peace proves that he is utterly opposed to the restoration of the rebels to power, except in such way as Congress, in its generosity, may provide.

Again: as Grant has not himself been suspected of any want of integrity, so he does not suspect the American people and Government of being any worse than himself. He is for the integrity of the Government, in the payment of all its obligations.

Lastly. Since the return of peace he has been untiring in his attempt to reduce the expenses of the army, and to introduce a rigid economy into all its Departments. The few days of his services as Secretary of War *ad interim* were signalized by the reduction of many expenditures, and his views on that subject have been fully proved by his conduct.

It is unnecessary to go into farther inquiries into his political opinions. If a public man be not honest in his character, it will be in vain to estimate his future conduct by his past opinions. He has a right to change them, and the vows written on the sand will be washed away by the first waves of interest and ambition.

From what is known to the public, and what I have recorded in this book, I infer and assert that on the great questions now before the people, Grant holds these views:

1. That he accepts all the results of the war, and is opposed to the restoration of rebels to power, unless by act of Congress.

2. That he is in favor of executing *all the laws of Congress, and will consider all laws Constitutional till declared otherwise by the Supreme Court.*

3. That he will conform to the Tenure of Office Act as long as it is in existence.

4. That he is in favor of *the reconstruction of the States on the plan of Congress.*

5. That he is in favor of maintaining the honor, credit, and faith of the Government.

6. That he is in favor of the most rigid economy in all departments.

These principles substantially cover the whole ground of our political conflict. In fact, from April, 1861, to the present time, there have been but two parties and two issues before the country. The one either directly aided or sympathized with the rebels, and constantly has endeavored to restore them to power. The other endeavored to destroy their power in war, and prevent its restoration in peace; and between these two there is no middle ground. General Grant has consistently opposed the rebels, and maintained the Government from first to last. He will take no backward steps; he will support the Congress and the Government of the United States. If this be not politics, what is? What politics had

Washington when the war of the Revolution ended?
Was it not to maintain the results of that Revolution?
And who has ever paid more respect to the acts and
opinions of Congress than did George Washington?
The idea that a President is deliberately to oppose
and counteract the acts and opinions of Congress is
wholly a modern one. It is contrary to the genius
and spirit of the Constitution, and it will be well
when we cease to look upon the President as the
fountain of power and patronage.

Since the foundation of the Government the patronage of the President has been increasing. When
the Constitution was formed, there were scarcely three
millions of people in the United States. The increase
since then has been *thirteen-fold!* But the number
of offices has increased at a more rapid rate; and the
necessity of raising an internal revenue, a necessity
which is not likely soon to cease, has multiplied them
yet more. The land is almost literally covered with
Government officers, and these officers are all looking
to Washington as their Mecca, and the President as
their Prophet. In an evil hour the first Congress,
acting in the presence of Washington, whom they regarded as the political Savior of their country, and
with reference to the small number of the people, decided that the President had the power of *removal*
from office. At that time it did no harm, nor for the
terms of the first three or four Presidents. Jefferson,
with whom the old Democratic party came into power,
made a few removals, and was censured for it by his
opponents. It was on that occasion that he made
the celebrated reply, "*Few die and none resign,*" as an

apology for the removals he had made. We should remember that, up to the administration of John Quincy Adams, this power of removal was never assumed to be exercised for mere party purposes, and for that reason was never really injurious. The right of the President to select his own heads of departments, (commonly called his Cabinet,) and the principal subordinates in the revenue, was not questioned, for reasons of propriety. After the formation of new parties, in the time of Jackson, the removal of old officers and the appointment of partisans was demanded as a party right. In fact, the number of active partisans and aspirants who were engaged in party warfare became too numerous and powerful to be disregarded. They demanded the offices of the country from the President whom they had elected. The result is, that for thirty years, on the incoming of a new administration, Washington has been crowded with office-seekers, entering, as a victorious army would a conquered city, and demanding of the President, not merely the political control, but the official patronage of the Government. This fact had become so obvious and so dangerous, in the time of Mr. Van Buren and his successors, that nearly all the great men of that day denounced it. Mr. Calhoun, Judge McLean, Clay, and Webster, all denounced and treated as dangerous this fearfully enormous power of patronage. Mr. Calhoun called it "the cohesive power of public plunder." Something may be abated from these denunciations by the fact that they were uttered by the opponents of the existing administration; but it was then, and is now, the conviction of calm and enlightened statesmen, that the immense increase of official patronage was a great, growing, and dangerous evil. How to lessen it, after half a century of usage, and to place the great offices of the country more nearly within reach of the people, was a problem which seemed almost impossible of solution. There was but one way. The Constitution has made the appointment of officers to depend on the "advice and consent of the Senate," and the Senate is the representative of the States, and, indirectly, of the people. Removal obviously ought to be made by the same power which appoints. Hence Congress passed what is called the "*Tenure-of-Office Bill.*" If this act continues in force, it makes removals depend on the consent of the Senate. General Grant's position on this act is, as it is on all laws, that an act of Congress is *the law* till the Supreme Court pronounces it unconstitutional. This is the true ground. To admit that any man in the country may violate laws because *he* thinks them unconstitutional, would be to make law a mockery, and give the power of revolution to every one who chooses to exercise it. Nor is it at all certain that the Supreme Court will choose to pronounce it a purely political act, or that the nation will justify any such proceeding. Hence the Tenure-of-Office Act must, for the present, remain the law of the land; to which Grant fully assents while it is in existence, and which he will cheerfully enforce, should it ever be his duty to act upon it.

Grant's published views and opinions on this subject were brought out fully in the course of his administration and correspondence while acting as Secretary of War *ad interim.* It has been said that Grant never speaks his opinions; or, in the phrase of the day, is reticent on all subjects. There is no more truth in this than in other slanders which have been so freely uttered against him. When should a general of the army utter his political opinion? Certainly, when his duties, his position, or his relations to public affairs demand it, and not till then. No political body has, I believe, asked Grant for his opinions; and, until they do, it may be safely assumed that they are willing to accept his acts for his words. But, on every *important issue* of the day, he has given his opinions. Let us take them up as he has given them:

1. As to the results of the war in relation to the negro. The grand fact in relation to that is the abolition of slavery. In the midst of the war, in that great campaign round Vicksburg, Grant wrote to Mr. Washburn, the representative in Congress from the Galena District:

"I have never been an antislavery man, but I try to judge justly of what I see. I made up my mind, when this war commenced, that the North and South could only live together, in peace, as one nation, and they could only be one nation by being a free nation. Slavery, the corner-stone of the so-called Confederacy, is knocked out, and it will take more men to keep black men slaves than to put down the rebellion. Much as I desire peace, I am opposed to any peace till this question of slavery is forever settled."

This was decisive of his views on the slavery

question. In 1864 he supported Abraham Lincoln for President, declaring that his defeat would be a calamity to the country.

When Congress came to act on the questions of protecting the loyal blacks and whites, securing the equal rights of all, and restoring the rebel States to all their practical relations, Grant was in full accord with Congress. It is known that among the most strenuous in carrying out the views of Congress was General Philip Sheridan. When the President became hostile to Sheridan on this account, Grant indorsed Sheridan in a letter. Senator Wilson says:

"When the pending Constitutional amendment was before Congress, Grant was for its submission to the people; and, when it was submitted, he urged the leading men of the rebel States to vote for its adoption. After its rejection by the rebel Legislatures, he pressed Southern men, who sought his advice, to reconsider their action, adopt it, and give suffrage to the freedmen. To leading Southern men he said: 'You must look to Congress. The Republicans have the power; consult them. Do not seek the counsels of men in the North who opposed the war. The people will never trust that class of men with power. The more you look to them for advice, the more exacting Congress will be, and ought to be. The rejection of the amendment, and the legislation against the freedmen, will cause Congress to require universal suffrage, and you should at once give it.'"

Observe, that Grant told them that, if they rejected the counsels of the Republicans, the more exacting Congress would be, and the more exacting *they ought to be;* and this in view, as he said, of the coming event of universal suffrage. On this subject, therefore, there is no doubt. Grant accepts, and, as far as he can, will enforce, the *results* of the war in the abolition of slavery, the political equality of the freedmen, and the bringing back of the rebel States under the acts and policy of Congress.

2. On the 12th of August, 1867, Grant was appointed Secretary of War *ad interim*, on the attempted removal of Stanton. He remained such till the subject of Stanton's removal was acted upon by the Senate, and, on the refusal of the Senate to advise or consent to that act, Grant quietly gave up his office to Stanton. The President asserted that this was done contrary to an agreement between himself and General Grant. This assertion Grant positively denied. A discussion and correspondence ensued, which is important on several accounts, and which I will analyze here, in order to bring out some of Grant's characteristics.

February 4, 1868, Secretary Stanton communicated to the Senate copies furnished by Grant of his correspondence with the President, of which the following are extracts:

GENERAL GRANT TO PRESIDENT JOHNSON.

"Head-quarters Army of the United States, }
"Washington, D. C., *January 25, 1868.* }

"To His Excellency, Andrew Johnson, President of the United States:

"Sir:—On the 24th inst. I requested you to give me, in writing, the instructions which you had previously given me verbally, not to obey any order from Hon. E. M. Stanton, Secretary of War, unless I knew it came from yourself. To this written request I received a message that has left doubt in my mind of your intention. To prevent any possible misunderstanding, therefore, I renew the request that you will give me written instructions, and until they are received, will suspend action on your verbal ones. I am compelled to ask these instructions in writing, in consequence of the many gross misrepresentations affecting my personal honor circulated through the press for the last fortnight, purporting to come from the President, of a conversation which occurred either with the President privately in his office, or in Cabinet meeting. What is written admits of no misunderstanding. In view of the misrepresentation referred to, it will be well to state the facts in the case :

"Some time after I assumed the duties of Secretary of War *ad interim*, the President asked my views as to the course Mr. Stanton would have to pursue, in case the Senate should not concur in his suspension, to obtain possession of his office. My reply was, in substance, that Mr. Stanton would have to appeal to the Courts to reinstate him, illustrating my position by citing the grounds I had taken in the case of the Baltimore Police Commissioners. In that case I did not doubt the technical right of Governor Swann to remove the old Commissioners and appoint their successors. As the old Commissioners refused to give up, however, I contended that no resource was left but to appeal to the courts. Finding that the President was desirous of keeping Mr. Stanton out of office, whether sustained in the suspension or not, I stated I had not looked particularly into the Tenure of Office Bill, but that what I had stated was on general principles, and if I should change my mind in this particular case, would inform him of the fact.

"Subsequently, on reading the Tenure of Office Bill closely, I found I could not, without violation of law, refuse to vacate the office of Secretary of War the moment Mr. Stanton was reinstated by the Senate, even though the President ordered me to retain it, which he never did. Taking this view of the subject, and learning, on Saturday, the 11th inst., that the Senate had taken up the subject of Mr. Stanton's suspension, after some conversation with Lieut.-Gen. Sherman and some members of my staff, in which I stated that the law left me no discretion as to my action, should Mr. Stanton be reinstated, and that I intended to inform the President, I went to the President for the sole purpose of making this decision known, and did make it so known. In this I fulfilled the promise made in our last preceding conversation on the subject.

"The President, however, instead of accepting my view of the requirements of the Tenure of Office Bill, contended that he had suspended Mr. Stanton under authority given by the Constitution, and that the same authority did not preclude him from reporting, as an act of courtesy, his reasons for the suspension, to the Senate; that having been appointed under authority given by the Constitution, and not under an act of Congress, I could not be governed by the act.

"I stated that the law was binding on me, Constitution or not, till set aside by the proper tribunal.   An hour was consumed, each reiterating his views on this subject, till, it getting late, the President said he would see me again.   I did not agree to call again on Monday, nor at any other definite time, nor was I sent for by the President till the following Tuesday.

"From the 11th inst., to the Cabinet meeting on the 14th inst., a doubt never entered my mind about the President fully understanding my position ; namely, That if the Senate refused to concur in the suspension of Mr. Stanton, my powers as Secretary of War *ad interim* would cease, and Mr. Stanton's right to resume at once the functions of his office, would, under the law, be indisputable ; and I acted accordingly."

Now, no matter what the misunderstanding with the President was, there are certain facts in regard to Grant established here.   1. Grant said, in the very outset, that the law was binding so far that Mr. Stanton could not be ousted till an appeal had been made to the courts.   This he illustrated by his former action in the case of the Police Commissioners.   2. He examined the Tenure of Office Act, and found that he could not remain in office after the Senate refused to consent to Stanton's removal.   Grant's position, then, is that all laws are to be obeyed till the courts have acted upon them.

GENERAL GRANT TO THE PRESIDENT.

"HEAD-QUARTERS ARMY OF THE UNITED STATES, }
"WASHINGTON, *January* 24, 1868. }

"*His Excellency, Andrew Johnson, President of the United States:*

"SIR :—I have the honor very respectfully to request to have in writing the order which the President gave me verbally on Sunday, the 19th inst., to disregard the orders of the Hon. E. M. Stanton as Secretary of War, till I knew from the President himself that they were his orders.

"I have the honor to be, very respectfully, your obedient servant,

"U. S. GRANT, *General.*"

THE PRESIDENT'S INDORSEMENT.

" The following is the indorsement of the above note :

" As requested in this communication, General Grant is instructed in writing not to obey any order from the War Department assumed to be issued by the direction of the President, unless such order is known by the General commanding the armies of the United States to have been authorized by the Executive.   ANDREW JOHNSON.

"*January 20, 1868.*"

GENERAL GRANT TO THE PRESIDENT.

" HEAD-QUARTERS ARMY OF THE UNITED STATES,
"WASHINGTON, D. C., *January* 30, 1868.

"*His Excellency, Andrew Johnson, President:*

" SIR :—I have the honor to acknowledge the return of my note of the 24th inst., with your indorsement thereon, that I am not to obey any order from the War Department, assumed to be issued by order of the President, unless such order is known by me to be authorized by the Executive, and, in reply thereto, to say that I am informed by the Secretary of War that he has not received from the Executive any order or instruction, limiting or impairing his authority to issue orders to the army, as has heretofore been his practice, under the laws and custom of the Department.

" While this authority to the War Department is not countermanded, it will be satisfactory evidence to me that any orders issued from the War Department by direction of the President, are authorized by the Executive.

" I have the honor to be, very respectfully, your obedient servant,
" U. S. GRANT, *General.*"

The point of this correspondence is this : the President orders Grant to disobey orders received from Stanton, unless they were known to be *authorized by him.* Grant goes to the War Department, and finds that the President has *not limited* Stanton's authority, and hence, that any orders issued from the War Department are presumed to be from the President.

The President answered Grant, differing with him as to the purport of their conversation, and charging Grant substantially with having deceived him. The letter contains this paragraph :

the Southern States, and who would embarrass the officers of the army in the performance of their duties.

In conclusion, Grant said:

"And now, Mr. President, when my honor as a soldier, and integrity as a man, have been so violently assailed, pardon me for saying that I can but regard this whole matter, from beginning to end, as an attempt to involve me in the resistance of the law for which you hesitated to assume the responsibility, in order thus to destroy my character before the country. I am in a measure confirmed in this conclusion by your recent orders, directing me to disobey orders from the Secretary of War, my superior and your subordinate, without having countermanded his authority, whom I am to disobey. With assurance, Mr. President, that nothing less than a vindication of my personal honor and character could have induced this correspondence on my part,

"I have the honor to be, very respectfully, your obedient servant,

"U. S. GRANT, *General.*"

Grant here charges upon the President what all intelligent men must have seen—that this was an attempt on his part, in a matter in which he hesitated to assume the responsibility, to involve Grant in a resistance of the law, and to destroy his character before the country." This was honestly said, and to its truth all the events of the day bore witness. A soldier, who is a true soldier, is always sensitive to his honor and his character. Hence Grant was indignant at an attempt to make him appear to do what of all things was most abhorrent to his character—an act in disobedience of law.

On February 11th, the President replied to General Grant, taking issue with him on matters of fact, and putting in the testimony of several Cabinet officers. In the course of this reply the President has this paragraph:

"You say that a performance of the promises

alleged to have been made by you to the President would have involved 'a resistance to law, and an inconsistency with the whole history of my connection with the suspension of Mr. Stanton.' You then state that you had fears the President would, on the removal of Mr. Stanton, appoint some one in his place who would embarrass the army in carrying out the Reconstruction acts, and add: 'It was to prevent such an appointment that I accepted the office of Secretary of War *ad interim*, and not for the purpose of enabling you to get rid of Mr. Stanton by my withholding it from him in opposition to the law, or not doing so myself, surrendering it to one who would.'"

Now it is this very point that, we should remember, as clearly proved, not only on the testimony of General Grant, but of the President himself, *that Grant was in favor of the acts of Congress; that he would not disobey them; and that he would not be made the instrument of thwarting them by aiding the President.* The position of Grant, therefore, on the acts of Reconstruction can not be mistaken. He was for crushing the Rebellion, not merely by armies in the field, but by such acts of reconstruction as would prevent the rebel element from regaining an ascendency in the Government.

In regard to the controversy as to an agreement with the President, and its non-fulfillment, the evidence seems to show that it was a misunderstanding on the President's part as to a subsequent meeting on the subject. This appears from the evidence of Mr. Seward, who says:

"General Grant admitted that it was his expectation, or purpose, to call upon you on Monday. General Grant assigned reasons for the omission. He said that he was in conference with General Sherman; that there were many little matters to be attended to; he had conversed upon the matter of the incumbency of the War Department with General Sherman, and expected that General Sherman would call upon Monday. My own mind suggested a further explanation, but I do not remember whether it was mentioned or not; namely: it was not supposed by General Grant, on Monday, that the Senate would decide the question so promptly as to anticipate further explanation between yourself and him, if delayed beyond that day.

"General Grant made another explanation, that he was engaged on Sunday with General Sherman, and, I think, also on Monday, in regard to the War Department, (with a hope, though he did not say so,) in an effort to procure an amicable settlement of the affair of Mr. Stanton, and still hoped it would be brought about."

Supposing this to be a misunderstanding on either or both sides, it is, in a public point of view, of little consequence. The point established most clearly is, that Grant sympathized with Congress, and intended to obey their acts and pursue their policy. The object of the President was to defeat that policy, and to secure his own; and what the correspondence most emphatically brought out was, that Grant was against the President's policy, and in favor of that of Congress.

General Grant made a final reply on February 11th, which closed the correspondence:

"Head-Quarters Army of the United States,
"Washington, D. C., February 11, 1868.

"His Excellency, Andrew Johnson, President of the United States:

"Sir,—I have the honor to acknowledge the receipt of your communication of the 10th instant, accompanied by the statements of five Cabinet ministers, of their recollections of what occurred in the Cabinet meeting on the 14th January. Without admitting any thing contained in these statements, when they differ from any thing heretofore stated by me, I propose to notice only the portion of your communication wherein I am charged with insubordination.

"I think it will be plain to the reader of my letter of the 30th of January, that I did not propose to disobey any legal order of the President distinctly given, but only gave an interpretation of what would be regarded as satisfactory evidence of the President's sanction to orders communicated by the Secretary of War. I will say here that your letter of the 10th instant contains the first intimation I have had that you did not accept my interpretation.

"Now for the reasons for giving that interpretation: It was clear to me, before my letter of January 30th was written, that I, the person having more public business to transact with the Secretary of War than any other of the President's subordinates, was the only one who had been instructed to disregard the authority of Mr. Stanton, where his authority was derived as agent of the President. On the 27th of January I received a letter from the Secretary of War (copy herewith) directing me to furnish an escort to the public treasure from the Rio Grande to New Orleans, etc., at the request of the Secretary of the Treasury to him. I also send two other inclosures, showing a recognition of Mr. Stanton as Secretary of War by both the Secretary of the Treasury and the Postmaster-General, in all of which cases the Secretary of War had to call upon me to make the orders requested, or give the information desired, and where his authority to do so is derived, in my view, as agent of the President. With an order so clearly ambiguous as that of the President's, here referred to, it was my duty to inform the President of my interpretation of it, and to abide by that interpretation till I received other orders.

"Disclaiming any intention, now or heretofore, of disobeying any legal order of the President distinctly communicated,

"I remain, very respectfully, your obedient servant,

"U. S. Grant, General."

This closed the correspondence, and no friend of General Grant's will wish to withhold it from the pages of history.

3. It remains only to notice Grant's position on the finances of the country. In his administration of the War Department, as I have said, he immediately retrenched all possible expense, and showed a great desire for economy. The same spirit which made him earnest for the supremacy of the Government during the war, makes him earnest for the support of the National credit, and General Grant does not withhold his opinion that the National faith and integrity should be sustained to the utmost extent. He is for sustaining the credit of the country, and, for this purpose, exercising the most rigid economy.

While I am writing these pages it seems quite manifest that Grant will be nominated for the Presidency by one of the great parties of the country. Looking to that possible event, we may look, for a moment, at some · of the objections made to him. Some persons seem to have the idea that he lacks the education or the business qualities which a President ought to have. Those who read this volume will hold no such opinion, for it is impossible to look upon his long and successful career at the head of great armies, at his letters, dispatches, and orders, without seeing at once that such a career is impossible without education and talent. An education at West Point is the very best the country affords. If it be said he wants literary ability, we need only refer to this correspondence with the President ; and, if more evidence be required, it may be found in his letters and dispatches throughout the war. What, then, *is* wanting? It can not be prudence, discretion, loyalty, or integrity, for if ever man came through a fiery ordeal safely in these particulars Grant has. In what respect, in any of these qualities, does he fall short of Mr. Monroe, who was eight years a most popular and successful President of the United States? The quality most necessary for a President, after the moral qualities, is *administrative ability.* And has not Grant given evidence of the highest ability in the administration of affairs? If any one has doubts on this subject, he may refer to Colonel Badeau's "Military History of Grant," and read the numerous letters and dispatches concerning the conduct of the war. It is impossible to be a great general without being a great administrator.

There are some persons, in fact a great number, who suppose that a President of the United States, occupying, perhaps, the most important executive office in the world, must be a man of shining qualities, whose genius, or manners, or dignity should command the admiration of mankind. But this has not been the opinion of those most competent to judge, nor has it been the practice of the American people, nor can such Presidents be easily found. Certainly, Monroe, and Van Buren, and Polk were not men of this description. When I was a student at law in Litchfield, Conn., Oliver Wolcott, who had been Secretary of the Treasury under Washington, was Governor of the State, and resident in the village. I used frequently to visit him, and converse on public affairs. He was a plain man, but thoroughly acquainted with the Revolutionary period. It was then a time of political calm, (1824,) and Mr. Adams, Mr. Calhoun, and Mr. Clinton were talked of for the Presidency. These were all, in some sense, men of genius—brilliant men. I was looking for men of illustrious qualities, and, on a bright summer afternoon, we talked over the subject. Governor Wolcott said that "it was a mistake to look for men of genius in the Government; that the administration of government did not require genius or eloquence, but plain business talents, with integrity and fidelity." Said he, "There is old S——, in Pennsylvania, would make as good a President as any man." I was struck with surprise, for I recollected S—— as industrious, and full of statistics, but as not at all representing the ideal of an illustrious man. I went away with my admiration for genius undiminished, and rejoiced in the election of Mr. Adams. It has turned out that the country has had Presidents whom it would gladly have exchanged for old S——, and I earnestly hope it may never have worse.

The moral qualities are far the highest; and if we can get a man of UNIMPEACHABLE INTEGRITY, who is FAITHFUL TO THE COUNTRY, OBEDIENT TO LAW, RESPECTFUL TO RELIGION, and LOYAL IN THE FIERY CONFLICT OF ARMS, we shall have secured enough, at least, to hope for a successful administration in the times of trial and of trouble which the country has yet evidently to pass through. The patriot will believe in its welfare. The Christian will do more. He will not believe that God has brought the Nation through great calamities only to cast it away on shallow sands. He will hope and believe that the great CHRISTIAN REPUBLIC will long survive, to be the Defense of Liberty and the Leader of Nations.

THE END.